Skies of Equus

Skies of Equus

Rebecca McCullough

Croft

Other Books by Rebecca McCullough

Battle for Equus Series:
Book 1: Planet of Equus

Other Titles:
The Light of Dark Things

I would like to thank Miss Bonnie for continuing to be my first reader and for all her editing suggestions.

Thank you to all the horses who have helped to bring the characters of Equus to life.

And thank you to all the cats, both barn and house, who added spice and intrigue as only cats can.

To Sydney,
Thank you for believing

Characters of Note

Thetis Stable

A. Bailus Zephyros
1. Ruling Stallion of Calabria
2. Chestnut with white stripe
3. Sire to Pyrios, Thracis, Aquina
4. Mate to Calypsa

B. Maestoso Calypsa
1. Mate to Zephyros
2. Dam to Pyrios, Thracis, Aquina
3. Gray shading to white

C. Zephyros Pyrios
1. Oldest son of Zephyros and Calypsa
2. Gray
3. Heir to Thetis Stable

D. Zephyros Thracis
1. Youngest son of Zephyros and Calypsa
2. Chestnut with white stripe

E. Zephyros Aquina
1. Youngest foal of Zephyros and Calypsa
2. Born dark but will lighten to blue roan

Augean Stable

A. Athene Hippolyta

    1. Queen of Diomedea

    2. Dam to Alastrina, Lachesis, Zeva, Psyche

    3. Pewter with dark mane and tail

B. Hippolyta Alastrina

    1. Oldest daughter of Hippolyta

    2. Heir to Diomedea

    3. Dapple gray

C. Hippolyta Lachesis

    1. Second oldest daughter to Hippolyta

    2. High Delphae of the Temple of Consciousness

    3. Black as onyx

D. Hippolyta Zeva

    1. Second youngest daughter to Hippolyta

    2. Exiled for attempted assassination of Psyche

    3. Black

E. Hippolyta Psyche

    1. Youngest daughter to Hippolyta

    2. Black and white pinto

    3. Seer and ammoni

Acadia Stable

A. Lord Quintus

    1. Ruler of Acarnia

    2. Sire of Aeos

    3. Buckskin

B. Quintus Aeos

    1. Only foal of Quintus

    2. Dam died shortly after his birth

3. Silver dun

Calpernia Stable

A. Lady Ithia
  1. Dam to Aethon and Phlegon
  2. Ruling mare of small but significant stable in Pendaria
B. Ithia Phlegon
  1. Oldest son of Ithia
  2. Gray
  3. Aide to Lord Kantaka
C. Ithia Aethon
  1. Youngest son of Ithia
  2. Gray

Mykenia Stable

A. Memnon Pedasos
  1. King of Myrmidonia
  2. Mate to Helena
  3. Sire to Salia
  4. Bay
B. Zeus Helena
  1. Queen of Myrmidonia
  2. Mate to Pedasos
  3. Dam to Salia
  4. Palimino
C. Pedasos Salia
  1. Only foal to Pedasos and Helena
  2. Buckskin

D. Desiree
   1. Lady in waiting to Queen Helena
   2. Originally from Emor in Acarnia

Hapsburg Stable

A. Favory Demas
   1. Oldest son of Hapsburg Stable in Levadia
      a) Hapsburg Stable is the ruling stable of Lipizzania
   2. Gray

Arion Stable

A. Dimitri Alexi
   1. Ruling stallion of Kigeria
   2. Mate to Nerissa
   3. Buckskin
B. Stephanos Nerissa
   1. Mate to Alexi
   2. Red dun

The Romanium

A. Commander Talos Dias
   1. Current Asapatish of the Hippikon
   2. Sire to Eno
   3. Bay with white stripe
B. Othello Iago
   1. Head student at the Romanium
   2. Andalusian

    3. Bay
C. Ilarches Platon
    1. Instructor to Thracis

University of Piber and Registry of Breeds

A. Lampos Nonios
    1. Head Sentinel
    2. Trakanian
    3. Gray
B. Xanthos Kantaka
    1. Representative of Mongolea
    2. Sorrel
C. Claudius Adonis
    1. Representative of Calabria
    2. Palimino
D. Lady Adelpha
    1. Representative of Courbettania
    2. Gray
E. Lord Nicodemus
    1. Welsh Representative
    2. Brown

Boudica

A. Alois Phrenicos
    1. Legendary trainer of the Romanium
    2. Mentor to Thracis
    3. White
B. Alcina

1. Diomedean mare in charge of Boudica
2. Nicknamed The Raven
3. Small main herd
    a) Dysis - Palimino
    b) Echo - Gray
    c) Haidee - Sorrel
4. Black

C. Titania
1. Barkeep
2. Clydesdale

D. Alcander
1. Companion to Kamuzu
2. Miniature gelding
3. White

E. Dias Eno
1. Only foal to Talos Dias
2. Longtime friend of Psyche
3. Brilliant in strategy and weaponry
4. Bay with white stripe and four white socks

Felisians of Note

A. Kamuzu
1. Companion to Alcander
2. Friend of Psyche, Eno, and Phrenicos
3. Orange

B. Neema
1. Constant companion to Titania
2. Calico

C. Lady Dendera

1. Lead cat of assassin cats
2. Special squad used by Queen Hippolyta
    a) Lisimba - male follower

<u>***Skies of Equus***</u>

Book Two of the Battle for Equus

Coming Soon:

<u>Battle for Equus</u>

The final book in the Battle for Equus Trilogy

CHAPTER 1

"This defeat is an outrage!"

The Baroquian High Commander's voice rang out over the Equine and Felisian assembly. The horses and cats flinched. Many gave furtive looks into the corners and at the exits, trying to decipher the safest retreat. All were huddled together, their natural herding instincts coming to the forefront in defense. The Dark Guard, the High Commander's personal defenders, stood at attention behind the pacing Friesian. A dozen in all, the Dark Guard were the most highly trained warriors in the Baroquian military, with the exception of Lady Zeva's mares. They would assassinate every animal assembled without question on the order of their leader. And the scouts and spies gathered knew it.

Off to the left, Lady Zeva stood with several of her most trusted mares. The rest were in the training fields, perfecting their skills. Zeva and her mares, like the Dark Guard, stood motionless. These mares, culled from Diomedean exiles, were not surprised by the Diomedean victory. Zeva had tried to warn her commander about the mares of Diomedea and their fighting skills. Like the stallions of the Imperial Cavalry, those of the Baroquian military had thought themselves superior. A deadly mistake. Zeva had done well to hide her smugness at the report of the total destruction of the Baroquian force sent to invade Diomedean territory.

"My lord," a quivering pinto began, "the Baroquians fought superbly, but the Diomedeans were as mares possessed. None could have stood against them. They fought until the breath left their lungs."

"As should have my soldiers," the High Commander hissed. "They should be thankful the Diomedeans cut off their retreat. Only execution would have awaited them here."

Several horses in the group shifted. Zeva knew the commander's rage, while justified, was not strong enough cause for him to attack members of this assembly. They were the best spies and scouts in Baroquia and were worth their weights in achillium. But it was wise not to let them know that.

The High Commander slowed his pacing, his expression becoming thoughtful. "We cannot change the past so let us look to the future. I want full reports on the battle. Diomedean strategies must be examined and understood. Fighting maneuvers must be studied. We have many months now to devote to training as no cavalry marches in winter."

Felisians pulled out pawheld computers and began making notes. Equine scouts moved forward eagerly to be given specific instructions by the High Commander's council members. The large hall became a flurry of activity as groups split off and others reformed. Through it all the Dark Guard and Zeva's mares remained impassive. Their orders would be given after the hall was cleared. Some things were not meant for everyone's ears.

Thirty minutes of instructions and scrambling and the hall was empty of all save the High Commander, the Dark Guard, and Zeva and her followers. The High Commander nodded to the Dark Guard. "Leave us. We will be going to Lusitania in the morning. Go prepare your supplies."

The stallions nodded as one and left the chamber. Zeva stifled the urge to snort at their retreat. No matter their training, she still felt stallions were inferior to her mares. The High Commander walked to her. "You better have good news for me."

Zeva bobbed her head. "We are very close to discovering the proper thruster capacity to make us airborne. A few more months and we should begin flying."

The High Commander nodded his black head. "That is good news. Speak with me privately, Lady Zeva." He turned away.

Zeva swished her tail. The mares gathered behind her knew a dismissal and filed out of the chamber. Zeva waited until she could no longer hear the echo of their hooves before addressing the High Commander.

"This defeat is a setback, my lord, but we will recover." She stretched her neck and back. "Once we conquer the air, no one will stand in our way."

The High Commander chuckled. "Confident as you are, I will not put my entire cavalry in the sky." He looked at her. "Zephyros Thracis is becoming more of a problem than is prudent. He should have died in the Diomedean battle. I will not see the prophecy come to light."

"We will continue our attempts to eliminate him. He has acquired some interesting friends as of late."

"Like your sister?"

Zeva stared at the High Commander in shock.

He snorted. "Do you think you are above my scrutiny? Even as my second-in-command, I do not grant you my total confidence."

"A wise decision." Zeva fought to keep her voice steady.

"When did you plan on telling me that Thracis' mate is that troublesome little sister of yours?"

Zeva stomped a foot. "It is a minor concern. I will deal with both of them in due time."

The High Commander reached out and nipped her shoulder. "Focus, Lady. We cannot allow our emotions to rule our actions. You must proceed with caution. Find a more subtle way of dealing with Thracis." He flicked his ears. "How is our associate proceeding with the other Zephyros colt?"

Zeva tossed her head, happy with the change of subject. "Things are coming along perfectly. She has him fully ensnared and will proceed with whatever action we wish."

"A truly wonderful find, that mare. She will be one to keep an eye on." He turned away. "I must say I am happy she is ensconced at the planet's capital. If she were here with you, I would worry about my standing. I would not put it beyond the two of you to decide you were better equipped to rule than any stallion."

Zeva laughed. "Why would we want to be in charge when it is much more educational to watch the missteps of others?"

The High Commander whirled to face her, his demeanor more amused than angry. He liked Zeva a great deal and she knew it. She could say things to him that would get any other horse killed. She rather thought he enjoyed their verbal sparring. "My steps may falter but, in the end, I will be known as the ruler of all Equus."

"To the glory of us all, my lord."

CHAPTER 2

The invigorating scent of salt filled the early morning air as Thracis trotted through one of his schooling patterns in the practice arena outside his teacher's stable. The patterns had become second nature to his hooves over the past months and the Calabrian stallion relished the exercise. The rolling sound of the ocean marked the tempo for the cadence of his steps. His ears flicked back and forth as his feet moved independently of his mind. The patterns were so familiar, he could perform them with a blindfold.

After long debate Thracis' instructor, Phrenicos, agreed that Thracis' required hour of meditation was best conducted while the young stallion's feet had something to do. Meditation was a requirement for any warrior. Phrenicos was fond of stating that to find balance a fighter needed a clear mind. It was during this time, while Thracis warmed up his muscles in preparation for the more demanding movements of the High

Dances, that the young stallion was able to achieve a state of mental balance and focus his thoughts.

His copper coat glimmered in the sunlight, not yet damp with sweat, as Thracis glided across the deep sand of the arena. It was mid-spring, the summer heat still a few weeks away. As the seasons progressed, Thracis would have to begin his exercises early in the morning or late in the evening to avoid becoming overheated. During this time of cooler temperatures, he entered the arena three and four times a day, if his muscles could take it. He moved from shoulder-in to travers to renvers to half-pass without a second thought. His mind was elsewhere, traveling roads in the past.

Eight months had passed since the Baroquian attack on Diomedea. The memory of the battle was still fresh in Thracis' mind. The shrieks of challenge, the screams of pain, the smell of blood bright copper in his nose. Thracis' body remembered the jarring crash of impact as he reared into another stallion, the hammer blows of another horse's hooves kicking against his armor. His feet stumbled as he felt the phantom pain of long-ago injuries.

Tossing his head in disgust, Thracis collected himself further, drawing his feet under his body and increasing his impulsion. A warrior, a hippeus, could not afford mistakes.

Shortening his tempo and pulling his head tighter against his neck to balance himself, Thracis began the stationary diagonal trot of the piaffe. He did this movement for twenty seconds before settling himself on his hind legs in the thirty-degree angle squat of the levade. He gritted his teeth. Keeping his head level, his neck arched, and his forelegs tucked up against his body, Thracis fought to keep his balance on his two back legs. He was able to pull himself together in the movement for three seconds before losing his concentration and coming back to all four feet.

"Very good, but you should be practicing the piaffe and passage this morning, as well as your canter changes. You have already performed enough combat maneuvers for the week. Your body needs time to recover."

Thracis' ears flicked toward Phrenicos as the white stallion stopped outside the arena. Phrenicos usually watched Thracis only when he was instructing the younger stallion in a new movement. After a few days of instruction, Phrenicos left Thracis to his own devices for the hours of practice he would have to log before achieving perfection. Thracis would be appalled to know that Phrenicos kept a much closer eye on him than Thracis thought. Phrenicos was no fool; young horses often pushed themselves beyond their limits.

"I've tried, but my mind keeps wandering. I need to do something different to keep my focus."

Phrenicos chuckled. "A good excuse but not one I accept. The advanced combat movements are only as powerful as their foundations and...," he trailed off.

"The foundation of advanced combat is the piaffe," Thracis recited.

Phrenicos nodded.

"You are right, as always." Thracis hung his head.

"It's getting hot. Come with me down to the beach. You can go for a swim and sooth your muscles."

Tossing his head, Thracis trotted out of the arena and followed Phrenicos down the path that would lead them to the beach close to Phrenicos' stable. As they walked Thracis glanced at the drying room Phrenicos kept for herbs. The room was filled with hanging plants, but to Thracis it seemed as bare as the Natarian Desert.

The drying room had been Aeos' favorite spot while the dun stallion had stayed with Phrenicos and Thracis. Thracis and Aeos had become good friends during their journey to the planet capital of Lipizza and then on to Diomedea. Thracis missed the dun stallion's sarcastic nature and sharp insights.

Aeos, more talented mentally than any other stallion Thracis had known, was studying the psychic arts in the Felisian city of Sanctuary. They had last seen each other at the Diomedean encampment after they had defeated the Baroquians. As Equines could use telepathy, the two stallions spoke at least once a week, but speaking with one's mind was different than being around that horse in the flesh. Without Aeos around to keep him on track, Thracis felt as if he were floundering through his exercises.

Aeos also gave Thracis a measure of how well he was performing the more advanced combat maneuvers. Like all young stallions, Aeos was trained in combat. He had attended the Romanium with Thracis before Thracis' dismissal and had been near the top of their herd. The dun stallion learned the movements quickly and didn't mind the hours of conditioning, but his interests lay in the healing and psychic arts. Good thing for Thracis because if Aeos had truly applied himself, he would have excelled beyond Thracis until the Calabrian found his balance. Thracis was destined for greatness, but was too eager to achieve it. He needed to learn patience. Aeos helped provide that patience and Thracis missed him greatly.

Thracis and Phrenicos walked out of the screen of trees that separated the beach from the meadow in front of the stable and onto the white sand of the beach. The light breeze that had tousled Thracis' mane in the practice arena was more forceful here where there were no trees to harness it.

The white stallion stopped with just his hooves in the churning waves. "It's still a little too cold for this old horse to go wading." He inclined his head at Thracis. "But it's perfect for overworked muscles."

"I have not been working too hard," Thracis mumbled as he walked into the water. He went in until the waves crashed against the middle of his belly, making sure that he was deep enough that his shoulders would benefit from the salinity.

"Given the defensiveness of your tone and your constant practicing, I would imagine Lady Psyche has been occupied as of late."

Thracis' ears pinned. He wished he could swim out farther so that the waves could drown out Phrenicos' voice, but the water was cold and even Thracis had limits. "She is studying some difficult exercises. At least that is what she tells me."

Phrenicos sighed. "The lady doesn't strike me as the lying type. She was quite pleasant on the days she came to visit."

Thracis pawed the ground making the water roil against his shoulders. "I'm sure she's busy. I just get the impression that it's Eno's experiments she's busy with."

"Why should that bother you? The mares have been friends for many years."

"I know, but Eno is getting closer and closer to giving Equines wings and I'm worried that Psyche will be her first test subject."

Phrenicos laughed. "Psyche is not so foolish. They will wait until you go to visit them again and send you into the air for the first attempt."

Thracis felt his tension ease. "And they'll likely have me jump off a cliff."

Phrenicos shook his head. "Psyche knows how important your own training is. She would not damage you so that you could not continue."

"Given Psyche's healing abilities, I could sustain a lot of damage before I return here." As his body became acclimated to the temperature, Thracis waded farther out into the water. He turned and began walking parallel to the beach.

Having come in so that the water was sloshing around his knees, Phrenicos paced Thracis. "Even though you cannot see it, your training is coming along well."

"I've a long way to go before I attempt a capriole."

"Not so long. If a hippeus you wish to be, you must learn patience."

Thracis flicked his ears. He wanted nothing more than to become a hippeus, a knight, the most elite warriors on all Equus. It was this desire that had led his hooves to the schooling rings of the Romanium. The Romanium was dedicated to teaching all the advanced combat maneuvers and principles that made a hippeus. The entry exams were brutal and quickly culled any stallions who viewed becoming a hippeus as nothing more than a passing fancy. Because of a political situation, Thracis had been accepted into the Romanium without having to complete the entrance exams.

Weakened from a Baroquian ambush and lacking the fundamental foundations that all the other cadets had, Thracis lasted a month before being dismissed for dishonorable conduct. The dismissal had shattered his belief that he could ever become a hippeus. Rather than wallow in self-pity, Thracis had journeyed to Diomedea with Aeos where the two stallions had found Alois Phrenicos.

Phrenicos had once been the headmaster of the Romanium. He had been exiled due to a difference of opinion with the current headmaster. Phrenicos, having come from a long-line of instructors, had believed that a stallion must first have a firm foundation in the movements of the High Dances, the passage, piaffe, and canter changes, before moving on to advanced combat. The current headmaster, realizing that a good foundation would take months of conditioning that the Imperial Cavalry did not want to invest, had held to the belief that the higher movements could be taught without a solid foundation. As a result of Phrenicos' exile, a lot of the hippeus' principles had been forgotten.

During their time at the Romanium, Thracis and Aeos had met stallions who upheld the hippeus ideals of honor, loyalty, and strength. But those horses had been few. The majority of the stallions at the Romanium wanted the prestige of being a hippeus without the humility. It was just such a stallion, Rodrigo Iago, who had been the culminating factor of Thracis' dismissal. Iago had been the lead student and had not wanted to share the spotlight with anyone. He had viewed Thracis as a threat to his position and so the Calabrian stallion had to be eliminated as a rival.

Iago instigated a fight with Thracis at a moment when Thracis was distracted and not able to hold his temper. The two stallions had clashed in private, away from the eyes of the ilarches, but that mattered little. Almost before Thracis returned to the cadet stables, Iago had whispered into the right ears that Thracis had attacked him without provocation. This incident, coupled with Thracis' inability to keep up with the rest of his herd, led to his dismissal.

Over the past months, Thracis had made an uneasy truce with himself over the treatment he had received at the Romanium. He had decided that he would become a hippeus without licking the proper horseshoes. With the support of his friends, Thracis had learned that a hippeus was not always forged in the rings of the Romanium. This realization had also raised the question in his mind as to where Diomedean mares were taught their superior combat techniques as mares were forbidden to enter the equine cavalry anywhere else on all of Equus. He had as yet not raised the subject with Phrenicos.

In Aeos' opinion, being dismissed from the Steppe was the best thing to have happened to Thracis. After his dismissal Thracis had learned that he was more of a knight than he knew. He already held all their ideals; now he just needed the training. This training period was what Phrenicos liked to refer to as a time of patience, a clarifying time during which a warrior could hone his skills and settle his mind.

It was the perfect time for such training. During this interlude when armies on all sides of the current conflict were reassessing their forces, those with any sense were sharpening their own fighting skills. At this moment three different forces were vying for power on Equus: the Baroquian Pact, the Elysian Alliance, and, most recently, the Diomedeans.

The trouble on Equus began when the Baroquian Pact, founded by the Friesians and Lusitanos, had threatened retaliation after the Registry of Breeds entered into alfalfa trade agreements with the Caprians. The Registry, aware that the Baroquians could cause problems with the coming agreements, had begun assessing the rest of the breeds on Equus to discern where Baroquian sympathies might lie. The outlook had not been promising. Many more breeds were siding with the Baroquians than the Registry had expected, but still the Registry tried to keep peace.

After the Baroquians attempted to invade Diomedea, the Registry knew they could not shy away from the obvious. They declared war on the Baroquian Pact and all their followers. The Registry gave the Elysian Alliance, the congregation of breeds opposing the Baroquian Pact, control of the Imperial Cavalry. As the Baroquian-Diomedean battle had been at summer's end, nothing much had occurred in the interim between then and now. Armies did not march in winter, not even the Imperial Cavalry.

The Caprians had withdrawn back to their home planet of Capra after the declaration of civil war on Equus. They were uneasy about signing trade agreements during such a tumultuous time. Goats and sheep were tough, but Equine weapons and spacecraft were far superior to anything the Caprians had developed. They did not want to make enemies if they could avoid it. Loss of the trade agreements, even a temporary one, had put the Equines supporting the agreements in a foul mood.

Tempers were further strained after Queen Hippolyta, ruler of Diomedea, sent representatives to the Registry to inquire about military assistance. Her forces had been significantly diminished after the Baroquian battle. Though they had fought well, mares were forbidden to join the Imperial Cavalry. While mares engaged in open combat in Diomedea, as the country was founded by mares, this practice was frowned upon on the rest of Equus. Queen Hippolyta had hoped that with the Diomedean victory the military commanders would see that mares were just as capable in battle as stallions. Her hopes had been misplaced.

After a heated discussion, the Registry informed the Diomedean queen that they would send Imperial soldiers to aid Diomedea against the Baroquians, but those soldiers would not fight alongside mares. Queen Hippolyta had thanked the Registry for their concern and then kindly told them all they could go straight to Pandemonium. Her mares were superior to most Imperial soldiers and she was not about to open her lands to herds of stallions with no respect for a mare's abilities.

With the closing of Diomedean borders, the planet of Equus was divided three ways: the Baroquian Pact, the Diomdeans, and the Elysian Alliance. The Baroquians were making it clear they wanted control of all Equus. The Alliance wanted Equus to remain as democratic as possible and proceed with the Caprian trade agreements. The Diomedeans didn't care one way or the other about the trade agreements as alfalfa did not grow well on the southern continent; they only cared about having an equal place in Equine society.

This nerve-racking environment covered Equus like a dark shroud, putting everyone, Equine and Felisian alike, on edge. Mares kept their foals close. Stallions didn't stray far from their home stables. Felisian mothers only allowed their kittens out to play under intense supervision. Strangers to any village were greeted with open hostility and suspicion, even here deep in the Diomedean province of Amazonia.

Thracis and Phrenicos stopped when they reached the post that marked the outer boundary of Boudica, a small sea-side town. Thracis looked at the post in surprise. With his mind wandering distant trails, he hadn't realized how far he had walked. He cursed himself soundly for forgetting his surroundings. He pawed the ground in agitation.

Phrenicos tossed his head. "I think you need a break. Take some time to balance yourself. Away from your studies and training," Phrenicos added.

Thracis walked out of the water and shook himself. "I don't want to leave for a week or more." It would take three days for him to get to the stable Psyche shared with the Felisian *ammoni*, Moirae. "Besides, I don't think Psyche will want me around."

"Why don't you go see Aeos, then?"

Thracis tossed his head. He stretched his neck and legs. "Aeos is undergoing some kind of intense training for the next three weeks. He told me about it when we last spoke." He looked out over the water. "Everyone is moving ahead, finding their places."

"Even your brother?"

Thracis pinned his ears. His brother, Pyrios, was an aide to the Mongol representative Xanthos Kantaka. This was an excellent position for the oldest Zephyros colt as Pyrios was the heir to their home stable of Thetis. Given Pyrios' disdain for combat and training it was better for him to follow a less demanding path in life. Such as a career in politics.

"I haven't shared a coherent conversation with him in months."

Phrenicos tossed his head at the irritation in Thracis' voice. "The Registry of Breeds is a busy place. I'm sure your brother is attending to the needs of Lord Kantaka."

"My brother is attending to someone's needs but I highly doubt that someone is Lord Kantaka."

"You have a mare that keeps you occupied."

"Yes, but my lady is available. I fear the mare my brother courts is part of a formal union."

Phrenicos sighed. "That is a dangerous game for some, but not unheard of in politics."

Thracis bent to scratch his nose against a foreleg. "It's not the fact that she is claimed. There is something...cunning about this mare. I don't like it."

"Given your experience with recent mares, your suspicion is understandable. I would hope your brother knows how to handle himself."

"He used to."

Knowing the conversation would only end in speculation as to what Pyrios was doing, Phrenicos changed the subject. "You've worked hard this morning and we're almost in town. Why don't we have breakfast and then I take you to see the delphae of Boudica? You could use some psychic training of your own."

Thracis' stomach rumbled.

Phrenicos laughed. "I guess that answers my question."

They walked in silence for a moment before Phrenicos asked, "Is something on your mind?"

Thracis hesitated. The mares of Diomedea were secretive about their training and any stallions fortunate enough to be accepted by them also held their secrets. He did not want to put Phrenicos in an awkward position. "I have spent a lot of time thinking about the Baroquian battle."

"And?"

"And many of the mares used combat techniques close to the advanced maneuvers taught at the Romanium, if not those exact maneuvers."

Phrenicos stopped walking before they entered the village. "And you are wondering how they came by such training."

"Yes."

Phrenicos tossed his head. "That answer is simple enough and not really a secret although it is not openly spoken of around newcomers." He shifted to stand hipshot. "The Romanium is where military stallions journey to learn advanced combat maneuvers and become a hippeus. To achieve this goal stallions who have completed their training must traverse the Barrens. A desolate, harsh landscape of sharp rocks, steep inclines, little water, and no vegetation. Many who begin this trek never reach the other side. If they are found before they perish, they can never become a hippeus."

Thracis nodded. He knew the history of the Romanium, the Barrens, and all the requirements to become a hippeus.

"As mares cannot join Equine military anywhere else on Equus, but are just as skilled as stallions, though lighter of bone and so must train slightly differently, Diomedean queens made their own training facility." Phrenicos flicked his ears. "It is called the Sphere, so named because the mares here are trained to be more in tune with their surroundings and so use everything around them when fighting."

"And I suppose is it closed to stallions?" Thracis said musingly.

"Of course, it is, foolish colt." They started into town. "They also have a rite of passage to traverse, by the way. They call it the March, after their foredams trek through the Natarian desert." Phrenicos waited a few paces before stating. "Your lady has graduated the Sphere."

Thracis gave Phrenicos an arch look. "Of course, she did."

CHAPTER 3

Pyrios shook his head and tried to focus on the current issue being discussed in the Registry of Breeds council chamber. As an aide to Lord Kantaka, Pyrios held the privilege of accompanying him to every meeting and social gathering. On the other side of Lord Kantaka, Ithia Phlegon, another aide, watched the debate with avid interest. Pyrios could hear the minute hum of the small computer that Phlegon used to record every discussion in the council chamber. This allowed Lord Kantaka to review the unspoken nuances in the room at his leisure if he chose. This was common practice among the representatives.

As the heir to Thetis Stable, Pyrios had fallen into great luck to have become an aide to such a respected representative. Most of this luck was attributed to his being Thracis' brother. Lord Kantaka and his associates had learned through their extensive network of spies that Thracis was of particular interest to the Baroquian Pact. This was the main reason for Pyrios and Phlegon's acceptance as aides to Lord Kantaka where the

Mongol could keep an eye on them. Thracis was to go to the Romanium where he would train in advanced combat maneuvers and be supervised by Commander Talos Dias, the current Asapatish of the Hippikon.

After Thracis' dismissal from the Romanium, Pyrios and his sire had tried to keep Thracis in the planet capital of Lipizza. They both felt that Thracis should enroll in classes at the University of Piber and attempt to gain reacceptance into the Romanium at a later date. Thracis had disagreed.

The younger Zephyros colt had always felt as though he were in the shadow of his older brother. While this knowledge had never bothered Thracis when the colts lived in their home province of Calabria, where their herd was the ruling herd, now that they were out on their own, Thracis felt the need to find his own path. Against the advice of Pyrios and their sire, Bailus Zephyros, Thracis decided to travel to Diomedea in search of a teacher. The only condolence in this line of reasoning was that Aeos would accompany him.

Pyrios and Thracis had met Quintus Aeos, heir to the Acarnian ruling herd of Acadia Stable, at the council of King Pedasos. King Pedasos was the ruler of the country of Myrmidonia. Myrmidonia was made up of the provinces of Acarnia, Calabria, and Pendaria. It was also at this meeting that the Zephyros stallions had met Ithia Phlegon who hailed from Calpernia Stable in Pendaria. Calpernia Stable was not the ruling stable in Pendaria, but Phlegon's dam had considerable influence with the ruling herds across Myrmidonia.

The four stallions, along with Phlegon's late brother, Aethon, had journeyed from Myrmidonia to the capital city of

Lipizza where they would discuss Myrmidon alliances with the Registry of Breeds. They had been in the Lipizzan province of Levadia when they had been ambushed by Baroquian supporters. In the subsequent battle, Thracis was gravely injured and Aethon had been killed.

It was only later, after the remaining stallions had met Lord Kantaka, that they learned the Baroquians had been looking for Thracis and had wrongly thought that in killing Aethon they had terminated the younger Zephyros stallion. This misunderstanding had bought Thracis several months before the Baroquian Pact tried another assassination attempt, this time using psychic means.

Though Pyrios had informed Lord Kantaka about the second attempt on Thracis' life, the Mongol, as well as Commander Dias, still felt that Pyrios was the more important of the Zephyros stallions. They ignored the attempt as a fluke and focused their attention on Pyrios. To an extent.

Even under the careful supervision of Lord Kantaka and almost constant attendance of Phlegon, Pyrios had still managed to get himself into a rather delicate situation.

Zephyros Pyrios had loved mares from the time he was a gangly colt. He lavished attention on them, made them feel special, and, with a talent that boggled the minds of all who knew him, could keep more than one lady at a time. Thracis was often heard to say that Pyrios had a mare in every town between Thetis Stable and the Myrmidon capital of Bucephalus. Sometimes two or three mares. Not only did he have several ladies, but in almost every instance, they all knew about each other. It was a strange arrangement that bespoke of how charismatic and charming Pyrios could be.

Until now.

Nearly a year ago Pyrios had met a striking Kiger mare at a social function. This mare was like no one he had ever met. She carried herself with the dominance of a stallion, she was intelligent and shrewd, and she could debate with students and politicians alike. And she was formally unified with the lead stallion of the Kigeria province, Dimitri Alexi.

Affairs were not unheard of in the Registry of Breeds. Many of the formal unions were of political necessity rather than mutual attraction. Even so, they had to be conducted with discretion. It was a game Pyrios was not only good at but excelled in. He understood all that was being risked and how careful he must tread. Besides, a single mare hardly kept his attention for more than a month and he thought he could handle the situation until then.

Lady Nerissa had other intentions. She was not only enjoying this affair, but loved the control she had over both Pyrios and her mate, Alexi. Not wanting to threaten her position as the Lady of Kigeria, Nerissa made sure that all of Alexi's needs and desires were sated. It was for Pyrios that she saved all her pent-up cruelty and frustration. She reveled in tangling the younger stallion in situations that pushed him to the brink of social embarrassment. She was calculating in her malice. She never pushed Pyrios away completely and stooped to every possible level to hold him to her. It was a vicious cycle the older Zephyros stallion found himself in. As a result, his attention was flagging when it came to his assistant duties.

"I say if the Diomedean queen wants to take a political stand against the wishes of the Registry, we should treat her no better than those aligned with the Baroquian Pact." This statement came from Claudius Adonis.

Adonis was the official representative of Calabria and had been a favorite follower of Bailus Zephyros. When the Calabrian representative stall in the Registry became vacant, Zephyros was more than happy to elect Adonis to the position.

Pyrios and Adonis had gotten along well enough in Calabria despite Adonis' additional ten years. Since coming to Lipizza and being an aide to Lord Kantaka, Pyrios had felt a coolness between Adonis and himself. If it hadn't begun before the mess with Nerissa, Pyrios would have thought the older stallion knew about the affair.

Lord Kantaka tossed his head. "That would be imprudent. The mares of Diomedea have already proven themselves in battle against the Baroquians. We cannot afford to divide the Imperial Cavalry between two competent military forces."

"That is a wise observation." Lady Adelpha, the Courbettanian representative, bobbed her gray head.

Lord Adonis snorted. "Feminine sympathy and nothing more. Those mares proved themselves against no more than the inferior warriors of the Baroquians."

The council chamber erupted in cheers. Pyrios tossed his head and took stock of the representatives that were left. As was expected, the representatives from both Friesia and Lusitania were absent. The Trakanean representative was also missing. That didn't surprise Pyrios, it was widely rumored that Trakanea was aligning itself with the Baroquian Pact. All the other stalls were filled. Even if their home provinces were siding with the Baroquians, many representatives were still trying to find a political way to avoid an all-out war. Pyrios thought this path a fool's errand at the very least. War was inevitable and they all knew it.

Lord Nicodemus, the Welsh representative, waited for the clamor to die down before speaking. "My ponies have had extensive dealings with both the Diomedean mares and the Felisians that call Diomedea home. I caution against inciting a war with the southern continent. The inhabitants there have psychic powers of which we could only dream."

Thoughtful mutterings followed this statement. They all remembered the stories of how Diomedea was colonized by the escaped slaves of Zaxas' army centuries ago. Those mares had dedicated themselves to learning both physical and psychic warfare. They could not simply be overcome by stronger opponents or larger numbers. It would take finesse to win a war against the ladies of Diomedea.

"A battle with the Diomedeans will have also shown the Baroquians where the holes in their training lay." All heads turned to see Commander Dias, Asapatish of the Hippikon. "They will learn from their mistakes."

Pyrios pricked his ears. Commander Dias did not often come to the council chamber, preferring to stay among his soldiers in the Hippikon. He hated politics and the intrigue that went with them. If he was here that meant he might have news on the condition of the Imperial Cavalry.

"Fine, let them learn. They still have a long journey before they reach the impeccable training of the Imperial Cavalry." Lord Adonis was on a roll today.

"Do not mock their training techniques. Many of the Romanium's finest students have left to join the Baroquian Pact. Some of the ilarches as well. And we have learned that the Friesians have built their own training complex that is very similar to our Romanium."

Silence met this. Pyrios, as well as most of the representatives, knew that with the open declaration of the coming war many students had returned to their home territories. It made sense that students would want to be with their kin in a time of turmoil. That some of the ilarches, the Romanium instructors, had left as well came as a shock.

"Shouldn't those instructors have been detained?" Lord Nonios, the Head Sentinel and not really a representative at all, drew the herd's attention.

"I have no authority to detain Equines who have not broken any law."

"Surely you could have found something to hold them on."

Commander Dias' ears lowered. "I have much greater concerns than the whereabouts of a dozen or so ilarches."

Hearing the threat, Lord Nonios fell silent.

Lady Adelpha addressed Commander Dias. "Is the Imperial Cavalry ready for battle?"

Commander Dias nodded. "The Cavalry will not fail against a single cavalry. Torn between two, the outcome may be in doubt."

"No one is marching to battle on this day," Lord Kantaka said, "I have it on good authority that the Baroquians lost many ships in their attempt to invade Diomedea. They will not set hoof on Lipizzanian shores for some time."

The other representatives muttered agreement. It was common knowledge that the battle would take place on Lipizzanian soil. If a stand the Baroquians wished to take, they must first overthrow their strongest opposition. With the Diomedean victory, many believed that the most likely place for the Baroquians to invade Lipizzania was from the north. They would use their tentative alliance with the draft breeds of the north to occupy the northern Lipizzanian province of Capriola.

Tossing his head, Lord Nonios garnered everyone's attention once more. "Ladies and Lords, the day grows late. Might I suggest we disperse and reconvene in the morning?"

The representatives agreed unanimously. It was late and many of the horses present had skipped the midday meal. The council chamber filled with sounds of rustling papers and hoofbeats as the Registry concluded another day of debate.

Pyrios tossed his head and stretched his back as he followed Lord Kantaka out into the hall. Phlegon walked beside him, but his interest was more on a pretty dappled mare following behind Lady Adelpha. The dapple was obviously an aide given her submissive demeanor. Her doe eyes looked about the hallway from beneath dark lashes.

At another time Pyrios would view the mare as a worthy quarry. He could charm such a shy and self-conscious creature with little trouble. They would spend a few days or even a week together before he moved on to another conquest. He would be kind to her and make sure the dapple mare was left with a tender memory, not a broken heart. It was in Pyrios' best interest to remain on an amiable basis with all his ladies.

Today he gave the dapple little notice. He did wish Phlegon well in his pursuit of her if Phlegon chose to pursue, but he had enough mare trouble without adding a third party.

"Your attention wandered much today," Lord Kantaka noted as the three stallions stepped into the afternoon sunlight.

Pyrios took a deep breath of the spring air. "I've much to think about as of late."

"I'm well-aware," Lord Kantaka said dryly.

Phlegon snickered behind the two horses. Pyrios pinned his ears. "This is no concern of yours, stallion of Calpernia Stable."

Phlegon's own ears flattened. "Don't take that formal tone with me, Pyrios, I'm not the one who holds Lord Kantaka's stable on the brink of shame."

"Children." Lord Kantaka's voice was amused. "If the two of you insist on squabbling at least wait until we are home and behind closed doors."

Pyrios opened his mouth to apologize to Lord Kantaka. Before he could speak, another mind contacted his. Lord Kantaka and Phlegon waited for Pyrios to complete the mental conversation.

Once it was evident that they had Pyrios' attention again, Lord Kantaka spoke. "Was that Thracis? Is all well in Amazonia?"

Pyrios shook his head. "It wasn't Thracis." He looked around at the other representatives all going their separate ways. He picked out the dun coat of Dimitri Alexi moving off toward the University of Piber. He bowed to Lord Kantaka. "Forgive me, Lord Kantaka, but I must go."

Pyrios didn't wait for a response but trotted out of the fence that encompassed both the Registry and the University. Phlegon and Lord Kantaka watched as the gray stallion trotted down the main road and into Lipizza.

"He's going to get himself killed over this mare," Phlegon said.

Lord Kantaka sighed. "Unfortunately, that is the fate of many young stallions. Let us hope that Thracis has more sense when it comes to feminine company."

CHAPTER 4

Psyche stood outside the circle of Queen Hippolyta's council of Equines and Felisians and watched the proceedings with unease. Her oldest sister, Alastrina, was speaking with ears pinned.

"The Registry has lorded over us for decades, refusing to see our worth. I say to Pandemonium with all those stallions." Her voice became a sneer on the last word. "It was our foredams who colonized the southern continent, our foredams who accepted the Felisians with pricked ears and lowered heads, and it was we who faced the Baroquians and turned them away from Diomedean shores."

The other members of the council cheered in response with whinnies and meows. Psyche shifted her feet and waited to hear what her dam thought of the situation.

Queen Hippolyta waited for silence before speaking. "We were victorious against the Baroquians. But Baroquian soldiers do not wear Imperial armor."

"Our weapons were designed to destroy Imperial armor." Lady Melantha, the queen's oldest advisor, a black Felisian, spoke with an even tone. Her black tail was coiled around her paws as she sat in her accustomed place on the queen's right.

"The lady speaks truth." Lady Dendera hopped up on a burlap pedestal. After destroying the Baroquian ships and eliminating any chance at retreat during the battle, Lady Dendera and her Felisians had achieved a new level of importance in Queen Hippolyta's council. "However, our forces are not yet strong enough to stand against the Imperial Cavalry and the Baroquians. Do not forget that many Felisians have sided with the Baroquians."

"A good point," Lady Melantha agreed.

Alastrina pinned her ears again. "We could hold them. We should have marched during the winter months. We could have taken the Baroquians by surprise on their home soil."

Queen Hippolyta shook her head. "Such things you do not know, my daughter. Armies do not march in winter because the weather makes moving equipment dangerous. Do not forget that we incurred heavy losses at the battle as well."

Lady Liana, new to the council, bobbed her sculpted head, her forelock bouncing. "Where do you feel the greatest threat lies, your majesty?"

This was the central problem. The southern continent was connected to the country of Lipizzania by the border between Courbettania and Artemia. Artemia, as the northernmost province of Diomedea, had always maintained a civil relationship Lipizzania and was more open to trade with other countries than the rest of Diomedea. This land connection would make the Imperial Cavalry seem the more imminent threat.

The Baroquian Peninsula was separated from Diomedea by the Backahasten Ocean. It was unlikely that the Baroquians would try to invade Diomedea again after the disastrous results of their first attempt, they had sustained substantial naval losses, but they would learn from their mistakes and come back eventually.

Queen Hippolyta flicked her ears. A cunning gleam sparked her eyes. "I believe we should let stallions be stallions."

She backed out of the council circle and went to stand in front of one of the few stallions in the room. He stood at attention, his tensed muscles ready for the queen to lash out her frustrations. Instead, she rubbed the side of her head against his muscled neck. The other mares in the group exchanged sly glances. The queen turned to look at her council.

"The best way to win a battle is to wait for your enemy to be at a disadvantage. We will hold our forces and continue our training. Dias Eno is inventing new weaponry that will raise our cavalry to a level never witnessed before on Equus. We shall be as a Felisian stalking mice and wait in the shadows. The Baroquians and the Imperial Cavalry will fight whether we engage in battle or not. It is the way of stallions."

She swished her tail and walked to stand before Psyche. She looked at her youngest daughter while speaking to her council. "We will wait until the dust has settled and then engage the remaining combatants. Whoever wins, their army will be weak and scattered. It will be the perfect time to pounce."

The Felisians in the room snickered.

"And this will allow us to measure their strengths and weaknesses." Queen Hippolyta nodded to Lady Dendera. "Set your cats to the task of ingratiating themselves among our enemies. I would know what our enemies are capable of."

Lady Dendera, head of the spy division, bowed low. "It will be done, my queen."

Queen Hippolyta looked at her oldest daughter, Alastrina. "Find a group of suitable stallions to infiltrate the Imperial Cavalry. The more spies we have the better."

Lady Alastrina lowered her head in a curt bow and trotted out of the chamber. The rest of the council, sensing the meeting had ended, filed out behind Alastrina. Queen Hippolyta stayed in front of Psyche, blocking her retreat until the chamber was empty.

"Come with me to my private garden."

Psyche hung her head and followed her dam down the warren of hallways that led to the queen's private gardens. Positioned in an open courtyard in the center of the queen's stable, the garden was a place of solitude for the Diomedean queens. Statues depicting all the queens ranging back to Lady Cassandra ringed the outside perimeter of the garden. The garden was surrounded by a raised walkway thirty feet high that was patrolled by both Equine and Felisian guards. Diomedea was one of the more tumultuous countries on Equus and it never hurt to be prepared. Assassination attempts against the queens of Diomedea had been tried even in times of peace.

Psyche felt anxiety flow through her body. She hadn't wanted to come to the Diomedean capital of Ruffiana. She still hadn't told her dam about Thracis though Hippolyta knew her youngest daughter was seeing the same stallion on a regular basis. This knowledge did not upset the queen in the least as she had bigger problems than who her daughters were spending time with, but Hippolyta was unnerved by the stealthy way in which Psyche was proceeding with this stallion. As far as the queen was aware, Eno was the only mare Psyche had formally introduced to this stallion. Hippolyta could go to Eno's laboratory and ask the bay mare about Psyche's interest, but Eno and Psyche had been friends since foalhood and their loyalty to each other ran deep.

The queen stopped in the center of the garden where the rose bushes were in full bloom. Psyche hung back outside the circle formed by the regal plants. She fought to remain still, keeping her ears from flicking and tail from swishing. Her dam would view any furtive movement as an inclination that Psyche was hiding something.

"You've been spending a lot of time away from the capital as of late." Hippolyta kept her tail to Psyche but the younger mare could see by the queen's ears that her dam was keeping an eye on her.

"My psychic studies with Lady Moirae have been keeping me busy."

"Not too busy to visit Eno frequently."

Psyche kept her ears forward. "She views those visits as much needed distractions from her constant inventing."

"I've heard from Lady Liana that you have not spent any time with her son, Belen."

Despite her best efforts, Psyche's ears lowered. Belen, oldest son of Lady Liana, her dam's newest council member, had been assigned to escort Psyche around the Diomedean encampment the night before the Baroquian battle. Lady Liana was hoping for a political alliance with the royal Augean Stable. Psyche and Belen learned to dislike each other within five minutes of their introduction. Fortunately, Psyche was saved the embarrassment of dismissing Belen herself by the arrival of Thracis, who challenged Belen for the right to escort the youngest Hippolyta daughter. Realizing a fight would lead to questions none of them wanted to answer, Belen had grudgingly stepped down and left Psyche with Thracis. Psyche had thought the incident forgotten. Until now.

Hippolyta turned her head to regard her daughter. "He is a fine stallion from a high-ranking stable. I received word that he fought well in the battle."

"I'm sure he did."

"You were not by his side? I thought you would stand by your escort."

"You raised your daughters to stand on their own. I need no stallion to fight for me."

Hippolyta's ears flicked. She had never seen such ferocity in Psyche. It intrigued her. "I was told you fought well." Hippolyta walked from one rose bush to another, sniffing the blooms. "You honored the Augean Stable." She waited to see if Psyche would beam her pleasure at the compliment. The queen was startled to see her daughter's ears flattened.

"You thought I would not."

Hippolyta stopped her flower inspection and stood to face her daughter. "I thought you would fight within a group and not out in the open alone as you did."

Psyche's squared herself. "I am not the foal of so long ago."

"And you are not yet a warrior," Queen Hippolyta snapped.

"I killed many on that day and still you treat me as an inexperienced filly," Psyche quipped back.

"More experienced as the days pass if I am to believe what my spies tell me."

Psyche was stunned into temporary silence.

Hippolyta tossed her head. "Do you really believe I do not keep watch over my daughters? I've known you've been with a stallion for months now. What I don't understand is why you refuse to bring him to court. Is he unworthy of the Augean Stable?"

He would be to your eyes. Psyche erased the thought before it was fully coalesced. Here in her dam's stable she had no idea how many eavesdroppers her dam employed. She cleared her throat. "I haven't had occasion to invite him here."

"You haven't made occasion."

Psyche tossed her head. "You do not make Alastrina or Lachesis bring their mates to you for inspection."

"That is because both your sisters are mares grown and are capable of making informed decisions."

Psyche stomped a foot at the insult to her intelligence. "That comment should explain to you why I abstained for so long." She sighed and looked away from her dam. "I am leaving. As it is, I will be late getting back to Moirae's home this evening." Moirae was a Felisian and though she lived in an abode made hospitable to Equines it would be a far stretch of the imagination to consider the building a stable.

"You will go when I give you leave."

"I am not one of your subjects to be ordered about."

Hippolyta's ears pinned at the open hostility in Psyche's tone. Her youngest had never spoken to her in such a way. "I wish to meet this stallion, Psyche, to be sure he is not of Baroquian descent."

"As if you are an expert on such matters." Psyche saw her dam flinch as the verbal thrust hit its mark.

Hippolyta's third daughter, Zeva, was the product of a mating with a Baroquian stallion of Friesian descent. Hippolyta had been unaware of the stallion's ancestry when he drew her amorous advances and he didn't think to inform her. Zeva was born as one of the strongest daughters of the Diomedean queen. Six months after Psyche was born, Zeva showed the evil in her heart when she tried to kill her younger sister. As a result, Zeva was banished from Diomedea. It was this darkness in Zeva that accounted for the coolness between Psyche and her dam.

"You are not as wise in these matters as you feel you are," Hippolyta said quietly. "What I do for you I do for your own protection."

"At this time, Mother, I feel I am capable of protecting myself."

Without waiting for a reply, Psyche bowed in mock respect and left the garden.

CHAPTER 5

Thracis lowered his head as he followed Phrenicos down the tree lined path leading to the residence of the delphae of Boudica. Thracis didn't know if it was a home or a stable as he wasn't sure if the delphae was an Equine or a Felisian since cats and horses were integrated here more than anywhere else on Equus. The path beneath his feet carried the scent of Felisians and Equines alike.

On the walk from Boudica, Phrenicos had explained that traditionally only a Felisian could become the delphae, the head of an *ammoni* coven, but in recent years Equines had proven themselves as delphae. The High Delphae herself who resided in the Temple of Consciousness was an Equine in point of fact. *Ammoni* was a Felisian term adopted by the Equines to describe a powerful psychic whose mental powers went beyond the common uses of telekinesis and telepathy. An *ammoni* was also a reference to an animal who practiced the occult or dark arts. Communicating with spirits or beings on other planes of existence was encouraged in Felisian society. It was a skill that was both coveted and honed.

Thracis, having come from a stable far from Diomedea, had never heard of an *ammoni* until he was wounded in a Baroquian ambush. His attacker's weapons had been dipped in a lethal poison. Thracis would have died if not for Kamuzu, a Felisian healer skilled in poisons, and his miniature horse companion, Alcander. They had been sent by Psyche. The mare had seen Thracis' fate in a vision and knew he would be unprepared to deal with such an insidious poison. It was Kamuzu who had first mentioned that Psyche was an *ammoni* mare.

Aeos was off in Sanctuary being trained by the *ammoni* healers in the city. The dun stallion, much more adept at psychic usage than Thracis, would have been right at home here on this shaded path walking toward the most powerful *ammoni* in five towns. Thracis himself was none too eager to meet with someone who could flay his mind open on a whim.

It was Thracis' inability to protect himself against mental attack that had led to this meeting in the first place. After the Baroquian ambush had failed to kill him, Thracis had been assaulted mentally by one of the Baroquian's *ammoni*. A mare disguised herself as Psyche in his mind. Having communicated at length mentally with Psyche, Thracis had opened his mind to her with little reserve. Fortunately, Thracis sensed the trap before the mare could fully ensnare his mind. He had a frightening few minutes before Aeos had come to his rescue, breaking the mental link between Thracis and the unknown mare. Thracis still shuddered when he thought of how close the mare had been to ripping through his inner barriers and destroying his mind from the inside out.

"You shouldn't dwell on the past. The delphae will treat you with all the respect you afford her."

Thracis lifted his head to the sound of Phrenicos' voice. "I'm sorry. It's only that I feel so vulnerable after that mind attack."

"I'm sure, but that is why we are here. You are of great importance to the Baroquians. We have to make sure you are just as strong mentally as you are physically."

Thracis bobbed his head. The path was leading out into sunlight, the trees giving way to a grass covered meadow. Thracis' ears flicked forward and his steps quickened. Phrenicos held back a little; Thracis wasn't a foal who needed minding.

The structure in the meadow wasn't a house or a stable, but a combination of both. The left side was designed like a typical Felisian house. Small windows with wide ledges were arranged in staggered placement in the solid walls of the house portion. Most of the windows were open, allowing easy passage from outside to inside for any Felisian. A gutter system zigzagged between the windows. The gutter served two purposes: it funneled water off the roof and gave the Felisians a pathway up and down the side of the house.

The right side of the house was more Equine friendly. It was set up in common barn fashion with large, room-spanning windows and wide, open doorways. While the house was two-story, the barn portion was only one floor. The gutter system crossed both sides of the building making bridges for Felisians to scamper across. Thracis had been inside very few Felisian homes as they were often too small for even a miniature to enter, but he imagined the inside of this one would resemble the outside of the house, with holes for doorways and ledges throughout.

Phrenicos walked past Thracis to the barn. He whickered a greeting to someone Thracis couldn't see. A few seconds later a white Felisian hopped up on a pedestal set just outside the barn door. The Felisian spoke to Phrenicos keeping its voice low. Thracis didn't believe that this hushed tone was an attempt to be rude; the whole area had a quiet, dozing feeling. Thracis guessed the Felisian was speaking low out of respect for anyone who might be mediating or studying. He waited for Phrenicos to motion to him before stepping up to the Felisian.

"I am Aahmas, assistant to the delphae of this coven. We have been waiting for you, stallion of Thetis Stable." Her blue eyes glittered with interest. Her white coat floated around her as if it were gossamer strands of spider's silk rather than fur.

"Do you know why the Baroquians want to kill me?"

The Felisian slowly blinked her eyes. Her tail curled around her paws as she sat on the pedestal. "All things in time, foolish colt. We have not decided if it is wise for you to know your future."

Thracis pawed the ground in agitation. "Hippolyta Psyche has told me a little."

Phrenicos turned his head to regard Thracis. The Felisian's gaze never wavered. When she spoke, her voice carried a deep purr. "The Lady is very talented and very wise. She would not have told you all. She would not have wanted you to believe your path is set. Even the High Delphae cannot see where all rivers flow."

Phrenicos nodded in agreement. The Felisian's eyes glazed as she contacted someone with her mind. Her lips curved into a small smile, revealing her pointed fangs. "The delphae is ready to meet with you. Follow me to the reflection pools."

Aahmas hopped off the pedestal and walked down a path to the right of the house. Her tail swayed in typical Felisian fashion as her hips swung. Thracis turned to follow her but Phrenicos stepped in front of him.

"Why did you not tell me of Psyche's vision?" The older stallion's ears were lowering.

"I did not think it important."

"One of the most talented *ammoni* in all Diomedea tells your fortune and you didn't think it might be important?"

Thracis flicked his ears. "It was…private. I didn't tell anyone exactly what she told me. Then I forgot most of it anyway."

"Apparently, even Lord Pegasus doesn't trust you with knowledge of your future." The white stallion turned away before Thracis could comment.

Aahmas was sitting on the path next to a decorated stone. The stone was covered with different colored runic symbols. Thracis felt his eyes being draw to the markings despite his attempt to look at the Felisian. The pattern of runes was just so intriguing. They almost seemed to flow and swirl together like the Calabrian grasses of his homeland. A sudden wave of homesickness flowed through him and Thracis thought maybe he should go back and see his parents and new sister.

The Felisian stood and walked in front of the stone, blocking Thracis' line of sight. As soon as the stone was out of view, Thracis felt his mind focusing again. He tossed his head in agitation. Why had he been thinking of going home? He was in the middle of training. Aahmas shifted, revealing a corner of the stone. Thracis was immediately caught in a hypnotic trance. He saw the turquoise water of the Pthian Sea, the emerald fields of grass. He smelled the roses in his dam's garden, the worn leather of the training harnesses in the schooling rings. His heart yearned to return home. He wasn't even aware of the other mind that had slipped into his as easily as an otter sliding into a pond without a ripple.

Sitting squarely in front of the stone, Aahmas began licking a paw. "He needs much work."

Thracis blinked at the Felisian. He was aware that time had passed. The shadows were longer and the air had the warm smell of afternoon. His feet hurt as if he had been standing in the same position for a while.

Phrenicos tossed his head. "His friend, Quintus Aeos, who has gone on to the delphae of Sanctuary, was very well trained in the psychic arts. It was he who ousted the mindreaper."

Thracis gave an involuntary shudder at the mention of the mare who tried to invade his innermost barriers and destroy his mind. A light sweat broke out on his body.

The Felisian stopped licking and looked at him. "This is a mesmer stone. We use it to keep someone occupied while we search their minds."

Thracis pawed the ground. "Does that mean you were in my head?"

"It was I who read your thoughts, stallion of Thetis Stable."

Thracis swung his head around and looked at a lithe gray Felisian with black spots. The Felisian walked with an air of royalty and Thracis had no doubt that this was the delphae. If Aeos had been present he would have explained to Thracis that cats with this coloring were called Maus and they were directly related to the royal families of Felisian society. It was rumored that the Mau cats were direct descendants of the Felisian deity, Bast. Aeos was not here, however, and Thracis knew nothing of the power, both psychic and political, that this Felisian wielded. Consequently, he continued the conversation in his less than tactful manner.

Thracis pinned his ears and glared at the newcomer. "What right do you have to search my most private thoughts?" An instant later he crumbled to the ground as a searing pain flashed through his head. He squealed in pain and thrashed his head against the ground trying to rid himself of the claws racking through his mind.

The spotted Felisian walked forward until she was just out of reach of Thracis' head. "I do as I wish, foolish colt. I am the delphae of this coven and it is my right to search all newcomers for potential threats. If you knew anything of covens, or *ammoni* for that matter, you would know that we are not as defenseless as we may appear." Her tail twitched. "A fact your lady should have enlightened you about."

Thracis had stopped thrashing and was lying flat with sides heaving. At the mention of Psyche his mind refocused. "What do you know about my lady?"

A slash of pain in his head reminded him who he was speaking to. He curled his neck down in a pantomime of a bow. It was the best he could do, lying flat like this. "I apologize. I should not be speaking to you in this manner."

At the sound of submission in the stallion's voice, the delphae released the mental hold she had on him. She looked up at Phrenicos. "He needs a lesson in humility."

Phrenicos chuckled. "He has received many. Fortunately, he learns from his mistakes rather quickly."

They watched as Thracis curled his legs under himself and rose shakily to his feet. His head pounded and his vision swam. He hung his head and waited for the ground to stop shifting under his feet.

Unperturbed by the horse's lack of balance, the delphae walked under him. She wove between and around his legs, pausing to sniff him occasionally. After a complete circuit, she flexed her haunches and jumped up on his back. She must have used some kind of psychic enhancement because the top of Thracis' shoulders were almost five and a half feet from the ground. She inspected his top as she had his underneath, then sat down on the top of his rump.

"He is a fine stallion, physically. And from what I have gathered, his mind is open to improvement." Thracis felt the delphae dig her claws into his skin. "I will accept him for training. He is of great importance to the Baroquians and they will send others to eliminate him. He will need all the defenses we are capable of giving him."

"In that case, I believe it will be good for him to spend a few weeks with you ladies." Phrenicos bowed his head. He turned to look at Thracis. "You see? I told you a break from training was needed and here one presents itself."

"I was not aware I would be gone for so long."

Phrenicos chuckled. "Several weeks' reprieve will do you good. Don't forget what you have learned from me in the past months."

Thracis bobbed his head. "I will continue to hone the skills you have already taught me."

Phrenicos tossed his head. "See that you do and I will come back for you when the delphae deems you capable of defending your own mind." As he walked off, the white stallion called over his shoulder. "And see that you treat all the ladies here with the utmost respect. They aren't accustomed to your usual brash demeanor."

Thracis rolled his eyes to look first at the delphae on his rump and then at Aahmas, sitting near the mesmer stone. After this meeting he would be absolutely sure to be on his best behavior. If word got back to Psyche that he had offended a delphae, Thracis would never hear the end of it.

CHAPTER 6

Psyche ducked as an unidentifiable metal object came hurling through the air at her head. She pinned her ears at the deafening clang as the object crashed into a pile of Eno's discards. The pile had doubled in size since Psyche's last visit only a month before.

Tossing her head, Psyche walked across the large indoor laboratory Queen Hippolyta had built for Dias Eno, Psyche's foalhood friend. Eno was the only foal of Commander Talos Dias, the current Asapatish of the Hippikon. Eno's dam had died not long after Eno was foaled. As a filly raised among stallions, Eno found it hard to associate with mares who were not of a Diomedean disposition. And since she was better at strategy and combat than many of the stallions under her sire's command, Commander Dias had thought it prudent to send Eno to a country where her opinions would cause less disruption. That she was working on a project that would allow mares to engage in open combat on the rest of Equus was something Eno was keeping hidden from her sire. Even though it was he who had put the idea in her head.

Almost three years previous, Commander Dias had made a bargain with his daughter. He promised her that if she could find a way for mares to fight in the sky without the benefit of aircraft, he would let them join the Imperial Cavalry. After sharing this news with the Diomedean queen, Lady Hippolyta was more than happy to fund Eno's experiments. Though the bay mare had yet to create a functional prototype, all Eno's theories were proving to be sound.

"I will find a way for mares to fly even if I have to pluck every bird from here to Lipizza to make feathered wings."

"Just don't fuse the feathers with wax. It didn't work out so well for Dalen Icaris."

Eno spun to face Psyche, her black mane flaring back along her neck. "Are you trying to make my mood worse?"

Ignoring the threat in Eno's voice, Psyche shifted to stand hipshot. "I was trying to lighten your mood. You've been especially snappish to everyone lately."

Eno flicked her ears and sighed. "It's only because I'm so close. The thrusters are perfected. I just need to figure out how to make the wings. The weight is the problem. Everything I come up with is too heavy."

Psyche tossed her head at the pile of metal. "What you need is something stretchy, something that can catch the wind, like a sail."

"Even sails are heavy."

"Lighter than metal."

Eno pinned her ears at Psyche and nipped the other mare's neck. "If anyone is going to be sarcastic, it's going to be me."

Psyche snorted. "I think being stuck in here surrounded by all this metal is ruining your customary less-than-cheerful attitude. You should come out for a while, it's a beautiful day."

Eno gave the lab a swiping, scalding look. "Maybe you're right."

The two mares headed out of the large room, their hooves muted by the rubberized flooring. Eno stole several glances at Psyche as they walked. Despite her nonchalant attitude, the black and white mare was lined with tension. Eno knew well of the dysfunction between Psyche and the rest of her herd. Eno was in a similar situation with her sire and was used to the formalities of having a parent who held such a high ranking. The difference between Psyche and Eno was that Eno's sire adored and praised her and never made the bay mare feel inadequate. When Hippolyta looked at Psyche all she saw was a foal in need of minding.

Eno had known Psyche was dreading her visit to her dam, but there was nothing either of them could do about it. Psyche had to play the dutiful daughter and show her dam respect. Eno wondered if Hippolyta had said something about either Psyche's lack of interest in Lady Liana's son or about Thracis directly. It was a sensitive subject for Psyche even in discussion with Eno and the bay couldn't imagine what would happen if the queen decided to provoke her youngest daughter on the subject of a suitable stallion.

"So, how did go?" They had walked out into the sunlight and Eno inhaled the sweet smell of summer grasses. Several fields in the area had been designated hay fields and were off-limits to grazing. The grass in those fields would be cut, dried, and baled for winter storage. The following year, the hay fields would be rotated to give the soil a rest.

Psyche tossed her head and snorted. "It went as well as could be expected."

"That doesn't sound encouraging."

Psyche lowered her voice. "She wants to meet Thracis."

Eno didn't bother asking which 'she' Psyche was referring to. There was only one mare in Ruffiana whose opinion mattered to Psyche, though the black and white mare would be loathe to admit it. Eno led the way into the field before speaking. She chose her words cautiously as she was having trouble reading Psyche's mood. "Do you think that's a good idea?"

Psyche only looked at her.

"Okay," Eno said, "We both know your dam treats you like a weanling. And we both know that if she comes into contact with Thracis all she's going to do is pick out every flaw she can find, either real or imagined." She waited for Psyche to nod. "But we also know that your dam won't give any peace until she meets whoever is courting you."

"I don't think she's going to bother me about Thracis anytime soon."

"Because she has so much to do with the coming war?"

"Because I told her to keep her nose in her own stable."

Eno stopped and stared at Psyche. "Really?"

Psyche swished her tail at a fly and stomped a foot. "Not in those exact words but…," she trailed off and looked away.

They were silent for a few minutes. The sound of bees and grasshoppers filled their ears in the lazy afternoon. The wind brought the smell of other fields, mixing with the smell of timothy, and the smell of rain in the west. By this evening the storms will have reached Eno's lab and stable and she would be working to the sound of falling rain. She found the idea appealing. Maybe she would talk Psyche into spending the night and the two of them could share a few buckets of wine. Psyche looked like she could use a drink.

"Well, after the way you handled yourself in the battle, your dam should accept that you are capable of making your own decisions. Especially about the stallions you want to be with."

"She doesn't think I'm capable of picking out which grasses to eat."

"Maybe some time apart would be a good thing. You were so much happier when you were in Iliad." Eno flicked her ears. "You could stay here for a little while. I know it's not that far from Ruffiana, but your dam hardly ever comes here."

Psyche considered, then tossed her head. "I can stay for a day or two but Moirae expects me back by the end of the week."

Delighted by the change of subject, Eno said, "How is your training going?"

At last Pysche's tension eased a little. "Very well now that Thracis has stopped contacting me every night, giving me a chance to concentrate. Moirae says I'm moving along and she wants to begin teaching me psychic combat."

"I think that's great given that your sister is trying to kill your mate."

"He's not my mate."

"He is right now."

"That's right now."

Eno pinned her ears. "Don't treat me like an idiot. We both know you're head over hooves for this stud of yours. And from what I've seen you have every right to be. He is quite yummy."

"Yummy? Are you running a fever?"

Eno twitched a shoulder. "The only contact with the outside world I get nowadays is the young Felisians that deliver my materials. I guess I'm picking up on their slang."

Psyche snorted. "You need to get out more."

The two mares lowered their heads and began to graze. The summer grasses were sprinkled with a hint of clover which lent a surprising sweetness with every second or third mouthful. They grazed for an hour before taking a break to get a drink from the stone trough in the stable garden. Eno herself wasn't much for gardening, but an older mare who lived a mile or so away came once a week to make sure Eno's garden was well-tended. Eno had to admit that the garden was a relaxing place to come and stand after several days of working in the lab.

"Since you're staying for a couple of days, I have some wine that I was hoping to open soon." Eno winked at Psyche.

Psyche tossed her head. "Is it Diomedean or is it something your sire sent for your birthday a few weeks back?"

"It is a birthday gift, but not from my sire, and it's Acarnian. I'm curious to how it tastes."

"Acarnian? The rumor is they make the best wine on Equus. Who do you know in Acarnia and what did you do to win such favor?"

"You should know; you're the reason we met. Or more correctly, your mate is the reason."

Psyche's ears, lowering in her confusion, pricked forward in surprise. "You have got to be kidding."

"Why? Just because I'm so technical that doesn't mean I can't be interested in someone who is a little more earthy." Eno ducked her head and looked at Psyche from under her lashes. "Besides, you don't think I wasn't appreciating his muscles when he was helping me off the battlefield?"

"I had a feeling leaving you and Aeos alone together, even in the medical tent, was a bad idea."

"It's not like it's serious or anything. We're not as physical as you and Thracis for instance." Eno flicked an ear as Psyche looked away in embarrassment. "We just contact each other once in a while and talk. And since his sire is the ruling stallion of Acarnia it's not as if it was hard for him to get the wine. Besides, he and I have a lot in common."

"Because both your dams died when you were foaled?"

Eno nodded. They stood in silence for a moment, each lost in their own thoughts.

Psyche tossed her head. "Still, your sire will be pleased to know you are talking to a stallion who was so favored at the Romanium."

"Such things don't concern him. He only wants his daughter to be happy. And find someone who can deal with my constant inventing."

"Not to mention arguing."

Eno knew Psyche was trying to sound flippant, but she heard the sorrow in Psyche's voice. "I'm sorry. I know familial interaction is a difficult subject for you." Eno dropped her head to show how sorry she was.

Psyche tossed her own head. "It isn't as if this is anything new."

"No, but you've never been interested in a stallion before. You can't blame your dam and sisters for being curious."

"The only one of my sisters who is interested is Zeva and she's the one who tried to tear Thracis' mind apart."

Eno took a sip of water before speaking. "Have you told him that?"

Psyche shook her head. "I have problems enough without telling Thracis my herd's dark secrets."

"What if she tries again?"

"She won't. You don't know my sister. She'll turn her mind to another form of attack."

Eno's ears fell a little. "You don't know your sister either. You were under a year old when she was exiled. You don't know how she's changed in the years between then and now. And she wasn't exactly pleasant to begin with," Eno finished under her breath.

Psyche pawed the ground. "Thracis told me Phrenicos was taking him to the delphae of Boudica for training. She should be able to teach him enough to keep Zeva out of his mind until he contacts someone else for help."

"Someone like you?"

Psyche pinned her ears. "You don't think I could protect him from Zeva?"

Eno sighed. This was always a sticking point with Psyche. Years of her dam not acknowledging her talents had driven

Psyche to take on the strongest opponents and most grueling training. Eno didn't doubt Psyche's abilities, but her sire had taught her not to underestimate her opponents. Eno thought that Psyche's need to prove herself was blinding her to the very real danger Zeva posed.

When she spoke, Eno chose her words carefully. "I think after years of training Zeva would be a formidable opponent for even Lachesis."

At the mention of the strongest of Hippolyta's daughters, Psyche raised her ears. "Do you really believe that?"

Eno bobbed her head. "I do. And I think that you will need help if you plan on challenging Zeva."

"Like help from a certain dun stallion?"

Eno twitched her shoulders. "He is very talented, Psyche. And he holds your skill in high regard. Unlike you he knows when to ask for assistance and when to yield a point."

Psyche's ears flicked at the smugness in Eno's voice. "Be that as it may, I have enough issues with one stallion. I don't need to listen to the 'good advice' of another."

Eno tossed her head and nipped Psyche's shoulder. "Fine then. Since you're here why don't you use that smart attitude of yours to help me figure out how to get us in the sky?"

Psyche sighed, resigned to spending the rest of the day in Eno's lab listening as the bay mare rejected one idea after another. As they walked back to the large building Psyche turned her face up to the sun. "Too bad the wings of Icaris melted. It would be something indeed to fly close to the sun's gold."

"You've always looked at things in a romantic light. Are you sure you're really one of Hippolyta's daughters?"

Tossing her head in the golden light, Psyche snorted laughter. "I'm the best of the lot."

CHAPTER 7

Thracis pinned his ears and stared at the delphae. Why couldn't she understand that he was not as talented in the psychic arts as the mares of Diomedea? Perhaps she had spent too much time in female company and didn't realize that males were lacking in some areas.

"I assure you, foolish colt, I am quite aware of masculine faults."

Thracis lowered his head and snapped his teeth in frustration. He couldn't stand that the spotted cat could read his mind on a whim.

"That is exactly what I am trying to correct." The delphae hopped up on a tree stump and sharpened her claws on the dry wood.

She and Thracis were in a small meadow not far from the reflection pools. The meadow was lush with summer grass, not that Thracis was allowed to sample any of it, and splattered with groups of blue and pink flowers. It was midmorning and they had been in the meadow since dawn. Having missed breakfast, Thracis was more irritable than usual and finding it difficult to focus on the simple tasks the delphae was asking him to perform.

A week had passed since Thracis began training with the delphae. His days were broken up into a series of sessions focusing on different aspects of psychic development. In the morning, Thracis spent two to three hours with the delphae herself, learning how to shield his mind from outside intruders. After a break for lunch and some light exercise, Thracis and Aahmas meditated at the reflective pools. It was more than meditation in Thracis' opinion, as Aahmas spent the time probing Thracis' mind and showing him how to do the same to hers. He had yet to invade her thoughts without her knowledge. Another break for dinner and some more schooling and then the evening was spent with the delphae again, learning how to project his mind to different areas in an attempt to gain information.

"Why do you take such delight in pointing out my failings?" Thracis tried to keep the frustration out of his voice.

"I have said nothing about your progress." She sat down and began to lick a paw.

"That's just the point. I've been here a week and every day is the same with no progress. At least in the schooling ring I can feel my endurance building and my muscles strengthening. Here I feel as awkward as I did when I first set hoof at your home."

"Perhaps I should see to it that you have time to eat a meal in the morning prior to training," the delphae said dryly.

"My mood has nothing to do with my growling stomach."

"I'm sure it doesn't." Her tone implied that she didn't believe him at all. "A true *ammoni*, much like a true hippeus, must learn to ignore physical discomforts. It is what defines a warrior."

"You and Phrenicos must communicate daily," Thracis said under his breath.

"Don't bother mumbling, I can pick your words right out of your thoughts."

Thracis snorted and pawed the ground in frustration. Doing this broke several blades of grass. His stomach growled louder at the sweet scent of fresh food.

"Enough complaining." The delphae jumped off the stump and walked over to stand before Thracis' front feet. "Time for you to learn to center yourself, stallion of Thetis Stable."

Thracis felt a slash of claws inside his head. He tried to jump back but found that his feet were secured to the ground somehow. He snorted and his ears ticked back and forth rapidly. "What are you doing?"

The delphae twitched her tail. "I am showing you that not only your mind is in danger during a mental attack."

Thracis fought panic at being unable to turn and flee from the delphae. He could feel her claws digging deeper into his mind. As he had with Zeva, Thracis threw up wall after mental wall around his core to keep the delphae at bay. With her momentarily blocked, Thracis closed his eyes and imaged himself in the meadow. He saw that mental tendrils, glowing blue in his mind's eye, were wrapped around his legs. The delphae had taught him that in psychic battle anything imagined became real, now was the time to test this teaching.

Without giving himself a chance to think of how impossible it was, Thracis imagined razor sharp blades coming out of his legs and cutting the restraints. He jumped back from the delphae and was startled to find that he could move. He was so unprepared that he almost fell down. The delphae used his surprise to squirm through several of his inner barriers. Thracis approached this threat with new confidence now that his legs were free.

Instead of facing her head on, Thracis choose to send something else. He imagined a huge owl with pointed talons and sharpened beak. Felisians had a deep fear of any raptor as birds of prey often hunted Felisian kittens. He chose an owl because they were silent and sent it to hover just behind the barrier the delphae was striking against.

The delphae pushed her way passed the barrier and Thracis felt a wave of satisfaction as she hissed in terror at the owl waiting in ambush. Thracis felt the delphae's mind retract from his own. Thracis couldn't see the delphae in his head as the Felisian had not formed an image, but he could feel her presence like a void. He manipulated the owl to follow the void as it retreated, making the bird swoop down and brandish it's deadly talons. Having enough of this plight, the delphae vanished from Thracis' mind. Thracis opened his eyes to see the delphae crouched on the ground in front of him, panting. It was the first time Thracis had seen the delphae lose her composure.

"That was impressive. Phrenicos warned me that you have a natural talent."

Thracis bowed his head in respect and in an attempt to catch his breath. The encounter had taken as much out of him as it had her. "It was difficult not to panic. I did not believe my attempts to dislodge you would work."

"This is the hardest lesson for even the Felisian *ammoni* to learn. When using the psychic arts all you can imagine becomes real. This time you caught me off guard with your boldness. Do not use the owl again as I will recognize the trap."

Thracis bobbed his head. "I did not think I could use the same ploy."

"It is the same with physical combat. An opponent will learn your tendencies and attack strategy. You must remain versatile and inventive."

"You sound like Master Phrenicos."

The delphae stood and stretched, her gray and black tail arching to form a half-loop. "We have been friends for many years. Come. After that display you deserve some breakfast."

"At this point I think it's closer to the noonday meal." Thracis tried to keep his grumbling low but he saw by the twitch of the delphae's tail she had heard him.

"I believe you are correct. Tell me, stallion of Thetis, when was it you last spoke with Lady Psyche?"

"It has been several days." *And my lady was not pleased with me by the end of the conversation.* He didn't think the delphae would be interested in his and Psyche's little snit and so decided not to add that last.

"Word has come to us that she and her dam have had a difference of opinion as of late."

"She does not share such things with me." Although this information did clarify the foul mood Psyche had been in lately.

"She does not share such things with anyone." The delphae looked at Thracis over her shoulder. "It was her sister, Alastrina, who told us there is distress in the Augean Stable."

"From what I've seen, Psyche is capable of taking care of herself. And if she were in trouble I would know." Even though he spoke the truth, Thracis' pinned his ears. As a stallion, and the one who was currently Psyche's mate though not formally acknowledged, Thracis was allowed the privilege of protecting his lady. As a Diomedean mare, Psyche claimed to resent his possessiveness. However, she seemed to preen even more every time Thracis pointed out that she was his mare until she turned him away and as such should be defended against other stallions. This hot and cold attitude of Psyche's was beginning to drive Thracis to distraction every time they spoke.

"It must be frustrating for a stallion such as you who wishes to become a hippeus, sworn to defend the weak, to be attracted to such an independent mare."

"It is frustrating, but well worth it. She is well worth it."

"You love her very much."

Thracis said nothing. His feelings were still something he discussed only with Psyche and then only when pressed. He didn't want to get into a personal discussion with the delphae. If she knew his emotions by looking into his mind, Thracis could ignore her, but if she connived him into an open discussion, Thracis would be forced to answer her questions.

Trying to lead her away from the private subject, Thracis said, "Lady Delphae, I have been here a week and still do not know your given name. Is it custom that you are only addressed by your title?"

The delphae gave a purring laugh. "It is not a custom unless you are addressing the High Delphae. She is the *ammoni* above us all. Only those she is closest to are allowed the privilege of addressing her by name."

Thracis listened politely. He couldn't imagine ever being in the presence of the High Delphae, but he knew better than to appear bored in front of a teacher. He would have listened with more interest if Psyche had told him her older sister was the High Delphae of Diomedea. The delphae of Boudica knew that Psyche was related to the High Delphae and found it interesting that Thracis didn't know about the connection.

"My name is Kasmut, a daughter of Ankah. You will address me as you already have or as Lady Kasmut."

"It would be the same if I were in the presence of a mare in a higher-ranking herd than my own."

"That would be difficult for you to do in your home province of Calabria. I was of the understanding that you are of the ruling herd in that land."

Thracis tossed his head as he walked. "Thetis Stable is home of the ruling herd. However, if I visited another stable in the province or journeyed to another province I would treat all mares with respect. Until we became more familiar with each other."

Kasmut smiled at the flirtatious tone in Thracis' voice, but kept her amusement hidden when she spoke. "Your dam and sire saw that you were brought up correctly."

"They only wished that I would behave properly when in the presence of potential political allies. My older brother Pyrios is the rightful heir, but my sire believes in contingency plans."

They reached the stable. The delphae walked past the water troughs and grain feeders and toward an open-air pavilion in the field behind the house. "Your sire knows that things do not always work out the way that we plan."

"Trust me, Pyrios was born to politics the way ducks are born to water. He would not be happy in any other station of Equine society."

"Choice of profession has nothing to do with your sire making sure you are capable of running the province. Sometimes things occur that are outside our control."

"You mean if Pyrios dies, my sire wants to make sure his line will continue."

"It is a realistic outlook given the current turmoil on Equus."

Thracis lowered his ears. He didn't like to think about the prospect of Pyrios perishing but he understood the delphae's meaning. This conversation was all the more unsettling to Thracis as Pyrios refused to contact him. Thracis hadn't spoken to Pyrios in weeks, his only communication to Lipizza had been through Phlegon. Pyrios had never ignored Thracis to this extent before and the younger Zephyros colt was becoming agitated. If Pyrios was chasing a mare in the Equine capital that was all well and good; Pyrios had been pursuing mares as far back as Thracis could remember. However, Thracis was much more involved with Psyche than Pyrios had ever been with any mare and Thracis was still finding a few moments every third day or so to contact his brother.

"A little time apart is never a bad thing once siblings reach adulthood," the delphae observed as she hopped up onto the pedestal on one end of the table that had been set up in the pavilion.

The table was loaded with fresh sliced fish, rice, sweet grasses, a variety of grains, and a small bowl of catnip. Buckets of water were set next to one of the pavilion's support posts. Felisians ate a variety of foods and, unlike Equines, preferred much of their food cooked. Rice was a particular favorite and they served it with most meals. Catnip was a treat and was offered out of politeness at most Felisian gatherings. In the delphae's home, Thracis had noticed wild catnip growing in the gardens as well as the fields. He gathered that it was the catnip's mood enhancing qualities that made it a sought-after herb among the Felisian *ammoni*. As there were no Equine *ammoni* training at this time, Thracis didn't know if catnip had the same effect on horses. He doubted it.

Thracis looked around for Aahmas but didn't see the white cat anywhere. She had been busy as of late and had spent little time with the stallion unless she was teaching him something. The delphae had explained that Aahmas, like many *ammoni* who assisted the delphae, often engaged in personal projects to strengthen and hone their psychic abilities. Thracis didn't see any of the Felisian students around either. He wondered how late it was, surely it wasn't that far past the noonday meal. He craned his head to look at the sun but it was hiding behind a scattering of clouds.

The delphae had filled her plate and was sitting on her pedestal, waiting for him to join her at the table. "It is well past noon. The others have eaten and gone about their afternoon duties."

Thracis tossed his head and drank deeply from one of the buckets before filling a low pan with a mixture of the grains provided. Felisians could fill their plates with their front paws as the gods had gifted them with opposable thumbs. Equines were forced to moved objects around with their minds. Not that this was a handicap. Equines often performed several actions at once after they developed their telekinetic ability. Felisians also used telekinetic powers but they relied more heavily on their dexterous paws. This was a quality Felisians shared with Canans and Mustels. It was also this quality that made those creatures prefer weapons such as swords, knives, and blasters.

"Why do you not have any other Equine students at this time?" Thracis asked around a mouthful of grain.

Kasmut swallowed the fish she was eating and twitched her ears. "I felt it better to keep you alone and focused. Besides the fact that most of my Equine students are mares."

Thracis pinned his ears. "Why should that make a difference? I am loyal to Psyche." He felt a guilty pang as he remembered the one night with an unknown mare on his journey to Diomedea. He hoped the delphae hadn't seen that memory in his mind or on his face.

"Loyalty has nothing to do with it. You might behave perfectly, treating another mare as nothing more than a fellow student. But I ask you, how do you think Psyche would address the idea of you spending so much time with another mare, innocent though it may be?"

"About as well as I would handle her spending time with another stallion. Even her infrequent communications with Aeos make me jealous."

Kasmut nodded. "So, you understand that it is easier this way."

Thracis bobbed his head and moved on to the sweet grasses. They ate in silence for a few minutes. Thracis' ears flicked back and forth as he listened to the messages the wind carried. He was proud of his accomplishment of thrusting the delphae from his mind but he was anxious to leave this place and return to schooling with Phrenicos.

Kasmut finished her meal and drank water from a crystal bowl set out on the table. She took a couple of sniffs of the catnip then jumped off the table. She walked to the edge of the pavilion and started licking her gray and black coat. She paused occasionally in her cleaning to flick her ears or look around the open field.

The clouds were thickening and Thracis could smell the copper tang of rain on the air. Thunder rumbled in the distance and the wind began to gust. The dishes and bowls on the table rattled. Cats appeared out of the tall grasses and began to clear the leftovers. Thracis had eaten most of the grain and all the sweet grass, so the cats were mostly retrieving empty serving platters. Thracis nudged the water buckets with his nose, dumping the remaining contents in the grass around the pavilion. He then stacked them within each other, picking the buckets up with his mouth instead of his mind. The Felisians paused in their cleaning of the table and watched with some amusement.

These cats were year-round residents of the delphae's home. They were servants and caretakers. Aahmas had told Thracis that many of the servants had come to the delphae in one crisis or another and had originally planned on staying here until they got back on their feet, then they just never left. Equines who came to the delphae in the same circumstance had a tendency to move on. There were two older mares who came to the residence once a week to spend time with the delphae, but they lived in the village. Thracis didn't mind Felisians but he was beginning to miss Equine company. So many things were lost in translation between cats and horses.

Working together, they cleaned up the pavilion before the rain and were all inside the home before the first drops fell. Felisians hated being wet as a general rule. There were exceptions but for the most part they liked to be indoors during rainstorms. Thracis didn't care either way during these summer storms if it was only rain. He, like other Equines, only wanted to be under cover when the lightning was bad or the wind turned to a gale.

As the storm gained intensity, Thracis was glad for the cover of the stable. He went to his stall and looked out the window. His stall was on at the front of the stable and he could see the lane leading to the village. The lane was filling with water as the rain poured down. If it kept up like this the front yard was going to be a muddy bog by morning.

Twitching his shoulders, Thracis walked to his bedding box. The grasses needed to be changed and he wanted to kick himself for putting off that task as it would take days for the fields to dry. He pawed the grass and walked around the stall some more. He knew he should doze away the afternoon since it was raining, but his mind refused to settle. He wondered if he should contact Psyche then dismissed the idea. She was busy with Eno and he didn't want to bother her.

Folding his legs under himself, Thracis lowered into the bedding box. He sighed and looked out the window. From this vantage all he could see were the trees waving in the wind. Lightning lit the sky and thunder crashed in response. Thracis sighed and laid his head down. Kasmut had said nothing on their short trip to the stable and Thracis hadn't seen Aahmas. Thracis hadn't felt that the delphae's silence had anything to do with discontent. If anything, Thracis thought the cat was excited by the prospect of snoozing the day away to the sound of falling rain.

As he lay listening to the soothing water and thunder, Thracis' eyelids began to droop. He didn't feel as if he were doing enough to be tired because he wasn't working as hard physically as he did when around Phrenicos but all this mind activity was exhausting him. As he drifted off to sleep, he wondered how Aeos was fairing in the far-off city of Sanctuary.

CHAPTER 8

Aeos walked along a street in one of the more insalubrious districts of the Felisian city of Sanctuary. The street itself was a clear indication of the corruption and overall rundowness of the area. It was overgrown with weeds, the cobblestone borders were cracked, and rocks were strewn across both sides in several areas. Aeos was careful to pick his way whenever walking through one of these rock-sprinkled regions. He had forgotten to get reshod the last time he had visited Thracis and a farrier was a hard thing to come by in a city founded and maintained by Felisians.

As a rule, Equines preferred to go barefoot whenever possible. Exceptions included military types and travelers simply because they couldn't count on always having smooth terrain. It was rumored that both the draft breeds in the north and the pony breeds of the east never wore shoes because their hooves were reputed to be the strongest on all Equus. For himself, Aeos had never met a draft or a pony who wore shoes.

Since he had not taken the opportunity to have his hooves filed and his shoes reset to fit him correctly, Aeos' feet were beginning to throb by the end of the day. The nails used to hold the shoes on were also beginning to give way and the shoe on his right front hoof slipped with every step. Cavalry soldiers used a strong adhesive instead of nails to save their hoof walls, but the farrier in Boudica didn't have any and so she had used nails.

Aeos looked at either side of the street as he wandered. All the homes, most falling down, were of Felisian creation. When he first turned onto this street he had thought the homes would be deserted, but he saw cats laying on roofs or in the branches of the few trees he passed. The cats were thin, their coats shabby. They watched his passage with slitted, suspicious eyes. Their tails twitched in the gloom of the overcast day.

The Felisian disdain did not bother Aeos in the least. Over the past months he had learned to be aware of the other minds in his vicinity. He would know the instant one of the Felisian's decided to confront him. In the event of an altercation, Aeos was confident that his weapons and armor would uphold against a Felisian assault. And none of the Felisians in this district would have the mind prowess of which he had become accustomed during his training with the *ammoni* of Sanctuary.

Still, he thought as his hoof clipped a sharp stone, it would not be wise to presume superiority. Thracis had shown him that courage and heart could balance an individual's lack of formal training in battle.

If he did have a problem in this seedy neighborhood, it would be Aeos' own fault. He shouldn't be in this part of the city and knew it but he had needed to get away. The delphae of Sanctuary was delighted with Aeos' ability and gave Queen Hippolyta frequent updates on his progress. In response to this, the queen suggested that perhaps he should travel to the Temple of Consciousness to be instructed by the High Delphae, Lachesis. The delphae of Sanctuary was so proud of this decision she beamed to all around and paraded Aeos through the streets like a prize.

The dilemma was this: Aeos didn't want to go to the High Delphae. He enjoyed his lessons and the challenges presented to him by the *ammoni*, but he cringed at all the attention. He had never wanted to be the center of attention, even as a foal, and hated it even more now. He missed his days at Phrenicos' stable, drying herbs and sparring with Thracis. Here he was allowed to continue his combat schooling as long as it did not interfere with his psychic development. Even with this compromise, Aeos was surrounded by Felisians and therefore was not getting the experience he would need against seasoned Equine fighters.

Besides the sparring, Aeos missed Thracis in general. He missed Thracis' camaraderie, his issues with Psyche, his constant questioning. In Thracis, Aeos found the brother he had never had, but longed for as a foal. He often wondered if Thracis missed him in the same manner. Surely, Thracis did not seem bothered by Pyrios' absence, but then, Aeos was under the impression that the Zephyros colts were not particularly close in the first place.

Along with Thracis, Aeos missed Eno as well. He spoke with her from time to time, mind to mind, but that was not the same as being in the same place with her. An observation Thracis often made about his interactions with Psyche. Aeos knew he did not feel as strongly about Eno as Thracis felt about Psyche, but the dun stallion knew there was potential for he and Eno to establish a relationship beyond friendship. Eno, he knew, would not hold his lineage against him as other mares might.

Because of the loss of their dams, Aeos and Eno had a bond few Equines understood. They knew what it was to grow up without a mother and therefore had shared a lot of the same experiences. It kept them close despite differing interests and activities.

On the advice of Phrenicos, Aeos had attempted to discover more about his dam during his stay in Sanctuary. She died giving birth and his sire, Lord Quintus, ruling stallion of Acarnia, refused to discuss her. Over the years, Aeos had gleaned precious little information about his dam. He knew she was originally from Diomedea but had no knowledge as to her herd or place of origin. Phrenicos had believed Aeos would find more answers in Sanctuary, but as yet no one seemed inclined to share any information. Most of the animals he spoke with were rude in their avoidance of any information about his dam, in point of fact. Their discomfort and evasiveness were much on his mind and the strain was beginning to show to his instructors.

Coming to a halt at the end of the street, Aeos blew out his frustration in a heavy sigh. He wanted to just keep walking until he left Sanctuary and returned to the warm beach and salt-laden air at Phrenicos' stable. The delphae would complain and Aeos was sure he wouldn't be invited to any social engagements in the near future, but that was a small price to pay for some semblance of mental peace. Besides, if he was going to find out anything about his dam, he was going to have to do it somewhere else.

"This isn't the type of area a young stallion like yourself should be wandering alone."

Aeos swung his head around and looked up at the nearest roof. A large orange cat sprawled on the sun warmed shingle. The cat wore a harness weighted down with various leather pouches and Aeos could smell the pungent aroma of herbs.

"I've been wondering when I would see you again. Well met, Kamuzu."

The orange cat stood and walked to the edge of the roof. "Well met, stallion of Acadia stable."

"Where is Alcander? I imagined that the two of you travel together."

Kamuzu nodded his orange head. "He is behind you."

Aeos swung his head around and saw the miniature standing a few feet away. The bells on the miniature's harness were conspicuously silent. Aeos thought Alcander must be using his mind to keep the bells quiet. "Well met, Alcander. It seems you're as stealthy as your traveling companion."

"I have my talents." The miniature's voice held a hint of amusement. He tossed his head and the bells tinkled.

"So, why are you wandering so far from watchful eyes?" Kamuzu had stretched out along the roof's edge. He was licking a paw and acting completely disinterested.

"I needed a moment alone."

"You need a month alone," Kamuzu observed.

Aeos sighed. "This wasn't what I expected. The training yes, and the challenge of learning how to control my abilities, but not the attention of every *ammoni* in Sanctuary. And now they're talking about sending me to the High Delphae to finish my training." He shook his head, his silver mane tousling. "I'm familiar enough with court society to wonder at the queen's insistence that I meet her daughter. Even if she is the High Delphae."

"A foal between the High Delphae and one so talented as yourself would be a strong asset to the Augean Stable." Alcander walked forward and joined Aeos under the sparse shade thrown by the tree nearest Kamuzu.

"Contrary to the belief of the mares in this country, I am not interested in studding myself out."

"It would be a high honor." Kamuzu didn't sound as though he really cared.

"I grew up with only one parent. I would not wish that on my own foal."

"Your sire was not sufficient?" This came from Alcander. Aeos wondered how the miniature could know about his history.

"My sire was wonderful. As was the wetnurse who raised me. It is because of the bond that I share with my sire that I will not abandon my foal. When I find a mare to have one with."

Kamuzu snorted. "Given that you don't appear to be courting anyone at this moment, where were you planning to run-away to?"

Aeos was about to argue then wondered what the point of that would be. Kamuzu was not as dull-witted as he presented himself to be and the Felisian would hear the lie in Aeos' voice. "I was just going to see how Thracis is fairing."

"And not come back for several months."

"If at all." Aeos and Alcander exchanged a look. "The truth of the matter is that I'm not made for this kind of attention. I've no issue with being trained in the psychic arts but I have no interest in court intrigue."

"It's a long journey to Boudica," Alcander said mildly.

"At least four days, if you make good time." Kamuzu stretched languidly in the sun. "Time might go a little faster if you have someone to talk to on the way."

"And you've shown how your defenses slip when you're preoccupied." Alcander tossed his head.

"Won't the two of you get into trouble? I was under the impression that you had obligations to the Augean Stable."

"Obligations are funny things. They shift like the sands of the Natarian Desert. You won't be able to continue your training until you have a clear head." Kamuzu jumped down off the roof. "Besides, not everyone benefits from traditional instruction."

"And city life leaves something to be desired," Alcander added.

Aeos felt his spirit lift at the prospect of beginning a journey with friends rather than alone. "I must have made the decision to leave without admitting it to myself because all my things are already packed."

"Lord Pegasus works best when we do not question his motives," Alcander said quietly.

"As does the Lady Bast," Kamuzu echoed.

Knowing they were talking about matters involving circumstances that had happened long before he met them, Aeos tossed his head to get their attention. "Are we to head directly to Master Phrenicos' stable?"

Kamuzu shook his head. "First we have to stop in and visit the Ladies Eno and Psyche. They will be the first to know of the queen's feelings about your abrupt departure. You should inform one of the delphae's assistants that you've left. Tell her that you feel the need to spend time with your old friends." He twitched his orange tail. "I would wait until we are outside the city walls, just in case she decides you should stick around for a little while longer."

The fresh air and sounds of birds singing in the trees woke Aeos the next morning. It was a welcome change to the noises of the other *ammoni* students preparing for their early chores before beginning their lessons. He stretched his neck and back, extending one of his back legs out until the joints popped. His stall at the *ammoni* school had been more than adequate, with plenty of room for him to roll and stretch, but it wasn't the same as being able to walk around with no barriers in site. And students clattering down hallways for classes were no comparison for birdsong first thing in the morning.

The delphae had handled Aeos' leaving far better than he had expected. She was aware of his disgruntlement and thought a few days or weeks away would do him good. He could come back with fresh eyes and a rested mind. For himself, Aeos believed that she was only telling him what he wanted to hear. He was adept enough to know she was hiding her true feelings. He let it go at that. If Aeos tried to pry her mind, the delphae would rip his own apart as punishment. Not enough that he couldn't heal, but it would be a painful process. In any case, he was sure he'd hear a more frank assessment of his vacation from Eno when he contacted her in a few days.

Alcander was already grazing in the meadow they had bedded down in the night before. Kamuzu was curled near the remnants of the fire. The orange cat had caught a rather plump woodpecker yesterday afternoon and, after gorging himself, had sprawled near the fire to sleep. Aeos and Alcander had spent the evening in conversation. Aeos had kept the subjects light and trivial; he didn't know the miniature well enough to ask anything private.

Moving quietly, Aeos joined Alcander in the meadow. The miniature looked up and flicked his ears in welcome. "Fine morning, stallion of Acadia Stable."

Aeos tossed his head and inhaled deeply. "Don't be so formal, Alcander. When not in my sire's stable or in a court under on some errand for my sire, I'm simply Aeos."

"You and Eno must get along very well. You both want to hide who you are when you are able." Alcander's voice held amusement. "Seems a lot of the young horses we've run into lately have the same desire."

"Trust me, if you had spent time with Pyrios around any mares you would have seen that the older Zephyros colt uses his title to his best advantage."

The miniature snorted. "We've had word that his addiction to the fairer sex may have him in a snare this time."

Aeos pricked his ears. "Is he in some trouble? Thracis has not mentioned anything in our communications."

"Thracis does not know. I'll wager Thracis has had little contact with Pyrios as of late." Alcander lowered his head for a mouthful of grass.

The dun stallion shook his head and took several bites of his own. He thought about the miniature's statement as he chewed. It didn't strike him as odd in the very least that Pyrios was in trouble over some mare. Aeos wondered how this debacle was affecting Lord Kantaka.

He finished his mouthful before speaking. "How will this affect Pyrios' standing in the Registry?"

Alcander swished his tail. "If this affair is discovered, some will use it as leverage to roust Pyrios from his position as Lord Kantaka's aide."

"Who is this lady he courts, that she holds such interest to those of the Registry?"

"None less than Lady Stephanos Nerissa."

Aeos tossed his head. The name meant nothing to him.

Seeing his confusion, Alcander clarified. "She is the mate of Dimitri Alexi, the ruling stallion of Kigeria. He has many connections among the Baroquians though he has not affiliated himself with either the Baroquian Pact or the Elysian Alliance."

"Another Equine trying to play both sides of this conflict?"

Alcander shook his head. "We don't think so. Lord Alexi is young, his sire passing unexpectedly and leaving him as ruling stallion. He is trying to find his way to do best by his horses."

"And his mate? Where do her alliances fall? Certainly not with him."

The miniature's ears pinned. "Her alliances fall to whichever stallion she feels holds the highest position. Zephyros Pyrios is the heir to the ruling stable of Thetis in Calabria. Calabria holds the deepest deposits of achillium on Equus. Thetis is far richer in material wealth than her home stable of Arion. More powerful as well."

"If it's power she's after, why not attract a Representative? They have all the social standing a mare like her would want."

Alcander sighed. "We are afraid she wants control of Calabria for a far darker purpose."

"You and your associates believe she wants to gain influence in Calabria and then offer a proposal to the Baroquians." Aeos bobbed his head as he spoke. It was the logical course of deduction, but it didn't feel right to him.

"You have another proposal?" Alcander was scrutinizing the dun stallion.

"Not one that I can give voice to. Your deductions are plausible, but they feel off to me. Let me think on it, when I put my hoof on what is bothering me, you'll be the first to know."

"Well, be sure to tell us at the same time so you won't have to repeat yourself."

Aeos and Alcander jumped as Kamuzu trotted between them, his orange tail twitching. Aeos tossed his head at his own lack of awareness. The Felisian was quiet but he was by no means trying to hide his approach.

"I fear I've been in the city far too long," Aeos said with chagrin.

"Your warrior skills will be quickly honed as we travel." Kamuzu licked a paw before sniffing the grass with interest.

"We won't have to wait for you to slaughter another bird, will we?" Alcander teased.

"No," Kamuzu burped, "I'll be fine until this afternoon. Better hunting then anyway. The sun's getting high now and the birds will be on alert."

Aeos shook himself to settle his harness and looked to the west. Eno's laboratory and stable were a day's gallop from here. He expected he and his companions would reach it the day after tomorrow as they weren't pressing themselves; it wasn't as if the mares were expecting them. And it sounded as though Kamuzu had every intention of stopping early for the night. As they started off Aeos wondered if he should contact Thracis and see if he wanted to come to Eno's lab. Boudica was only a couple days' travel and Thracis would likely gallop the whole way. Tossing his head as he walked, Aeos decided to wait until he reached Eno's stable, then he could persuade Psyche to invite Thracis for a visit.

CHAPTER 9

Eno stood with a back foot cocked and ears pinned. Her mouth worked as she chewed on a tough piece of hay. Her eyes fired steel sparks at the prototype harness Psyche wore. Aware of Eno's considerable temper, the other mare was trying to hold as still as possible to give Eno the best view of the harness. Sighing, Eno spit out the piece of hay and began to circle Psyche.

"How does it feel? The weight, the tension. How comfortable is it?"

"Do you want the truth?" Psyche's voice was hesitant. Eno knew her friend was dreading another frustrated outburst.

"If you want me to make it work I have to know the truth."

"Fine." Psyche took a deep breath. "It is heavy, but I think that's mostly do to the wings. The idea of micro thrusters made out of achillium is a good one, but light as achillium is it's still too heavy. As for the rest of it. The harness fits good. I can't feel any rubbing or chafing and you saw how I was galloping around the field. I think everything is coming together except for the wings."

Eno kicked a metal bin across the floor. "And those are the most important parts."

"Eno, you're not giving yourself credit for how far you've come. You'll get us in the air."

"But will I do it before the next battle?"

"What does your sire say?"

Eno flicked her ears and tossed her head in agitation. "He says the Baroquians are up to something but they've withdrawn all contact with the Registry. They've also closed their borders to all but native breeds." She took a deep breath. "But that's the least of my sire's concerns. Several stallions who were set to graduate from the Romanium bolted. They were the top students. My sire fears they may have allied themselves with the Baroquians."

Psyche's ears lowered. That was grave news. "Has your sire told you their names or lineages? Perhaps Aeos knows them."

Eno shook her head. "My sire holds many things close. He won't tell me who the stallions were for fear that my queries about them would draw the attention of Queen Hippolyta." She gave Psyche a shrewd look. "I don't have to tell you to keep quiet about this to your dam. With tensions already high, the Augean Stable doesn't need to know the Asapatish of the Hippikon has misplaced some very dangerous warriors."

"My dam and I have little to talk about these days." Psyche tossed her head. "If she finds out about the cadets who turned rogue she'll have to get the information somewhere else."

"It's been weeks. Is she still pushing about Thracis?"

"I wouldn't know. I haven't spoken with Queen Hippolyta in some time."

Eno sniffed. "I had just thought maybe one of your sisters had mentioned something."

"My sisters want even less to do with me than my dam does." Psyche tossed her head. "I think they feel my enticement by a young, flashy stallion who'll keep me out of trouble is a good thing."

"Maybe they're just jealous." Eno was nudging through a pile of metal discards with her nose. She was only discussing this topic with Psyche to give the front of her mind something to do. Deep down, she was gnawing over the problem of the wings. She needed something light but durable, like a fabric of some kind. Then there was the problem of fuel for the thrusters. The thrusters themselves weren't that heavy but the fuel cells were. If she could minimize the thrusters to only being on the harness and not the wing frames and if she could find a way to power the wings without fuel cells.... Her eyes fell on a woven banner draped across one window.

The banner was a gift from the mare who saw to Eno's garden. She was an older gray mare who came from a little village deep in Athenia. She said the banner was created by weavers who only came from a specific herd. The weaving was a craft that was passed from dam to filly through the generations. It was a beautiful piece of work. Eno had asked the mare about another weaving to give to Psyche as a birthday gift.

This banner was colorful array of threads woven into an intertwining pattern. The pattern had no symbolism as far as Eno knew, but it was very pretty and she liked to let her eyes travel the colored paths. It was calming and as close to meditation as Eno was apt to get.

Her ears flicked back at Psyche who was shifting on her feet under the weight of the harness. "Do you know anything about a herd of weavers in Athenia?"

Psyche bobbed her head. "The Arachne Weavers. They're known throughout Equus for their talent."

"I'd never heard of them until Laria gave me that banner."

Psyche looked at the banner, then inclined her head at Eno. "That explains why you've never heard of the Weavers. That's the most artistic thing I've ever seen among your belongings. If you knew more mares with more, um, domestic tendencies, you would have heard of Arachne Stable."

"As if you're a little stablemaker."

Psyche twitched a shoulder. "My dam insists on promoting local artists and guilds. She says it creates good standing between herds."

Eno wasn't listening. She didn't care about Queen Hippolyta's political intrigues; what she cared about was the way the colored threads meshed seamlessly together. She pulled the banner down and tugged on it with her teeth while standing on one end of it. The banner resisted tearing with surprising tenacity.

"Don't take all your frustration out on a defenseless bit of weaving," Psyche said dryly, "If you find it that offensive, give it to me."

"I'm testing it's durability."

"Planning on using it as new harness material?"

Eno shook her head. She wasn't sure what she was planning but she felt that the seed of an idea was planted. Now she needed to give it time to germinate. She would know if it would bear fruit within the next day or so. Until then, she and Psyche could take a much-deserved rest.

Eno tossed her head at Psyche. "Come on. I'll help you out of that harness and then let's go get something to eat."

"You seem to be giving up rather easily today." Psyche's voice betrayed her mistrust of Eno's sudden change in attitude.

Eno bobbed her head, trying to show Psyche she really was in a better frame of mind. "I might have an idea, but I have to let it form. Until it reveals itself I'll be useless in this laboratory."

Still acting cautiously, Psyche let Eno help her out of the harness. They put the prototype on the model horse in the center of the laboratory. Eno gave the harness an appraising look before bobbing her head and walking out of the room. Psyche trotted after her. The black and white mare looked back over her shoulder at the model and therefore didn't notice when Eno abruptly stopped. She bumped into the bay and Eno lashed out with a back foot, catching Psyche above her left front knee.

"What in Pandemonium was that for?"

Eno turned and pinned her ears at Psyche. "You should have been paying more attention. Someone is here. I can smell them."

Psyche took a deep breath. The scent of familiar herbs filled her nostrils. She tossed her head at Eno. "It smells like Alcander and Kamuzu. What a nice surprise." She ducked around Eno and cantered out into the open field.

Sighing, Eno shook her head and trotted after Psyche. She blinked as she stepped out into the full sun of midday. When her eyes refocused she saw not only Kamuzu and Alcander standing in front of Psyche, but Aeos as well.

Eno froze, her mind filling with what she must look like. She and Psyche had been in the lab for several days, only taking meal and restroom breaks. She never gave any thought to what she looked like when Psyche was around. She felt a flush of embarrassment rise to her cheeks.

"I might have taken a moment to groom myself if I had known you were coming." Eno hoped her irritation at being caught with her coat roughened and mane tangled didn't show.

Aeos bowed his head. "You look lovely as ever, Lady Eno." He turned to Psyche. "As do you, Lady Psyche."

"Thracis should warn you that flattery gets you nowhere with mares such as us."

"Maybe not with a mare like you."

Psyche blinked at him. Eno would have gladly kicked the dun stallion for speaking so openly about their private interactions.

Finding her tongue before Psyche could begin asking a lot of questions Eno would rather not answer in the presence of Kamuzu and Alcander, the bay mare stepped forward to get the group's attention. "We were just breaking for a meal. Would you care to join us in the timothy meadow? I've noticed several fat field mice who have become too brazen as of late," she added with a nod to Kamuzu.

The newcomers bobbed their heads. Kamuzu left the horses to sharpen his claws on a tree before disappearing into the tall grass. The Equines, respecting the Felisian's need to hunt, went in the opposite direction. Psyche and Alcander held back, encouraging Aeos and Eno to walk together. The pinto and the miniature exchanged several speculative glances as they followed the other two.

Once in the meadow, the horses spread out as to not crowd each other. Aeos, acting as any stallion, grazed off to one side of the others. He lifted his head frequently to sniff the wind. Eno watched this display with the corners of her mouth twitching. She knew his male nature was likely getting under Psyche's skin, but the other mare was ignoring him as much as possible.

Eno wondered how Psyche put up with Thracis, who was far more dominant than Aeos. Aeos would stand as lead stallion if pushed, but was more than happy leave Eno in charge. He would do well to settle with a dominant mare who would run Acadia Stable. In Eno's opinion, Aeos was more than capable but lacked the ambition needed to be an effective ruling stallion.

Now, if she were in charge of such a stable as Acadia. Eno's mind filled with the possibilities. She could triple the wealth of that entire province by fortifying and encouraging the wine guild. The Acadian wine Aeos had given her for her birthday was the best Eno had ever tasted. And with the fruit orchards the winemakers could create vast varieties and flavors.

Eno tossed her head and nipped at a fly on her shoulder. Such thoughts were not for the likes of her. She was an inventor and a builder, not a vineyard keeper. She knew about the ingredients that went into good wine but not the care that gave it voice or the song that gave it body. Her sire was often heard to say that the best winemakers sing to their grapes as they grow. Maybe it was true. Still, she wouldn't meddle in the process or creation, only make sure it could continue.

Besides, she thought with a glance at Aeos, a stallion like him would quickly grow exasperated with her constant curiosity and need to dismantle everything. They would enjoy their friendship and the benefits that came with it for a time, but once the world settled itself Aeos would look for a mare to carry on his line. A mare from a good farming stable most likely.

"Will you be staying long?" Eno heard Psyche ask.

"For a few days at least. Perhaps longer if you request your mate to come for a visit." Alcander answered.

There was a pause. Alcander filled it, his voice apologetic. "I am sorry, lady. I only thought you and Lord Thracis were a mated pair."

"We are not formally acknowledged." Psyche said in low voice.

"The situation is a bit delicate where the Auguean Stable is concerned," Eno explained.

Alcander bobbed his head. "Understood. I will be more discreet."

Eno tossed her head. "For love of Pegasus, it's not as though everyone doesn't know."

"Yes, but I can see that the lady wants to be subtle." Alcander looked at Eno. "Until she formally introduces Thracis to Queen Hippolyta, it would be best to avoid as much of a scandal as possible."

"As if the Auguean Stable is not familiar with scandal." Psyche pinned her ears and swished her tail.

"That may be true, but tensions are high between Diomedea and Lipizzania at this moment. The Registry will use any excuse they can find to discredit the Augean Stable." Alcander spoke with the patience of an older horse.

Eno flicked her ears at Aeos. The dun stallion seemed thoughtful. She wondered if he knew about the cadets who had fled the Romanium. She would have to find a private moment to ask him. She knew she could count on Aeos' discretion in this matter.

Deciding to lighten the conversation, Eno said, "Enough evasion, Psyche. Will you contact Thracis and ask him to come play with us or not? I'm sure he could use a furlough."

"And I haven't seen him in months," Aeos added.

Psyche swished her tail and stomped a front foot. "I guess since all of you want him to come the least I can do is send the invitation."

"Excellent," Kamuzu said around a mouthful of fur. He was carrying the dead body of a plump field mouse in his mouth. He dropped it on the grass and licked a paw. "I feel we should all be together. Ask Phrenicos to come as well. He can continue the stallions' training while we are here."

"You sound as though you plan to stay for more than a few days," Eno said with a look at Alcander. The miniature looked just as confused as everyone else.

Kamuzu nodded. "I've had a communication from Sanctuary. The Baroquians have landed on the shores of the northern continent. They have not caused issue as of yet but the Alliance is up in arms and readying the Imperial Cavalry."

"This close to winter? Are they mad?" Psyche inclined her head at Eno. "My dam told me cavalries never fight in snow if they can help it. The footing isn't good and the heavy equipment causes accidents."

Kamuzu nodded. "Your dam speaks true. It is dangerous on the ice. Especially for shod Equines. Our sources do not believe that the Baroquians had any intention of beginning a conflict before spring. The snows come early on the northern continent. We believe this contingent was meant to establish an outpost to be used as a staging point."

"As they tried to do here." Eno was referring to the battle between the Baroquians and the Diomedeans the previous summer. The Baroquians were hoping to secure a military outpost in Diomedea and invade Lipizzania from the south. The Baroquians were most surprised when the Diomedean mares, led by Queen Hippolyta herself, annihilated the cavalry sent to invade their territory.

"They will have better luck on the northern continent," Aeos opinioned.

The northern continent was home to the country of Vanneria. It was made up of the provinces of Clydesdalea, Belgia, and Shira. Those were the home regions of the draft breeds of Equus. Heavy and thick coated, the draft breeds were the best adapted to handle the cold, open tundra and rolling, rocky hills. They lived for blustery days and rainy mornings. Eno had visited the north once with her sire and found it a miserable experience. She preferred sunshine and warmth.

Aeos shifted his feet to stand hipshot. "The draft breeds have made it clear in the past that they do not wish to be engaged in any conflicts. If they had their way we'd still be using wooden wagons and living in caves. I doubt they will have much opinion about a Baroquian outpost on one of their more isolated shores."

"Not to mention I'm sure the Baroquians have offered something in trade to ensure a warm welcome." Kamuzu was getting to the work of dressing the mouse carcass.

Eno watched how quickly the Felisian worked with fascination. As a horse she had no need for meat, though Equines did use leather. In that case, the deer were dispatched by a group of Felisian hunters, or farmers if the deer were raised, the hides removed and sold to Equine merchants and the meat sold at Felisian markets. The deer hooves were made into adhesive material and the bones had a variety of uses, from occult items to fine-toothed combs. On Equus everything was used to its fullest potential.

"They would be fools not to. Even if the Vanners state that they have no intention of officially entering into this conflict, many individuals will make their own decisions," Alcander pointed out. "Titania is a Clydesdale, yet she fought most ferociously at the Diomedean battle."

Eno nodded but she was looking at Psyche. The other mare seemed worried. She kept swishing her tail at nothing and bobbing her head in agitation.

Something the matter? Eno felt Psyche closing her inner barriers against intrusion.

I do not want Thracis to come here. It is too close to Ruffiana and my dam will insist on a formal meeting. And if Psyche were to ignore such a request, she would be shaming herself as well as her herd. Eno didn't understand Psyche's determination to keep Thracis away from her herd, but the pinto was well versed in the seer's gifts and Eno was sure Psyche had her reasons.

Eno flicked her ears. *Perhaps I can offer a better solution.* She tossed her head to get the males' attention. "Maybe here is not the best place for a reunion."

The males gave her quizzical looks. Eno lightly pawed the ground. "I've been trying to fulfill my promise to Queen Hippolyta for several months, yet have reached a point of impasse. I feel I need a change of scenery but it has been impossible for me to move my necessary equipment." She inclined her head to look at everyone with a sidelong glance. "With you here to help navigate a mover and aid with difficulties on the journey, I believe a seaside landscape might bring inspiration."

The three males puffed their chests at the compliment of their abilities, whether or not it was intentional. Psyche was staring at Eno with slack-jawed wonder. Eno ignored the other mare for the moment and focused on the males. "I have a clear idea of what I need to bring. It wouldn't take me more than a couple of hours to pack a mover, if I had assistance."

Aeos flicked his ears, an indication that he knew he was being manipulated. However, Eno could tell by his posture that he was all but dying to show how helpful he could be. It was a stallion thing, this need to be useful. An aspect of their sex that Psyche should be more aware of, Eno mused.

"If we begin packing now, we should still have several hours of daylight left." Alcander was looking up at the sun. "We could cover a few miles, even with a mover." Movers were big and bulky. Most came equipped with heavy tread tires and could traverse rough terrain, but the group would be obliged to avoid closely growing trees or marshes. Had they been in Lipizzania Eno would have had access to a hover-type mover, the kind used by the military. These movers used thrusters to hover three feet off the ground and could be manipulated with little trouble as the slightest push would shift their course.

Kamuzu patted his gutted mouse. "Let me get him in my belly and I will join you in the laboratory. I feel the craving for some ocean fish."

They shared a laugh, then Eno led the others to her lab. Inside, she immediately began directing Aeos and Alcander as to what they should load and what they should leave. She sent Psyche into the stable to get grain and healing supplies for their trip. After ascertaining that the males would be okay on their own for a few minutes, Eno went to the stable to pack the few private items she carried with her everywhere. Before leaving the laboratory, Eno carefully packed the woven banner in with her things. She felt strongly it would hold the key to giving her wings.

CHAPTER 10

Nerissa shook her head, her damp mane flapping against her neck. She could use the blower to dry her mane as she had her coat, but she would lose her natural appeal. And she had no intention of appearing any less attractive to the stallions she was currently having relations with. That would not do at all.

Such a wonderful young stallion she had found, so strong and virile. And well-connected. To think she had formed a relationship with the heir to Thetis Stable, the ruling stable of Calabria. Nerissa's mind spun with all the political implications of that title. Pyrios, eldest son of Bailus Zephyros, was poised to take control of the richest achillium deposits on all Equus. It wouldn't matter which side of this conflict Pyrios chose to ally himself with, both would need achillium for weapons and armor. After all this disruption was settled, Thetis Stable would still be raking in hooffulls of creos as achillium comprised most of the equipment on Equine spacecraft.

It was a deliciously perfect and profitable arrangement, if only Nerissa could get the younger Zephyros son out of the way. She swished her tail. Thracis, the foolish little colt who managed to get himself thrown out of the Romanium, which resulted in shaming himself and his herd. As if that wasn't bad enough, her contacts in Friesia were telling her that the younger Zephyros stallion was of some importance to the Baroquian Pact.

Nerissa walked to the floor to ceiling mirror on one wall of her private suite in the town stable she shared with her mate, Dimitri Alexi. She regarded her reflection as she pondered this rock in her foot. Her coat was the characteristic red dun of the Kiger breed. Her red dorsal stripe and leg markings were more crimson than sorrel, lending the horizontal stripes on her legs a brilliant contrast to her tan coat. Her mane and tail were the same deep red.

She shifted this way and that, her dark eyes looking for any flaws. She saw none. Good. She had things to do today and hadn't planned on spending a substantial amount of time smoothing stray hairs. Nerissa swished her tail and shook her head again, thoroughly ruffling herself. Alexi liked her a little rough around the edges. She would have to appease him this morning if she planned on spending the afternoon with Pyrios.

Leaving her private stalls, Nerissa trotted down the short hallway that connected to the double suite she shared with Alexi. Her keen eyes scrutinized the hall for any dirt and the flower arrangements, changed daily, for wilting blooms. She herself had hired the staff of this stable and had made sure that several Felisians complemented the standard Equine servants.

The stable was to be kept spotless at all times, the flowers always fresh, and the wine cellar and grain pantry always full. Unfortunately, Nerissa had been forced to terminate several employees who could not keep up with her high standards. She tossed her head as she walked. Letting those individuals go was just the warning needed to keep everyone else on their toes.

She entered the double suite without knocking. It was, after all, her stall as much as Alexi's. Nerissa didn't really expect to find him here, but thought she would stop in on her way to his private suite of stalls. Alexi spent much of his time there or in the study, going over communications sent from Kigeria. As the ruling stallion, Alexi was kept informed of all that transpired in his absence.

While Nerissa had no intention of returning to her harsh environed homeland, it wouldn't do to soil her own bedding box. Nerissa was a mare who believed in contingency plans. If her plans with Pyrios did not work out to her liking, she wanted to be sure to return to her mate unscathed.

The shared suite was empty. Swishing her tail, she left the stall to follow the hall to the study. Halfway to her destination, she was stopped by a harried looking younger mare. After a moment, Nerissa placed her. A five-year-old chestnut from a herd of no importance. Nerissa had selected her because the chestnut was eager to please and would be little trouble to dispose of if she stepped out of line.

"My lady," the chestnut bowed low, her nose nearly touching the floor, "Lord Alexi sent me to find you."

Nerissa pinned her ears. She had not expected him to leave before she had spoken with him. "Well, what does he wish?"

The chestnut spoke to the floor, her words muffled. "He wishes to meet you for the evening meal in the Pegasus Pavilion. He sends his apologies at not meeting with you this morning."

Or mentioning any pressing engagements last night. But that was something she would not bring to a servant's attention. Nerissa stomped a foot and the chestnut jumped. "Stop cowering, you stupid filly. Go and find something useful to do." Nerissa snapped her teeth in anger.

The chestnut bounded away, her hoof beats echoing down the hall. Nerissa snorted. Well, since her formal mate was unavailable at the moment she would find someone else to occupy her time.

She took a deep breath and reached out with her mind. As she brushed against Pyrios, a tingle of anticipation flowed through her. *It appears my plans have changed. Sneak away for a few hours and meet me for some fun.*

My apologies, Lady, but I cannot join you at this time.

Nerissa kicked a wall at the curtness of Pyrios' response. How dare he dismiss her so casually. *Whatever can be so important in that stuffy council chamber?*

Something has occurred that concerns us all. It is the reason for your availability this morning.

So, something significant really was happening or had happened. Still, it hadn't occurred in Lipizza which meant one of her stallions should be accessible.

Can you not even get away for an hour? Nerissa tried to show more disappointment than irritation.

No. I cannot leave until the debate is over. Perhaps in the after-noon.

Do not bother. Now Nerissa did let her anger flow through the link. *I will not be kept waiting as some tavern wench with quivering flanks.* She felt his surprise and confusion at the feel of her fury. *You wait for me, foolish colt of Thetis Stable.*

Nerissa broke the link. She felt Pyrios scrambling against her mind, begging for access. She put up a wall between her mind and his and stalked down the hallway. The males in her life felt they could treat her as nothing more than an amusement to be kept for their entertainment. She tossed her head as she stepped into the sunlit street. Both Alexi and Pyrios would learn that she was not a mare to be dismissed so easily.

Turning her tail to the more respectable sections of Lipizza, Nerissa sauntered down the street in search of more devious company. As she walked, she noted the appreciative glances cast her way by every stallion she passed. Some she returned, others she ignored. If the stallion were walking next to another mare, Nerissa made sure to cast him a flirtatious gaze, holding his eye until his companion voiced her discontent. As the stallion hurried on behind his own lady, no doubt counting the favors he would need to perform to gain forgiveness, Nerissa chuckled to herself. How she enjoyed this game of power.

CHAPTER 11

"Your lady still angered by your lack of attention?"

Pyrios pinned his ears at the snicker in Phlegon's voice. The younger stallion saw far too much and Pyrios worried that the gray would get tired of keeping quiet and tell Lord Kantaka of the less than honorable actions taking place under his roof. Pyrios had hoped that Phlegon would find a mare of his own to occupy his time. However, though Phlegon had entertained several ladies, none of them seemed to be a permanent arrangement.

"She is not my lady and I'm sure she has other business that has nothing to do with me." He and Phlegon were having the noonday meal at a café near the Piber University. They could have dined in the restaurant favored by the Representatives, but Pyrios wasn't in the mood for the speculative stares he had been receiving as of late.

"Lord Alexi was in the council chamber. What other stallion might be occupying her time?"

Pyrios snapped his teeth at Phlegon. "There is no other. She has more discretion than that."

"She has discretion enough when it suits her." Phlegon's words were strong but he lowered his head in submission.

"I've kept our affair a secret from most."

"But not all."

"If something is on your mind, Phlegon, then speak it and stop prancing around the subject."

Phlegon took a long drink of water. Pyrios waited. He had gained patience growing up with Thracis. He nibbled the salad in front of him, though he didn't have much appetite.

At last Phlegon spoke. "Your, entertainment, has kept your mind busy and distracted from matters in the council. Lord Kantaka worries that you are not as aware of the other Representatives and their aides as you should be. Do not forget that Lord Kantaka's spy network has suspicions that you are of some import to the Baroquians."

"That network has found that Thracis is of interest."

Phlegon shook his head. "Lord Kantaka and Commander Dias both feel you are the more likely target. They feel the spies are mistaken."

"And you agree?"

"It does make more sense that the heir to Thetis Stable would be a greater threat to the Baroquian Pact than the younger brother, shamefully dismissed from the Romanium."

"That was not the case and you know it," Pyrios snapped.

"Lower your voice," Phlegon hissed with a quick look around, "What I know and what is perceived are two different subjects."

Two mares walked by on the street. Before his appointment as one of Lord Kantaka's aides, Pyrios would have been calling to them, inviting them to join he and Phlegon. Now the sight of them only made his stomach turn. He never believed that a mare would cause the turmoil he felt. He wished he had taken Thracis' advice and been more considerate of the mares he courted. Perhaps his involvement with Lady Nerissa was a punishment for his earlier disregard to those of a female persuasion.

He turned his attention back to Phlegon. "And what is perceived in the Registry?"

"Nothing that is spoken of, not in public hearing at least. Lord Alexi could be an important ally for the Alliance. The Registry wants to keep him on welcome terms."

"If the affair is that obvious then Lord Alexi must know."

Phlegon twitched a shoulder. "If he suspects he gives no sign. He has many matters on his mind at present."

"As do I."

"When was the last time you spoke with Thracis?"

Pyrios flicked his ears. What was Phlegon playing at? Why did he care whether or not Pyrios had spoken with his brother?

"That long, is it?" Phlegon took a large bite of salad.

"I spoke with him…." Pyrios' voice trailed off. He couldn't remember. How long had it been? A week? A month? He tossed his head. "It has been some time."

"I'm well-aware. I fear Thracis has spoken more to me in the past months."

Pyrios snorted. "And what has my brother told you?"

Phlegon shook his head. "Not much. He is training with the delphae of Boudica and finds it not to his liking. I feel he may return to Phrenicos soon."

"He is better suited to fighting than mind games. He does need more training in defending his thoughts, however."

Phlegon gazed at the other patrons of the café. "Why don't you contact Thracis yourself? He would be glad to hear from you?"

"I fear he would see too much of my situation in my mind. And I have other reasons to avoid contact."

"You do not trust your lady?"

"No," Pyrios said. He signaled to the waiter for the bill. "She keeps much from me. I do not trust her motives."

"Nor do most horses. She is surrounded by mystery."

"We should be returning to the Registry. The council chamber will be filled for several more hours." Pyrios thought about contacting Lady Nerissa again to tell her of his delay.

Phlegon caught his eye. "Let her wait and wonder what is so important that it keeps you from her beck and call."

"I do not think that is a wise course of action. I fear she is more dangerous than she has let show."

Phlegon held his tongue until they were walking down the street toward the University. "You fear retaliation from her?"

"Fear? No. Anxiety, most definitely. She has a calculating manner. She will punish me for this day, of that I am certain."

"More reason for me not to promise myself to any one mare." Phlegon spoke casually enough, but Pyrios knew the other stallion secretly hoped to find to a mare who would capture his heart. Phlegon was as much a romantic as Thracis was showing himself to be, despite the Calpernian stallion's philandering.

As they passed through the University gates, Pyrios caught the eye of the spotted sentry that had first greeted him a year ago. The mare looked away quickly, ducking back into the gatehouse. Pyrios felt a stab of guilt at her reaction to him. They had spent a brief time together during which he made no promise of loyalty. He had thought they had parted on good terms, but her aversion to him suggested otherwise. He knew Phlegon had tried to have a relationship with her but the spotted mare refused his advances. Probably because she still harbored feelings for Pyrios.

Phlegon gave the gatehouse a cursory glance as they passed. He apparently had given up on the spotted mare and had turned his efforts elsewhere. At least that was how it appeared to Pyrios.

"You would think she would have put in for a transfer to another position so that she would not have to see you walking through the gate every day."

Pyrios tossed his head. "She is good at her occupation. And it is only for a few seconds each day."

"You left her heart more than a little bruised."

"A miscalculation on my part. I didn't realize she had such little experience with stallions." The spotted mare's inexperience added chains to the guilt Pyrios already felt on her behalf. Phlegon was adding weights.

"I have heard she is being courted by a young officer at the Hippikon. He comes from a good herd and has treated her with respect and patience."

Pyrios gave Phlegon a sidelong look. "You seem to know a lot about her private matters."

"She and I have kept a close friendship. I think she needed a friend after your dismissal."

Pyrios flinched.

Phlegon continued. "She is strongly attracted to this officer and think they may have a future together."

"That's good to hear. It makes me feel a little better."

"I thought it would."

They were entering the Registry of Breeds. On either side of them the walls were covered with the name of every breed on Equus. Next to each breed was the representative that stood for them in the Registry. Not every breed had a representative. In those cases, either the breed had exercised their right not to have representation or had withdrawn from the Registry when war became imminent. It was a loose way of keeping track of contacts in various countries.

Their pace slowed as they approached the council chamber. Neither stallion was in any hurry to go back to what they considered pointless discussions about trying to resolve this conflict in a peaceful manner. In Pyrios' opinion they had reached the point of zero negotiations. With a heavy sigh, he walked into the chamber and took his place behind Lord Kantaka. Phlegon took up an identical stance next to Pyrios. As the conversations resumed, Pyrios' mind turned to Thracis. He hoped his brother was enjoying a more entertaining afternoon.

CHAPTER 12

Thracis galloped across the meadow behind the dephae's stable. He came to a sliding stop ten feet from the white form of Alois Phrenicos and bowed his head low in respect. "I'm so happy to see you, Master."

Phrenicos tossed his head. The brisk wind tousled his snowy mane. "I've had word from the delphae that you have achieved as much training as she can give you this moment."

Thracis raised his head. "I have tried to keep to her standards."

"She stated as much when she contacted me." Phrenicos didn't try to hide the amusement in his voice. "She feels you have enough skill to protect yourself until help arrives. She wants you to continue your combat training with me and your psychic training with your friends."

Thracis danced in place. He was excited to finally be leaving the delphae's training. "May we be off?"

Phrenicos shook his head. "First we have to thank the delphae for all her generosity in teaching you. Then we must go to Boudica and pick up supplies. It seems we will have company for the next several weeks. I haven't a clue as to where everyone is going to sleep."

Thracis listened to the older stallion's grumblings as they headed to the reflection pools. Lady Kasmut and Aahmas were deep in meditation this time of day and the reflection pools were the cats' favorite place for privacy. Thracis hoped they would not be too angered by the interruption. He wondered who could be coming to visit Master Phrenicos. More students perhaps?

Phrenicos stopped at the edge of one of the pools and bowed his head low. "Forgive me for the intrusion, Lady Kasmut, but this was the earliest I could arrive."

The gray and black cat opened her oval eyes and gazed at the Equines. "It is alright, Master Phrenicos. I was aware of you the moment you arrived. We have been discussing Thracis' progress since you first brought him here."

"I hope he has come far."

The delphae licked a paw. "He has done well. Lady Psyche should be able to complete his training. He will never be overly strong in the psychic arts but he will be able to defend himself."

"That was all I wanted to hear."

Aahmas stood and stretched. "May fortune favor you in your endeavors, stallion of Thetis Stable."

"And you as well, good Aahmas." Thracis turned his attention to the delphae. "Thank you for your generosity and patience, Lady Kasmut. I know how frustrating I can be to instruct and I thank you for not casting me out."

"Spoken with true humility. Keep an eye on this one, Phrenicos, he learns quickly from his mistakes."

"A fact of which I am aware. Good day to you, Ladies, and may Lord Pegasus and Lady Bast grant us all a mild winter."

The horses bowed again to the Felisians before turning and leaving the premises. They remained at a walk until they reached the main lane. As his hooves touched the dirt path, Phrenicos broke into a brisk trot. Thracis drew abreast of him before opening his mouth.

"Who will be coming to visit? More students? Old friends?" Thracis was all but bursting with curiosity.

"A little of both. You will have competition in your training with me. A good thing. You've kept yourself conditioned but the time has come for you to advance."

Thracis stumbled to a halt. Phrenicos had never spoken of advancement before. His version of enlightening Thracis meant he would tell the Calabrian in the morning the exercises he wanted completed by that afternoon. Thracis tossed his head and cantered to catch up.

"You are going to teach me the higher movements? I thought I had not yet mastered the levade."

Phrenicos tossed his head and lowered his ears at Thracis. "You haven't mastered the levade. Or even the piaffe or passage, though your canter changes are well-controlled. I would like it if you had more time to establish a stronger foundation, but I fear another battle is on the horizon." He was silent for a moment, lost in thought. "I will teach you the capriole first. It will be easier for you to learn and more efficient for your fighting style. But that will be a month off yet. First you must hold the levade to my satisfaction. I have no doubt you can accomplish that feat."

"I confess I have not practiced the levade overmuch. I have concentrated more on the passage and piaffe. I have collected my canter almost to the point of performing a pirouette."

"That is very good to hear. I looked at your haunches and legs and knew you were doing something to strengthen your stamina. Your physique has changed in the last weeks. I feel you will surprise yourself when next you sit in the levade." Phrenicos tossed his head. "Come now, let us stretch our legs on the road to Boudica."

The white stallion sprang into a gallop, racing ahead. Thracis blinked in surprise, then tossed his head and bucked before bolting in pursuit. The autumn sun flashed off their armor harnesses as the two horses raced along the winding road. Even though he was far younger, Thracis was finding it difficult to keep up with Phrenicos. The older stallion tossed his head and laughed at the younger horse. Thracis lowered his head to streamline himself as much as possible and found another burst of speed. He pulled even with Phrenicos only to see the white stallion pull ahead once again.

They came into a copse of trees and Thracis could see one of the huge old elms had fallen across the road. Other horses were present, devising a way to move the tree. Phrenicos didn't check his speed in the very least. Thracis watched in awe as the older stallion surged forward, his haunches bunching to launch himself over the trunk. Thracis slid to a stop, knowing he could never clear the tree, and looked after the diminishing white blur.

"That was some jump, I'll say," said a red and white pinto to the left of Thracis.

Thracis turned to regard the other horse. "I can't believe it and I was right behind him. There was no way I could have cleared this tree. It must be six feet high with the branches."

"And that horse had a foot to spare at least." This came from a buckskin standing a few yards away. She was a pretty little thing that immediately caught Thracis' eye. Noticing the new stallion's stare, the mare moved closer to the red and white paint. The paint took a stance between Thracis and the mare.

Not wanting a confrontation, Thracis bobbed his head. "I'm sorry to stare, but you are very pretty. I've never seen a buckskin with white markings before."

"My dam is a spotted breed. I get my unique coloring from her." The mare was buckskin, true enough, from her haunches forward. Her front legs had the characteristic black coloring to the knee but her back legs were white. She had a dark dorsal stripe but it stopped just before her rump which was coated by a white blanket with tan spots. Her mane was black but her tail was a mixture of white and black.

The paint was still standing with ears lowered. Innocent as Thracis' interest was, this stallion did not like the idea of another male noticing his lady. Thracis averted his eyes to the fallen tree. "Neither of you was injured when the tree fell?"

The others shook their heads. The mare tossed her head at the tree's base. Thracis saw the splintered stump where the tree had broken. He could smell rot and decay. The tree must have been ready to fall for a while but it needed the push of today's brisk wind to finish the job.

"We saw it fall but we were at least a hundred yards away." The mare's voice was low, submissive and shy. Not the voice of a Diomedean mare.

"You are not from here." Thracis spoke without thinking and the paint's ears pinned. The buckskin sidled farther behind him, giving him space to maneuver. Thracis looked more closely at the two strangers. They wore armor harnesses, though he could tell they were of poor quality, and heavy pouches hung from leather straps. The horses' hooves were chipped and in need of filing and their coats were ragged. These two had been on the road for a while.

"Why should it matter?" The paint's voice was a challenge and brought Thracis to focus.

"It does not matter to me, but the mares of this country do not take kindly to dominant stallions."

"I do not force her to stay with me."

No, Thracis could see that he didn't. But what Thracis saw as a stallion and what a Diomedean mare would see were two different things. "I did not say that you do. She is not frightened of you but of me." Thracis lowered his head but kept his eyes on the paint. "I am Zephyros Thracis of Thetis Stable and I mean you no harm."

The paint didn't move but the buckskin took a hesitant step forward. "I am Tansy, this is Zotico."

Thracis waited for lineage names. With none forthcoming, he addressed Zotico, "I am a traveler here myself, though I came through the Andromedan Gate a year ago. Have you had much experience with the mares of this region?"

The paint shook his head. "We've had no contact with anyone."

"Then how did you pass through the gate?"

"We crossed the mountains."

Thracis only stared. The Pleiades Mountains were a harsh and formidable territory. The only safe passage was through the Andromedan Gate. Equines had crossed the mountains but they did so at their peril. Thracis regarded the two horses again. "It was only the two of you?"

The mare's eyes filled with tears before she looked away. "My sister traveled with us, but the mountains proved too much for her." She took a watery breath. "She is with Lord Pegasus in Tranquility."

"I am sorry for your loss. What could prompt you to attempt such a dangerous crossing?"

"We've our reasons," Zotico snapped.

"And you'd best be sharing them before you get close to the village by the sea. The mares living in Boudica will skin you for your arrogance."

Tansy nibbled the paint's flank. He looked at her and Thracis knew they were communicating mind to mind. He waited.

After a private argument, which Tansy appeared to have won, Zotico turned back to Thracis. His ears came up a little but tension lined his body. "We are from Trakania. Our parents made us leave when the Baroquian raids threatened our village.

We didn't know where to go, but Tansy's sire thought we would find refuge in Diomedea."

"He probably thought the two mares would find refuge here," Thracis said. He saw the defiance in Zotico's eyes when he mentioned Tansy's sire. Thracis thought it likely that Zotico had not been the sire's first choice for his daughters but when time ran out the paint was all that was left.

"I would not leave Zotico, even when he tried to chase my sister and I away," Tansy shifted so that her shoulder touched the paint's flank.

Thracis felt a strong longing for Psyche. She and this little mare would have much to talk about, he was quite sure. With his lady in absence, Thracis decided on the most logical course of action. He wished Phrenicos had turned around and come back to check on him, but the white stallion had apparently gone on to Boudica.

Taking a deep breath and hoping he wasn't insulting Phrenicos too much, especially with the knowledge that the master already had guests, Thracis said, "You both look tired and in need of assistance. My master has a large stable and a larger heart, perhaps the two of you would like to stay with us until you come up with a plan."

Zotico's nostrils flared as he tried to sniff out any deception. Thracis remained relaxed. They would either take his offer or leave it. It was the knowledge that Tansy couldn't go much further that decided Zotico, Thracis was sure of it. The paint bobbed his head. "We will accept your offer, but only until we have rested and looked at our situation with clear heads."

Thracis bobbed his head. "Whatever you think is best. Come on, it looks like it will be easier to get around the base of the tree. I have to stop in Boudica to get supplies. We will tell them about the blockage of the road."

"Shouldn't we try to do something about the tree?" Zotico was following behind Tansy who was behind Thracis.

Thracis shook his head. "No, the mares will come out and decide how best to handle this situation."

"It is a stallion's privilege to help mares with any manual labor."

Thracis snorted. "Trust me, around here a stallion is lucky to ask a question, let alone give an opinion."

"I wondered what was keeping you," Phrenicos said as Thracis approached with his two charges. He was standing outside Boudica's large tavern.

"Your curiosity was not enough to coax you to turn around." Thracis was hardly annoyed, he was more concerned about his next statement. "I've offered your stable for them until they get back on all four feet and have an idea as to what they are going to do."

Phrenicos turned to the two newcomers. Zotico, all outward aggression gone, still made sure to keep himself between the white stallion and Tansy. Phrenicos kept his demeanor relaxed and inquisitive. "I don't see where these two could cause much inconvenience. My name is Alois Phrenicos, a former military instructor, among other things."

Taking a more open stance, Zotico said, "I am Zotico and this is Tansy. We are from a village in Trakania and we prefer not to divulge our lineages if that is possible. We will gladly tell anyone in authority who wants to know but we do not want our heritage to become common knowledge."

"A frequent request from those who seek refuge. You will, of course, have to stand before the delphae of Boudica and the ladies who rule this village, but you will be judged by your actions, not your ancestors."

The paint and buckskin released dual held breaths and began to look around their surroundings with more interest. Tansy spotted the gang of foals that habitually wandered the streets of Boudica and her body sagged. Thracis felt the urge to comfort her, but knew it would only result in a challenge from Zotico. The paint looked distressed, as if he wanted to go to her but not knowing how. This paralysis confused Thracis, it made him question the relationship between Zotico and Tansy. Fortunately, Phrenicos had the experience Zotico lacked.

He stepped forward and stretched his neck toward the mare. "I see your sorrow. You must have lost someone close."

Tansy's body shook with suppressed emotion. "My younger sister. She fell in the Pleiades Mountains." If Phrenicos thought it was strange that they crossed the mountains rather than used the gate, he didn't show it.

Pushing his limits, at least in Thracis' opinion, Phrenicos reached out to nuzzle the mare's shoulder. "There are many here who have known loss. You will find companions in your pain who will lead you back to the light."

Tansy's voice shuddered with emotion. "Thank you for your kind words."

"Think nothing of it," Phrenicos replied, pulling back. "We've all lost someone close." He regarded Zotico. "Step forward, young stallion, so that I might have a better view of you."

Zotico stepped up and squared himself. Because they were in the main street, they had drawn the attention of passersby. Phrenicos walked around the paint, noting his strengths and weakness. Thracis knew exactly what Zotico was feeling as he had undergone the same inspection upon introduction to Phrenicos' teachings.

"Narrow chest, weak hindquarters, thin neck." Phrenicos shifted his head this way and that. "Nice long legs, straight back, deep girth." He nodded. "I can work with this. Come and train with me and your inadequacies will slowly diminish."

"You can make me a warrior?" It was impossible to miss the eagerness in Zotico's voice.

"I can make you capable of defending yourself." Phrenicos spoke with patience. Thracis wondered if he was remembering Thracis' first weeks under his tutelage. "A warrior must devote his life to combat." Phrenicos inclined his head at Tansy. "I feel you may be traveling a different path."

Zotico gave a shy glance at Tansy, but didn't comment on Phrenicos' observation. Phrenicos tossed his head at Thracis. "Why don't you go the store and see about the supplies I've ordered. I've arranged for them to be delivered this afternoon, but we will have to add to the order now that we have more company. After you've seen to that come and join us for the midday meal."

Thracis bobbed his head and turned down the street. As he walked he saw Kebi, the black cat who first met him and Aeos when they arrived in Boudica, pacing him on the opposite side of the street. After a year of living in the area, Thracis was still unsure as to what position Kebi held in the village. The black cat always seemed aware of the going's on whether she was directly involved or not. Thracis was under the assumption that Kebi was the unofficial mayor of the small town.

He walked into the general store, the smell of herbs and foodstuffs making his stomach growl. He wanted to get this over with and go have something to eat. Thracis walked to the counter and waited until the proprietress was finished with another customer.

"How can I help you this fine day?" Her eyes sparkled with interest. Thracis sighed as he realized everyone in town would have known about Zotico and Tansy by this time.

"As you are undoubtedly aware, Master Phrenicos is expecting company."

The mare nodded.

"Thanks to my meddling, we now have two more mouths to feed. Master Phrenicos has sent me to add more supplies to the order to account for the extra horses."

"They are a complicated pair, are they not, foolish colt?"

Thracis sagged as he felt Kebi hop up on his back. He was irritated that the black cat felt she could treat him as her own pedestal, but he would not insult her and, as a result, insult Master Phrenicos. "They have an unusual relationship."

Thracis spoke with caution. He knew Kebi was adept at mind reading and would know more about Zotico and Tansy than anyone thus far.

The Felisian stretched along Thracis' back. The shopkeeper busied herself with fixing the order, but her ears flicked in Thracis' direction. Kebi's voice purred behind him. "It is interesting, no? The way you males try to seem so dominant, yet fall over yourselves to please a chosen lady?"

The shopkeeper snorted laughter.

"Maybe if you ladies weren't so hard to please, we wouldn't be so flustered."

Thracis winced as Kebi dug her claws into his back. "You would be less amusing."

The shopkeeper laughed heartily at that and came to stand across the counter from Thracis, no longer bothering to eavesdrop.

Thracis lowered his ears and turned to face the cat on his back. "Since you are so well-informed, what is the status of their relationship?"

Kebi laid on his back, tucking her paws under her body and wrapping her tail along her side. "The male wants desperately to lay claim to her. And she would welcome his advances. However, in light of their journey and the recent loss she has suffered, the male does not feel this is the proper time to make his intentions known."

"Maybe, he is trying to let her decide if she wants to be with him with a clear mind." Thracis saw the shopkeeper pin her ears from the corner of his eye, just as Kebi sank her teeth into his skin. Thracis gave a little buck of surprise and asked both females the same exasperated question, "What? Aren't you always complaining about how males take advantage of you when you're most vulnerable?"

"We only mean that when the male intends to take advantage. If his feelings are true then a male's advances will be welcome when we need comfort." Kebi was all but spitting her frustration.

"How am I supposed to know that? It isn't as if females don't come with their own complications."

"We are not so complicated as you make us," the shopkeeper quipped.

"Let us agree to disagree on that subject, dear lady."

"The point is," Kebi said, using her claws to make the subject clear, "the red and white horse must make his intentions clear before she seeks solace from another source."

Thracis pinned his ears. "I would never be disloyal to Psyche."

"What makes you think you're the stallion she'd choose?" the shopkeeper asked. Thracis assumed she meant Tansy and not Psyche.

"The fact that there is a lack of unclaimed stallions in the area and I doubt she would be interested in Master Phrenicos."

"A logical deduction." Kebi hopped down from Thracis' back to the counter. "I've given you as much warning as you need. Hurry along before your master comes searching for you."

Thracis bowed his head. "Good day to you, ladies."

Back on the street, Thracis noticed that things had returned to normal. The shopkeeper had likely contacted as many mares as possible and shared the news about Zotico and Tansy. It was to Zotico's benefit, Thracis knew. The mares of Boudica regarded any new stallion with high suspicion and open hostility.

The tavern was full of patrons at this time of day. Thracis scanned the room and saw Phrenicos, Zotico, and Tansy at a corner table. At this distance Thracis could see the table was nearly overflowing with grain, sweet grasses, and hay. He wondered if he should have told the shopkeeper to add four horses instead of two.

He wove his way through groups of Equines, mostly mares, and around tables. The tavern catered to horses and cats, but the Felisian tables were on the upper level to keep them out from under the Equines feet. The arrangement also gave the cats a bird's eye view of the room below.

When he reached the table, Tansy immediately shifted, making room for him between her and Phrenicos. Giving an uneasy glance at Zotico, Thracis stepped forward and looked at the food spread out before him. His greatest interest was the full bucket of water Phrenicos was nudging toward him. He took several large swallows before starting on a portion of grain.

"Is everything in order?" Phrenicos would know if it wasn't, but Thracis answered the question anyway.

"The additions weren't a concern."

Tansy was looking all around and shifting from foot to foot. Her shoulder brushed against Thracis' side. He wanted to move away from her, but to do so he would have to push Phrenicos out of the way. He hoped Zotico remembered Thracis telling him about Psyche at the fallen tree.

A Felisian trotted up one of the ramps to the second level. Tansy jumped, bumping hard into Thracis. She lowered her head in embarrassment. "I'm sorry. I've never been around so many Felisians before or in a place designed for them. It is a little overwhelming."

"If you are done eating, perhaps you and Zotico should take a walk around town," Thracis suggested. "We won't leave without you."

The mare looked disappointed at Thracis' dismissal, but before she could say anything, Zotico spoke. "I think that's a good idea. It will give us a feel for this place and let everyone see us for themselves." He backed away from the table before Tansy could argue.

"If you've a mind, two stalls down from here is the farrier. Tell her to put the cost of your hooves on my account." Phrenicos tossed his head to the left of the main doorway.

Neatly herded by the three stallions, Tansy led the way through the tavern and out into the street.

"I feel trouble may be brewing." Phrenicos sidled over to the opposite side of the table to give Thracis more room.

"Kebi warned me of the mare's interest." Thracis looked about the room and sighed. "I wish Psyche were here. I think the presence of my lady would be enough to dissuade Tansy's advances."

"Perhaps, but then she would move on to another stallion." Phrenicos tossed his head to get the attention of the waitress.

"Who she moves on to is not my concern. If Zotico wishes to become her mate he will have to win her favor as he would that of any other mare."

"And if he does not know how to go about doing such a thing?"

Thracis lowered his ears. "I've better things to worry about than teaching a younger stallion how to entice a mare."

"A hippeus has many responsibilities."

"Well, since you are already a knight, you can pass on your experience."

Phrenicos laughed so loud he drew the attention of several nearby tables. The white stallion tossed his head and stomped his foot. "I've missed you, foolish colt. It will be good to have you back in my stable."

Thracis had to toss his head in amusement. "And twice as entertaining with those other two to keep us company."

Phrenicos paid the bill then looked at Thracis with a sparkle in his eye. "With the company I'm expecting, things should be very exciting around the stable in the coming weeks."

"Perhaps we should add wine to the supply order."

"Foolish colt, I've ensured that I, at least, will be well-supplied with something more whole grain in composition than wine."

CHAPTER 13

By the time the foursome was walking up the path to Phrenicos' stable, Tansy was being obvious in her flirtation
with Thracis. He tried to avoid her without giving insult, but
she was proving more determined than he expected. Zotico,
realizing he was no match for Thracis, was walking ahead
with Phrenicos. The paint was trying to appear unaffected by
Tansy's interest in the other stallion, but Thracis could see
Zotico's ears were pointed back in the mare's direction.

"The beach is different here than what I am used to." Tansy
had stopped at the end of the path by the sand. Thracis stopped
and turned, but didn't join her. He could hear Phrenicos and
Zotico proceeding into the trees. Tansy swished her tail and
pawed the ground. "The beaches I've seen were covered in dark
pebbles."

"I'm used to it. I grew up on the Pthian Sea and our beaches
are all white sand." He wondered at the difference from shy filly

to bold mare. Especially since she was upwind of him and he could smell her anxiety.

She inclined her head at him. "Will you walk with me, Thracis? Just to the rocks."

Thracis looked down the coast. The rock outcropping was at least two hundred yards away. Plenty of distance for a heartfelt discussion. The incident with Desiree, Queen Helena's lady-in-waiting, flashed in his mind. She had thrown herself at Thracis during a quiet interlude at a social gathering. It seemed the Zephyros brothers shared a magnetism when it came to the opposite sex.

Hoping to end this infatuation before it could grow roots, Thracis bobbed his head. "To the rocks, but then we must join Master Phrenicos."

Satisfied, Tansy waited for him to join her before walking toward the outcropping. She walked close, too close for Thracis' comfort, but she was young. He hoped he could convince her to show her affections to a more receptive stallion, like Zotico.

They walked in silence. As he was sure she had something on her mind, Thracis wished she would get to it already and stop stalling. He was looking at the line of trees that flanked the beach and thinking about asking Psyche to come visit when Tansy's voice broke into his thoughts.

"Do you have a lady, Thracis?"

"I do. A very fine lady. With a wicked temper, I might add."

Tansy's disappointment was evident. "Is she here at Master Phrenicos' stable or in Boudica?"

"She is with a friend near Ruffiana. That is the Diomedean capital. We are both in training for different things and have to be separated for the time being."

Tansy's ears pricked. "It must be hard, being far away from the one you love."

"You've experience with this?"

She looked out over the water, her voice holding a slight stutter. "I've...my sire was very strict. I was not permitted to enjoy time with the stallions of the herd. Neither was my sister, though she was only three and therefore not interested yet."

"You must have known Zotico if your sire was willing to let you and your sister leave with him."

Tansy sighed. "Zotico's sire and my own were friends since foalhood. Zotico's sire was the village magistrate. He has some combat training and he and his sire often wander the mountains in our region. When it was decided we should leave, he was the best option."

"You don't sound as though you agreed."

She tossed her head. "Zotico and I have always been close. But I don't think he sees me as more than a friend."

"Would you accept his advances if he pursued you?"

"I might have." She looked at him through her lashes. "Before I met a stallion like you."

They had reached the rocks. Thracis turned to head back the way they had come, but Tansy stood broadside in front of him, blocking his path. He was struck again by how young she was. Young and lost. Kebi was right; Tansy did need a strong stallion to support her right now. But Thracis was not that stallion. He was smart enough to know that she was drawn to him because he made her feel safe after her ordeal. It was a sound reason to become attracted to a stallion but not a good one. She was fortunate to be here with Thracis rather than his brother, Pyrios. Thracis had no doubt Pyrios would exploit Tansy's inexperience as much as possible.

"Tansy, I am in a committed union with a mare. I am not free to pursue another."

She swished her tail and looked away from him. Thracis saw her disappointment and embarrassment. "I guess that means I'm tethered to Zotico."

"You could do worse," Thracis said, thinking of Pyrios.

She snorted.

Thracis nudged her shoulder. "Listen, Zotico does not seem a bad stallion. After a couple months of training with Master Phrenicos, Zotico's physique will look like mine. He brought you this far, didn't he?"

"He had a lot of help from my sister and I." Tansy sounded defensive.

Taking care not to stir up too many feminine emotions, Thracis said, "I'm sure he did. A stallion needs a mare as much as she needs him." He paused, a memory of Psyche and his first meeting flitting through his mind. "I have seen that Zotico cares for you very much and is willing to challenge a much stronger stallion just to keep you safe." He pushed against her with his nose and then stepped back.

"Don't judge him too quickly. I doubt you would have found me this intriguing if you had met me last year."

Tansy tossed her head. "I'm a fool, aren't I?"

Thracis stepped around her and began down the beach. "You are searching for strength and comfort after a painful experience. I don't think there's much foolishness in that."

Tansy trotted to catch up with him. Thracis stopped and looked at her. Before he could react, Tansy reached over and touched noses with him, nipping lightly at the side of his lip. When she pulled back her eyes held nothing but the affection of a younger sister for an older brother. "Thank you, Thracis, for not taking advantage of a silly mare's idea of romance."

"You're more than welcome, Tansy." Movement up the beach caught Thracis' eye. He turned his head in that direction, thinking it was Phrenicos come to hurry them along. His heart stopped in his chest as he saw the black and white patchwork coat, the mane shot through with silver.

Psyche's ears pinned flat to her head. She glared at Tansy, but her eyes sparked pure fury at Thracis. She uttered a screaming whinny at both of them and reared, striking the air with her hooves. She dropped to all fours, snapping her teeth and stomping her front feet.

Without another word, Psyche spun on her hindquarters and cantered up the path to Phrenicos' stable. Thracis groaned and cantered after her, Tansy all but forgotten on the beach.

Thracis made it to the stable door just in time to have it slammed in his face. He couldn't stop fast enough and whacked his sensitive nose on the wood. Stomping his foot, he yelled at Psyche hiding inside the stable. "You have no idea what was going on. I have no interest in her whatsoever. Psyche, open this door before I kick it down."

"You will do no such thing." Master Phrenicos walked up next to Thracis. "I don't know what's happened but you will not take out your frustration on my belongings."

Thracis hung his head and took a deep breath. He became aware of eyes other than Phrenicos' watching him. He turned his head to see Zotico, Eno, Aeos, Alcander, and Kamuzu watching in fascination. His joy at seeing his former traveling companions shriveled in the light of Psyche's fury.

If you're going to make an ass out of yourself, you may as well have an audience, Thracis thought with disgust. He struck the door with a hoof, though not hard enough to mar the wood, and stepped away.

"It appears nothing has changed since the last time we were all together." Aeos tossed his head at the stable. "You and your lady are getting along as well as ever."

Thracis trotted to Aeos and bumped his chest against the dun's shoulder. They rose up on their hind legs and swung their heads around each our, nipping lightly. When they were back on all fours, Thracis shook his head at the stable. "A misunderstanding that I will explain after her temper has cooled."

"You will be waiting a long time given the way she galloped through here," Eno snickered.

"Perhaps you should lend a feminine shoulder," Thracis shot back.

"I've known Psyche far longer than you have, Thracis. I won't be the first target she strikes in her current mood."

Thracis turned his attention back to Aeos. "I had no idea you were coming. Master Phrenicos said we were having guests, but he neglected to identify them."

"It was a spur of the moment decision to come here. As was my leaving Sanctuary."

Thracis ducked his head. "You are not in trouble with the delphae for this decision, are you?" He was thinking of Lady Kasmut's quick reprimands when he disobeyed.

"The overall consensus is that I was in dire need of a distraction from my duties."

"Whatever the reason, I am glad you've come." Thracis turned to Alcander and Kamuzu. "Well met, Kamuzu and Alcander. I am excited to see the both of you as well. I will be forever in your debt for what you did for me."

Alcander shook his head as if saving Thracis' life was nothing. "We were doing as you lady requested."

The lady in question was now thumping around in Phrenicos' stable. Thracis was sure the mare wouldn't damage another horse's property, as long as none of it belonged to Thracis, but it sounded as though she were taking the place apart.

Kamuzu hopped up on a nearby stump. He looked at Phrenicos and then at Alcander. "I fear we will not have a relaxing autumn while all these children reside under one roof."

"Don't worry, I ordered plenty of liquor," Phrenicos laughed. "It is good to see old friends again."

Tansy was sneaking into the stable yard. She gave Aeos an appraising eye as she approached but stopped next to Zotico. Phrenicos took the opportunity to introduce all who were present.

Eno ducked her head close to Aeos' shoulder and spoke in a low voice that would not carry. "Thracis will have to grovel for some time to win back Psyche's favor."

Aeos brought his head to nip her cheek and give Tansy a signal that he was unavailable. "Do not delight too much in his embarrassment. He is a good friend."

Though Thracis couldn't hear the conversation between Eno and Aeos, he envied Aeos' position. He wished his own lady would allow him the honor of caressing her cheek. He would help settle the others and unpack the mover they had brought. That should give Psyche enough time to calm down. Perhaps in the evening he might be able to convince to her go walking with him. Not along the beach, though, that would only bring disaster.

"Come," Thracis said, tossing his head at the mover, "let's unload this. By then Phrenicos will have figured out where you will all be sleeping."

"Is there enough room in the stable for all of us?" Tansy's voice held a hint of nervousness. Thracis thought she was likely worried about sharing room and board with Psyche. Well, he had tried to warn her.

Phrenicos tossed his head in the direction of a copse of trees that Thracis had yet to explore. "I have been a trainer for many years and used to have many more students. Behind those trees is another stable with six stalls. It will have to be cleaned and repaired but should be suitable for you young stallions." He glanced at Tansy and Eno. "I think it best that the mares stay in my stable with Alcander, Kamuzu, and myself."

Alcander tossed his head. "I would rather stay with the stallions if you don't mind, Master Phrenicos. They might need the experience of an older male, gelding or not."

Kamuzu twitched his tail. "Alcander has a point."

"My old friends, you may sleep wherever you choose. I only thought you might be more comfortable in my stable."

"I don't think any of us will be comfortable until the Lady is settled," Kamuzu said dryly with a nod at the stable.

Phrenicos bobbed his head. "I will go and see if she needs anything. The rest of you should either help unload Eno's equipment or see to making the student stable livable."

CHAPTER 14

"I think you might be misunderstanding what you saw on the beach." Eno was keeping her head low, her voice soft.

Psyche pinned her ears and stomped a foot. They were standing in Aeos' old stall. They had finished the evening meal an hour before. It had been an arduous, unpleasant experience with the tension between Psyche and Thracis almost palpable. Coupled with the knife-sharpened glares Psyche kept cutting at Tansy and depression that was hanging over Zotico, every one bolted as soon as their plates were empty. Psyche and Eno had gone to Eno's stall and Tansy had left the stable for the time being. Psyche thought the young mare would slink in later when she suspected Eno and Psyche would be asleep.

"She's little more than a filly, Psyche. And Thracis loves you too much to be unfaithful."

Eno's words made sense, but logic had no place in a wounded heart. Psyche tossed her head and walked to the large window. Night had fallen, the cold weather rendering the sky so clear the stars appeared close enough to touch if one stretched their neck far enough. Its beauty jarred with the churning emotions in Psyche. She wanted to see storm clouds and turmoil, not sparkling stars and serenity.

A snort on the other side of the stall brought Psyche's head around. Eno was sniffing the bowls of dried herbs that Aeos had placed on the shelves along one wall. Psyche wondered why the stallion hadn't put the herbs in pouches which was customary. She enjoyed the various scents and realized that many of the herbs were used for relaxation. That knowledge didn't sit well with her mood either.

"I wish you would let me stay in Thracis' old stall. All these plants will give me a headache before the night is through."

"These herbs are used for relaxation and focus. They will ease you into sleep."

Eno snorted again as she sniffed a pungent mixture. "Maybe you should use some then."

"Are you saying you believe I'll have a restless night?"

"Oh, come off it, Psyche. You're being a bigger jackass than your dam and sisters combined." Psyche flinched at the verbal thrust, but Eno continued, "you and I both know that Thracis is attractive. He's also polite and thoughtful and considerate. If Tansy has little experience with stallions, then she may have mistaken compassion for interest."

Psyche glared at Eno. "Why are you taking the side of some strange mare?"

"I'm not taking anyone's side, except maybe Thracis'. Psyche, the way he looks at you. There are no other mares as far as Thracis is concerned."

"How can you be so sure? What experience do you have with stallions? You use them the same as any Diomedean mare, for a moment's satisfaction." Psyche's vehemence was fueled by Thracis' indiscretion, not Eno's logical deductions, but with Thracis absent, Eno was the only target Psyche had in the stall. She was stunned when she saw the fury in Eno's face.

"What I do with any stallion is none of your business, Hippolyta Psyche. You are not the only one who shares feelings with another. Now, if you're quite through insulting me, I would appreciate if you would take your tail out of my stall. I refuse to deal with you until you treat me with the same respect I grant you."

"Fine." Psyche walked to the door.

Behind her, she heard Eno say, "May Lady Serene take pity on your arrogance, Psyche. You are destroying the greatest thing that has ever happened to you."

Psyche's ears flicked back as she heard the snick of the lock on Eno's door. She was still unnerved by Eno's fury. Was there more between Eno and Aeos than friendship? Given Eno's reaction it seemed like there was. Guilt ripped through Psyche. She shouldn't have spoken to Eno like that whether or not Eno and Aeos were romantically involved.

Her neck and tail drooping, Psyche walked into her stall. Thracis' stall. She hadn't had time to change the grasses in the bedding box and Thracis hadn't emptied the box before leaving for training with the delphae. Psyche lowered her head and inhaled deeply. Thracis' scent permeated the dry grass. She felt a tightening in her chest. Eno was right. She was being stubborn and foolish. But she couldn't deny the stab of jealousy she had felt when she had seen Thracis touching noses with that, that....

Psyche spun and kicked a wall. On the other side she heard Eno utter a rather explicit retort. Pinning her ears, Psyche raised a hind foot to kick again, then thought better of it. A fight with Eno she didn't need. Mostly because she was fairly certain Eno would win a physical confrontation. The bay mare had picked up more than a little combat training during her time among the cavalry soldiers.

Snorting in frustration, Psyche headed out of the stable. She stood on the front porch and sniffed the air. A lingering odor of Tansy's scent, mixed with the smells of the stallions. Not Thracis, but Zotico certainly and Aeos. Psyche lowered her head and sniffed closer to the ground. The trio of horses had split after meeting in front of the stable. Tansy had gone to the beach and the two stallions had taken the path to the student stable. Good for Aeos. Not that Psyche expected anything less from the dun stallion. He would be careful to avoid Tansy until things smoothed over.

The ground was free of Thracis' scent.

Psyche raised her head and blew out her nostrils, trying to catch his smell on the wind. She didn't think he had gone to the student stable. Knowing Thracis as she did, Psyche tossed her head and walked around the stable. As she passed the window of the main room, she saw Phrenicos, Kamuzu, and Alcander playing some kind of game involving colored stones and a wooden pegboard.

She followed the path past the drying room, slowing her gait as she approached the training arena. When he was agitated, Thracis found solace in the flowing movements of his training exercises. Psyche knew that better than anybody as Thracis usually contacted her as he was cooling himself out. She stopped in the shadows of a tree, out of sight and watched Thracis on the white sand of the schooling ring.

Thracis seemed oblivious to her anyway. He moved in perfect cadence as he shifted from collected trot to ground-covering extension. Psyche hadn't seen Thracis practice in months and she was awestruck with the improvement. He was balanced and relaxed, enjoying himself instead of stumbling through a difficult transition. Hidden from everyone and able to drop her own guard for the moment, Psyche let her eyes wander over the other improvements that had occurred in the past months.

Thracis was more muscled for one thing. He chest had broadened and deepened, his hindquarters half again as big as they had been when he and Psyche first met. He walked with a new maturity now, a confidence that drew her to him in a different way. It was no wonder Tansy was throwing herself at him.

That observation made Psyche pin her ears again. Well, she was going to find out what was going on. She marched out into the schooling ring. Her abrupt arrival startled Thracis and he settled back onto his haunches. The movement pulled him together, making him an impressive figure. Psyche tossed her head, refusing to lose her anger. And never mind the look of muscles flexing in starlight.

"I thought you weren't speaking with me?"

Psyche heard the restrained anger in his voice. If she provoked him things would only get worse. "I had reason to be angry."

Thracis' ears lowered. "You should have let me explain. How could you believe I would do something so stupid?"

"I have had a lot on my mind." She pinned her ears at him. "If it had been me in such a situation, you would have challenged the stallion and the two of you would have been fighting on the beach."

For that Thracis had no reply, as she knew he would not. Lifting her ears, Psyche pawed the ground. "These are trying times for me, Thracis, my dam, my sisters. They still do not see me as an equal."

Thracis reached out with his nose. Psyche could sense that he was afraid she would shun his advances. She lowered her head to meet him halfway. She breathed deep of the breath he blew against her. "You should have told me you were having difficulties. You no longer have to carry these burdens alone."

"I have done so for such a long time." Psyche was silent. Thracis waited and she loved him for it. She wanted to reach out to him but wouldn't be able if he forced her. She reached up and nibbled the soft spot behind his ear. "I don't even trouble Eno with the most personal of my issues."

"I'm sure she's had an earful of my failings." Thracis nipped the underside of Psyche's neck.

"Especially the most recent ventures."

"I swear by Lord Pegasus that what you saw was all there was. She's young and confused and doesn't see the stallion standing right in front of her."

"Zotico."

Thracis snorted. "Obvious to all but her."

"I don't want to speak of her anymore. It's bad enough I will have to make amends at some point."

"If it will ease your guilt, she was pursuing me, just not at the time you saw us."

She nipped his neck. "That does make me feel a little better, oddly enough." She pushed against him, laying her head along his back. "I've missed you, Thracis. In retrospect I don't think we should have parted after the Diomedean battle."

He nuzzled the lock of hair that fell against her withers. "I agree. No just about you and I, but Aeos and Eno as well. I feel settled. It is as if something inside me has been waiting for all of us to come together."

Psyche's shoulders twitched. She had felt the same, even in her anger at Thracis. It was as if the world around her had been holding its breath, waiting for something. As soon as she and the others reached Phrenicos' stable, that breath was expelled in a soothing sigh of relief. From where her head lay, Psyche could view the entire schooling ring. The light sand would be glaring in sunlight, but the stars gave the area a pleasant glow at night.

"You spend a lot of time here." It wasn't a question.

"Many hours. It is the place I feel most at home."

"Do you miss Calabria?"

He sighed against her. "I do. I don't miss the land as much as my herd. I've never met my younger sister and she will be a year soon."

"You could have returned for a time before completing your training."

He shook his head, his mane tickling the front of Psyche's shoulder. "Until the threat of the Baroquians has passed I will not return to my home stable. I can't bear the thought of my herd becoming endangered because of my doing."

Understanding the loyalty he felt, Psyche rubbed her cheek against his back. "Thracis, there is something you should know about the attacks on you. The mental attack anyway."

"You've discovered the source."

"I," she paused, "have known who it was for a long time."

He stepped closer to her, his neck curving around her own in an embrace. "Why haven't you told me?"

"Because the mare who attacked you was a member of my herd. She is my older sister, Zeva."

A silence followed. Psyche fought hard not to twitch or fidget. She hoped he would say something, at least give her a chance to explain before walking away.

He stepped back a little, pulling away so he could look at her directly. "I would hardly think that Queen Hippolyta would condone such an action on a stallion who has committed no grievance."

"The queen had nothing to do with the attempt. Zeva was exiled many years ago after she tried to rid the herd of the youngest daughter."

"She tried to kill you."

Psyche nodded. She didn't think Thracis was asking a question, it had sounded more like a statement, but it gave her the excuse to move. "One of my other sisters saved me. It was that incident that led to Zeva's exile and my forever being labeled as incapable of taking care of myself." She stomped a foot and swished her tail. "It is a shadow I have lived under almost my entire life and I wish you hadn't been brought into it."

"When we met in Iliad there were many things you and I did not know."

Psyche pawed the ground in distraction. "I saw many things involving your future, but never my sister's attack. I swear by Lord Pegasus I did not know she would try to assassinate you using me."

"It is in the past. She isn't the only one who has tried to kill me."

They stood in silence. Psyche shifted her weight from foot to foot, fretting. There was more she wanted to say, more she wanted to explain, but words were lost to her. She looked at Thracis in desperation.

Thracis shifted to stand hipshot, his demeanor relaxing. "I think when the planet is settled again, you and I should spend some time with my herd."

Psyche blinked at him. "You aren't going to leave?"

Thracis tossed his head. "Why would I leave?"

"My sister tried to rip your mind apart," Psyche said dryly. Thracis twitched a shoulder. "Every herd has its problems. For instance, I think my brother is about to completely scandalize the Registry of Breeds."

Psyche stretched her neck, relieving the tension in her back and shoulders. She did want to hear about the capital gossip but not at the moment. She stepped forward and nuzzled Thracis' cheek. "You can tell me about Pyrios and his conquests later."

"Would the lady care to join me for a walk along the back meadows? They are the farthest from the beach."

"Keep that up and you'll be walking alone."

Thracis tossed his head, but kept his mouth shut.

Psyche looked back at the lights of Phrenicos' stable. "I'm sure Master Phrenicos won't wait up for me to return."

"In that case, maybe you shouldn't wake him. It's not that cool tonight and the grasses out here are softer and fresher than the ones in my old bedding box."

"Are you attempting to seduce me, stallion of Thetis?"

"Attempting."

Psyche trotted down the path that led to the back fields. "If that is your intent you will have to catch me first." She burst forward into a gallop, the wind carrying her laughter back to chestnut ears.

CHAPTER 15

Eno and Psyche watched as Thracis, Aeos, and Zotico trotted through a series of warm-ups. Master Phrenicos stood at one end of the schooling ring calling out instructions, encouragements, or criticisms. Zotico was having little trouble keeping up the pace, but Eno caught several stumbles as the patterns changed. She thought he would learn the sequences soon enough. Alcander grazed along the side of the ring, occasionally looking up but clearly happy that he was not required to participate in the training. Kamuzu had gone fishing early that morning. Tansy was nowhere to be seen.

As Psyche had not returned the night before, Eno and Tansy had shared a light breakfast with Phrenicos, discussing the day's activities. Tansy had been anxious, her eyes constantly flicking to the door and jumping at every little sound. Eno knew the young mare was worried about confronting Psyche when the pinto decided to come back to the stable. Eno wanted to tell Tansy not to fret; Psyche wouldn't cause a stir with the buckskin as long as there was tension between Psyche and Eno. However, Eno couldn't say that without bringing up the incident with Thracis, which Tansy seemed eager to forget.

Psyche had come wandering into the stable with a look of embarrassment at staying out all night just as the other three were finishing their meal. Tansy immediately found an excuse to leave the table. Minutes later they heard the back door open as the young mare escaped outside. Phrenicos stayed, more as a buffer than for any interest in what Psyche had been up to the night before. Eno thought this action was more a protective gesture for his belongings than an attempt to keep peace between the two mares. He needn't have worried. Eno and Psyche shared half a dozen words before Eno excused herself and began clearing the table and cleaning the dishes.

Eno had been planning to start working on designing an outdoor lab this morning, but Master Phrenicos had invited her to watch some training and it would have been impolite to refuse. She knew she and Psyche would have to speak again but she was still hurt by Psyche's words the night before. If Psyche wanted to mend feelings between them, she would have to find the way herself.

"Zotico shows promise. Perhaps not as a hippeus, but if today is any example, he will grow into a formidable opponent in basic combat." Psyche was trying to start a conversation using a trivial subject. If she thought she things would be better between them without an apology, she was grievously mistaken.

Eno twitched her shoulders noncommittally.

"Aeos has come far since I last saw him. He must have been keeping up with his training while he was in Sanctuary. I give him credit for that. When I began my studies with the Felisian *ammoni* I hardly had time to breathe."

"I really hadn't noticed. When you only use stallions for one purpose you don't pay attention to their advancements." She saw Psyche flinch from the corner of her eye.

"Eno, last night," she paused, gathering herself, "last night I spoke out of frustration and anger and said things I never should have. I know you have soft memory for each of the stallions you have spent time with. I also know that whether or not you and Aeos are anything more, you are good friends and that friendship should be respected. I am sorry for what I said."

Eno turned her head. "I know you were angry, but you should not have vented your anger at me."

"A lesson that has been well learned."

Eno inclined her head. "I'm not the only one with whom you will have to make peace if we are all going to be comfortable."

"Oh, come now, Eno." Psyche's voice became a whine. "She was blatantly trying to entice my stallion."

"She is young. You can't blame her for being attracted to Thracis. He's a gorgeous stallion."

"Wait until she moves on to Aeos, then we'll see how forgiving you can be."

Eno lowered her ears. "Why would she be interested in Aeos?"

Psyche's voice turned innocent. "Why wouldn't she? He's well-built, intelligent, sensitive. He may be a better fit for her than Thracis, if you stop to think about it."

Eno nipped Psyche's neck. "If you're trying to get back on my good side, this tack is not working."

"I'm only stating the obvious. From what Thracis has said, Tansy has no preference for Zotico."

"If Aeos wants to entertain another mare, he's welcome."

"Funny, you actually sounded like you meant that."

Eno stomped a foot, making the stallions in the arena shy away. Aeos and Thracis quickly regained their composure, but Zotico was thrown off and stumbled several steps before coming to a stop and starting over. "I'm going to go lay out my lab. You can join me if you plan on being civil."

Psyche snorted. "A bit touchy, aren't you? I'm sure Aeos would never entertain two mares at the same time."

"Keep it up and I'll show you the stallions aren't the only ones good at close combat."

Eno spun and walked down the path and passed the student stable, her ears flicking back to Psyche's following hoofsteps. The area to the left of the stable was flat and open with all of Eno's equipment stacked on one side. Eno was already planning on converting the mover to a temporary table that would keep her prototypes out of the dirt. She had also packed several tents that would keep her equipment out of the elements. With the stallions busy training, Eno took the opportunity to set up her lab exactly how she wanted it without a male pointing out the impracticalities of her layout. Psyche had worked with Eno long enough to keep her mouth shut and put things where Eno told her to. Eno wished everyone she knew was so good at following directions.

Psyche held up the banner with her teeth. "What do you want to do with this?" she asked around the fabric.

"Attach it to that tree branch there. That way it can blow in the wind and still be relatively protected in case of a storm."

Psyche did as was asked then stood regarding the banner. "It's very pretty. It must have been expensive. The Arachne Weavers are not cheap."

"Do they sell in the markets or do they only produce commissioned pieces?"

"I think the works done by the apprentices can be bought at the marketplaces. I know they do export a fair amount of weavings. But if you want something done by a master, I think you have to commission the work."

"Have you ever been to the Arachne Stable?" Eno tried to sound casual. The idea for how the banner would help her create wings wasn't fully formulated in her mind yet.

The other mare snorted. "I went there a couple of times before Lachesis went to the Temple of Consciousness. She was in love with the designs of a particular apprentice. I think that apprentice has since moved on to master. Lachesis purchased several weavings."

"Are they open to strangers?"

"They are if your purse is well filled." Psyche walked to one of the tents and tied back the front flap. She used her lips to do this, giving her mind a break for the time being. Eno knew Psyche would be getting back to her mental exercises soon and was relishing the time off.

"Hmm. Do you think some of the other mares in Boudica would come up here and let me try the prototypes on them?" If

Psyche thought the abrupt change of subject was strange, she gave no sign.

"I think they might. Did you get inspired on the journey here?"

Eno shook her head. She turned her head to see the stallions walking this way. She didn't feel like dealing with them at the moment. "I'm going for a swim."

"Don't you think the water's a little cold for swimming?"

"It will wake me up and clear my head. You can endear yourself to me further if you stay here and keep the colts busy. I really do need some time alone."

"Fine," Psyche sighed, "but I feel you're using my outburst to your fullest advantage."

"My sire taught me to never miss an opportunity." Eno tossed her head at the stallions, then turned and trotted down the path that would take her to the open sand of the beach. Not giving herself a chance to think, she cantered straight into the foaming surf. Her hair stood up on end immediately. Psyche was right, the water was freezing.

Ignoring the cold as much as she could, Eno swam out several yards to get her heart pumping. She turned and stroked parallel to the shore for a little while, then came back to shallow water. She felt invigorated. Heading in the direction opposite the rock outcropping, Eno galloped down the beach, chasing the seabirds foolish enough to get in her path. Out of breath, she slid to a stop and looked back the way she had come.

The first thing she noticed was how all the birds were gliding on the wind, waiting to see if the creature that had disrupted their foraging would return. As they hovered on drafts of air, the sunlight glinted off their white wings, making them glow gold. A movement over the water caught Eno's eye. A pelican, targeting on a fish, tucked its wings close to its body and dove. Eno watched in envy. She knew in her heart she could create wings to let a horse soar and dive like the birds if only she could figure out the weight problem.

She started walking back to the stable as she thought of her predicament. She could make the wings out of achillium, but even if the sheets were pounded thin the weight would still be too much. Especially with the batteries. What she needed was a way for the thrusters and the wings to recharge themselves without using an additional weighted source.

She kicked a large shell out of her way. She may as well find a way to use the air to power her wings. The shell flipped several times before coming to lay with its shiny inner surface pointed up at the sun. Eno blinked as a sun flash shone off the shell and into her eyes. While she waited for the colored spots to leave her field of vision, something Psyche had said occurred to her.

Too bad the wings of Icaris melted. It would be something indeed to fly close to the sun's gold.

"Something indeed," Eno murmured. The colorful banner flashed in her mind. "It might work." She was talking out loud to no one, though a few birds cocked their heads. "I will have to speak to the Arachne Weavers and see if it can even be done."

Her decision reached, Eno cantered up the beach to Phrenicos' stable. Behind her, the cries of seabirds filled the blue sky.

CHAPTER 16

Aeos and Thracis looked at each other over the table set with the midday meal. Psyche and Tansy had set out grain, grass, and fruit as well as buckets of fresh water, but neither stallion had much appetite. The two mares were tense around each other even though they were trying to be civil. Most of the trouble came from Psyche. It was obvious to everyone that she was still angry. She made a point of standing between Thracis and the other mare whenever Tansy came close and had threatened with a back foot on more than one occasion.

Tansy herself seemed preoccupied. She walked around the small group tossing her head occasionally, as if flies were bothering her. Several times during the conversation her eyes became fixed and she had to be asked the same question repeatedly. To Thracis she seemed as though she were mulling over her behavior and he gave her strangeness little thought.

Thracis had hoped the appearance of Eno would ease things, but after a few quick mouthfuls, the bay mare had excused herself to her lab. It would be in Tansy's best interest to stand near Zotico, but the buckskin had settled herself between Alcander and Aeos. Thracis didn't like that. And it didn't look like Psyche was happy with the arrangement either. Well, Thracis had smoothed Psyche's hard feelings. Aeos would be on his own where Eno was concerned.

The chestnut stallion didn't think Eno had noticed Tansy's placement; the bay mare had seemed preoccupied before leaving. Thracis knew that if Eno missed how close Tansy was standing near Aeos, Psyche would bring it to the other mare's attention. Thracis liked Zotico and Tansy, but he was wishing Phrenicos would find another establishment where the mare could stay while Zotico continued his training.

Thracis nibbled a few more bites of grain and was readying himself to ask Psyche if she'd like to go for a walk down the beach when a loud whoop sounded from the direction of Eno's lab.

"She must have made a breakthrough," Psyche mumbled, stepping away from the table.

"I'll go with you," Aeos said.

Thracis reached for another mouthful when he felt a bite on his flank. He turned his head to see Psyche glaring at him. "I think you should come to. Eno might need help moving something heavy, maybe even as heavy as a horse."

Not sure if the statement was a threat or not, Thracis bowed his head at Master Phrenicos and left with Psyche and Aeos. He heard the white stallion begin a lecture on the importance of foundation training as Aeos led the way to the student stable. Thracis knew Zotico wouldn't be moving anytime soon and

Tansy wasn't brave enough to enter Eno's territory without the paint stallion in tow.

As they approached the clearing, Thracis saw Kamuzu talking with Eno. They were both looking at a multicolored banner hanging from a tree. Eno was gesturing with a front hoof as she spoke and Kamuzu was nodding in agreement.

"Seems she may have made The Breakthrough, not just a breakthrough."

Thracis jumped at the sound of Alcander's voice. The miniature had the uncanny knack of moving in total silence.

"Looks like it. What is that banner they keep looking at?"

Alcander sniffed. "It looks like a weaving from the Arachne Stable. Their works are unique in Equus."

"A stable of weavers? Are you sure you don't mean a house?"

Alcander rolled his eyes. "Do you think the only animals that can weave threads are Felisians and spiders?"

"No. I'm sure the Mustelideans and the Canans are capable as well."

Thracis uttered a short squeal as Alcander bit his tender underbelly. He sidestepped away from the miniature in case the gelding decided to bite a more private area.

Alcander pinned his ears. "A smart ass is still an ass."

"Point taken. Don't ever let anyone tell you your stature makes you less of a threat, Alcander."

"I make my points known."

"You've spent too much time among the mares of Diomedea."

The miniature tossed his head. "Perhaps."

They came to a stop behind Aeos, who was standing next to Psyche. Eno was paying the new arrivals no attention. She was too involved in the conversation with Kamuzu. Thracis knew the mare well enough to know that did not bode well for the rest of them. He predicted nothing but pain for himself as a result of this conversation.

"So, do you really believe it is a possibility?" Eno was all but dancing.

"I believe if any creature on the planet can do what you want, it will be the Weavers." The orange tail flicked back and forth as Kamuzu thought for a moment. "For this invention of yours to work, you will have to combine technology and, for lack of a better word, magic."

"Magic?" Aeos snorted.

Kamuzu shrugged. "Well, let's say otherworldly assistance. It has long been whispered that the Weavers sing spells into their threads to make them stronger and keep the colors vibrant for years to come."

"That could be nothing more than using their mental powers in a different way," Eno said.

"The *ammoni* tell us that those with the strongest psychic powers have simply learned to use more of their brains than the rest of us." Psyche twitched her shoulders and glanced at Aeos. "It's as good an explanation as any."

Eno shook her head. "I won't think about that aspect just yet. Right now I am interested in the theory, not the application."

"Why don't you let the rest of us in on your newest inspiration?" Thracis suggested. He hadn't liked the way Eno said 'theory'. He knew that when it came time to apply her latest inspiration, she would not be the one testing her theory, he would.

"Alright. As Psyche and I have discovered, it's not flying that is the issue but the weight of the equipment. Mostly due to the energy packs used for wings. I can design wings with miniature thrusters that will lift a horse with little trouble and they themselves have little weight. But the batteries to store the energy are too heavy to carry around while a horse is earthbound."

"Not to mention the battery packs get hot," Psyche murmured.

Eno nodded. "We played with the idea of sails that would allow a horse to glide on the winds, but then again the weight was a problem. Sail material is heavy."

"Which leaves?" Thracis was becoming bored.

"Solar sails."

The four other horses stared at Eno.

The bay mare tossed her head and pawed the ground. "Look. If I can find someone who can weave metallic threads that can be energized by sunlight it would eliminate a significant amount of weight. And metal can be woven thin enough that it will not weigh as much as bulky canvas sails."

Thracis and Psyche exchanged a look but Aeos was bobbing his head. "It is a sound theory. The sails will need some sort of framework."

"I'm working on that. Achillium is the best choice as it is the lightest and since it is so strong the frames could be very thin."

Aeos cocked his head. "You realize if the frames are built correctly and the sails are strong enough, you may be able to eliminate thrusters entirely."

Eno's eyes beamed with the possibility. Thracis felt his unease grow. He knew Aeos was trying to endear himself to Eno so that he would not be the first to test this apparatus. Thracis didn't like the idea of not having thrusters in case the wings ripped or folded or something and he said so.

Eno rolled her eyes at him. "Don't worry, Thracis. I would never do anything to hurt you. As long as you stay on Psyche's good side."

Thracis pinned his ears at the last bit, but couldn't say anything. He had rectified things with Psyche; an argument with Eno he didn't need. So he changed the subject. "How do you know these weavers will do this for you anyway?"

"I don't," Eno glanced at Psyche, "but I think if I bring along a friend they might be convinced."

"I will go with you."

They all jumped at the conviction in Alcander's voice. Thracis turned to look at the miniature. The white gelding was standing with legs braced and ears lowered as if he planned to go into battle. His tail was low and his jaw set. Little as he was, Alcander appeared more warrior than healer as he stood before the others.

"You are most welcome to join Psyche and I," Eno said.

"You're not leaving without us," Aeos protested with a head toss at Thracis.

"A merry group the five of you will make." Kamuzu was cleaning his paws and watching the horses.

"You aren't coming?" Psyche asked.

"I believe Alcander can foalsit you."

"I was going to ask Master Phrenicos to join us," Eno said.

"And he may, but I wish to stay here. It has been long since I spent any time in Boudica."

Thracis flicked his ears. It didn't matter to him if Kamuzu wanted to stay behind. What mattered to the chestnut stallion was whether Tansy and Zotico would remain here. A journey into the mountains would be difficult enough without Tansy and Psyche sniping at each other with every opportunity.

"Do we at least get a reprieve before we have to repack all your supplies and drag them up hill and down dale?" Aeos sounded exasperated.

Eno nodded. "Yes. I want to draw a few frameworks and re-design the harness. Aeos, stay with me and speak up. I am open to any suggestions to remove the thrusters. As well as anything else you can come up with to eliminate excess weight."

"It will be my pleasure, lady."

Well, this arrangement will ensure that Aeos is under Eno's super-vision at all times, Thracis thought. He said, "You can have him after morning practice. If I have to work, then so does he."

Aeos reached over and nipped Thracis' neck. "I would not leave you to the admonishments of Master Phrenicos. I heard a whisper that he may teach you to jump the capriole within the next few days."

Thracis had heard that same from Master Phrenicos himself during morning warm-ups. "Yes, he thinks I have the concept of the levade and should move on to something more challenging. I will have to alternate days on which I practice the levade and the capriole."

"Not to mention piaffe and passage," Aeos muttered.

"I haven't seen you holding cadence for more than a few seconds since you returned to the sands. You must have spent much of your time in Sanctuary learning to flex your mind as opposed to your body."

"I kept myself toned." Aeos was turning defensive.

"Yes, you didn't break a sweat until after the warm-up."

"And after Zortico. I'm in better shape than you give me credit for."

"Colts, colts," Psyche said in a clucking, maternal voice, "I'm sure we can make a schedule that will allow you to play together."

Both Thracis and Aeos pinned their ears at her. She pinned hers in return.

"Now children." Kamuzu stretched and hopped off the mover. "It would be rude to start a skirmish in your host's backyard."

"He's right. I have a lot of rearranging to do. Most of the items we brought from my lab might be useless now." Eno paused as the others who came with her to Boudica groaned. "I saw an empty stall in the student stable. Aeos, help me go through everything we brought and we can store the extra stuff in the stall."

"Do you want us to help with anything?" Thracis didn't want to unpack boxes. He wanted to go for a swim and then doze for a little while before spending some time in meditation before the evening meal.

"I don't think that will be necessary, Thracis." Eno was nosing through the items on the mover. "I will need you later, after I come up with a framework. I'll need as many different Equine bodies as possible actually. I know the wings are for mares but some mares are quite bulky."

"If extra bodies are what you want, I know several mares, including a Clydesdale, who will be most willing to learn how to fly." Thracis was thinking of Alcina and her small herd. They were warriors of the highest grade and would jump at the chance to improvise on their talents.

"Really?" Eno turned from the mover. "Perhaps they should join us on our journey to Arachne Stable. If this all works out we should train while in the company of the weavers so they can add their input and adjust their spinning."

"A herd trip with Alcina and her ladies. What fun we'll all have." Aeos sniffed the covered items in the mover. "Let's get on with this, Eno, if you want to unpack it all before sunset."

Thracis tossed his head at Aeos' disgruntled tone. He must have known immediately who Thracis was thinking of when he suggested the mares to Eno. Belatedly, Thracis remembered that Aeos had shared an intimate evening with one of Alcina's herdmates. Well, at least he wouldn't be the only one getting the sharp side of his lady's tongue. Although, looking at Aeos and Eno, Thracis doubted the bay mare would be as temperamental as Psyche. Good thing for Aeos.

"Yes, right." She turned away, but spoke over her shoulder. "I would like to meet these mares, Thracis, at a more convenient time."

"Of course." Thracis shifted his attention to Psyche and Alcander. "Would either of you care to join me for a swim?"

"I will," Psyche said. She regarded her dusty coat. "I need a good scrubbing. It will get harder and harder to keep my coat clean as my winter hair grows in."

Alcander snorted. "By mid-December I'll look like an overgrown Felisian. It is the curse of being a gelding, this overgrowth of hair. I never had this problem when I was a stallion."

"When you were a stallion, you were also much younger," Psyche noted.

"Very true. I guess I can go down and soak my legs. I don't think the water is warm enough for a swim but if the two of you don't mind the company I would be glad to join you."

"I've no objection." Thracis was walking the path to the beach. He was curious about the rapport between Psyche and Alcander. It sounded as though she knew the miniature before he was gelded. Thracis wondered if she knew the miniature's story. However, if he asked, he was likely to get a hard kick for his query.

CHAPTER 17

Pyrios trotted through a basic trotting pattern in one of the many open schooling rings on the university campus. These arenas were made available for horses who did not have any military affiliations and could not afford to rent a private ring. Lord Kantaka had his own private ring at his stable of course and the representatives and their aides were allowed access to the Registry arenas, but they lacked the privacy of these rings.

Pyrios enjoyed working in the university rings, it gave him the chance to speak with other horses who did not involve themselves with politics. It also gave him a place to hide from Nerissa without anyone asking embarrassing questions.

Lady Nerissa, and his involvement with her, was driving Pyrios well beyond distraction. In response to his absence, Nerissa had shown up at several social functions attended by Pyrios and Lord Kantaka. In every instance, Nerissa had been cold to him, shamelessly flirting with other stallions while constantly sending Pyrios provocative images via their mind connection. By the end of each event Pyrios was begging her for forgiveness. After two weeks of enticement, Nerissa finally allowed Pyrios access to her again. But she often reminded him of his transgression.

"Well, well. It appears one of the Zephyros colts have yet to be turned out of the schooling rings."

Pyrios lowered his ears at the sound of Favory Demas' voice in the morning air. This he didn't need. The oldest son of the Hapsburg Stable and the future king of Equus, if the sources could be believed. For some reason unknown to Pyrios, Demas had decided he didn't like Pyrios much. And made his displeasure known at every opportunity.

"The university arenas are open to everyone." Pyrios would be as civil as possible but his nerves were reaching the breaking point.

"An unfortunate byproduct of the professors' need to seek balance." Demas fell into step next to Pyrios. Pyrios noticed that the older Conversano stallion, the one Phlegon and Lord Kantaka were so curious about, walked behind them at a prudent distance.

"To what do I owe the honor of this conversation."

Demas tossed his head, his feet falling to the pattern Pyrios set with no discernable thought. As a member of Hapsburg Stable, Demas had undergone extensive military training and would have been in line to become the next Asapatish of the Hippikon if not for his ambitions to become king. "I simply wish to spend time with a fellow politician."

Pyrios snorted. "I am an aide, a far cry from politician."

"I wish to spend time with a familiar face then."

Tossing his head in the Conversano's direction, Pyrios said, "You've brought a friend. Why not talk with him?"

The Conversano was of great interest to Lord Kantaka and Commander Dias. The gray stallion was too much in the background, his ears always pricked. He never left Demas' side, as far as Pyrios was aware, and was quick to come to the aid of the Favory stallion. Though he made no effort to conceal himself, the Conversano was a mystery to everyone. No one seemed to know anything about him other than he had the knack to make everyone around him uncomfortable.

"I would rather speak with you." Demas' voice had dropped several degrees as they trotted around the arena. Apparently, the bantering was at an end.

"What is it you want?"

"I want to know where that disgrace of a brother of yours is hiding."

"Why would he concern you?"

Demas laughed. "He does not. But several of my acquaintances are interested in his whereabouts. It seems they have things to discuss with him."

Pyrios sighed. "I do hate to disappoint the king's oldest son, but I have not been in contact with Thracis in some time. I've no idea where he is." He was aware that Demas was slowly pushing him out of the ring and down a shadowed lane. The Conversano had closed the distance between them, cutting off Pyrios' retreat back to the ring.

Demas sped up to step in front Pyrios. "Do not play me for a fool, Pyrios. Contact your brother and find his location."

Pyrios pinned his ears. "I will not put my brother in danger. I don't know why you are so interested in his whereabouts but I will not help you." He pushed against Demas. "Excuse me, I've errands to run."

A sharp pain erupted along Pyrios' left flank as the Conversano struck out with a front foot. Fortunately for Pyrios, Thracis was not the only one in Thetis Stable to have natural talent. He rose on his hind legs and pivoted, surprising the Conversano with a hoof to the face. Without thinking, Pyrios kicked out with both back feet, striking Demas in the shoulder. Demas squealed and jumped away. Pyrios took the opportunity to dodge through the gap between the Conversano and Demas.

Knowing going back to the schooling rings wouldn't help him, Pyrios cut across the campus at a fast canter toward the main gates. A few students, out for a stroll between classes, gave him curious looks but no one stepped in his path. He slowed to a trot before proceeding through the gate. The spotted sentry gave him a startled look as he passed the gatehouse.

He moved at a steady trot until he reached a more populated area. Even Demas would not try anything with dozens of witnesses present. He kept glancing over his shoulder and stumbled into another horse.

"I hope Thracis is more observant than you are."

Pyrios turned his head to see Phlegon shaking himself.

"What are you doing here?"

Phlegon glanced passed Pyrios and down the street. "The spotted sentry alerted me to your hasty retreat from the university."

"Did she say anything else?"

"She said Favory Demas and his Conversano companion left the campus shortly after. I don't see them now though."

Pyrios took a deep breath. "They've probably skulked off to find another way to get what they want."

"News about Thracis?" Phlegon turned and began walking in the direction of Lord Kantaka's stable.

Pyrios fell into step beside the other horse. "Yes, and they weren't being nice about it either."

"You seemed to have done alright."

"Only because I caught them off guard."

"There will be repercussions from this, have no doubt."

Pyrios' shoulders slumped. "My dismissal from the council chamber."

"It would plummet Thetis Stable into dishonor. To have one son dismissed from the Romanium and the other from the Registry."

"Do you think Demas will succeed?"

"Possibly. Lord Kantaka has some pull and it would not be good for a colt from Calabria to be dismissed during this time of unease." Phlegon tossed his head. "Your herd does control the wealthiest achillium deposits. The Registry will want to make sure you are sympathetic to the Alliance."

"My sire would never aid the Baroquians."

"Never is a long time. And I can't speak for your sire, but my dam would never forgive the Registry if I was wrongly accused and dismissed. My stable may be small, but my dam has influence."

Knowing exactly the kind of influence Lady Ithia possessed, Pyrios bobbed his head. "You have a lot of understanding for a horse who doesn't speak much."

"That's because you talk enough for both of us."

They were nearing Lord Kantaka's stable. "I think I should contact Thracis."

"I don't think so. Demas would have employed eavesdroppers to keep an eye on you. I think it would be better to wait for Thracis to contact you."

"Can't the eavesdroppers track him?"

"Maybe not if he's with that mare of his." Phlegon stopped outside the stable door.

"Speaking of mares, I think-," Pyrios trailed off as someone contacted his mind.

Phlegon sighed. He knew it was Nerissa from the look that crossed Pyrios' face.

Several minutes later, Pyrios focused his attention back on Phlegon. "It appears my afternoon has been booked. Lord Alexi must journey to Courbettania for a few days. Lady Nerissa wishes for company."

"I'm sure she does. Pyrios have you given any thought to the possibility that Nerissa might be involved with the Baroquians? The lady has some suspicious activities."

"If she is, she's keeping it well-hidden. All her contacts are solidly backing the Elysian Alliance. Besides, what would she have to gain by siding with the Baroquians?"

"If they become more powerful, they could make her the sole ruler of Kigeria. It would not equal the Diomedean queen, but it would be a start."

Pyrios snorted. "Why would she bother? I am under the impression she enjoys the freedom being a ruling stallion's lady gives her. If she were ruler, she would be harnessed by her political obligations."

"To some power is more enticing than freedom."

Pyrios shook his mane. "I still don't believe it." He opened the door. "I have to go and get cleaned up before I meet my lady."

Phlegon nipped Pyrios' flank to get his attention. "Look, just do us all a favor and don't discuss Thracis with Lady Nerissa."

"Why would I discuss my brother with Lady Nerissa? She never asks about him."

CHAPTER 18

"I'm not so sure about this arrangement." Thracis shook himself, trying to settle the packs carrying Eno's equipment more comfortably on his back. The packs were situated up against the back of his armor harness and hanging onto either side of his body. "I'm not a packhorse."

"Stop whining, Thracis." Aeos was rechecking Titania's packs. Neema, Titania's calico companion, was supposed to be checking the packs and supplies, but was currently finding excuses to rub against Kamuzu.

"I'm not whining, I'm complaining. Are you sure my armor will work with all this extra baggage?"

Aeos sighed. "The pack harnesses have quick-release catches. You have to release the pack before you can activate your armor. It will only take a second, you'll be fine." Aeos nodded at Titania. "That should do it."

The Clydesdale mare tossed her head. "Is everyone else packed? I'm anxious to be on the road."

"We're waiting on Psyche and Eno. Phrenicos is already here to see us off."

Alcander came trotting down from the direction of Phrenicos' stable. He passed under Titania's belly with a foot to spare between she and him. Titania, used to the miniature, shook her head and walked off to collect Neema.

In all Titania, Neema, Psyche, Eno, Alcander, Alcina, Dysis, and Haidee would be joining Thracis and Aeos on the journey to Arachne Stable. Thracis was worried about the size of the herd, there were nine horses in all, and that added many more supplies. Between grain, water, and equipment, they were all weighted down pretty good. He worried about what effect the added weight would have when they began to climb the Pleiades Mountains.

The miniature addressed Aeos, "The ladies are on their way. There has been a dispute but I think they have sorted it out."

Aeos and Thracis exchanged a look. Another dispute. Thracis would bet it was between Psyche and Tansy. In the week since Eno had decided on this course of action, Psyche and Tansy had been at each other's throats. Thracis had hoped the two mares had reached an understanding. That was until Tansy decided to join Thracis for an early morning swim. In his defense he hadn't seen the mare until he angled back toward the beach and by then she was already in the water and stroking toward him.

Thracis had tried to get away and back to the schooling ring before anyone was the wiser even though nothing had happened. Unfortunately, Psyche had decided to come down to the beach and surprise Thracis with some impromptu companionship. The sight of him, soaking wet and an equally drenched Tansy at his heels, sent Psyche into a rage. She had charged at Tansy and landed several solid kicks before Thracis could break them apart. Then she turned her fury on him. He refused to fight back even when Psyche kicked him hard enough to send him to his knees. She had stormed off the beach, leaving a panting Thracis and quivering Tansy in her wake.

It took Eno three hours to convince Psyche to come back to the stable and then only on the contingency that Tansy be removed from Phrenicos' stable to the student stable and Thracis moved in with Psyche. Phrenicos had been happy to comply, but Tansy demanded Psyche be disciplined for her outburst. Psyche explained that the next time Tansy came near Thracis, Psyche wouldn't bother kicking the little hussy, she would just eliminate her altogether.

This was the point at which Phrenicos commanded that Tansy stay away from Thracis at all times and Aeos remain with Thracis to keep the peace. So it was that Thracis was foalsat for the week while they prepared for their journey. For his part, Zotico had been so embarrassed by Tansy's behavior that he had thrown himself into training, hardly making eye contact with the mare whenever the two of them were in the same area. Aeos and Thracis sympathized with the other stallion, but he had never made a claim to Tansy and therefore could not challenge her or Thracis about the situation.

"Please tell us this argument did not involve bloodshed." Aeos was craning his neck to look at Phrenicos' stable. "I thought Tansy was barred from Psyche's territory."

"She is, but apparently the buckskin has decided she wants to travel."

Thracis groaned. "Psyche will push her off a cliff at the first opportunity."

"She'll have to stand in line." Thracis jumped as Alcina strode between the two stallions. Alcander prudently slipped out of her way as well. "That buckskin wench is more trouble than she's worth. The nerve she has, trying to seduce Psyche's mate."

Haidee and Dysis had come up behind Alcina. Dysis inclined her head at Aeos, her golden coat shining in the early morning sun. Aeos nodded at her but didn't approach. They had spent time together the night before the Diomedean battle. Since then they had shared a mutual friendship, but nothing more. In Thracis' opinion, that was all to the good. Eno seemed a much better match for Aeos in the long run.

"If she were not after Thracis you would likely recruit her into your herd for her tenacity." Aeos was trying to lighten the mood but Alcina lowered her ears.

"There is something strange about that mare, Aeos. She feels off to me."

"She's had a hard road, Alcina," Thracis said, "she's trying to find her place."

"Right under you," Haidee smirked.

Thracis pinned his ears. "I would never betray my lady."

It was Dysis' turn to speak. "We know that, Thracis. It is not your integrity we are questioning. Besides, Psyche is under a lot of stress from her herd and this little tramp is the last thing she needs."

Alcina swished her tail, whipping both Aeos and Thracis. "If that buckskin thinks she's coming with us, I'll kick her back to the student stable myself."

"Now, ladies, that is not the sort of tolerance I teach in my arena." Phrenicos sauntered into the group and stood beside Titania. Kamuzu was sitting on the white stallion's back. "If Tansy insists on going the least you can do is allow her to trail you."

"Are you mind-addled, Master Phrenicos?" Alcina's astonishment was obvious. "Psyche will have a complete melt down. She's under too much pressure."

"We all have our burdens. Besides, if Tansy is hiding something, I would think she is among the best mares to find out what that something is."

Alcina's ears rose slightly. "It would be my pleasure."

"I thought so." Phrenicos raised his head. "Here they all come, the rest of you better be prepared."

Thracis tensed as Psyche led the way down the path. The black and white mare's ears were pinned and she was grinding her teeth. Her haunches were tensed and her tail swished wickedly from side to side.

"Let's get moving." Psyche glared at the gathering, ready to pounce on the slightest challenge.

"I wish you luck," Phrenicos walked along beside Aeos, keeping pace with the herd. Kamuzu was having a mental conversation with Alcander and ignoring the other horses. Aeos was the most settled in the group and Phrenicos knew the dun stallion would look after the others. "Zortico, Kamuzu and I will remain here. By the time you and Thracis return, Zortico will have little trouble keeping pace in the schooling ring."

The topic of the conversation was standing at the perimeter of Phrenicos' territory. The red and white paint was pawing the ground apprehensively.

"It will take several days for him to settle into a routine," Aeos observed.

"He will settle faster with the mare leaving."

Aeos swung his head around to look at Tansy. The buckskin was walking with head down and tail drooping. She was the last in the line as they walked along the path. Her packs bulged more than any other horse's, leading Aeos to believe she wasn't as experienced at packing as the rest of them.

The other horses each nodded at Zotico as they passed the waiting stallion. Haidee stopped briefly and shared a few words with the paint before moving on. Zotico watched her go before turning to Phrenicos and Aeos. The three stallions stood as the rest of the herd passed. Tansy didn't even offer Zotico a glance as she passed him. The stallion's hurt was evident as he turned his rump toward the retreating herd.

"I've not much experience with heartache, but I have heard it eases with time." Aeos was trying to be sympathetic, but Zotico's lowered ears indicated Aeos was talking to himself.

"Aeos is right. If that mare does not value your worth after all you have done for her, she is not worthy of you." Kamuzu hopped from Phrenicos to Zotico. "Trust me, young Equine, there are plenty of mares even here in Diomedea who will see your merit."

Zotico nodded but kept silent for a moment, then, "I should not keep you, Aeos, have a safe journey." He looked at Phrenicos. "I will go and start on the morning schooling, with your leave."

Phrenicos nodded. Zotico, with Kamuzu balancing on his rump, trotted back to the arena. Phrenicos said, "He will mend. A first love is a hard stumble."

Aeos shook his head. "I still do not understand that mare. The others may be right in their belief that she is hiding something. Zotico seems to be evasive as well when you ask too much about their journey here."

"I have noticed that. I will try to get him to confide in me more. I will have plenty of time to do so as I believe he will be in the ring until he collapses."

"He and Thracis have much in common."

"They do. Better hurry along, Aeos, else the others will leave you behind."

"I will see you soon, Master. Hopefully by then Eno will have made us all airborne."

"Well, at least the mares may have earned their wings. I fear you and Thracis will only be used for practice."

"It might not be so bad. Her advances will be tempered with all the other mares around. I think Alcina is looking for any reason to skin Tansy alive."

Thracis was trying to lighten Psyche's mood. The mare was ignoring him. The two of them were yards ahead of the rest of the herd which wasn't a problem now, but as they entered more dangerous territory, they would all want to keep close. Thracis looked back often and could just make out Eno leading the rest of the group. Eno was keeping her distance, giving Psyche and Thracis some privacy.

Psyche was forging ahead along a forest trail as if she planned on reaching Arachne Stable tonight. Thracis felt sweat gathering under his harness straps. It was midday and they would be stopping in the next meadow for something to eat. Thracis thought everybody would welcome the reprieve, though few would admit it.

Lost in thought, Thracis bumped into Psyche when the mare stopped abruptly. She kicked him in the chest for his lack of attention.

"What was that for?"

"You should be more observant."

Thracis tossed his head, his patience at an end. "I've had enough of this, Psyche. I understand your jealousy. I would be out of my mind if another stallion were vying for your affections. But what more do you want of me? I ignore her, I avoid her, I'm rude."

Psyche was listening to his tirade with lowered ears. Her head was raised to watch for the others. Her skin twitched as a fly landed on her flank.

Thracis pinned his ears. "Could you at least do me the courtesy of looking at me?"

"Come with me."

Thracis tossed his head at Psyche's new inscrutability. He didn't like it. Nevertheless, he followed her when she turned off the main trail and walked several yards into the trees. She turned and looked back the way they had come, waiting for the others to pass. Thracis sighed and was about to ask what they were doing when Psyche pinned her ears at him. *Open your mind as they pass, Thracis, and listen.*

Twitching his shoulders, Thracis did what she said.

The first horse to come down the path was Eno. Aeos was walking at her shoulder. They were discussing the wing frameworks again. As they passed, Thracis could see the affection they felt toward each other clearly in their minds. It gave him a start to perceive their private feelings and he felt ashamed. Psyche must have sensed it because she nipped his neck. Her eyes told him to keep quiet.

Next came Alcina and her herd, moving in a loose group. Thracis felt their suspicions toward Tansy and their excitement about the journey. Discussion-wise, the ladies were talking politics. The only one who kept her thoughts guarded was Neema. From her Thracis had the sense of a brick wall in her mind. He guessed this was normal for a Felisian who would have grown-up knowing others could read their minds. Alcander walked next to Titania and he also had a wall shielding his thoughts.

Tansy came last. The buckskin mare was beginning to labor under her heavier packs. She was wearing a bare basic armor harness from the design and Thracis had no doubt it had been provided by Phrenicos.

The oddest thing happened as the mare passed in front of Thracis and Psyche. Thracis could feel nothing from her. No wall shielding her thoughts, no emotion, no interest in her surroundings. He flicked an ear at Psyche. The mare shook her head slightly, indicating he should be quiet.

After the others were well up the trail, Psyche led him back out of the trees. She tossed her head in the direction of the herd. "Now do you understand that it is not just you I'm concerned about?"

"Why is her mind blank? And how did you know I could see their feelings?"

"Sensing the surface emotions of others is not difficult. And I helped you a little, raising your perception. All animals give off some signs to what they are thinking, signs that are obvious whether you can read their minds or not."

Thracis bobbed his head. His training required he become adept at gauging his opponent's reactions. "Tansy's intentions have been clear before. Why is she shrouded now?"

"I do not know. This absence of thought or emotion began two days ago, around the same time I banished her from Phrenicos' stable."

"Talking more and more like a princess," Thracis mumbled.

Psyche ignored him. "Zotico still shows much emotion and indecision, as was evident when we left this morning. The mare shows nothing."

"Maybe she's intimidated by all you mares waiting to attack her."

"Then she would show fear or anxiety."

Thracis had no comment. It was strange to feel that blankness. He shifted to brush shoulders with Psyche. "You don't think the Baroquians are using her in some way? Is that even possible?"

Psyche shook her head. "A puppet master can manipulate a creature but they have to be close to one another and I haven't sensed any other animals around." She rubbed her cheek against Thracis' neck. "And a puppet master takes years to learn their craft. An animal of that caliber would be sensed by the rest of us. Especially Neema."

Thracis nodded. He knew the Felisians were more attuned to the occult. He pawed the ground. "What do you want to do?"

"I have told the others to keep their mind contact to a minimum. We don't know what purpose Tansy is serving. I have heard that a mindreaper can sometimes transform an Equine or Felisian into some kind of transmitter."

"Like the equipment used by spacecraft to enhance mind contact when Equines are off planet?"

"Exactly. The transmitter has no purpose other than recording and broadcasting information from the animals around it." Psyche tossed her head. "I have never encountered one or a mindreaper who could produce one."

"Did Phrenicos know of your suspicions?"

"It is the reason he forced me to allow her to come. He knows we are the best equipped to deal with a Baroquian threat if threat there is."

Thracis began walking. Psyche followed along behind him. "How long are we going to allow her to transmit us? Surely not once we get to Arachne Stable."

Psyche swished her tail. "No, Alcina and I hope to deal with the issue before we reach the mountains. We can't change the fact that she knows we are going to see the Weavers, that information was given before we suspected anything, but we don't want anyone to know the path we will take."

"Where have you two been hiding? Stepping out for some privacy?" Eno's voice was teasing, playful.

"Apologies. I just can't seem to keep her off me." Thracis dodged away from Psyche's hind foot as she lashed out.

"If that's how you feel, you can be replaced quick enough." Psyche was talking to Thracis but looking at Tansy. The buckskin mare was standing with head drooping, her pack on the ground beside her. The others were grazing in the large meadow Eno had found, but Tansy was dozing. She would have to eat before they moved on or risk passing out from lack of sustenance.

"I'm hurt that my lady would dispose of me so quickly." Thracis chomped into a mouthful of grass. It was a mixture of brown and green, the higher meadows had already felt the autumn's cold bite.

"It's nice that the two of you are behaving normally again." Aeos had removed his pack and was grazing alongside Alcander. "We were wondering if you would be civil at all during this trip."

Dysis swished her tail and raised her head. Her mouth was stuffed with grass. She swallowed and bobbed her head in the direction of the Pleiades Mountains. "Storm coming. A big one."

The other horses looked up.

"We should find shelter for the night before the rains come," Titania said. "The trees are old, their branches full and broad. We should be able to find a fairly dry spot deep in the forest."

"Excellent idea." Alcina shifted her pack. "Let's finish this meal and move on."

"Should we carry grasses for later in the evening?" Haidee asked. She was sniffing the air. "It is only mid-afternoon."

"We should. The grass won't add much weight. We can secure it to our backs with mental straps." Alcina engaged her armor. She walked away from the group and extracted two wicked-looking hooks from the shoulders of her armor. The hooks were razor sharp and made of achillium, ensuring they could cut through any other metal. Alcina swung the hooks back and forth like scythes, cutting large amounts of grass with a single swipe. After several passes, the black mare retracted the hooks and her armor.

"That was courteous of you," Alcander commented.

Alcina tossed her head. "I thought it would make things go quicker. That storm is really moving."

The horses moved quickly, bundling grass and securing it among their packs and harnesses. Tansy had to be nudged more than once by Titania to complete the simple actions. It was as if the buckskin was asleep on her feet. Following a discussion with Psyche, Neema left Titania's back to ride on Tansy. The Felsian would secure the grass so that Tansy wouldn't lose her dinner on the trek into the forest.

The wind was beginning to blow as the horses headed back into the trees. Thunder rumbled in the distance. The horses would do well to get out of the open and they knew it. Lightning strikes were deadly. Thracis and Aeos waited until all the mares had left the meadow before following behind. In Equine society, the stallions took up the rear in the instance a mare needed assistance with anything. At least that was the way it was on the rest of Equus. Neither Aeos or Thracis knew if it was true in Diomedea where the mares were dominant and didn't ask. If these mares were going to travel with them, they were going to have to compromise. A little.

As Thracis fell into step behind Haidee, he noticed Tansy stumble not once but twice. The second misstep caused a collision with Dysis. The palomino mare restrained kicking and helped Tansy regain her balance.

"I don't think Tansy has the stamina for this journey," Aeos whispered.

"I don't think it's Tansy anymore," Thracis whispered back. Behind them the wind began to howl through the trees.

CHAPTER 19

Lightning illuminated the sky making the horses stand out in stark relief under the trees. The subsequent thunder shook the ground beneath their hooves. Thracis felt Psyche quiver against him and dropped his head to nuzzle her. Psyche lipped the front of his chest in response. She was uncharacteristically on edge tonight and Thracis could sense her anxiety. He looked around in the next flash of light.

Alcina and her herdmates were clustered around the base of a huge oak. The tree was broad but squat and not a candidate for a lightning strike. Titania was standing with Aeos and Eno. The Clydesdale's one eye glimmered in the flickers of light. Neema was curled on Titania's back, a piece of canvas from the equipment laying atop her. She was the only dry one of the lot. Tansy was nowhere to be seen.

Where is Tansy? Thracis thought at Aeos. Stallions were natural sentinels, centuries of instinct compelling them to watch over the herds. They were the first to notice if something was amiss.

Aeos roused from a restless doze. *The last I saw, she was standing next to Haidee.* He shook himself. The rain had started as soon as they settled in for the storm and all of them were soaked through, with the exception of Neema.

Thracis waited for light, then looked at Alcina's group. The black mare was in the middle, Haidee and Dysis flanking her. Tansy was not with them.

Aeos stepped away from Titania and Eno.

"Something wrong?" Eno asked. She had to shout to be heard over the rain.

"Tansy is missing." Aeos was swinging his head from side to side, looking around as much as he could in the flashing light.

Eno swished her tail and tossed her head. "Why would she wander in something like this?"

"There is something else controlling her." Psyche was shaking against Thracis. "I can't figure out what it is but it's very strong."

Alcina came to stand next to Psyche. "Do you need my help?"

Psyche nodded.

Alcina swung around and began giving orders. "Psyche and I will have to merge our power. We will need to concentrate. Eno, Aeos, and Thracis will have to guard us. The rest of you search the immediate area for the mare. Do not wander far. You will get lost."

Titania, Dysis and Haidee dispersed into the rain. Neema bounded up a tree and hopped from branch to branch above the Equines. Psyche moved up to Alcina and the two mares rested their foreheads together. Aeos, Eno, and Thracis formed a nose to tail circle around Alcina and Psyche.

Thracis' muscles tensed. His ears pricked and his nostrils flared. Psyche's warning had sent a chill through him and he was on edge for the slightest threat.

How are we supposed to protect the mares if we can't see in the dark?

The question was addressed to Aeos but the dun took several seconds before responding. *We will feel the change in energy. Dark things are sometimes easy to discern.*

Thracis' ears flicked back and forth as he strained to make out the sound of hoofbeats. All he could hear was the rush of falling rain, the wind sawing through the trees, and the crash of thunder. If any of the other mares needed help, they would have to make mental contact.

Psyche shuddered behind Thracis and he swung his head to look at her. At that moment a hoof caught him in the back of the head just below his ears. The blow sent him stumbling, but Thracis caught himself before falling into Psyche. He turned to see Tansy in broken light. The mare's ears were pinned, her teeth bared. She reared, meaning to strike him again, but Aeos slammed into her side, sending her sprawling.

The buckskin was on her feet in an instant. She spun and began kicking. Aeos shied back, his perception thrown off by the lightning. Thracis darted forward to strike the mare's unprotected flank. She swung her head in his direction. She opened her mouth and screamed.

Thracis slid to his knees as pain ripped through his head. Aeos was in a similar position next to him. The dun was rubbing his head on the ground, trying to drown out the mare's shriek. Thracis wished he had paws to cover his ears. All he could do was pin his ears flat and duck his head to his side to block the sound.

Eno, unaffected by the noise, jumped over the prone Aeos and reared, striking Tansy in the jaw with a front hoof. The buckskin's jaw broke and hung, unhinged, from her face. Her eyes, burning red, focused on Eno. Tansy rose on her hind legs and jumped forward, hopping toward Eno.

The bay mare didn't flinch. She didn't enact her armor either. Instead she whirled and jumped straight up, her back legs pistoning out parallel to the ground, her front legs tucked underneath herself. If Thracis hadn't been burrowing his head against his shoulder he would have be astounded at the perfection of the mare's capriole. According to hippeus doctrine's mares were forbidden to learn advanced combat maneuvers. How shocked Commander Dias would have been to see how much his daughter had learned as a filly raised among the military stallions.

Eno's back feet connected with Tansy's belly. The buckskin mare crumpled to the mud. She was trying to get her feet back under her, but the lightning showed twin trails of blood flowing from her nostrils. Eno was standing above Tansy's head, pawing the ground hard enough to send clods of wet earth flying. Thracis and Aeos were getting unsteadily to their feet.

Tansy dragged herself to a standing position and swayed from side to side. In the flickering light, sometimes she looked buckskin, sometimes she looked black. She charged at Eno. Eno sidestepped and swung her head around to bite down on Tansy's withers. The buckskin mare screamed in anger and struck with a front hoof, catching the side of Eno's knee. The bay lifted the leg before it buckled under her and popped her shoulder up, throwing Tansy off balance.

The buckskin wasn't going to be dislodged so easily. She reared, hooking a foot over Eno's neck, driving the other mare's head down. Eno went with the motion, turning her head sideways to bite Tansy's soft underbelly. Tansy ignored the pain and tried to strike at Eno with her back leg, kicking in a sideways fashion. Eno threw herself back and to the right in a roll, pulling Tansy with her. The two mares scrambled to untangle themselves and get to their feet.

Thracis and Aeos tried to engage Tansy but as soon as the mare focused on them again, that ripping pain went through their minds. They were knocked back to their knees in seconds. Eno would have to win this fight on her own.

The mares reared again, locking their legs around each other's necks. They battered each other with their heads. Tansy's broken jaw swung grotesquely. Several seconds later they dropped to the ground. Tansy was heaving, the blood coming from her nose was thicker, running faster. She came at Eno again and the bay swung and kicked. A crack, much louder and closer than the breaking branches, shattered the air. Tansy squealed and somersaulted forward.

Eno stood, panting and waiting to see what the buckskin mare would do. Tansy lay for a moment and then, incredibly, she struggled to get back up. She hobbled toward Eno, ears pinned, trying to gnash her teeth. Eno didn't flinch. The bay mare reared and struck out, pummeling Tansy in the face. The buckskin fell back on her haunches. The front of her face was caved in, her nose broken. She staggered to rise again.

Psyche and Alcina voiced simultaneous gasps and their bodies shuddered. At the same moment, Tansy's body slumped back down. The fire left her eyes and she started to gasp and cough, choking on the blood flowing down her throat. She lay flat on her side and panted, her body shivering in the cold rain. Eno walked forward cautiously and sniffed the fallen horse. Tansy's head twitched and her ears flicked lazily.

Thracis and Aeos approached carefully, wary of the mare's painful attacks on their minds. Psyche walked over to lean against Thracis. He could feel the heat of exertion baking off her. Steam rose from her coat to mix with the rain. "We freed Tansy's mind from the puppet master, but we were too late to save her."

Thracis watched as the buckskin's breaths came slower and slower. She was close to the end. Aeos reached out to nudge Eno's hip. The bay mare turned to bury her face in the dun's shoulder. He arched his neck around her, resting his head on her withers. Alcina, who would except comfort from no one, whinnied loudly, calling the rest of the herd. Thracis had a moment to wonder why they hadn't come running to the sound of fighting before they all showed up.

"We tried to get to you, but we kept getting lost." Dysis was breathing heavily, evidence that she had been running around.

"Something was keeping us confused. I could not find you even from the trees." Neema was in her customary place on Titania's rump.

"The one we were grappling with had much help," Alcina spoke calmly enough, but Thracis detected the slightest tremble in her voice.

"Help and talent," Psyche said, "we were forced to destroy part of Tansy's mind to dislodge the other presence. Unfortunately, we didn't accomplish that task soon enough."

They all looked to the buckskin as she drew her last shuddering breath. Nothing filled the silence but the falling rain, even the wind and thunder had quieted.

"We must grant her proper burial. The attack was not her fault." Titania's voice was a deep rumble.

"How long do you think she was being manipulated?" Haidee asked.

"Only a day or two before we left." Psyche shook her head. "Phrenicos suspected something as well, but neither of us could pinpoint the problem. Tansy was too erratic from the very beginning."

At this last, Thracis nodded. "She was always off-balance." He was quiet for a moment. "I don't believe she was malicious, though, only young."

The others nodded agreement. Neema shook herself and looked up at the trees. "The rain is stopping."

Eno stepped back from Aeos. Unlike a Diomedean mare, she didn't look embarrassed or chagrined by the need for support from a stallion. She was tired and shaken and would want the support of the other mares in the coming days.

Psyche stepped forward. "Let me work on that knee, Eno. I may not be able to do much but I can try to make you comfortable for the rest of the night."

Eno sighed and relaxed against Aeos again. She looked at the fallen mare. "We will bury Tansy at first light. That way we can find a good place."

Aeos tossed his head. "You ladies pick the spot and Thracis and I will dig a grave." He looked pointedly at Eno. "You will need time to recover and redistribute the equipment before we move on."

Eno nodded. The suggestion that she recheck the packs and equipment settled her in a way comforting words could not. She needed a job to occupy her mind while she dealt with what had just occurred.

Dysis stepped forward. "Haidee, there is canvas in my packs. Help me cover her until morning."

As the two mares set themselves to the task, the others drew together in a loose group with Psyche, Alcina, and Eno in the middle. Thracis felt exhausted. He also grieved for Tansy with a sense of loss he hadn't thought possible. She had been an annoyance for him almost since their meeting but he didn't harbor any hard feelings. He wished she had stayed with Phrenicos and Zotico, but understood that the decision had been taken out of her hooves.

Feeling Psyche rest her head on his back, Thracis shifted to stand hipshot. The last thing he saw before closing his eyes and succumbing to sleep was the canvas draped Tansy.

CHAPTER 20

Zeva and two other mares stood in a group with their heads pressed together. They had been merging their mental powers in order to control the drone so many miles from their current location. Others, spies implemented all across the distance between Zeva and the drone, had also shared their power. The others acted like boosters, catching Zeva and her helper's instructions and passing them on. When the link was severed, all contact was lost.

The two mares backed away, their sweat-coated bodies trembling from the psychic exertion. They had long experience with Zeva's temper and neither wanted to get kicked simply because they were standing too close. They needn't have worried; Zeva herself was too tired to punish them for the failed attempt to separate Thracis and Psyche.

The black mare stretched her neck and rolled her shoulders. She was sweaty and hot and hungry. Zeva's goal had been to destroy the relationship between her youngest sister and the

Zephyros colt. It had been more of an amusement to alleviate the boredom of the past weeks than anything more focused. However, she had gleaned some intriguing information.

"Leave me." Zeva tossed her head at the chamber door. "Go cool yourselves and get something to eat. I will be out to oversee today's drills in half an hour."

The two mares didn't hesitate. They trotted out, making sure to close the door securely behind themselves.

Zeva bobbed her head in satisfaction. These mares understood discipline. They understood swift punishment following any act of insubordination, either real or imagined.

She walked around the circular chamber she used whenever engaging in strenuous mental activity. Her pace was quick and sure. She was very pleased with what she had learned.

So, the little military brat thought the weavers could give her wings. Zeva's shoulders twitched as she walked. Too bad Eno couldn't be enticed to join the Harpies. Zeva could use someone with the bay mare's expertise. Brilliant as Eno was, she was still behind in her invention. Zeva's mares were already in the air and learning to dive and swoop like eagles. At least this little adventure would keep Psyche, Eno, and their pet stallions occupied for a while.

Her breathing normal and coat dry, Zeva left the chamber to go to her private stalls. She needed to contact her commander but wanted to do so in an area she knew was secure from eavesdroppers. As she passed other mares in the stable, she told them to be ready for practice in ten minutes.

Alone in her stall, Zeva cleared her mind. She reached out and waited for her commander to grant her access to his mind.

What is it?

I have gained interesting information, my lord.

The other mind focused more eagerly on the communication. *Something to aid our cause?*

Zeva's ears twitched. *In a way. I have found that the Asapatish's daughter is close to unraveling the secret of flight and the location of Zephyros Thracis.*

The commander's pleasure flowed through the link. As always, the good feeling was tainted with something dark and menacing. *Good, good. Let her continue. I want you to show our superiority in the air. It will make for a more crushing defeat.*

Zeva felt her chest expand in pride and anticipation. She was more than willing to attack Eno and Psyche from the sky. *What of the Zephyros colt, my lord?*

Leave him as well. I have a special surprise in store for him. How is our lady in the Capital?

She continues to string her stallions along. She is waiting for further instruction.

The commander waited a few seconds before replying. *Tell her the time has almost come. Everything must be in place before the final assault.*

Yes, my lord. Zeva waited for more but the link broke. She walked around her stall for several minutes, giving the commander time to contact her again if he wished. When her mind remained clear, she trotted down the hall and outside to the training fields.

Her Harpies were already assembled. They were the best of the best of Zeva's personal soldiers. All were mares who knew the importance of victory, the sacrifices that must be made so that their leader would prevail. These mares were better trained than any stallion or mare who had ever set hoof in the Romanium or the Sphere. Zeva made sure they spent hours conditioning their muscles and increasing their stamina. However, as she had never studied the training principles of the High Dances, Zeva did not understand the importance of proper collection and balance. An oversight that would have been apparent to those who had been trained correctly.

Zeva stood in front of the ten mares and waited as her assistants dressed her in the flying harness worn by all the Harpies. The harness was like any other, save for the ultra-thin metallic wings that crossed over the mares' backs. The mares used thrusters to become airborne, then stretched their wings for flight. The wings were thin enough to float on the air currents, but thrusters had to be used to keep the mares up. The thrusters were insulated as to not burn the mares too badly.

Like Eno, Zeva's scientists had discovered the problem with excess weight. Zeva would hear nothing of failure. To accommodate the wings and thrusters, the Harpies were not allowed to wear armor as they flew and their weapons had to be kept as minimal as possible. This meant they had to excel at basic combat. Another problem with the wings was their overall bulkiness. It was hard for the mares to turn quickly and malfunctions with the thrusters had resulted in three deaths already. After every setback, Zeva would point out that with great reward comes great sacrifice.

"Our commander is pleased with our progress." Zeva raised her voice to be heard by all. "He has given us leave to crush our opposition, but wishes that we destroy them in the air to show all our superiority."

Cheers and whinnies filled the air. The ground shook from all the stomping hooves. Zeva tossed her head and pawed the ground. Silence fell. "Take to the sky and continue your training. Our enemies have not yet even learned to make wings. Once they have, we will send them to the earth like the ungainly fledglings they are."

More whinnies as mares started their thrusters and lifted off. Shadows blotted out the sun as the Harpies circled the sky over their leader. Zeva waited for a clear space before launching herself upward. She opened her wings as soon as she gained altitude. Soaring over the open practice field, Zeva saw other contingents of horses, mostly mares, trotting patterns and moving in combat formations.

Their loss at Diomedea had been bad, but not nearly as devastating as Queen Hippolyta would like to believe. And with more contention in the Registry, the Baroquian ranks were swelling each day. The Belgians were coming around. They had granted the Baroquians access to their lands. A small port only, but enough room to establish a significant military presence. From Vanneria, the draft country, it was a short sail to the northern shores of Lipizzania and Myrmidonia.

"I want defensive and offensive patterns. Make sure to push yourselves to the limits of your endurance." Zeva's voice rang out to her Harpies. "This skirmish against Eno and her followers is our first battle. We must learn as much as possible from the experience."

The others flew in rank behind her, forming a spear with Zeva at its point. They moved as one, daring the birds to cross their path. Zeva whinnied as she led her mares down into a deep canyon. Here was where their skill was put to the test, flying through winds and crosswinds. The sheer cliffs gave no purchase for emergency landings and the rocky ground would grant no mercy to any horse who fell from the sky. It was a good place to cull out any who were not worthy enough to fly with Zeva and her chosen.

CHAPTER 21

"She will rest easy here," Alcina said quietly as Aeos and Thracis finished covering Tansy's grave. The mares had chosen an open area surrounded by trees. When the cloud cover burned away this glade would be filled with sunlight. As it was now, the glade held a gloomy, dank quality. After a brief pause the rain had continued through the night, but it had become a soft drizzle and the thunder and lightning had moved south.

Thracis stretched his neck and back and shook the dirt from his coat. Psyche, conscious that both he and Aeos were recovering from the mind attacks, helped him into his armor harness and pack. The pack was slightly heavier now. Eno had parceled out Tansy's belongings among the other horses in the group. After a heated debate with Psyche, Eno had agreed to parcel out some of her supplies as well to lighten her load. Her knee was not permanently damaged, but it would need time to heal and they couldn't afford to slow down because of Eno's stubbornness when it came to carrying equipment.

The buckskin with the golden-spotted white blanket on her rump had been carrying enough supplies for a two-week journey. Psyche and Eno didn't kid themselves that whoever had been controlling Tansy would continue to use her after her purpose was fulfilled, but a horse under as much strain as Tansy would have needed more food than normal.

"Why do you think Tansy was the target?" Thracis asked.

Neema answered him. "She was unfamiliar with mental infiltration. These mares are trained from foalhood to protect themselves. Aeos was undergoing training in Sanctuary and you are still spooked by your earlier encounter with a mindreaper." The Felisian shook her wet fur. "Tansy would have been open to suggestion, given her attraction to you in the first place."

"You think someone destroyed her because of me? Wouldn't the stallion have been a more suitable pawn if killing me was the point?"

"It wasn't you that was meant to be hurt," Eno said. She tossed her head in Psyche's direction. "Tansy was meant to drive a wedge between you and Psyche."

Thracis felt his stomach clench before anger flooded through him. Someone trying to sever him from Psyche? Unthinkable. He would die before he left his lady. But if she turned him away he knew he would leave to make her happy. After a hard-fought battle, of course. "Who would do such a thing?"

The mares exchanged looks before Alcina said, "That is something for you and your lady to discuss."

Aeos asked a question. "Why wasn't Eno affected by Tansy's attacks? Alcina and Psyche were protecting each other, but

Thracis and I and the rest of you were all halted in our attempts to fight her."

"I have been friends with Psyche for many years. She and her herd have taught me a great deal concerning psychic defense and attack." Eno was watching the clouds as she spoke. "We should get moving. It looks like today's trek will be wet and miserable, but we must hurry. The Baroquians will know where we are and what we are doing."

Titania nodded. "I will take the lead. Rest assured that I am more surefooted than most of you."

Thracis and Psyche held back as the others started up the path into the mountains. He waited for her to begin walking then fell into step next to her, on her left. This granted her the position of dominance. He hoped it would ease her nerves.

They walked in silence for several minutes. Psyche was trying to find the right words to begin the conversation and coming up short with every sentence. How did one tell their mate that their sister was trying to assassinate them, again? She thought it best to just come out and tell him straight, but what if he wanted to leave now? Well, she would worry about that when and if it happened.

"Thracis, there is something about my herd you don't know. It's a sort of scandal."

"All herds have scandals."

"Not like this." She took a deep breath. "When I was six months old, my older sister Zeva tried to kill me. She was stopped by my sister Lachesis."

"The High Delphae? You told me this already."

Psyche seemed not to hear. "As a result of the attempt, Zeva was banished from Diomedea. She went to the lands of her sire's herds. In Baroquia."

She waited for Thracis surprised outburst. Instead of getting angry, Thracis asked, "I know that also. What became of her?"

"It is widely rumored that she is second in command of the Baroquian cavalry. She is very strong in the psychic arts. Her coat is pure black."

They were silent for a few heartbeats. The rain fell in a silver curtain all around them. The leaves of the trees dripped and ran. Thracis took a deep breath. "She really hates you, doesn't she?"

"Zeva's heart was blackened long before I was foaled. Her cruelty is well-known."

"Is that why your dam is so overprotective?"

Psyche sighed. "I suppose."

Thracis nuzzled her withers. "Don't worry about your dam so much. She is only doing what mother's do."

"You wouldn't be so agreeable if you knew what she was saying about you."

Thracis twitched a shoulder. "I am not what she expected?"

"You are not worthy in her eyes, after your dismissal from the Romanium."

"It's not her eyes I wish to please."

Psyche stopped walking and turned to nuzzle noses with Thracis. She lipped his jaw lightly. "You please me very well, foolish colt."

He nipped her cheek. "I'm glad to hear it, Lady Psyche."

"Hey," Aeos called, making Thracis and Psyche jump, "are you two coming or what? We need to stay together as we move higher."

"We're coming. Honestly Aeos, you sound like a worried dam." Thracis nudged Psyche forward. "Let's get going before he decides to come back here and herd us along."

"How much farther is it to Arachne Stable?" Thracis was walking at a fairly good clip. It was the first open ground they had seen in days and he was relishing letting his legs stretch.

"We should reach it by sundown." Dysis was walking with him. In the time they had spent together, Thracis was discovering he liked all the members of Alcina's little herd. They were tough and blunt and quick to point out his shortcomings, but this they did in a sisterly way, always softening the criticism with a laugh or head toss.

"Do they know we are coming?"

"They've been informed and are excited by the prospects of Eno's invention."

"She's described what she wants to them, then?" Thracis slowed his pace as the path narrowed.

Dysis nodded. "In great detail. From what she's told Alcina, the weavers already have several pieces of material completed."

"That's pretty quick, isn't it?"

"They aren't the best on Equus without reason."

Thracis stopped walking. The movement, or lack thereof, was so abrupt that Dysis bumped into him. "What is it?"

"Do you feel something?"

Dysis cocked her head. "Maybe a shift in temperature."

"No, I feel eyes on us. You don't feel like you're being watched?"

The palomino shook her head. Thracis felt his protective instincts rising to the surface. The others would be joining him and Dysis in a matter of minutes. Thracis couldn't let the whole herd fall in to an ambush. He moved to block the path in front of Dysis, dropping his pack and engaging his armor. The mare didn't question him. She only followed suit, dropping back into a more defensive position.

"Whoever is there, show yourself," Thracis snapped. "I'm in no mood for games."

A beat of silence, then the bushes ahead of Thracis rustled. He braced himself, ready to launch into battle at the slightest provocation. He heard Dysis shifting behind him to face whatever was coming out of the brush.

When the gray Felisian with the black spots hopped out of the bushes, Thracis felt himself tense even more. He had never fought a Felisian, but he had seen the cats do plenty of damage in the battle against the Baroquians. The Felisian, Thracis caught her scent and knew it was female, walked to the center of the path and sat down.

"Impressive that you felt the eyes of my birds." The cat's voice was a deep purr. As she spoke two owls, little screeches, broke cover and flew to land in the tree closest to the Felisian.

"Lucky." Thracis waited for the cat to say more. He didn't want to retract his armor until he was sure she was a member of Arachne Stable.

Dysis edged passed him. Her armor was retracted and she was buckling her pack straps. "My name is Dysis. This is Thracis. We are part of Eno's herd."

"Oh, yes. We've been waiting for you. I was sent to lead you into the stable." The cat rose and walked to Dysis. She stood on her back legs and put a paw on Dysis' lowered nose. "My name is Anneke. I am a descendant of the Queen Nefertiti and one of the master weavers of this stable."

Thracis retracted his armor and bowed his head. "I am sorry if I gave offense, Lady."

Anneke dropped to the ground and regarded him. "No apology needed. I am happy you are so perceptive, stallion of Thetis Stable."

The rest of the herd joined them. Dysis made the introductions. Eno addressed Anneke, "I hope to get started attaching the weavings to the frameworks as soon as possible."

"All in time, young Eno." The Felisian watched as Thracis replaced his pack. "This one will have to speak with Lady Aldara. He and his *ammoni* mate."

Thracis heard Psyche's intake of breath behind him, but didn't turn around. If she thought she was going to hide their relationship from this stable she had another thing coming. It was time for Psyche to accept him openly around strangers.

Anneke raised her voice. "The rest of you will be shown to the visitor's stable. Stalls have already been prepared and a meal has been set out. Take the rest of the day to see to yourselves. Then you will begin tomorrow with fresh minds."

Felisians emerged from the bushes along the path. They were a variety of colors, but Thracis saw several with gray coats and black spots. Those individuals must all be related. At a bend where the path cut back into the trees, a young dappled filly stood. She was watching the other Equines with interest.

As Anneke led Thracis and Psyche forward, the filly said, "I am Beryl. I will take you to Lady Aldara."

Thracis stood aside and allowed Psyche to walk between him and Beryl. The dapple seemed more relaxed with this arrangement as mares were not accustomed to having unknown stallions walk along at their heels. It also wouldn't put Thracis close to another strange mare who might be enticed by his physique.

Beryl took them down a winding path flanked on one side by a shallow stream and the other by a meadow flowing with fragrant grasses. A few mares grazed in the meadow. They raised their heads and watched as the trio strode passed. Thracis couldn't tell for certain, but he had an idea that the mares in the meadow were young, maybe five or six. He wondered if they were students sent here to learn how to weave the intricate patterns the stable was famous for.

The dappled mare entered a large, sprawling stable. Thracis looked around at all the weavings hanging from the walls. Several were strewn across the foyer hall's rafters, lending the entrance a festive impression. The rubber flooring was a mixture of colors ranging from white to black. They were entwined in such a way that they complemented rather than clashed with each other. Reds and greens and blues and yellows; they dazzled Thracis' eyes.

They walked along two corridors before turning down a short hallway that led to an inner stall with a heavy door. The door was carved with runes and other mystical symbols. Beryl stopped outside. She tapped the door with a front hoof. After a moment the door swung slowly open.

Beryl turned to Thracis and Psyche. "The Lady Aldara will see you. I will wait here and escort you to the visitor's stable."

Psyche and Thracis bowed their heads to Beryl. Thracis waited until Psyche entered the stall before following.

If he had thought the weavings in the main hall were impressive, Thracis had been mistaken. The ones that hung in this stall were the most beautiful pieces Thracis had seen yet. Their swirls of color drew his eyes deep into their contemplative depths. He could stand and look at them for hours. Eno's experiments aside, Thracis would have been happy to stay in this stall and study each of the numerous weavings in turn. Not that he would admit it to any other stallion, even on pain of death.

"I see you admiring my works of art, stallion of Thetis Stable."

Thracis jumped at the musical voice issuing from the back of the stall. He followed Psyche to a rounded corner whose walls were made up of large windows. Fading daylight flooded the area in gold, making the mare standing in its middle a bronze-tinted shade of pewter. The mare was standing in front of a large loom, a weaving secured to its frame. Thracis was reminded of Queen Hippolyta, whose coat truly was pewter no matter what the lighting. He didn't think there was any relationship between the two mares. If there was, Thracis was sure Psyche would have mentioned something.

"They are very beautiful, Lady Aldara." Thracis stopped in front of the lead mare of Arachne Stable and bowed low. "Are they your own works?"

"They are. Although Lady Anneke sometimes comes in and gives me another opinion if she feels I am wandering off course." Lady Aldara's eyes flowed over Thracis before fixing on Psyche. "Daughter of Queen Hippolyta. You are most welcome at my stable, though I wonder why you did not contact me yourself. Perhaps you are hiding feelings you do not wish to have examined?"

The older mare's teasing voice sent a visible ripple through Psyche. Thracis wondered if it was a pleasurable ripple.

"I have not yet divulged my relationship with Thracis to my dam." Psyche tossed her head, her black forelock falling over one eye.

Lady Aldara stepped back from the loom and snickered. "A good thing that. Your dam is not the most open-minded about the stallions who court her daughters."

"As if she is such a good judge of character." Thracis' ears lowered at the venom in Psyche's voice.

"Little filly, you will make mistakes in time."

"But they will be mine to make, not those my dam has chosen for me."

Thracis was lost in this conversation. Psyche did not speak with him about her family herd unless he pressed, which he rarely did. Given the tension filling the stall, Thracis decided to stand back and listen. He didn't want to garner any attention from the mares.

Lady Aldara took a deep breath. "No matter what the issue between you and your dam, you should not let your anger blind you to real danger."

"Thracis is not dangerous. Not to me," Psyche huffed.

"Thracis is in danger." Lady Aldara's voice was taking on the patient tone known to both Psyche and Thracis. "And that puts you in danger by association."

"My dam doesn't think that way, believe me Lady Aldara. My dam is only concerned with the fact that Thracis was dismissed from the Romanium and that he is not the heir of a ruling herd." Psyche walked around the stall, her tail swishing. "I am not concerned with such things."

"Of course, you aren't." Lady Aldara was moving closer to Thracis, inspecting him. Thracis felt the feathery touch of someone searching the front of his mind. He waited for Lady Aldara to identify herself before allowing her access. He locked down his innermost barriers, only giving her passage to his feelings toward Psyche.

"Do you think that makes me naïve?" Psyche was randomly looking at weavings as she walked.

"It makes you young." Lady Aldara glanced at Thracis, catching his eye. "And in love. It's this strong feeling that scares your dam more than anything."

"Because she feels stallions are only breeding stock?"

"Because at times love is stronger than family." Lady Aldara addressed Thracis, "I have heard the tale of how your parents met one moonlit night. Your sire risked much to win your dam."

Thracis bobbed his head. "He did and would risk more now that his herd is established."

"What are the two of you talking about?" Psyche snorted.

"Something your mate should share with you in a private moment. The purpose of this meeting was not to discuss your relationship, however." Lady Aldara cleared her throat. "I have reviewed Eno's design and the weavings the members of my stable have been creating. I believe you will be in the sky sooner than you think."

"Eno will be pleased to hear that," Psyche said.

"Of course, she will," Thracis muttered.

"What I wish to discuss is what role you, Psyche, will play in the coming battles."

Silence filled the room.

To Thracis, the question was redundant. He fully expected Psyche to find herself as Eno's second in command. Finally, free of her dam's overbearing protection, Psyche could literally spread her wings and take her place as the warrior Thracis knew she was.

"Eno and I have not discussed it, Lady." Psyche was ducking her head, her shoulders hunching, her tail drooping.

Lady Aldara walked forward to nudge Psyche. She waited until the black and white face was even with her own. "If you truly wish to find your path, you must first discover your courage. The others will follow you, youngest daughter of Augean Stable, but you must have the strength to lead them."

The older mare's head tilted toward Thracis. "Your mate knows you can do this, but you must accept it for yourself."

"I will think on it, Lady." Psyche's voice was humble.

"See that you do. I have arranged that the two of you will share a stall. It is always best to mark out your territory first thing."

Thracis nodded emphatically. He didn't want any of the younger mares at this stable causing trouble for him and Psyche. He also wanted time alone with Psyche where they wouldn't have to worry about another horse coming upon them at an inconvenient moment.

"A smart stallion. I like that." Lady Aldara turned back to her weaving, dismissing them.

CHAPTER 22

"Stop struggling, Thracis. We have to make sure the straps are secure."

Thracis pinned his ears at Eno. They had been out in this open field since first light. The sun was past its zenith and angling toward the west as Eno and Alcina checked the winged harness Thracis wore. He was hot and tired and his head ached from trying to control the wings. He had yet to achieve a liftoff that would satisfy Eno. And he was starving. This combination had put him in a foul temper.

So far Thracis had managed the wings well enough to raise all four hooves about five feet off the ground. It was difficult to get the right balance and all his muscles were quivering from strain. He was also stunned at the amount of mental energy he had to expend to keep himself straight as the wings pummeled the air around him. He was still amazed by the wing's existence in the first place, which only added to his mental agony.

The weavers of Arachne Stable had outdone themselves on Eno's behalf. The multifaceted wings shimmered in a rainbow of colors in the sun's rays. Thracis marveled at how much these prototypes looked like actual wings. The weavers had made the materials resemble feathers as much as possible. From a distance, the Equines wearing these harnesses would look like Lord Pegasus himself.

As instructed, they had devised the weavings out of a solar material. Unlike the legend of Icaris which warned of flying too close to the sun, these wings gained all of their energy from sunlight. This energy was in turn transferred to the thrusters located at key points along the harness. These thrusters ensured the that the wearer would be able to stay airborne in the event something happened to the wings. The thrusters were insulated with a lightweight, nonconductive metal that ensured the horses would be safe from burning. It was an ingenious design, both light and practical. The only thing left was for the Equines to learn how to fly. This aspect of the plan was proving more believable in theory than in practical application.

Aeos stood in front of Dysis and Psyche. The dun stallion spread his wings, flaring them out so the mares could inspect for tears or rips. Eno and Psyche had decided by mutual discussion that Psyche and Thracis should be separated during training. This was certainly for Thracis' benefit as Psyche had enough of her dam in her to push Thracis to exhaustion.

"Perhaps if we jumped into a capriole first? It would give a little more lift," Aeos suggested.

Eno shook her head. "No, I think a running start is better. At least until you're more adept with the thrusters."

"Why don't we just jump off a cliff?" Thracis mumbled.

"Keep it up and I'll help you do just that," Eno snapped.

Thracis tossed his head. Eno's anger didn't bother him. He was annoyed and frustrated by his own incapability to master these cursed wings. Shrugging away from Alcina, Thracis took a step toward Eno. "How is it that you know how to perform a capriole anyway?"

The others looked at him in puzzlement. Eno twitched a shoulder. "A filly has to learn how to take care of herself."

"By practicing forbidden maneuvers?"

"Forbidden only because stallions have large egos and tiny minds."

"Those egos make up for other small aspects of their physiques," Alcina commented. This enticed laughter from the other mares.

Thracis refused to be baited in that direction. "You know how to perform advanced combat maneuvers. Who taught you?"

Eno sighed. "No one, Thracis. All I know I learned through observation and practice. And practical application. You see, I know how the mechanics of the movements function. From that beginning I only needed to condition my body to endure the standards of training."

"The daughter of the Asapatish is as talented as his hippeus. How delightfully funny," Haidee all but giggled.

"Funny and embarrassing. My sire will never accept my combat skills." Eno pawed the ground.

"He might. He was the one who invited you to conquer the sky, after all," Psyche said.

"He was."

Thracis gave these comments little notice. He was still fixated on the other matter. "Without Phrenicos I can't move on. You know the next steps, you could teach Aeos and I the capriole."

Eno shook her head. "No, that won't work. I've never taught anyone else before."

"I'm sure you could if you gave it a try." Aeos had folded his wings and walked up to Eno. He nuzzled her shoulder. Their relationship had bloomed into something beyond friendship in the last days. It was a touchy subject and one they all avoided. This show of affection was taking them all by surprise.

"I could only explain to you how I do it. You would have to find your own technique." Eno was looking at Aeos, blotting everyone else out.

"Master Phrenicos teaches us in much the same manner," Aeos said. His nose had moved up her neck to her ears.

"You could teach us all, Eno," Alcina suggested. "My mares and I already know the basics of the advanced combat maneuvers. We trained in the High Dances and have achieved adequate levades. And do not forget we have all completed the March and graduated the Sphere." She looked at Thracis. "I do not mean any insult, Thracis."

Thracis, far less touchy about his dismissal from the Romanium, tossed his head. "It's fine, Alcina. If Master Phrenicos has his way I am sure both Aeos and I will have to complete something comparable to the graduation requirements of the Romanium."

Eno looked around at the others. "It is something to think about. First, we have to learn to fly. If I thought the capriole would help you with lift-off, I would teach you in a moment. But I think you have to master the thrusters first."

"We have to keep things simple," Psyche said. "Maybe you should try to fly, Eno, then you could explain it to us."

"A good idea. Aeos give me your harness. It will have to be tightened for me."

Watching the other mares scamper toward Eno, Thracis felt his patience was at its limit. He turned his head. The north end of this field ended in a sheer drop of thirty feet or so. Not enough to kill him, not if he landed properly, but far enough for him to break a leg or maybe his back. It was risk he would have to take.

Shifting the harness on his back and spreading his wings, Thracis bolted toward the drop. As he ran, he engaged the thrusters just enough to propel himself a little faster.

Seeing what he was doing, Psyche screamed, "Thracis!"

His ears flicked back and he heard the pounding of hooves behind him. They were trying to catch up with him. He had only a few seconds before one of them got the idea to use a mental lasso to contain him.

Lowering his head, Thracis pushed with his hind legs, launching himself off the edge of the field. At the same time, his wings spread wide, catching the wind. He dropped a few feet before he diverted more power to his thrusters. He didn't disperse the energy evenly and the burst of force threw him forward into a somersault. His front hooves clipped the edge of the shelf he would have fallen on. Beyond the shelf the drop fell a hundred feet straight down.

Panic flared in his mind but Thracis fought it back. He concentrated on getting his thrusters to expend equal amounts of energy. He regained his balance, coming up even. His wings, catching the drafts of wind in the gorge, opened further, stretching to their limits. Thracis was jerked to a halt.

Not giving himself time to think, Thracis flapped his wings and flew with instinct. He dove down to the bottom of the gorge and followed the stream that would take him alongside Arachne Stable. The young mares weaving in the stable's open courtyard looked up in surprise. Flapping harder, Thracis shot straight up until he was even with the lowest clouds.

Thracis had never felt such freedom. He looked down. The ground below became a patchwork of fields, forest, and rock outcroppings. The clouds around him were tinted pink as the sun lowered. Thracis passed birds, their startled squawks making him laugh. He flew higher, above the clouds, his wings barely moving as he drifted on shafts of warm air. Thracis couldn't wait to share this with Psyche. She would love this experience.

Feeling like Lord Pegasus himself, Thracis dove and hovered, darted and drifted. He experimented with his feet, wondering how he would fight in the sky. He folded his wings and dove, aiming straight for the practice field. He pulled up twenty feet from the ground, soaring over the heads of his companions. He laughed at their astonished expressions.

Prancing on air, Thracis wheeled around to land. Then his smugness gave way to nerves. How was he supposed to land? It was something they hadn't even discussed. Panicked, flapping back up for another pass, he contacted Eno.

Eno, how in Pegasus' name do I get down?

You'll have to come in as level and slow as you can. Use your wings and thrusters to stop your forward motion.

Thracis nodded and swooped down. As he approached the field, Eno's voice filled his head with one last bit of advice. *If you get into trouble, remember to tuck and roll.*

He tried to slow and remain level but that was a lot more plausible in theory. Thracis began running as he got lower to the ground so that he was moving when his hooves touched the grass. It worked at first, then he tripped over a root or a stone and was catapulted forward. Thracis ducked his head, sending himself into a roll. He ended up in a heap of scrapes and bruises and torn wings inches from Psyche's front feet.

"You stupid, stubborn, arrogant jackass," Psyche sputtered, "You could have killed yourself. What in Pandemonium were you thinking?" She was sniffing him as she shouted, checking to make sure he didn't need medical attention.

"I love you too, sweetheart." Thracis pulled himself to his feet and shook. He tried to fold his wings, but the weavings were too damaged. They hung along his sides like party banners after the celebration.

"Apparently the landings will need some work." Eno was tugging on the shreds of weavings with her mouth. "At least the frame isn't tweaked."

"What was is like?" Aeos asked.

"It was fantastic. I've never experienced a bigger thrill." Thracis glanced at Psyche. "Well, almost never."

Psyche huffed and bit his shoulder.

Aeos spread his wings. "I want to try."

"No," Alcina and Haidee said in unison.

Aeos tossed his head at them. "Why not?"

Dysis tilted her head at the west. They all looked to see thunderheads gathering on the horizon. "That could be one reason," the sorrel mare commented.

"And I don't like the idea of you plummeting a hundred feet to your death," Eno said. She had folded the weavings along Thracis' back and secured them with twine. "We have to build a ramp. Fifty feet high. We will water the ground below to make it soggy and soft. It will help in the event of a fall. And now that we know it can be done, I will design harnesses for all of us."

The mares whinnied in excitement. Thracis nuzzled Psyche, asking forgiveness for his rash action. After a moment, the black and white mare lowered her head to nuzzle noses with him and nip his lips.

"I guess you were right to try what you did." Psyche's breath was warm against him.

"It was reckless," Thracis conceded.

"But necessary." Eno was looking at the storm. "Let's get back to the stable. I want to discuss the needed weavings with Anneke and Lady Aldara." She was already moving across the field.

Aeos folded his wings and trotted after her. Thracis and the other mares stayed in the field, feeling the cold wind blowing before the rain.

"There'll be hail with that storm," Haidee said.

"Winter is on its way," Alcina said, her voice muffled against Dysis' coat. The two mares were standing side by side, facing each other's tails. They had swung their neck's over each other and were diligently grooming each other's backs.

"Will we be back at Master Phrenicos' stable before the first flurries do you think? He is farther south." Thracis was asking Psyche but Haidee answered.

"If we take to flying as easily as you, then I imagine we will."

"We can learn combat maneuvers in Boudica. That way we can enlist other mares." It was the first time Titania had spoken and Thracis jumped. He had forgotten the Clydesdale was with them. For such a big animal, Titania walked on silent Felisian feet.

"Your wings will truly look like sails to lift you off the ground," Haidee teased.

Titania arched her neck, the long scar prominent in the yellow light. "Then I should have the weavers place the symbol of my herd into the fabric. That way all my enemies will know who it is that pursues them."

"Well said, Titania." Psyche was nudging Thracis toward the stable.

The other mares fell into step behind them. They walked in silence for a few minutes before Alcina asked, "Do you think Eno will teach us advanced combat, Psyche?"

Psyche tossed her head. "Eno may have been playing modest, but I believe she was pleased beyond measure that you feel she would be a worthy instructor."

"It is a great loss to them that the Imperial Cavalry ignores Eno's talents." Titania's gait sounded like the distant thunder.

"It is," Alcina agreed, "but stallions are not known for their fairness where mares are concerned."

"I have to disagree, Alcina, at least on behalf of Aeos and myself." Thracis knew he was baiting a dangerous mare, but her snide comments were getting to him.

"And what do you believe, stallion of Thetis?" Dysis asked.

"I know how terrifying it is for me to watch Psyche march into battle even though I know she is more than capable of defending herself." He noted the rise in Psyche's shoulders. "As stallions, as honorable stallions, we have a hard time not protecting the weaker sex. We want to protect you. We want to make sure you and your foals and our foals are safe. It's been our job for millennia."

The mares digested this bit of information. Finally, Alcina broke the silence, "I apologize, Thracis. My own experience with stallions has been less than honorable, and I have a rather cynical view."

"I am sorry for your experience," Thracis said. He had known something bad had happened to Alcina on their first meeting and had always been cautious when dealing with the black mare.

"I am glad you and Aeos are showing me a different way." Alcina nuzzled Thracis' withers. He accepted the affection graciously. They were becoming a true herd, these eight, nine if you counted Neema. A herd all their own. And these mares, like it or not, were his and Aeos' mares. The two stallions would care for these ladies as they would their own sisters or cousins. Only Psyche and Eno would be treated with deeper respect.

Lady Aldara was standing at the entrance of the main stable, her black mane blowing back in the wind. "Come along. The evening meal has already been set out. Thracis, go and remove your harness and rinse yourself so that you will be more comfortable."

"I'll help him, Lady Aldara," Psyche called.

The Lady bobbed her head and waited for the other mares to join her. Aeos and Eno must already be at the visitor's stable, Thracis thought. He couldn't see them anywhere.

Psyche led Thracis to the equipment stall situated at the front of the visitor's stable. She told him to hold still while she removed his harness and hung it on the hooks Eno had set up. Aeos' harness was already hanging, the wings pulled out. He followed her down the hall to the stall they shared. Once inside, Thracis walked into the wash stall to shower. Psyche waited in the main room, watching the gathering storm out a window and trying to make sense of her clamoring thoughts. She jumped when Thracis came up behind her, nuzzling her hip. She kicked out and he dodged, his ears lowering in confusion.

"I'm sorry, Thracis. I wasn't paying any attention."

"Good thing or you would have broken my knee." He stood next to her and nuzzled the top of her neck along her mane.

"You're in a very forgiving mood."

"I know you've had a lot on your mind since Lady Aldara's conversation."

Psyche turned her head to bury her face against his shoulder. Thracis arched his neck over her, tucking her close.

"My dam would be devastated if she knew how deep my feelings for you run."

Thracis pulled her close. "My dam would be delighted. I think she worries you'll break my heart."

"She should worry that I will kill you for your own stupidity." She huffed against him. "I thought you had fallen to your death, Thracis, you nearly made my heart stop."

"I'm sorry. I wasn't thinking."

"You never do when you're at your most brilliant." Her voice held tired frustration.

"Don't worry so much about your dam, Psyche. She has two other daughters to herd."

"Yes, but Alastrina and Lachesis have proven themselves. I haven't. The queen doesn't believe I am capable of making my own decisions."

"You have to believe, that's all that matters."

Psyche relaxed against him. "Do we have to go to the evening meal?"

"On any other night, I would say no and spend the evening alone with you." He nipped her neck and pressed against her to get his meaning across, as if Psyche could miss it. "But I'm starving after the day's activities and if Eno expects me to help build a fifty-foot ramp I'll need all my strength."

"I don't want to be responsible for making Eno wait," Psyche grumbled. She pulled away from Thracis. He waited until she had smoothed her coat and mane before opening the stall door. Aeos and Eno were already in the hallway.

"Aeos and I were discussing the most efficient way to train combat while still learning to fly," Eno said with a head toss.

"And what did you decide?" Thracis asked dryly.

"That you'd better eat well and get a good night's sleep if you're going to keep up with the pace we set."

CHAPTER 23

Lady Nerissa whipped her tail back and forth in annoyance. Her ears were pinned. Her dun coat was several shades darker due to the sweat that dripped down her sides. Snapping her teeth, the Kigerian mare whirled and kicked out with both back hooves, catching her opponent squarely in the chest. The stallion hobbled away, coughing.

Frustrated by the inferior male's lack of stamina, Nerissa turned her attention on another stallion, a flea-bitten gray, who had entered the practice ring. She flew at him, biting down hard on the side of his neck. The gray squealed and struggled away from her. Snorting loudly through her nose, a challenge usually voiced only by a stallion, Nerissa pivoted in a circle looking for her next victim.

"My dear you seem to be of a mood tonight."

Nerissa spun around to the sound of Alexi's voice. Her mate stood hipshot, looking bored. Nerissa snapped her teeth at him.

"Come now, my lady, why are you venting your frustrations on these poor guards? You know well enough that I have forbidden them to cause you harm."

"Then perhaps I shall hire my own sparring partners. These stallions are little more than geldings in a practice arena."

Every male in the area winced at the verbal thrust. To call a stallion gelded was the ultimate insult. Alexi pinned his ears. "Whatever issue you may have, I will not have you speak to my guards in such a manner. Remember that it is these stallions who keep you safe whenever you venture beyond the city walls."

"Believe what you will, but I am more than capable of defending myself." Nerissa turned on her heels and stalked out of the training arena.

Sighing loudly, Alexi regarded the two guards Nerissa had been sparring against. "Go and see the asklepiade if you feel the need, then take the rest of the night off. I know well how difficult my mate can be when she's in this kind of mood."

The other stallions bobbed their heads and walked off in the direction of the examination rooms. Alexi watched them go. He liked both of them. They were courageous and loyal, but he felt it might be time for them to move on. Before his mate could spoil them against him and his stable. Unfortunate, but a consequence of Nerissa's moods he had become accustomed to.

Swishing his tail, Alexi walked down the hall leading to Nerissa's private chambers. They shared a stall with a bedding box large enough for both of them, but they also each had the luxury of their own stalls in the event they wanted some space.

To Alexi it seemed his lady had wanted a great deal of space in the last months.

He paused outside her door and tapped it politely with a front hoof. No answer but he could hear the sound of the shower. Bracing himself for the scolding he was likely to get for barging into her stall uninvited, Alexi pushed open the door.

As always, he was astounded by the difference in their private areas. While he tended more toward neutral colors and wooden furniture, Nerissa liked bold colors and the cold gleam of metal. Her stalls were decorated in reds, blacks, and stark whites. The silver flash of steel glinted along her bookshelves and glass-topped tables. Looking at Nerissa's stalls made Alexi wonder, and not for the first time, if he had made a mistake in choosing his mate.

At the time Lady Stephanos Nerissa was the most intriguing mare Alexi had ever encountered. Beautiful, intelligent, and most importantly, a member of a prominent herd, Nerissa was the most likely choice for the future ruler of Kigeria. He courted her for nearly six months before winning her favor. Once ensconced as his mate, Nerissa had shown her talent for flattery and manipulation, always to the benefit of Alexi's stable. It made him proud that his lady was competent enough to run his country in the event of his untimely death. It gave him a sense of peace and gave him no urgency to sire an heir immediately. That was a good thing because Nerissa had voiced even before their formal union that she did not want a foal any time in the near future. Delighted in the talents of his lady, Alexi didn't want a foal underhoof either.

He wondered now if that was a mistake. A foal might have settled Nerissa a little. Kept her eyes in her own stable and on her own stallion. Much as it might distress his lady, Alexi was aware of her transgressions.

The first time it had happened, it had been in Kigeria and Alexi had wanted to confront her and the stallion she was sneaking around with. He had wanted to challenge the strange stallion to a fight to the death, wanted to kick and scream and tear the intruder apart. What stopped him was the realization that a ruling stallion's responsibilities outweigh the disruptions of his own stable. So, he had cooled his heels while he waited for a spy to find out the identity of the other stallion. After he found out, Alexi didn't know whether to laugh or cry.

The stallion Nerissa was spending her afternoons with was a young, unestablished six-year-old who knew even less about mares than he did about politics. Curious, Alexi had confronted Nerissa to find out what the attraction was. To her credit, his lady didn't waste time with tears or denials. She simply told him the truth. He, Alexi, was a busy stallion, running the province, dealing with representatives, playing politics. She needed more attention and so she had found it in a stallion that was no threat whatsoever to her formal mate. As she still fulfilled all her duties to Alexi, Nerissa argued that she was doing nothing wrong. Besides, she was quick to point out, most of his council members were having affairs.

After the young stallion ceased to amuse her, Nerissa discarded him and had remained loyal. Until they had come to Lipizza.

For the first few weeks, Nerissa had been so consumed with shopping and sightseeing and lunching with other representatives' mates, that she had seemed content.

Then all the old signs began to appear. She began to be busy most afternoons, shielding her thoughts so that Alexi could not contact her. She always left the stable in perfect condition, her coat glossy, her mane and tail red silk in the light breezes of Lipizzania. She became more complimentary at social engagements, more insistent that Alexi take her to every engagement. It was in this manner that Alexi had reached the conclusion that she had taken another politician for a lover. It never occurred to him that she was stoop so low as to entice a representative's aide. He had considered finding out this new stallion's identity, but what would be the point? She would only tell him the same as she had the first time. And she would keep her lover, only once Alexi informed her that he knew what was going on she would likely let her discretion slip.

No, it was better this way, with at least the guise of secrecy. He only wished Nerissa had given him an heir before she began to stray. That way Alexi could be sure the foal was his.

Nerissa's temper flared as she heard the outer door of her stalls open. How dare he come into her private chambers uninvited. Formal mate or not, Alexi knew his place. He knew how much it angered her for him to intrude on her privacy. Stomping a foot in the flowing water swirling down the drain, Nerissa shook her head and snapped her teeth again.

Stallions. They were so much more trouble when they didn't behave properly. Nerissa was in no mood for Alexi's whining. She had problems enough without having to comfort and reassure. She had explained their relationship well enough in Kigeria after she had taken that young stallion for some relief. Alexi had prided himself so much for finding out about that affair. Well she had to give him something to stop his persistent questioning. So, she had made her activities with the younger stallion obvious, making sure that Alexi's spy couldn't miss what was going on. And then she had continued with the other three stallions she had been entertaining. A mare could never have enough suitors.

Turning off the water, Nerissa stepped out of the shower and under the blowing air of the drying tubes. She took her time, making sure her coat, mane, and tail were completely dry. If Alexi wanted to speak with her that badly, he could wait. As she dried herself, Nerissa contemplated the events of the last weeks.

Her contact with the Baroquians had informed her that it was time to stop toying with Pyrios and end the affair. End it completely. This order was the reason for her constant training in the practice arena. Pyrios may not have much combat background and he was getting soft and slow from too many days in the council chamber, but Nerissa had learned at a young age to never underestimate an opponent.

She could poison him, she supposed, but that would take away her chance at crowing superiority when Pyrios fell beneath her hooves. A combative victory would also show the Baroquians that she was more than just a mare to be used as bait for any stallion they wished preoccupied. Nerissa had made it her business to know her rivals in the Baroquian Pact. Her greatest threat was the Lady Zeva, second to the High Commander. High as her ambitions were, Nerissa had no desire to clash hooves with Zeva. However, a general in the Baroquian cavalry, or a trusted council member would make an adequate replacement for her current mate. Of course, the High Commander had already promised Nerissa the province of Kigeria once the takeover of Equus was complete, but Nerissa wanted to rule more than a single province. A country now, that would be sufficient.

Turning off the blowers, Nerissa spent several minutes smoothing her coat and mane before walking into the main stall. Alexi was standing near the outer door, looking around with interest and appreciation. When she emerged from the wash stall, his eyes locked on her. Even with the knowledge that she was enjoying another stallion's affections, her mate still craved her company. It bolstered her and made her walk with confidence in her ability to make stallions do whatever she wished.

"You have more business with me?" She turned slightly, giving him a full view of her muscled flank. She saw hunger fill his eyes before they shifted away.

"You should not treat the guards in such a manner."

"Alexi, you sound like a parrot. Repeat, repeat, repeat." She tossed her mane and walked to the window that encompassed the entire east wall.

"Parrot I may be, but you owe your safety to those stallions." He squared his feet. "I know you have been spending many afternoons without their company."

Nerissa glanced at him over her shoulder. "I would think you would prefer that I do not spend copious amounts of time with other stallions."

Alexi stomped a foot, a sign that she was beginning to antagonize him. "Nerissa, these are dangerous times, even here in the capital. No one knows who to trust. I hired those guards to keep you safe."

"To keep watchful eyes on me, you mean."

He sighed. "My lady, you explained our relationship not long after our union. If you have taken a lover, I commend your discrepancy, but be wary."

Nerissa came to stand next to him. She rubbed her cheek against his neck. It would disrupt her plans terribly if Alexi decided she required an armed escort at all times. "Darling, I am always aware of my surroundings. I know how to be careful." Her lips nibbled at his withers, making his skin twitch. "I make sure those guards are present whenever I travel in unsavory portions of the city."

Nuzzling her soft belly hide, Alexi snorted. "I don't know if that reassures or concerns me more."

She lay her head against his back, a subtle show of dominance. "Let it be a reassurance." She bit his withers and spun away from him, tossing her head and playfully striking out with a front foot.

Caught by surprise, Alexi jumped back then advanced, all thoughts of another stallion fleeing his mind. Let her do what she wanted. At the end of the day, it was his stable she slept in.

Watching him come towards her, Nerissa stifled the urge to laugh. Stallions simply were too easy to manipulate.

CHAPTER 24

Aeos watched as Eno and Thracis dove and spun around each other in the crisp autumn air. He was gliding on warm drafts of air, using minimal effort to stay aloft. Psyche was soaring along to his left and slightly behind him. The black and white mare had learned the delicateness of flying as quickly as he had and the two of them spent much of their time instructing the others in the art of using the winds to their advantage.

At this point, only four harnesses were fully functional. Eno had devised that everyone would spend at least two hours learning to fly each day until the rest of the harnesses could be constructed. The weavers, learning from their mistakes much as Eno did, improved with each set of wings. Thracis and Aeos wore the original designs, which were bulky and difficult to manage. Eno's harness was much more aerodynamic and the wings took only slight mental direction. The most recent harness was Psyche's and the *ammoni* flew as if she were the daughter of Lord Pegasus himself.

The others had wings that shimmered in a rainbow of colors in the sunlight. Psyche's wings, specifically designed for her alone according to Lady Aldara, gleamed in silver and gold. It was as if the weavers had taken the colors of the dawn and woven them into the metal and fabric of the wings. Psyche's wings were different in another way as well. Her wings were connected to her muscles with a mesh covering and each flex of shoulder made the wings flap and spread. The black and white mare did use her mind to control the wings, but nowhere near to the extent the others did. Dangerous as Psyche was on the ground, she was unconquerable in the air. Aeos had also heard a rumor that Eno's harness would be replaced shortly with something the weavers were keeping hidden from the visiting Equines.

"Thracis is learning well," Psyche commented.

Aeos looked at her. "Yes, but I feel he prefers to stay on the ground."

Psyche laughed. "I believe you're right." She shifted her wings to glide farther away from him, angling toward a plateau. Aeos followed her. Thracis and Eno would be a good thirty minutes yet and Aeos and Psyche had been in the air for most of the day.

Landing close to Psyche, they had spent days learning to land without somersaulting hooves over rump, Aeos folded his wings over his back. He turned his head in time to see Eno diving at Thracis. Thracis whirled away from her, regaining his balance before flying back into the fight.

"They have spent a great deal of time together lately," Aeos said.

Psyche shook her head and began to check over her wings. This was a requirement of all Eno's followers. They were instructed to check their wings and harnesses every time they had opportunity. "I'm glad. She will begin teaching you and him the capriole and it's all Thracis talks about."

"You lack the jealousy of most mares." Aeos began to check his own harness.

"Only where Eno is concerned. Her affections lie elsewhere."

Aeos twitched his shoulders. "I am not sure they are falling on the right stallion."

Psyche swished her tail and lowered her head to graze. She spoke around a mouthful of grass. "I would not spend too much time worrying about where your relationship will end. Eno is simply enjoying the moment. She is aware of your ambitions and how much they differ from her own."

Relief swept through Aeos. "That is good news indeed. I do care deeply about Eno, but it is not the same depth of emotion Thracis feels for you."

"I think Eno would be reassured to hear those words."

Aeos spread his wings in the afternoon light. The color spectrum spread across them from left to right. "She is more of a dreamer than she is willing to admit to devise these. To believe that horses would fly without ships. Eno is not as technical as she wants everyone to believe."

Psyche laughed. "She has always been that way." She swallowed her last bit of grass. "Tell me, Aeos, what plans have you after we return to Boudica?"

"Does Eno wish to know?"

"I wish to know."

He sighed. "I will continue and complete my training with Master Phrenicos. After that I will beginning training with the delphae of Boudica. Sanctuary is a wonderful city but it is not for me. I was lonely and unable to concentrate."

"I would learn with you if you do not mind the company." Her voice was soft, ready for rejection.

He stepped close her. "You do not think Thracis would disapprove of our spending that much time together?"

Psyche looked up at Thracis, gliding next to Eno. "I think he would like me to study closer to him and farther from my family herd."

Thracis had told Aeos a little of the trouble between Psyche and her herd. It was something Aeos had trouble understanding as he and his sire were close as brothers. Thracis was close to his family herd as well and so did not know how to support Psyche other than stand by her decisions. "Perhaps that is best if you and your dam have a tumultuous relationship."

"I think it might be. Thracis has invited me to journey with him to visit his herd. Perhaps once we all learn to fly Eno will allow us to travel."

"It would be an exciting journey, I'm sure." He flapped his wings slowly. "Care to join me?"

Psyche opened her own wings and raced across the plateau. She sprang into the air, accompanied by a powerful downward movement of her wings that made her airborne. Aeos mimicked her takeoff and the two of them soared high to catch Eno and Thracis.

Aeos angled himself to push between Eno and Thracis, the downdrafts of his wings buffeting Thracis farther away.

"Hey, you don't have to be rude." Thracis tossed his head and pulled back, winging his way around the others to fly next to Psyche.

"You should be on alert. Don't you know you're not the only thing up here?" Aeos teased.

"Why didn't you keep him on the ground?" Thracis asked Psyche. "Eno has already worked me almost to exhaustion. I only want to go back to the stable and take a long shower."

"Oh no you don't," Eno said, "you have to stay out with us while I instruct the other mares. It will be a good time for you and Aeos to practice your High Dance movements. Your levades still leave something to be desired."

"Perfect. Thracis, why did you have to get me in trouble?" Aeos tossed his head and struck at the air with a front hoof. The movement was comical and made the others laugh.

"We may as well practice on our way back to the stable. V formation. Aeos take lead. Psyche, you will be between Aeos and Thracis."

They switched around. As the leader, Aeos took the brunt of the wind and broke it apart for the others. He didn't mind. He liked the open view, the mountains and valleys spreading out below him. Birds fluttered away from him in surprise and Aeos tossed his head. He led the group down into the valley, tilting in the crosswinds to keep from losing control and plummeting to his death. They had all had their share of close calls in the past weeks, with Haidee's being the most disastrous. The mare had gotten caught in the back draft of one of the other horses and had spun out of control. She was only able to break her fall enough to keep from breaking her legs on landing. She was just beginning to fly again after seven days of recuperation.

Aeos saw the other mares waiting for them in the practice field. He opened his wings to stop his forward momentum and landed gracefully between Haidee and Titania.

"Show off," Titania snickered. For all her bulk, the Clydesdale was learning fast and was more agile in the air than Alcina, Haidee, or Dysis. Neema, after a heated conversation with Eno in which the Felisian insisted Titania needed her at all times, had been granted a harness attaching her to the Clydesdale's broad back. The calico wore a parachute and thruster pack that would allow her to land safely in the event she was dislodged from Titania. Together the two of them made a formidable team as Neema was in charge of the projectile weapons on the Clydesdale's harness. Or would be. At this time Titania and Eno were sharing a harness.

Aeos mentally unfastened his harness buckles and hovered the whole thing over to lay on Dysis' back. The palomino began securing straps. Alcina was already wearing a harness. It must have just been completed or the black mare would have gone out with the others. Eno and Thracis removed their equipment and helped secure it to the other horses. Psyche stood a few feet off, looking distracted.

Confident that all the buckles and straps were secure on Dysis' harness, Aeos walked to the black and white mare. "What troubles you?"

She jumped a little and gave a nervous laugh. "Nothing specific. A feeling just crept over me. I should speak with Lady Aldara about it."

Aeos turned his attention outward, opening his mind. He felt something as well, a smudge on the horizon was the best description he could come up with. He said this to Psyche.

She nodded. "Yes, like a shadow on my mind. It is strange."

Aeos probed the smudge deeper and it broke apart, making him lose his focus. "Could it be an Equine who doesn't want to be found?"

"Perhaps, but...for just a minute I thought the feeling was familiar. As if it is someone I know or knew."

He pawed the ground and looked at the others. Thracis was arguing with Neema about something and Alcina was showing her harness to Eno. "Is it a relation to one of them? I didn't feel any connection to the thing."

"It could be. I'm confused because I can't discern its location." She sighed and stomped a foot in frustration. Thracis looked over and Neema took the opportunity to hop on his back and claw his withers. He squealed and bucked, sending Neema flying over his head and the others into gales of laughter.

Psyche turned her head to speak in Aeos ear. "Do not bring attention to this. It's nothing solid and I'd hate to spoil their good cheer. Let's just tell them to be cautious."

"I'll tell them we saw something strange from the plateau."

She nodded in agreement and followed him back to the herd. Thracis was rolling, trying to ease the sting of Neema's scratches. Neema was strapping herself to Titania's harness, pointedly not looking in Thracis' direction.

"Can't we have a single conversation without you children having a tantrum?" Psyche came to stand beside Alcina. "Nice harness. I noticed you had them attach your weapons already."

"I like to be prepared," Alcina said, angling her body this way and that to give Psyche a good look. "The weavers gave these wings a little more achillium because according to Lady Aldara 'Alcina is a temperamental creature who will fight with the eagles if given a chance'."

Psyche laughed. Thracis took a moment to shake the dust from his coat before joining Aeos. "Have a care with that cat. She's got daggers instead of claws."

Neema rolled her eyes. "Don't be so dramatic, Thracis. I hardly nicked you."

Thracis snorted.

Aeos took the moment to caution the others before another fight broke out. "Psyche and I saw something funny out in the training area." The others looked at him. "It was a shadow on the horizon, maybe nothing but an eagle or crane. We've seen a lot of them lately. Just something to be aware of."

Alcina and her mares nodded. They had been dived at by several female eagles when the horses strayed too close to their nesting sites. Alcina walked away from the herd and spread her wings. "Let's get going."

Eno waited until the others were aloft and flapping strongly before approaching Aeos. "You didn't mention this shadow earlier."

Aeos twitched a shoulder. "We didn't think it was important, but the thought nagged."

"Uh huh."

"If you're so curious, why don't you call them back and ask for a harness to go with them."

Eno nipped his shoulder. "Don't get snappy. I was only interested."

Thracis stretched his neck and nuzzled Psyche's shoulder. "Is it really nothing?"

"I'm not sure," Psyche admitted. "I didn't want to spoil their good time without proof."

"They'll be fine." Thracis trotted to the make-shift arena at one end of the field. It was surrounded by tall trees with thick branches. Most of the branches were bare now, but they had provided needed shade when Thracis and the group had first arrived.

"I should be joining him." Aeos slunk away before Eno could ask more questions. She was Psyche's friend; she could ask the black and white mare.

Thracis tossed his head as Aeos entered the ring. "Coward."

Aeos fell into step next to Thracis. The two stallions trotted around the perimeter of the arena. They moved in sync with one another, their legs lifting and dropping at the same exact moment. If not for the different coats, they could have been one animal.

After several rounds, Aeos pulled away from Thracis and moved to the center of the ring. He pulled himself together, his back feet moving farther under his body until he lifted himself up into a levade. His balance was perfect and he held the position for several long seconds before slowly settling down to all fours. Aeos repeated the movement several times, always proceeding the maneuver with the piaffe. His hips and flanks were beginning to ache by the time Eno and Psyche walked to the ring.

"You've both come a long way," Eno commented.

Until that moment, Aeos had forgotten Thracis was sharing the ring with him. Like Thracis, Aeos allowed his mind to wander where it would while he practiced the physical movements. He looked over at Thracis who was likewise coated in a sheen of sweat. "It has been a long journey."

Thracis nodded in agreement and cantered slowly around the ring, building momentum. Eno had already instructed them in the ballotade, the preliminary maneuver to the capriole. In this maneuver, the horse jumps straight up, lifting all four feet and tucking them close to its body. The final movement of the capriole was to kick out straight with the back legs and therefore cause the most amount of damage possible. Executed correctly, the capriole was the most lethal of the advanced maneuvers.

Aeos moved out of the way as Thracis came to the center of the ring and jumped up, his legs tucked.

"Very impressive, Thracis." Eno was standing hipshot next to Psyche. "You came up about four feet. That's good. It's time for you to learn how to kick out without falling down and injuring yourself."

She walked into the ring and began to canter. "Let me show you and then you can try to copy me."

As she passed Aeos, Eno tossed her head. "Are you ready to begin the capriole or are you still satisfied with the levade?"

Aeos trotted along the ring's perimeter. "I will wait a bit. I have already begun the ballotade if you remember correctly."

Ignoring him for the moment, Eno pulled herself into a tight collection and sprang into the air, her front legs tucked to her belly and her back legs striking out. The force of her kick made a brief whistling noise in the still air.

"That would have hurt," Aeos said, coming to stand by Psyche.

"It's supposed to." Eno turned her attention to Thracis. "Come on, Thracis, give it a go."

Thracis tried to replicate Eno's capriole five times before admitting defeat. He was close on a couple of attempts, but his lack of confidence had him waiting until his front legs were extending to break his fall before he kicked out, making the movement resemble a buck.

"I thought this would be easier since I am comfortable with the ballotade," Thracis panted as he walked around the ring to cool himself out.

"It takes practice just like everything else." Eno was watching the sky, looking for the other mares. "Aeos, take a turn. I want to see what you can do."

Fighting the urge to roll his eyes since Eno was in an instructor position, Aeos cantered around the perimeter of the ring. He pulled himself together and began to rock himself as he slowed, almost cantering in place before springing in the air and striking out with his back legs.

"Excellent," Eno said, "Thracis you should watch Aeos."

"That was only luck," Thracis muttered. He walked over to Aeos and bit his neck. "You're making me look bad."

Aeos pulled away and shook his head. "It's not intentional. I just learn better through observation. Besides, you'll note I only made it about two and a half feet off the ground.

Mollified, Thracis pawed the ground. "I think I will try to shorten my strides to canter in place. It looked like it gave you a little extra momentum."

"Tomorrow we can assemble targets for the two of you to kick at. It will help to--Psyche, are you alright?"

Psyche was standing with her head down, her nose touching the ground. Her muscles strained against each other. Thracis jumped the arena rail and slid to a stop beside her. He reached out to touch her neck with his nose and she reared, striking out and connecting with his cheek. Thracis stumbled back, more out of surprise than pain. Eno stepped between Thracis and Psyche.

"Leave her alone. She's having a mental confrontation with someone. Aeos, try to get into her mind and help her."

Aeos cleared his mind and connected to Psyche. Her barriers were fortified against all intruders. He waited patiently for her to recognize his mind. As soon as she gave him a crack he slipped through. And walked into chaos.

Psyche's mind was a cyclone. Mental gusts of wind buffeted Aeos as he strove to keep the projection of himself from being blown apart. The ground beneath his hooves felt unsteady, as if it would fall away at any moment. Drawing on his training from Sanctuary, Aeos imagined himself with wings. After all the training he had endured with Eno over the last weeks, he could now effectively imagine flying.

Hovering a few inches above the ground, Aeos searched for Psyche. He was in her mind, and could feel her all around him, but he should be able to see some representation of her. Instead, he saw a black shape, a wraith, coming toward him. He ducked out of instinct and felt claws rake along his sides. The wraith whirled, returning for another attack. Aeos imagined armor encompassing him. He made sure to leave openings for his wings. Unfortunately, that would leave them open to attack.

Psyche! Psyche, where are you? The wraith flew at him again. He dodged. The thing screamed and spun away.

I am here. Her mental voice was drained. She sounded out of breath. He wondered if she were injured.

What is this thing? Aeos soared the canyons of Psyche's mental landscape, the wraith right behind him.

I do not know. Do you remember the eagles?

Aeos tossed his head and flew lower. Psyche was changing the canyon below him to resemble the training area. The wraith gave no notice; it was too concerned with catching its prey.

Folding his wings and plummeting, Aeos dove to a certain outcropping where in reality a very large golden eagle had built her nest. The real eagle was a fierce creature, ruthlessly chasing the flying Equines until they were beyond her territory. Several of the mares had sustained rakings from the eagle's sharpened claws. The eagle was an ambush hunter and Aeos knew exactly what Psyche had in mind.

Diving under the outcropping and spreading his wings to glide, Aeos led the wraith beneath Psyche's hiding spot. He heard a muffled shriek of surprise, heard the sounds of collision. He wheeled around in a semicircle and faced the wraith and Psyche.

Psyche had flown straight into the wraith. She was wearing her flying harness complete with weapons and Aeos saw that she had contained the wraith somehow. It shrieked and wiggled, trying to break free. Psyche's wings were spread, working like a parachute to lower her slowly.

Aeos wanted to help her, but had no idea how. He would have to wait until they all landed. Then he remembered the deathshrouds Eno had designed. Imaging that his armor came equipped with one, Aeos flew above and to the right of Psyche.

Let it go, Aeos called.

Psyche complied. The wraith shoved backwards and tried to fly away from both of them. Aeos didn't give it the chance. He deployed the deathshroud. The metal net entwined itself around the wraith, binding it. The thing fell like a boulder, screaming in terror.

Aeos and Psyche followed it until it landed on the canyon's rocky floor, splattering in a crimson spray of blood.

A good idea, Psyche said, *we must get back to our bodies. This was a distraction.* She vanished.

Aeos pulled himself back together. He did it too quickly and stumbled on his feet as a wave of vertigo swept through him. Confused images swam in front of his eyes. Titania, blood dripping down her flank. Neema, pointing to the sky with one paw and talking rapidly. Psyche, on her knees and heaving air into her lungs. Then sound flooded his ears. Neema's voice, panicked. Eno asking questions. Thracis speaking softly to Psyche. All this bedlam was giving Aeos a splitting headache.

"What's going on?" His voice was unsteady.

"They were attacked." Eno was shrugging into Titania's harness. Aeos was aware others were running toward them from the stable.

"Attacked by what?" Aeos was still a couple steps behind.

"Other horses with wings."

"What?" Thracis was helping Psyche to her feet.

"Apparently I'm not the only genius around," Eno smirked.

"The wings are not like ours," Titania gasped, "They look like bat wings. And they shimmer like silver."

"Must be metal," Eno grumbled, fastening the harness buckles. "That will mean they're heavier than ours and it will impede their soaring capabilities."

"They didn't seem impeded at all. Have a care, Eno." Titania was regaining her breath.

Psyche was spreading her wings and preparing for takeoff. Thracis saw this and stood in front of her, cutting her off. "You and Eno can't go alone. Someone else has to go with you."

Psyche pinned her ears but her retort was interrupted by Lady Aldara. "He is right. You must be on your guard and need as many with you as possible."

"Time is short and we have only two harnesses here." Eno sounded frustrated.

"You have three." Lady Aldara tossed her head at two younger mares floating a harness between them. "This was designed for Haidee, but it will fit one of the stallions."

Thracis and Aeos exchanged a looked. "You go," Thracis said, "I am too tired from the arena." He lowered his head. "I don't want Psyche in danger because I'm too exhausted to help."

Knowing how difficult it was for Thracis to leave Psyche's side, Aeos walked over and nipped Thracis shoulder. "I will take care of her." He looked at Eno who stood with lowered ears. "And you as well."

The mares helped Aeos fasten the new harness and then he, Psyche, and Eno were taking to the sky. They flew in a V, Eno on the lead. Psyche glanced at Aeos. "Titania says there are six mares in all. She doesn't know what happened to Alcina, Haidee, and Dysis. The last she saw they were all tangled with opponents."

Aeos nodded. "Are her injuries bad?"

Eno answered him. "No. She will take to the air by tomorrow. Neema made sure to get them away so they could warn us and get help."

They flew to the training area. The mountain cliffs were scored with marks from explosives. Aeos wondered what kind of weapons these others had been carrying. Eno led them in a sweep of the entire area before dropping lower to look for Alcina and her mares.

It was as they were coming down to land on the plateau that a shadow moved across the sun. Not giving in to surprise, the trio split apart as two horses dove at them from above. Aeos wheeled away and then dove into the fray. His wings clipped one of the strange horse's and both of them plunged toward the ground.

Aeos engaged his thrusters, trying to stop his downward momentum. He was trying to think as clearly as possible as the ground rushed up to meet him. His opponent was not. Aeos heard the horse's terrified whinny, saw it try to open its wings and engage its own thrusters. The thrusters fired but it looked like the wings were too heavy. The other horse began to roll as it fell. Aeos spread his wings and hovered, watching as the other horse collided with the earth.

He was so fixated on his fallen opponent that he was sideswiped by another horse. The two of them struggled to keep from falling as they fought with each other. Aeos was astounded by how good this new horse was at air combat. He was kicked and bit several times before he got enough distance between the two of them to soar higher.

The other horse flew up in pursuit, but Aeos saw the problem with the other's wings immediately. Where the harnesses designed by Eno were created to act as actual wings, which was why the weavers' help was necessary, these others were more like bat wings and therefore depended a great deal on the thrusters connected to the harness.

Aeos spread his wings to hover and waited for his opponent to come to him. They engaged again, but this time Aeos didn't worry about inflicting damage on the horse's body. Instead, he focused his kicks and strikes on the thrusters. The horse, realizing what was happening, tried to get away, but one of the thrusters was already sputtering.

Taking advantage of the other horse's distraction, Aeos attacked again. He flapped his wings to pull himself into a rear and struck at the horse. His hoof connected with the horse's face and when it dodged away, it went into a roll. Unlike his previous opponent, this horse didn't panic. It fell a few feet before using its wings to glide away as fast as possible. Aeos wanted to pursue but he had promised Thracis. He wheeled back to see Psyche engaged with an opponent.

Thracis needn't have worried. Psyche was pummeling her opponent with little trouble. Aeos turned his attention to Eno. Eno was having a more difficult time. Two horses were attacking her. One would come in for a fast strike then dodge away as the other struck from the other side.

Pinning his ears and whinnying a challenge, Aeos launched himself at one of the attacking horses. It tried to turn and face him head on, but Aeos was too close. He rammed the horse in the shoulder. The horse lowered its wings and went with the movement. It snaked its head around and clamped its teeth on Aeos' left wing. He heard a tearing sound as the wing ripped. Aeos threw himself forward at the other horse, climbing on top of it. If he was going down he was taking the other horse with him.

They fell together, the other horse spreading its wings and trying to slow their decent. Aeos helped as best he could with his one intact wing. They weren't slowing. Having no other choice, Aeos turned on his thrusters. The horse beneath him screamed as the thrusters burned into its back. It bucked, but Aeos held on. They hit the ground with a bone crunching collision. Aeos was thrown forward. He rolled onto his legs and stood, whirling for battle.

His opponent lay in a heap. Blood poured from the charred holes the thrusters had burned into its back. The horse gasped and struggled to its feet. It took a couple of steps and collapsed to the ground. Blood began to drip from the horse's nostrils. It lay flat on its side and looked at Aeos with dying eyes. Aeos felt no sympathy. This horse had attacked his friends, his herd.

Aeos shook with the realization that he was capable of an unmerciful killing. Was this what the coming war would turn him into? A warrior without compassion? No, he would end this horse's suffering. He was a foot away from the horse when it gasped a final time and lay silent.

Psyche and Eno landed close to Aeos and looked at the fallen horse. Psyche walked forward and sniffed the dead horse. "This is a mare. That symbol on her hoof. That is Zeva's design. My sister sent these horses."

CHAPTER 25

"We have to search for survivors." Eno's voice was quiet on the plateau.

Psyche ignored the statement for the moment. Questions crashed into each other in her mind, distracting her from what Eno was saying.

How could Zeva have discovered the secrets of flying? And why? As far as Psyche was aware, the Baroquians had no problem with mares fighting alongside stallions.

This indifference to female cavalry was something the Baroquians tried to use as a bargaining chip when they tried to establish a military outpost in Diomedea. That was appealing to Queen Hippolyta. It was the idea of having to answer to a stallion commander that she wouldn't accept.

"What was that, Eno?"

"I said, you and Aeos should go look for Alcina, Haidee, and Dysis. They may only be injured. If they are dead, they deserve proper burial." Eno looked at the mare laying a few feet away. "I want to inspect this harness, figure out how it works. We will have to put energy fields around them until we can move them since it's impossible to get to this plateau on foot."

Psyche glanced past Eno to the fallen bat-winged horse. Psyche couldn't believe these horses hadn't tried to retreat when they had been out fought. Instead, they had continued until the bitter end. Zeva's cruelty must have increased rather than diminished over time. Psyche shuddered to think of the punishment for failure.

"Let's get going." Aeos was exchanging harnesses with Eno.

Psyche took the opportunity to contact Thracis.

Are you safe? His worry filled the link between them.

We are all fine. These warriors were sent by my sister.

Is she close? Do you need help?

Zeva was smart enough to stay away. Psyche didn't try to hide her bitterness. *I or my sister, Lachesis, would have recognized her at once.*

Thracis' love and affection surrounded her. *Don't fret about your sister. You have to keep your mind clear.*

I have to go. Aeos is ready to leave. We have to look for Alcina and the others.

Take care, my love. The link broke. Thracis was relaying information to the horses at Arachnae Stable.

Psyche turned her full attention to Aeos. He was taking off. Psyche nodded to Eno before joining him in the sky. "You lead the way. I think it's better if we travel together."

Aeos bobbed his head and dove into the valley.

The valley had been carved thousands of years ago by a deep river. Now the river was little more than a shallow stream for most of the year, only swelling to substantial size in the spring after the winter melt began. Because of the yearly flooding, the banks were wide and flat, the perfect place for emergency landings.

Psyche and Aeos scoured the area, finding two more bodies. Both were from the group of attacking horses. They had ricocheted off the mountainside as they fell, dying before they reached the ground. Psyche turned her eyes quickly from their mangled bodies. They should be buried but Psyche doubted they would be. She didn't think there would be time.

Aeos led her through several passes, both of them whinnying frequently. No answers came on the wind. Psyche opened her mind and began searching for the others, trying to contact them. No one answered her probing, but Psyche didn't feel the blankness that indicated the others were dead. It was disturbing to Psyche that she could not locate them. Her mind was still too confused from the wraith's attack. She wondered how Aeos was fairing but didn't ask. He was too concerned about finding the others.

They were returning to the plateau and Eno when Psyche felt a tug on her mind.

Here.

Psyche turned her head back and forth, trying to locate the source.

Here.

To the left, in a collection of boulders.

"Down there, Aeos, among those rocks."

He turned to follow her. Psyche folded her wings and dropped, gliding down to a sloping bank scattered with mid-sized boulders. Her hooves made hollow clicking sounds as she landed. Aeos made more of a racket, nearly colliding with a dead tree. He must be getting used to the different harness. Psyche would have to be more assertive until Aeos was confident.

Where? She inquired.

Here.

Psyche recognized Alcina. She walked around a large boulder and saw the black mare, her wings folded protectively around her body, standing guard over a fallen Haidee. The sorrel mare's side rose shallowly and blood dripped from a clotted gash across her chest.

"Where is Dysis?"

Alcina tossed her head across the stream. Psyche could see Aeos approaching a golden heap wearing a crimson blanket.

"She was in the lead. Four took her all at once. She never had a chance." Psyche heard the sorrow in Alcina's voice. "I could do nothing for her. The remaining two came for Haidee and me. I dispatched one but by then Haidee was wounded and falling. I had to help her land." Alcina lifted her wings and Psyche saw the scratches and abrasions that covered her coat. Every movement would be painful for a while.

"Psyche, where are you?"

Psyche walked around the boulder to the sound of Thracis' voice. How was he flying? She looked up to see him hovering in the air above the slope. The harness he wore looked like metal sticks wrapped in rags. "We are here. Alcina, Haidee, and I."

He landed a little more abruptly than was prudent. He folded his wings as best he could and trotted around Psyche to check the other mares. "We will have to rig some kind of net to carry Haidee back to the stable. It would take three days to get into this valley on hoof." Thracis looked up at Alcina. "Can you fly?"

"I will manage."

He backed away. Psyche looked at his harness. "What is that?"

"Improvisation. Lady Aldara fastened cast off wings to one of Eno's prototypes. The thrusters are a little warm and the whole thing is heavy, but we felt you might need help." He twitched a shoulder. "Where is Aeos?"

"Aeos is digging," Psyche said. "Dysis has fallen. He will need help."

"I will help him. Do what you can for Haidee. I will get the harness off Dysis. Hopefully the wings will be undamaged."

Psyche went back to the other mares. "Alcina, you have to come forward so I can attend to Haidee."

The black mare hobbled out of the way, groaning with every step. She stopped and watched Aeos and Thracis. "She was a good companion. Dysis was with me the longest."

Psyche was gently removing Haidee's harness. Everything appeared to be intact. She placed the equipment in a pile out of the way and began to mend the other mare's wounds. She couldn't do much but she could start the healing process. She had nothing with her to dress the wounds.

"Dysis told me the two of you met as foals." Psyche only spoke to have something to say. Alcina was tightlipped when it came to her emotions and after this brief exchange Psyche doubted the black mare would speak with anyone about the incident again.

"My dam was her wetnurse. Dysis' dam died after Dysis was born. Foal colic."

Foal colic. The most feared affliction after a mare gave birth. Essentially, it was like any other colic with one exception: the mare's already weakened body was more prone to the more dangerous effects of colic. Twisted guts, hernias, hemorrhaging. One or all could happen if the mare wasn't seen too as soon as she reported stomach pain and upset. Treated quickly and correctly most mares recovered with nothing more than a sleepless night. Left to run its course, the colic would almost certainly end in death. Psyche wondered if neglect or inexperience had led to the dam's death.

But Alcina was moving on. "We spent our entire foalhood together. We were only separated for a few years when I had some trouble."

Her voice trailed off and Psyche didn't comment. Given the way Alcina acted around stallions, Psyche was pretty sure she knew what the trouble had been.

"Dysis was the one who found me. Rescued me. She was my strength." Alcina looked at Psyche and tears streamed down her face. "I need a few moments."

Psyche watched as Alcina staggered away. She didn't know what to say, what words of comfort Alcina would accept. Haidee groaned, drawing Psyche's attention. She began a thorough investigation of Haidee's injuries. It was a preoccupation from grief.

An hour later, Eno was gliding down with Neema on her back, the wings of Aeos harness repaired for the time being. They brought the supplies Psyche needed to finish bandaging Haidee. Neema was using the harness designed to keep her attached to the flying harness while she and a horse were in the air.

"I've taken the other harness back to the stable. The design is very strange, not user-friendly at all. I'm surprised these mares even made it here from wherever they came from." Eno was prattling on, but Psyche didn't mind. It was comforting in its familiarity. "I'll take Dysis' and Haidee's harnesses back now and tell the weavers we need some sort of net. Titania is ready to fly so I will give her a harness. Thracis can use the other harness."

"I will stay here with you." Neema was unpacking salves and bandages. "Alcander sent these. He said they are of your design."

"Good." Fully ensconced in her craft, Psyche was barely listening.

Eno left her to work and asked Neema to secure Haidee's harness to her own. After that, the two of them went across the stream to get Dysis' harness. Eno lowered her head to the body and Neema placed a paw on Dysis' cheek before Eno launched herself into the air to return to Arachne Stable. Neema came back to the boulder to help with Haidee.

Pysche was already finished by that time. Haidee was sleeping as comfortably as possible. Psyche was sure the other mare would live, but her recuperation would take a long time. Even so, Haidee would be back in the air by the first snow. "We'll let her sleep. Are they almost done?"

Psyche was leading Neema away from the boulder as she spoke. The Felisian was looking around alertly, getting a feel for the area. "They have finished digging. You must say your farewells."

The two of them walked to the new grave. Thracis and Aeos waited off to one side. Alcina stood a few yards away. Psyche and Neema said their goodbyes. Neema placed a paw on the fresh earth that would cover Dysis and uttered Felisian words no one present understood. Psyche nuzzled Dysis with her nose then motioned to the stallions and the four of them moved off to give Alcina her privacy.

By the stream, Aeos said, "It will take her a long time to get over this. She will wall herself off even more and be alone."

"Not as alone as you think." Neema pointed with a paw. "Don't you see what stands beyond Alcina?"

The Equines shook their heads. All they saw was Alcina, her head lowered to speak into Dysis' ears. Neema narrowed her eyes at Psyche. "I would think an *ammoni* mare such as yourself could see who stands watch."

Embarrassed, Psyche said, "I see nothing, Neema."

The Felisian brushed against Psyche's mind. *Open your eyes and see, mare of Augean Stable.*

Psyche did as instructed, looking beyond the veil of reality. Her eyes widened.

Behind Alcina and Dysis, Psyche saw a shimmer. As her mind opened further, the shimmering focused, became more coherent. Then the image sharpened, became real.

A horse, more beautiful and regal than any Psyche had ever seen, stood with wings spread wide to catch the light. While Eno and her followers' woven wings shimmered in the colors of the rainbow, this horse's wings truly were rainbows. Noticing Psyche, the horse turned to face her.

Psyche's breath caught. She dropped to her knees, her words spilling over each other. "My Lord, forgive me. I had no right to look on you."

A soft laugh was carried to her on the wind. "Do not fret, daughter of Lady Hippolyta. If I did not wish for you to see me you would not have. Rise."

Psyche got unsteadily to her feet. Now that her initial shock was over, she noticed another horse, a palomino with golden wings, standing next to Lord Pegasus. Dysis. How it would gladden Alcina's heart to know her friend had been given wings of gold to fly with their lord in an endless sky.

Lord Pegasus looked at Psyche again, marking her, then turned and galloped away. Dysis waited a few seconds longer, watching Alcina. She dipped her head low then turned and followed Lord Pegasus. Psyche watched until they both disappeared.

Color flowed back into the world. Psyche was aware the others were looking at her as if she had lost her mind. All but Neema, who sat with a satisfied grin on her face.

"Are you all right?" Thracis' voice filled with awe.

"I'm fine."

"Who were you talking to?" Aeos was searching the area with his eyes.

"Lord Pegasus."

They stared at her. Before they could ask any questions, Psyche said, "I must speak with Alcina."

Watching her walk away, Thracis asked, "Was he really here?"

Neema sneezed. "Has the Lady ever lied?"

Thracis and Aeos stared at each other. Neema laughed and walked to Psyche and Alcina. Her tail twitched with each step.

CHAPTER 26

"These harnesses were obviously designed with gliding in mind."

Eno was walking around the table in her workshop. One of the enemy's harnesses was laid out for inspection. "They're impractical for upward momentum. That is why this harness has so many thrusters."

She moved the wings with her nose. "See here? These wings are too small. They should be three times this size to lift a horse. And they are more metal than cloth. I want to put one on and attempt to use it but I can tell you all that this harness is at least five times heavier than ours."

"No wonder they set up an ambush." Neema was walking on the table.

"Whatever their reasoning, it worked." Alcina's voice was roughened by grief.

"It did. We have to learn from their tactics." Eno was trying her best for patience but her excitement at a new challenge was shining through.

Alcina sighed, pulling herself together. "Titania, Neema, you tell them."

The draft nodded. "We were flying in V formation. Dysis was in the lead, then Alcina and Haidee. I brought up the rear.

"Four fell on Dysis the moment she flew under a rock out-cropping. They seemed to drop from the sky. The impact sent Haidee into a spin. Another went for Alcina. She was trying to get to Dysis. The one who struck us did so from underneath."

"Underneath?" Eno asked.

Neema spoke, "Yes. Our attacker shot up at us like an arrow. It must have had its thrusters on full."

"It hit like a hammer on an anvil," Titania explained, "took my breath. I didn't realize I was wounded until we were flying back to get help."

"Titania and I tried to take the other horse but the creature fought as a thing possessed." Neema shuddered at the memory.

"If you had ever met my sister, Zeva, you would know a far worse fate than death awaited them if they failed on whatever mission she devised." Psyche was standing in a corner of the workshop next to Thracis. She wanted to get back to Haidee, sleeping soundly in the stable medical stall. Lady Aldara employed her own healers, but Psyche felt bonded with the sorrel mare.

"I have had the displeasure of meeting Lady Zeva. The mare is a demon spawned of Pandemonium."

They all looked to see Alcander standing in the doorway. His small frame was quivering.

Titania nuzzled the miniature. "You are safe with us, little friend. I would end your life before I saw you returned to her hooves."

Alcander nodded in acceptance of the offer. Given Alcander's attitude and the way the attackers had sacrificed themselves, it appeared even death was preferable to punishment.

"What happened after you hid?" Eno brought everyone back to the important subject.

"They circled. Like vultures," Alcina spat.

"They didn't try to land? Not at all?"

Alcina shook her head.

Eno bobbed her head and looked back at the wing design. She sniffed the thrusters. She had inspected the dead bodies as well and noticed the old burn marks on the horses' hides. Apparently, Zeva's version of combat preparation did not take into account the damage caused to her soldiers. Some of the burns were so deep, Eno wondered how the horses' muscles could function.

"Given this design, I suspect they didn't land because they couldn't be sure of taking off again. The crosswinds in the valleys are tricky and these wings are meant for darting, not hovering. Even with the thrusters, a liftoff from those slopes would have been difficult. My design has no such problem." She added the last with a marked sense of pride.

"You have taken the time to make your wings correctly," Neema said, "It looks like whoever did these was in a bit of a hurry."

"My sire often states that haste leads to pain." Eno swished her tail. "I saw enough accidents in the Hippikon to believe that truth."

"More proof stands before you." Alcina pawed the ground. "If they had landed, they would have killed us all. After our landing I was in no condition to protect Haidee and myself from trained assassins."

"Something bothers me." Thracis drew everyone's attention. "Why would Zeva send these soldiers in the first place, unprepared as they were?"

"To learn how far we've come in Eno's endeavor," Aeos stated. "The fact that Eno is trying to put mares in the air is no secret in Diomedea and I'm sure the Baroquians have spies in the country. She sent these as sacrifice to see what we could do."

"You noticed the relay equipment on the harnesses?" Eno inclined her head at a camera-like device, broken and not transmitting any longer.

Aeos nodded. "I did, but it is also something a good tactician would do. Learn about your enemy. Find a way around their defenses. To do this, sacrifices must be made."

"Not always," Psyche interjected.

"No," Aeos agreed.

"What do you think she will do with the information?" Thracis asked.

"Improve her design." Eno twitched a shoulder. "It's what I'd do."

Later that night, after the evening meal and everyone had gone their separate ways, Psyche walked along the paths of the private gardens. Unlike most gardens, this one was comprised entirely of native plants. The plants were encouraged to grow as they would and were not restricted in any way. Psyche thought this an excellent way to live in harmony with the surrounding area.

Thracis had wanted to join her, but Psyche had refused the offer, stating that Aeos needed more support than she did at the moment. He was quite rattled by Dysis' death, though he would not admit it openly.

In reality, Psyche was more upset than she wanted to admit as well, but she needed time alone. Her vision of Lord Pegasus coming to get the fallen Dysis was clear in her mind.

Psyche had spoken to Alcina, telling her that Lord Pegasus had taken Dysis and given her golden wings. Alcina had fought tears at the news, but Psyche sensed that it had settled something inside the black mare. She had spoken to Thracis as well, but had been more evasive. Psyche knew he was uncomfortable with her abilities and he was under enough stress with Aeos. It would be better, Psyche explained, if he and Aeos stayed close to Eno and helped her in the lab. Aeos should also be available in the event Haidee or Titania was in need of care.

The wind had died down as night fell, but the air was cold. Psyche's winter coat was beginning to grow but she still felt a chill. She should have put on a light blanket before venturing out for a walk. Well, she wasn't going back to the stable for one now.

She meandered through the garden, letting her mind wander. Too many questions kept her distracted. Who had Zeva commissioned to create the bat-winged harnesses? Eno wasn't the only genius on Equus, but usually horses with that much intelligence had a reputation. Besides, as the daughter of the Diomedean queen, Psyche was kept informed of all possible threats.

The identity of the horse responsible was a mystery to Eno as well. She had been trying to remember all her fellow students during her time at the Piber University. None stood out in her mind as being particularly brilliant. But Eno did admit that just because neither she nor Psyche knew of anyone didn't automatically mean the Baroquians hadn't kept this horse a secret for years.

In addition, Psyche was having a difficult time reconciling the fact that Zeva had sent her mares for sacrifice just to learn the inadequacies of the harnesses. Zeva was evil, but until today Psyche had hoped that there was at least some good in her older sister. This attack had only proved that all the stories about Zeva were true.

Her hoof stumbled over a stone and Psyche nearly fell to her knees. As she regained her feet, a shimmer of light caught her attention.

"It seems you have caught the attention of my mate, mare of Augean Stable. I have come to find out why."

Psyche raised her head to look on Lady Selene, mate and escort to Lord Pegasus. Lady Selene was the goddess preferred by the mares of Diomedea. She was mystery and danger and strength. The moons were hers and like the moon, the color of her coat fluctuated. As the strongest mares of Diomedea wore the darkest coats, so too did the Lady Selene when she was at her most secretive. When the moon was full, Lady Selene was said to be cloaked all in white with a silver mane and tail. As the moon darkened, so did the lady's coat until she was purest black. Tonight, the moon was new.

"I apologize, Lady. I have not tried to win his favor."

The black mare circled Psyche. Her ears were lowered and her tail swished occasionally. "I did not say you have won his favor, I said you have drawn his attention."

Deciding silence was her best course of action, Psyche lowered her eyes and waited to hear what the goddess had to say. The gods could be finicky; their moods changing from pleasant to cruel in the blink of an eye.

After circling several times, Lady Selene seemed to come to a conclusion. "Walk with me, daughter of Queen Hippolyta."

Knowing she couldn't deny the request, Psyche fell into step beside and a little behind Lady Selene.

"I believe now I know why you are so interesting." The black mare looked back at Psyche. "You are very powerful, Psyche, but your power is tempered by your inability to believe you are special."

"I am not as special as those around me."

Lady Selene struck out with a back foot, kicking Psyche high on the front of her shoulder. "Stop being so modest. You are special. More so now that you have something to fight for. Your stallion needs you; your friends need you. You are the strength that binds them together."

Psyche couldn't speak. She didn't know what to say.

"You have always been strong. That is why your sister tried to destroy you so long ago. She knew what you would become. It is not your skill that raises you above the rest of your herd, but your heart."

Lady Selene stopped walking. They were out in the open, standing in the training field. Lady Selene looked up into the star-filled sky. "You will be more important in the battles to come than you know. Like Thracis, you will turn the tide of battle in your own way."

"Why have I not sensed this during my meditations?" Psyche kept her voice meek.

"You have not been ready. Also, it is not in our best interests to tell our children everything their destinies hold." An amused slyness had crept into Lady Selene's voice.

They stood in silence for a few moments before the goddess shook her black mane. "I must be off." Black wings, invisible until this moment, unfurled on her back. She looked at Psyche. "Take care, mare of Augean Stable. You are the heart that beats for your friends, in their time of doubt you will bring them hope."

Lady Selene launched herself skyward, her lift off more graceful than anything Psyche and the others could accomplish with their created wings. Psyche watched until the goddess became a shadow in the night. She listened to the rustle of small animals in the training field. Her ears flicked back toward the stable. She would have to talk to Lady Aldara about this, but not tonight. Tomorrow, after the morning meal, that would be the best time.

Shaking her head at the strangeness of the entire day and feeling the weight of sorrow and exhaustion settle on her back, Psyche turned and walked back to the stable.

CHAPTER 27

"You wish to speak with me." Lady Aldara was standing behind a loom setup on the balcony outside her private stalls. The balcony was ringed with columns that were draped with heavy linens that could be dropped in foul weather. This enclosure was set in the center of the stable giving Lady Aldara a bird's eye view of the entire complex.

"Lady Selene came to speak with me last evening." Psyche was walking around the terrace in a slow circle. She couldn't seem to make her feet hold still.

"I am not surprised." Lady Aldara's tone was dismissive, uninterested. "We see the Lady frequently at this stable."

"I know you and my dam were foalhood friends. Were you still close when Zeva was a foal?"

Lady Aldara paused in her weaving. A few heartbeats passed before she began twisting the strands again, more slowly than before. "I was at the Augean Stable until your sister was exiled.

Your dam needed support, though she would not admit it. A trait she has passed on to all her daughters."

"Was she always evil?"

Lady Aldara shifted to stand hipshot. "There was always a darkness in Zeva, always a void. As an *ammoni* you are taught to sing with the world around us."

Psyche nodded.

"It was as if your sister had no voice."

"My dam never loved me after Zeva. Never bonded to me as she did my sisters."

The pain in Psyche's voice was a thing both heard and felt. Lady Aldara chose her next words carefully. "Your dam and I are of the same age. For reasons of his own Lord Pegasus withheld the joy of motherhood from me, but I always felt like a favored aunt to your sisters. I saw more clearly than anyone what Zeva's deception did to your dam." She took a deep breath. "Hippolyta wanted to love you, Psyche. She wanted to fix what had gone wrong with Zeva by making sure you were always taken care of, always watched."

Psyche snorted. "Her watchfulness became smothering. She treats me like a weanling."

"You are different from your sisters."

"I am less."

Lady Aldara pinned her ears. "You are different. And your dam knows it. You have been touched by Lord Pegasus and Lady Selene in a way your sisters have not. Of all her foals, you are the one Lady Hippolyta cannot understand."

"What are you talking about, Lady?"

"Alastrina was born to be Queen Hippolyta's heir, her destiny chosen from birth. Then Lachesis came and showed her power of mind and spirit and so was the natural choice to be groomed as the next High Delphae. Zeva showed her steel and cunning as a six-month-old. She was to become your dam's military commander. Queen Hippolyta planned on laying the entire Diomedean Cavalry at your sister's hooves before she attempted to assassinate you."

Lady Aldara turned to look directly at Psyche. "And then there is you. A black and white filly who plays at her craft as a foal plays with toys. A filly who left Diomedea to be educated at the University of Piber. Then, rather than return to your place in your herd, you ensconce yourself in Iliad, under the guise of a talisman merchant and wait for a stallion you've had visions of but have told no one about." The older mare snorted. "And you wonder why your dam is reserved?"

Listed in such a way, Psyche had to admit that there might be something to her dam's hesitancy. "But why does she treat Eno so differently? Eno is more of a conundrum than I am."

"Eno is someone else's foal."

"Thracis says his dam doesn't worry about him like this either."

"Stop whining, Psyche. What Thracis' or Aeos' or Eno's parents think is not the point. What matters is what your dam thinks." Lady Aldara reached out with her nose. "You must accept that your dam may never approve of your chosen path. The question is: can you live with her disapproval?"

Psyche had no ready reply.

Lady Aldara didn't seem interested in one. She walked to the edge of the balcony and looked down into the stable yard. "Your mate is searching for you."

Psyche nodded, hearing the dismissal. "Thank you for your advice, Lady Aldara."

"Any time, little filly."

"I wish you would speak with me about what's bothering you." Thracis was trotting beside Psyche in the schooling arena. They were exercising alone, Aeos helping Eno reconstruct the bat-winged harnesses to discover what type of weapons Zeva's mares might use.

"I don't know that you would understand."

Thracis tossed his head. "I want to try. If we are a pair then you will have to confide in me sometime."

"I've confided more than I feel comfortable with already."

Her voice sounded amused and Thracis relaxed a little. He had been on edge since yesterday's attack and Psyche's avoidance was making it worse. He knew she liked to work things out for herself just as he did, but he was hurt by the efficient way she was shutting him out.

She broke into a light canter. Thracis followed her. "When will Eno let us into the air again?"

Psyche tossed her head. "I'm not sure. She and the weavers are repairing the damaged harnesses but I think we might be leaving soon. Probably as soon as Titania can take wing."

"Something's happening isn't it?"

Psyche stopped cantering and looked at him. "I'm not sure. The winds feel wrong. I can't explain it any better than that. And I don't like that I wasn't even aware of the danger of that ambush."

"No one is perfect all the time," Thracis said, thinking of the ambush that had almost resulted in his death. "Besides you mentioned that you did feel something."

"Yes, but, Thracis, none of us felt the danger, just something off. It wasn't just me. All the mares here, not to mention Aeos, are trained to pick up on the slightest change in their surroundings and most of us keep ourselves open to identify dangerous influences."

He thought about that. He still didn't understand the way Aeos could feel what was happening even if he couldn't see it, but Thracis found it unsettling that no one had noticed the apparent danger. "Do you think it's because we've all been so busy?"

"That makes sense for us, but Lady Aldara has Felisians as well as Equines posted as sentries and none of them sensed anything either."

Thracis twitched a shoulder. "Like I said, no one's perfect all the time."

"This time that lapse was fatal."

"It was the last time as well." Thracis was thinking of the ambush that led to his friend Aethon's death.

Psyche stepped forward to rub her head against his shoulder. "I know. I remembered this morning. How are you?"

"Pretty fair mostly because I know the ambush was aimed at all of us and not just myself. It relieves a lot of my guilt in a strange way."

"That is odd."

"What?" Thracis was nipping the underside of her neck. He couldn't help himself. Every time Psyche was close enough to touch he took full advantage.

"The Baroquians have been trying to kill you for over a year."

Thracis nodded against her.

"They've tried assassination on two separate occasions and if you had been killed in the Diomedean battle it would have been worth all the Baroquian losses." Psyche's voice was taking on a contemplative tone.

"Don't forget Tansy."

"That's it." Psyche raised her head, almost smacking the bottom of Thracis' jaw. "Tansy. Going after you and causing friction between us was just a bonus for Zeva. Tansy's real usefulness had been to listen to everything Eno was creating."

"You think your sister created her wings based on what she heard through Tansy?" Thracis found that hard to believe.

"No, I think she has someone like Eno who has been trying to develop flight for some time. But Tansy was letting Zeva know the differences in Eno's design as well as where we were going. Zeva attacked us to find the flaws in her own design and in ours."

"And using Tansy to get under your skin kept you distracted. Not to mention the weavers have been so excited about the wings, I'll bet they've let a few things slip."

"Exactly. Zeva isn't the Baroquian second-in-command for no reason. My sister is very smart and she knows all the training we Diomedeans go through for attack and defense."

Thracis didn't know if he should be appalled by the realization that Zeva was just as well-trained as Psyche and Eno or not. Both mares had held their own in battle and Psyche was not as devious as her older sister. Thracis had only had a glimpse of Zeva when she had tried to trap his mind at Phrenicos' stable. He had no desire to engage with the mare again, either in his mind or on a battlefield.

"What does she want?" Thracis thought if Zeva was still under orders to assassinate him, she would have sent her mares after him instead of Alcina and Haidee.

"I think she's planning her own attack. Something more personal."

"Wouldn't her commander be angry at a show of hidden weaponry?"

"Not if she is attacking Diomedea again."

Thracis tossed his head. "Why does the rest of Equus need to worry since this is becoming a conflict between Diomedea and Baroquia?"

"I could be wrong." Psyche began to walk around the arena.

Thracis stayed where he was, watching the flex of muscles as Psyche moved.

"See something interesting?" she asked.

"Always."

Flicking her ears at him, Psyche moved toward the exit. "We should get back to Eno. She wants to get all our harnesses finished in the next few days."

"Sometimes I don't think you relax enough."

"Maybe I should spend more time with Aeos then. I'm sure he could teach me a few things."

Thracis cantered to catch up with her. "He'd have to go through me first."

CHAPTER 28

Pyrios shifted his weight as he stood behind Lord Kantaka. The council was discussing sending ambassadors to Vanneria, country of the draft horses, in an effort to discern if they were taking sides in the conflict between Baroquia and Lipizzania. So far as anyone knew, Vanneria was remaining neutral. Both Belgia and Shira had representatives in the Registry, but they had returned to home soil after Baroquia declared open war.

Stop fidgeting. You are drawing attention.

Pyrios jumped at the sound of Lord Kantaka's voice in his head. The movement elicited a glare from Phlegon.

The Calpernian stallion was coming along nicely, surpassing Pyrios in his understanding of politics. He spoke with his dam routinely and she was boasting his accomplishments to all who would listen. Her stable was gradually climbing higher in Pendarian society and it was rumored that she may be granted a position in King Pedasos' court. As a result, Phlegon was taking his position as Lord Kantaka's aide seriously and had little patience for Pyrios' floundering.

The council debate dragged on for another few hours before the mediator called for an end of the discussion. It was decided that two horses would be sent to Belgia to ascertain the Belgian ruling stallion's stance on the coming war. The council members filed out amid many mumblings and grumblings. Pyrios thought the whole idea of the Registry ridiculous at this point. In his opinion, the countries were well beyond negotiating a settlement.

Not that he planned on joining the Imperial Cavalry any time in the near future. Thracis was the fighter. Pyrios couldn't stand the idea of weeks or months out in the open, no mares around and training day in and day out when the soldiers weren't fighting.

Although, given his current situation, a lack of feminine attention might be a good thing.

As he stepped into the cool autumn evening, Pyrios quickened his pace. He had tried, unsuccessfully, to avoid Lady Nerissa. But even three days away from the Kigerian mare was too much. She was like some kind of drug he couldn't live without. He wondered, not for the first time, if she had put some kind of spell on him. He had heard such things were possible with the aid of love talismans and mental suggestion.

At this point it doesn't matter, Pyrios thought as he trotted down an avenue to the secluded spot where he and Lady Nerissa had been meeting recently. Earlier in the affair they had met at upscale boarding stables, Nerissa always insisting on superb service staff. Just lately, she had been bringing him to more natural settings, far from the interior bustle of the city. Pyrios had thought this change odd, given Nerissa's preference for her creature comforts, but she explained that she missed her Kiger homeland and wanted to get back in touch with a semblance of wildness. Pyrios wasn't sure if he believed this explanation, but he did like the privacy. He was tired of judging glares and open curtness.

By now Lord Kantaka and Phlegon had stopped asking Pyrios where he spent the majority of his afternoons. Both had given up on him as a lost cause and Lord Kantaka's only conciliation was that at least Pyrios was being more discreet. Pyrios believed that if Lord Kantaka didn't believe he was important to the Baroquian Pact, he would have been sent back to his home stable of Thetis long ago. Phlegon didn't bother hiding his disapproval any longer and often made snide comments whenever Pyrios came stumbling into Lord Kantaka's stable late at night.

Pyrios turned down a tree lined lane and entered a small park. The first time Pyrios had met Nerissa here he had noted that the park was surrounded by large trees which created a privacy screen. The park boasted several secluded meadows, most overgrown with witchgrass and brambles, testifying to their lack of use. In all their meetings here, Pyrios could only recall meeting one other couple, two younger horses who were obviously embarrassed that their sanctuary had been discovered. Pyrios hadn't seen them since that one encounter.

Lady Nerissa was standing in the center of the meadow farthest from the park's entrance. Her sides with damp with sweat, as if she had been running. Her mane was in disarray.

When Pyrios approached, she swung to face him and flared her nostrils.

Instinct gripped him, adrenalin pouring into his system. A mare, any mare, in this physical state and nervous at the approach of a known stallion brought all a stallion's protectiveness to the forefront. He raised his head and sniffed the air. No scent of a male horse anywhere, no mare's scent either, other than Nerissa's. He was confused. Maybe she had outrun whoever had done this to her.

"What has happened?" he demanded.

"My guards. One of them attacked me. I fought him off. I don't know what happened to the other. He wasn't around when I was attacked." She spoke as if she were trying to catch her breath. Her sides heaved slightly and she looked around the meadow. "I ran away after I kicked in his knee."

"Where did this happen?"

"A few streets from here."

"Why didn't you find a constable?"

She barked harsh laughter. "And what would I say? 'Could you please arrest this stallion, sir? He's keeping me from my lover'?"

Pyrios felt his anger begin to ebb. "You wouldn't have to say it like that. What were your guards doing with you anyway? I thought you made them stay at the stable when you came to see me." Actually, she had made a point of telling him that she left the guards to their own devices on purpose to anger her mate.

"I tried to make them stay. He must have followed me and found out what I was doing. He was forcing me to go back to the stable and wait for Alexi."

Panic flared in Pyrios' mind. "Will he tell your mate?" *Because if he does, the scandal will ruin Lord Kantaka*, he thought but didn't add.

"No. With these bruises all I have to do is bat my eyes and tell my mate that the guard wants me for himself and will tell Alexi anything to have me turned out." She was moving closer to him.

He reached his nose out to reassure her and something in her scent made him pause. She smelled anxious, which he expected, what startled him was the hint of anger. He stepped back. "Won't Lord Alexi wonder what has happened to the guard?"

Nerissa pinned her ears at his withdrawal. "I told you. I'll tell him the guard wanted me for himself. I am adept at controlling my mate."

I'm sure you are. "I was only asking. You do not need to vent your anger on me."

She blinked at him. "I have to vent it at someone. That guard had no right to treat me like common street trash. I am lady to the ruling stallion of Kigeria. I will be treated with respect."

Pyrios had heard a variation of this speech before. Lady Nerissa liked to have her station in society addressed with every opportunity. He let her continue her tirade for several minutes before saying, "Why does your mate insist that you have guards in the first place? Doesn't he know you're safe in Lipizza?"

"He still thinks we are in our home territory. Kigeria is not as, civilized, as Lipizza." She was moving against him, rubbing her cheek along his spine.

Normally, that sensation would have him begging for more, but today it made his skin twitch. Something was off here. He shifted, trying to put space between them. He remembered trying to get away from her weeks ago and now wondered if he had made a mistake by going back to her.

"After this maybe we should spend some time apart."

Nerissa stiffened against him and Pyrios knew he had made a mistake.

"Are you trying to leave me, stallion of Thetis Stable?" Her voice was ice.

He walked away to the far side of the meadow. Had Thracis been there, he would have scolded Pyrios for letting a potential threat get between him and the meadow's exit. But Pyrios didn't really believe Nerissa would hurt him physically. She was more apt to try and destroy his reputation. "I just think we should let things settle. You know all your society lady friends will want to talk to you about the incident once they find out."

"They can wait."

Thracis would have heard the threat, felt the danger, but Pyrios continued to leave his back to her. "I'm sure Lord Alexi will want you to stay close to the stable in the coming days."

"I've had quite enough of a stallion's control."

Pyrios' ears flicked back as he heard the sound of armor being engaged. Her harness was so decorative, Pyrios hadn't noticed it was an armor harness. He only thought she was wearing the harness as some new societal fashion. He whirled around in time to for a raptor to slice through his shoulder. Pain, sharp and burning, rushed up his chest.

Confused, aware that he wasn't wearing his harness and therefore had no protection, Pyrios backed away. "What are you doing?"

"Something I would have done a long time ago if you hadn't proved so amusing." She fired another raptor, this one at his face.

Pyrios jumped sideways, avoiding a direct hit, but feeling the blades sliding along his flank. He was no match for her without armor. He bolted toward her, intending to dodge around her and out of the park.

She saw him coming and rather than yield to the heavier opponent, she threw herself at him. They collided with a metal hitting flesh sound. Pyrios was knocked back a few steps, more out of surprise than because Nerissa was any stronger. Before he could get space between them, he felt spikes drive into his skin, burying themselves into his muscles.

He squealed and pulled back, trying to get away. She was on him again, this time spinning around to kick his already damaged shoulder. Pyrios went down on one knee and she kicked again, connecting with his face.

White sparks bloomed in Pyrios' mind as blood began to drip from his nostrils. In his panic, he didn't think to contact Phlegon or Lord Kantaka. Scrambling to his feet, he shoved forward, the spikes on her armor making new holes, and pushed around her.

The exit was in reach but before he could make a run for it his legs were entangled by wire. Bolos were a common weapon used by Equines, especially mares. Pyrios collapsed to the ground, trying to keep from straining against the sharp wire and straining anyway, his panic stampeding out of control.

Nerissa came to stand over him. "And to think my contacts thought you would be too much for me to handle."

CHAPTER 29

Thracis! Thracis, wake up!

Thracis rolled over, gathering his legs underneath himself, shaking his head to clear away the sleep. Next to him Psyche shifted but didn't wake.

Thracis.

The mind contacting him was familiar, but Thracis couldn't place it. Mostly because the other horse was in such a state of panic. It wasn't Pyrios. Was it Phlegon?

Phlegon? Is that you?

Yes. Are you well? Are those around you safe?

What was Phlegon prattling on about? Thracis got to his feet and stepped out of the bedding box. His mind was getting sharper by the moment, but he still felt two steps behind this conversation.

Everyone is fine. What has happened?

The link filled with despair. *It's Pyrios. He's gone. We've searched the entire city and found nothing except a park meadow sprayed with blood.*

Pyrios? Blood? That got Thracis' attention and he focused on the voice in his head. *What's been happening?*

Phlegon immediately filled Thracis in on his brother's affairs in Lipizza, both ethical and unethical. It didn't take long with their minds linked the way they were. Most of what Phlegon explained Thracis could see for himself, shining bright in Phlegon's mind. Phlegon, like Thracis before his weeks of training with the delphae, did not know how to shield the inner layers of his mind from another horse. Thracis felt angry frustration surge through him. Pyrios and his mares, Pyrios and his ladies, his ridiculous philandering. Now it had finally caught up with him.

Was it a jealous stallion? The lady's mate? That made the most sense to Thracis.

We don't know. We don't think so. The lady in question, Lady Nerissa, is mate to the ruling stallion of Kigeria, Thracis felt his stomach turn at the sound of that. Phelgon didn't notice the revulsion and continued, *has gone missing as well. We think she may have Baroquian contacts.*

What does her mate say? Thracis could hear Psyche getting up behind him. Soon she would start asking him what was going on and he wasn't skilled enough to hold two conversations, one in his head and one in the stall, at the same time.

*He says he hasn't seen his lady for two days. He also says she's been sparring extra hard the last few weeks._*The last line carried an ominous weight.

What is being done? Psyche had come up behind him and was resting her nose against his flank for support. Thracis silently thanked her for giving him the chance to finish with Phlegon.

Lord Kantaka has informed your sire. The soldiers around your home stable have been doubled. Commander Dias is using every resource to locate Pyrios.

I'll be there as soon as I can.

A pause in the link between them. Then, *Lord Kantaka thinks you should either stay put or go to Thetis Stable. In reality, there really is nothing you can do here.*

I can bring horses who can help.

Lord Kantaka wants you to stay away. Sympathy filled the link. *He worries the Baroquians are using this as a trap to get to you. I will make sure no one stops looking for Pyrios.*

Not wanting to ask the question, but needing to know, Thracis said, *Have you tried to contact Pyrios' mind?* His muscles felt like wire-wrapped frames as he waited for Phlegon to respond. If he said he felt nothing then Pyrios was already gone to Tranquility and Thracis could mourn his passing.

When I try to contact him, all I see is mist.

Mist, not the nothing of death. Thracis exhaled an explosion of pent-up breath. *Fine. I will discuss the matter with my companions and then most likely return to my home stable.*

I am sorry to bring you such ill news. Travel safe, Thracis. May Lord Pegasus watch over you. The link broke.

Thracis closed his eyes and took a few steadying breaths before turning to Psyche. "My brother has gone missing."

"There is no question that Thracis must return to Thetis Stable. He needs to be with his herd at this time."

Lady Aldara's voice rang out in the informal meeting chamber. Eno's herd was present, as well as Anneke and Beryl. Thracis had told them all what Phlegon had told him and then Lady Aldara had spent several hours contacting her own spy network to confirm what Phlegon was saying. Like those helping Lord Kantaka, Lady Aldara's spies had been unable to locate either Pyrios or Lady Nerissa. However, one spy did verify that Lady Nerissa did have Baroquian contacts and that it was rumored that she had been planning on joining the Baroquian forces in Friesia.

"My suggestion is for all of you to join him." She stomped her front foot at Eno and Alcina's protests. "Haidee will remain here to recover. When she is well, I will have an escort sent for her to take her back to Boudica. In the meantime, Eno has made a stock prototype from which more flying harnesses can be made." Lady Aldara nodded to Beryl. "Beryl will notify a herd of Morgans known for their metal crafting abilities. We will coordinate a group to join you in Calabria where achillium is abundant so they may harvest as much as they need to make the equipment you require. In the meantime, Master Phrenicos will begin construction on a building for the creation and assembling of the harnesses. I am sure Queen Hippolyta will help him."

"Will you begin creating more harnesses even if I am detained in Calabria?" Everyone could hear the hurt in Eno's voice.

"We will only if you give us leave. However, I would discourage this course of action. Eno should be present when the harnesses are being assembled to halt mistakes before they happen."

Eno breathed a sigh of relief. In time she would likely be persuaded to yield some of her control to a few choice horses, but not in the near future.

"When will our harnesses be ready, Lady?" Thracis tried to keep his voice polite, but the delay in leaving was chafing him raw.

Anneke answered. "You will be ready to depart at first light. We will see to the preparations. You should all rest tonight. Your journey will be long and hard, even with the wings."

Thracis glanced at Titania. The Clydesdale pinned her ears at him. "Don't fret over me, foolish colt. Neema and I will keep up."

"In truth I was wondering if you would be able to carry any extra supplies."

Titania snapped her teeth at him. "You are not safe from my hooves just because you are Psyche's mate."

"I hadn't thought so."

"If the two of you are quite finished," Lady Aldara said dryly, "I think all of you should begin preparations to leave. Psyche, I will need a list of all the salves you are using on Haidee. Eno, make sure to leave specific instructions for what you need to create your harnesses."

Having received their instructions, the horses left the meeting chamber. Thracis wanted to go out into the arena and work off some of his nervous energy, but knew he would need all his strength in the days to come. Snorting in frustration, he decided to go for a walk instead.

"Care if I join you?"

Thracis eyed Alcina, not sure if he had a choice in the matter. "Are you sure? Do you need to help Eno?"

Laughing a little, she fell into step next to him. "I think Eno has all the help she needs. And Psyche is helping Aeos, so you can keep me company."

He didn't trust this new, almost flirtatious attitude. Alcina was blunt and driven and never hid her distrust or dislike of stallions for the injuries she had suffered long ago. Asking if she could follow him around the Arachnae Stable's lands put him on edge.

"You can relax, foolish colt. I need to stretch my muscles as per Psyche's orders. I'm still stiff from the other day." Her voice lowered. "And it would be good for me to get away from the others for a little while."

From the other mares was what she meant and Thracis knew it. Alcina was strong, but she was also a horse and not made of achillium. She felt great sorrow for the loss of Dysis, it was in every line of her body. She wanted to grieve for Dysis but wished to do it in her own way. And that meant not feeling pitied by the other mares. Thracis had never asked Aeos, who had spent a night with Dysis, but he had a feeling the two mares shared a bond that went much further than friendship. In the short time he had known them, that night with Aeos was the only time Thracis had seen either mare with a stallion. Alcina wanted to spend time with Aeos or Thracis because she knew the stallions wouldn't ask if she were well and if she needed anything. They were too scared of retaliation, if the truth be known.

"The snow is beginning to stick. It's good we're leaving in the morning." Alcina's coat had lost its summer gloss and looked thick and rough. Thracis doubted she was very uncomfortable in the day's cold.

"Is Eno worried about ice forming on the wings?" Until Alcina noted the snow Thracis hadn't thought about what would happen if they tried to fly in frigid air. Of course, if the air was cold enough that ice formed on the wings or on the frames, the Equines themselves would not survive. Unless they wore the stretchy body coverings used by the Imperial Cavalry soldiers or those Equines that insisted on exercising outdoors no matter what the weather.

"No, she worked heat tapes into the frames that will help melt any ice. She thinks of everything, Thracis, that's why she's so methodical."

"And why her harnesses are superior to the ones made by the Baroquians."

"Exactly. Except that Zeva is very smart. She will take this attack as a learning experience and improve her design, like Eno said." Alcina shuddered. "I think her design works well enough already."

"Are you nervous about flying again?" Alcina had not been in the air since the attack.

She thought about it. Weighing whether or not she was going to show any weakness, Thracis thought. "A little, but not because I fear another attack. The fall scared me. It was the first time I lost control. It was a sobering experience."

"Well, I hope you get your spine back fast because I have to get home and I don't want to hear you whining about not being able to keep up." She reached over and bit him. Hard. Thracis didn't mind though. That was the Alcina he knew. Besides, pricking at her pride was the best way to make her prove a point.

They were walking down a lane that would have been lined with thickly leaved trees in the spring and summer, making it a cool and shadowed place for a stroll. Today, with all the leaves fallen and blown into drifts, the lane led between skeletal Felisian arms reaching up to the sky, the tallest branches hooked into sharpened claws. Beautiful in their way, but Thracis had a new respect for the trees now that he had flown above them. Falling into one of these would guarantee torn skin and broken bones.

"Eno has decided on both projectile and close combat weapons for the harnesses. She has also converted our original armor harnesses to engage around the flying harnesses."

That was something else Thracis hadn't thought about. When they practiced flying, none of them used their armor. Thank Lord Pegasus Eno had the foresight to realize they would need armor in combat. "Do you think we should be armored on the journey?"

"It would be prudent."

"May I ask you a question?"

He saw her stiffen next to him. "You may ask but I withhold the right not to answer."

He nodded. "Why do you think no one can find my brother?" Thracis had his own suspicions, but he needed to hear them echoed by another horse.

Alcina seemed to try several responses and found none of them to her liking. Finally, she said, "He has been taken for questioning."

"You mean tortured until he tells them what they want to know."

"Yes."

Silence. The sound of hooves on dirt and light snow. A crow cawing. Small rustlings in the fallen leaves as little animals foraged for the last nuts before the true snows fell.

Alcina kept her peace, waiting for him to begin the conversation again. Thracis thanked her for that. He knew he should share his fears with Psyche, but he was too close to her, and he knew she would only try to make him feel better about the situation. What he wanted was someone who would tell him the truth. Alcander would have been the most logical choice, but Thracis had enough worry without bringing up bad memories for the miniature.

They all knew the miniature was embroiled in his own emotional distress over Pyrios. He had met Pyrios when Thracis had been injured and had liked the older brother. Pyrios had treated Alcander like an equal, like something more than a gelding. Alcander would never forget that. The thought that Pyrios would share Alcander's fate had crossed all their minds.

"If we find Pyrios, if we get him back, he will not survive as a gelding." Thracis' voice held all his anger and worry.

"A gelding may still perform."

Startled that Alcina knew exactly what the problem was, Thracis stared at the mare.

"Psyche has told us of your brother's affinity for mares. As has Aeos. No, he will not be able to produce heirs, but he can still manage. I have heard that others have."

He wondered if she was speaking of Alcander and thought it better not to ask. "He will never be accepted into the life he knows, never be welcome back to any court. The taboo of being gelded is too strong."

"So, he will have to make a new life. Settle down near your herd and maybe find a mare to be loyal to. Perhaps one that already has a foal or two."

"I expected you to be more harsh." Admitting that took courage, but he was so stunned by the turn of conversation that he hardly noticed.

"I am being realistic. Your brother is young, if Lord Pegasus is kind he will learn to adapt."

Thracis tossed his head. "He is very stubborn."

Alcina gave him an even stare. "Thracis, if you find your brother or if he escapes where he now is, you will find him much changed. Whether he is gelded or not."

They had reached the end of the lane. He stood and pawed the ground, trying to get rid of some of his anxiety. Alcina took the break to stretch her back and neck. In his preoccupation with Pyrios, Thracis hadn't noticed how stiff she was moving.

"I wish I had been with him."

"Your paths were meant to part. If you had been in Lipizza, it might well be you in Baroquian hooves."

"I'm stronger than he is."

Alcina twitched a shoulder. "None of us know how strong we can be until we are tested. He may surprise you."

Thracis turned and began walking again. He needed to walk, needed to move. Standing would only aggravate him more. "I hope you're right."

Alcina flicked her ears as they walked, listening to the sounds of the winter forest. "Have you spoken with your parents?"

"Yes." He had contacted both his parents after Phlegon's frantic report. They already knew of Pyrios' disappearance and were concerned about Thracis. Neither had wanted him to come home if it would disrupt his training, but their relief was palpable when he told them he would be coming regardless of training. He had not told them he would be bringing friends. He was deciding whether he should or whether he and his herd should just show up. "I haven't told them yet that you are all coming with me."

"Maybe you should wait on that. Playing host to the daughter of the Asapatish, several rogue mares, not to mention a princess, would be intimidating to anyone."

Thracis laughed. "You've never met my parents. They'll welcome the company and all the disruption that comes with it."

"You've been away for a long time?" She sounded curious. Thracis noticed her stiffness and checked his stride to walk with her. If Alcina noticed, she gave no sign.

"Too long. My dam was still round with my younger sister before I left. Now she's passed her first year." Thracis regretted not seeing his youngest sibling, but it hurt his heart more that Pyrios had not met her either. And now he might not ever.

Not wanting to sour his uplifted mood, Alcina said, "Well then we'll see what this filly is made of when we all arrive together. Perhaps Eno should bring an extra harness."

Thracis' laugh startled several starlings. They flew into the gray sky, filling the air with the sound of flapping wings.

CHAPTER 30

To what do I owe the honor of this contact?

Psyche fidgeted. She was taking a large risk by contacting Lady Dendera. The Felisian was a member of Queen Hippolyta's council and leader of the most lethal Felisians known on the planet. Her group was trained in covert battle operations and unconventional attack strategies. They were the ones responsible for the destruction of the Baroquian ships during the Diomedean battle which cut off all retreat for the invaders. They would be Pyrios' best chance of rescue. However, as a member of Queen Hippolyta's court, Psyche couldn't be sure Lady Dendera would keep Psyche's request to herself.

The black and white mare took a deep breath to settle herself. *I need a favor.*

Personal or a favor to the court?

Here was the problem. While rescuing Pyrios would be beneficial to everyone, Diomedea had withdrawn from the rest of Equus because of the unfair treatment Diomedean representatives received from the Registry of Breeds. Psyche would have to tread carefully. *Personal, but beneficial to my dam.*

Amusement filled the link. No doubt all of Hippolyta's court knew about Psyche and Thracis. *Does it have something to do with the stallion you're playing with?*

Refusing to rise to the bait, Psyche kept her mind neutral. *It does. His brother has been taken by the Baroquians.*

Unfortunate, but I fail to see how this is a Diomedean problem.

His name is Zephyros Pyrios. His sire is the ruling stallion of Calabria. That should be of interest to my dam.

Lady Dendera's mind sharpened, Psyche felt it. It was like claws sharpening on fabric. *They could use him as a bargaining tool to obtain achillium or find out about hidden deposits and Calabrian defenses.*

Psyche was quiet. In the link between them she could sense Lady Dendera thinking about the ramifications of Pyrios' capture. After a few minutes the Felisian said, *I will have to tell Queen Hippolyta, but I will keep the personal connection out of it for the moment.*

My dam will still know.

Lady Psyche, I must inform the queen of all my operations. She must be made aware that I will not be at her disposal for some time.

Psyche felt hope pulse through her. *Does that mean you will help?*

It means I will do what I can.

Sighing, Psyche left her stall and went to find Thracis. He should be back from his walk with Alcina. She wouldn't tell him about her conversation with Lady Dendera for the moment. Not until the Felisian contacted her and let her know if she and her cats had leave to rescue Pyrios. No point in getting Thracis' hopes up.

CHAPTER 31

"Slow down, Thracis, you'll tear your wings if you keep up this pace."

Thracis pinned his ears but dropped back to soar next to Aeos. He was flying point, the others forming the rest of the V behind him. They were supposed to rotate the point position, but Thracis had insisted on leading since they left Arachnae Stable three days ago. He was also carrying more than his share of equipment. Knowing this stubbornness couldn't last forever, that his body would give out eventually, the others had decided to humor him.

"We've got the wind at our back and are making excellent time." Aeos spoke with his customary bored expression. "Why don't you relax and enjoy the scenery."

"We have to push in case we run into weather. That will be more likely the farther north we get."

"I'm sure. I know there's usually a foot of snow on the ground in Acarnia this time of year."

"So we have to keep going."

Aeos snorted. "No one has suggested we stop early, although we will have to stop for the midday meal soon."

"And spend two hours wandering the countryside."

Aeos flew close, the wind from his wings buffeting Thracis and sending him into a wobble. Thracis snapped his teeth. "What was that for?"

"For acting like an idiot. You know we all have to walk around to keep ourselves limber."

"This is still taking too long. Maybe we should have hired a transport."

"With a lot of stallions asking questions about a herd of Diomedean mares traveling to Calabria? Thank you but I'd rather fly."

Thracis tossed his head.

Ignoring him, Aeos scanned the ground for a suitable place to land. They were carrying as much grain as they could because grass would be scarce with the snow. So far they had stayed in the wild, avoiding settlements and questions. They would continue to do so for as long as they could, but they would have to make a supply stop somewhere between here and Calabria, no matter what Thracis thought.

Seeing an open field with plenty of room for landing and take off, Aeos called, "Down there."

The mares angled themselves downward. Thracis tossed his head again and followed. He hated to delay but he thought they could go longer in the afternoon if they stopped this early. If not Aeos would have to deal with his complaining all night and into the next morning.

Landing close to Psyche, Thracis was appalled when he sank into snow up to his knees. "Well, this is just wonderful."

"Stop whining so much, Thracis," Psyche snipped. The mare had been in a bad mood since they took off this morning. Thracis chalked it up to a rough night and thought nothing of it.

"Snow feels good on my legs," Titania said. "How are you fairing, Alcander?"

The miniature was standing higher up on the snow but the white drifts were touching his belly. "Quite fine. We should move that way, the wind will have dusted off that end of this plateau."

They breasted their way through the snow. Alcander went last, after the others had created a clear path for him to follow. Neema had no difficulty with the snow. The calico hopped along as if she were walking on solid ground. She had a pouch filled with dried meat but so far had been able to hunt for meals. Thracis doubted she would bring down any game here, but she had surprised him before.

Alcander was right, the northern area of the plateau was only covered with half a foot of snow. Here and there tufts of winter grasses peeked through the layer of white. Neema immediately began inspecting the area for foolish mice who had grown sluggish with the cold. Thracis pawed the ground until he had a clear patch on which to eat his grain. He unpacked a small amount and dropped it on the ground.

They ate in silence for a little while, then a rustling caught their attention. Neema, her jaws clamped around a very fat rodent, strode through the group with tail high. She settled herself between everyone and began to dissect her meal. Thracis watched, fascinated, for several minutes before realizing his own appetite had vanished.

"Must you share that with everyone?" Aeos was nibbling the last few bits of grain from the dirt.

"Equines are so squeamish about hunters. Not all of us can live on bits of grass and dried seeds."

"Equines are squeamish because your large cousins, the ligers, see us as prey and will take one of us down if given half an opportunity," Eno observed.

"How are you feeling?" Aeos was moving to inspect Titania's wounds. They were healing well, but she was still pained by the deep gash she had gotten at the Diomedean battle. That wound would pain her for the rest of her life on cold and rainy days.

"I am doing well."

"We will slow the pace a bit." Aeos cocked a back leg at Thracis as he spoke, ready to kick. "You will have to be in the best possible shape when we arrive in Calabria. We have no idea what will be waiting for us."

"What do you mean?" Thracis lowered his ears.

"That the Baroquians may not be content to capture one member of your herd."

Thracis flinched away from the thought of his dam and sister being attacked.

"They are being protected by Imperial soldiers. You would be informed if anything out of the ordinary happened." Psyche's voice was soothing but not patronizing. "We must arrive ready for battle just in case."

"You're both right, but I can't help feeling worried."

"We all know that, Thracis." Eno spoke distractedly. She was inspecting harnesses and shifting equipment. "That's why we haven't been arguing with you over every little thing." Her tone implied this was a great kindness on her part.

Alcina and Alcander looked over from a private conversation. "We think that if the weather holds, we should be at Thetis Stable in a week. Maybe less if the wind stays at our backs," the miniature explained.

"I don't think we'll be going anywhere for the rest of today," Neema said mildly.

Thracis looked at her, puzzled. She pointed with an orange paw. Dark clouds were gathering in the direction they had to travel. The wind changed and Thracis felt the icy bite of a winter storm.

"We must find shelter," Alcander launched himself skyward. "I'll fly over the valley and see what I can find." He flew off before anyone could protest.

Thracis opened his mouth to complain about the delay when pain ripped through his mind. He squealed, dropping to his knees and slamming his head into the ground, trying to get those claws out of his head.

Instantly Psyche was in his mind, wrapping him in a protective shield. He could see her, shimmering as if a sheet of falling water were separating them. She reared, striking at an enemy he couldn't see. Then she dropped to all fours, and Thracis could feel her trying to communicate with whatever was in his head. Aeos appeared looking surprised and concerned. He brushed up against Psyche, laying his head along her back.

Thracis felt a pang of jealousy before he realized what Aeos was doing. The dun stallion was giving Psyche access to his mind, boosting her own mental reservoirs. Alcina wavered into view and pressed herself to Psyche's other side.

Thracis could no longer see the thing that had flown through his mind, ripping and tearing its way through his various layers. Psyche was concentrating on something, though. Thracis saw the shield around himself slowly dissipate. He approached the others in his mind. Psyche turned to looked at him, her eyes liquid pools of compassion.

Your brother is alive.

Thracis' heart began to pound. *Where?*

I can't. The others began to waver, their bodies beginning to fade. Psyche tried again. *We can't talk here.* They all vanished.

Thracis blinked his eyes and was confused to find himself laying in the snow. His head ached and his mind trembled. Why did everyone have to attack his head?

"Are you alright?" Eno was looking from Psyche to Thracis to Aeos to Alcina seeming unable to decide who was in the most distress.

"We're fine," Aeos said. He searched the sky for Alcander, they needed to find shelter to rest.

"Was that Pyrios? Was he trying to contact me?" Thracis couldn't believe his brother would try to hurt him, but if Pyrios was being tortured, he might not know what he was doing.

"It was. His mind is fragmenting, trying to find solace in the familiar." Psyche kept her voice even. The others found reasons to move off a little and give them privacy. "I calmed him down a bit and gave him a place of refuge. Creating for a mind that far away, even with help from others, is difficult and draining." She did look diminished. Thracis was suddenly glad they wouldn't be moving on today.

"Will it keep him sane?" Thracis wasn't sure if he wanted the answer.

"For a time. I hid it as well as I could but my sister will find it eventually."

"Then she'll come after you for interfering?"

Psyche tossed her head and barred her teeth. "I welcome that confrontation. You are my mate and that makes Pyrios part of my herd by default."

Thracis was staggered by her ferocity. He had never thought of mares being that territorial. It was a new facet of her personality and something that made him want her with deeper passion. A mate who was also strong enough to protect what she held dear.

Alcander hovered above them. "Follow the valley ridge. A hundred yards that way." He struck out with a hoof. "A line of spruces will give us cover from the wind on one side and the mountain wall rises on another."

"Can we fly?" Titania was looking at the snow drifts between them and the trees.

"Yes."

A gust of wind tore through their manes.

"We had better go then," Alcina said.

The short flight and subsequent landings tested all their ability. Alcander was right; the spruces did give them adequate cover. Between the mountain and the snow that had filled open spaces between the trees, the area was well protected. Their heavy coats would keep them warm but they were each carrying winter blankets. They removed their harness, stacking the equipment in a niche in the rock, and shrugged into the heavy blankets. By then the storm was almost on top of them. They huddled together, turning their rumps into the wind and burying their heads against one another.

As they settled in to wait out the storm, Thracis hoped that whatever sanctuary Psyche had created for Pyrios would be enough to keep him sane until he was rescued.

CHAPTER 32

Pyrios shuddered in the small cave he had found in this world of swirling mists. If he had ever pursued an *ammoni* mare she could have told him about the Deceptive Mists, and that would have allayed some of his fear. But he had not and so was terrified. Besides the monstrous predators that lurked in this place, the lack of a name for where he was made his panic even greater. His complete disorientation was compounded by his lack of knowledge of how he came to this place.

He remembered meeting Nerissa in the park and he remembered that she seemed unhappy with him about something. However, Pyrios had no memory of the fight that had followed. Zeva's first order for the Equines who were transporting Pyrios to Baroquian lands had been to erase his short-term memory. The transporters were not fully-trained *ammoni* and therefore Pyrios retained partial memories.

When he awakened, Pyrios had been in this strange world made of gossamer mists and spongy ground that gave him no firm footing. Horrified, Pyrios had bolted, running in a frenzy of different directions until he was exhausted as well as scared.

As his heart began to beat more slowly, the voices had begun. Sneering female voices asking him question after question about Thracis. Why did everyone want to know about Thracis? While the voices spoke out of the surrounding fog, Pyrios felt sharpened hooves pawing at his mind.

Pyrios had never received any training in the psychic arts and relied entirely on instinct. Like his brother, he had a formidable, though undeveloped, talent, and was able to avoid Zeva and her assailants with more tenacity than the mares expected. He broke free every time they ensnared him in invisible ropes and dodged around all the monsters they projected into his mind to drive him insane. But even instinct has limits.

He was nearing the end of his endurance and his sanity, when another voice called to him. At first Pyrios shied away, afraid it was some new trick devised by his captors. Then the voice had begun to whisper instructions and when he let himself reach out to that mind, he felt the familiarity. Psyche. Thracis' mate. The mare from Iliad. She led him to this place and shrouded it somehow. She told him to be still and help would come.

Hours passed, maybe days. It was impossible to tell time trapped in his own mind. Occasionally a predator would pass by the entrance of the cave, but they never noticed Pyrios' hiding spot. He didn't give himself the luxury of believing he could hide in this cave forever. Eventually, the mares, most importantly the one who called herself Zeva, would discover his location. But for the moment, he would thank Lord Pegasus and Lady Psyche for this reprieve.

And he would wait.

CHAPTER 33

Concealed under a smooth blanket of snow, the rolling hills of Calabria spread out beneath Thracis and his small herd. Ten days had passed since the storm that had kept them in the mountains for almost two days. It was the only one they encountered and they counted themselves very lucky. Thracis had slowed the pace a bit, but the wind had been steady at their backs, pushing them towards his homeland.

Lady Dendera had contacted Psyche and the black and white mare reported that the Felisians had been granted leave to attempt to locate and rescue Pyrios. Psyche had neglected to tell anyone other than Thracis about the thorough scolding she had received from Queen Hippolyta. To Thracis, Psyche seemed pleased rather than embarrassed by the scolding. He thought it strange but knew better than to mention it. He still refused to allow himself much hope but it was impossible to block out that glimmer completely.

Looking down at land that would be familiar even in the darkest night, Thracis felt his heart swell at the prospect of home. He had contacted his parents earlier in the day to let them know he would be bringing friends and that they would be arriving by air. He didn't want the soldiers protecting his family herd to open fire on he and his herd. He wanted to take Psyche on a private flight and show her all the places he held dear, but that would have to wait. He couldn't let the others arrive alone.

"We're almost there," Thracis called back to the others.

They whinnied in response. Psyche pumped her wings harder and drew abreast of Thracis. It was strange to see another horse fly, Thracis thought. Since they used their minds rather than their muscles to use the wings, it looked as though the wings moved of their own accord.

Psyche saw him watching her and tossed her head. "What?"

Thracis shook his mane. "I can't get used to the fact that our wings move even if our legs are still." Not that they kept their legs still. When using their wings, it helped them focus if they moved their legs as if running.

"I guess I never thought about it." She stretched her neck and looked into the distance. "Is that Thetis Stable?"

Thracis looked down at the cluster of buildings in the distance. He voiced a loud whinny and darted forward, forgetting Psyche and the others in his excitement. Home. It had been so long since he had seen the low buildings and gentle pastures. Diving low, he made a complete circle over the entire compound, whinnying frequently to call everyone out into the open.

Satisfied that he had sufficiently announced his presence, Thracis dove down to land in the center of a semi-circle of horses formed in the field in front of the main stable. The horses on the ground backed away in wonder of the multi-faceted wings. Thracis kept them open for a couple of minutes to give everyone a good look before folding them over his back. He was used to this attention. He and the others had caused quite a stir when they stopped to resupply during their journey.

He tossed his head at the collection of Equines. "Where is my sire?"

The horses moved, creating an open aisle. Thracis whinnied at the sight of his sire trotting toward him. Zephyros whinnied in response. He stopped in front of the son who had left a gangly youth trying to find his way and returned a muscular stallion confident of his place in the herd. The two horses danced around each other, both speaking at the same time so neither knew what the other was saying. Their chatter stopped as the mares and Aeos landed in the field behind Thracis.

"When you said you were bringing friends, I assumed you meant stallions," Zephyros observed. "This is much more interesting."

"Don't let any of those mares hear you say that."

"Are they all Diomedean?"

"More or less." Thracis cocked his head at Eno. "She is the daughter of the current Asapatish."

Zephyros walked toward the small cluster of mares and one stallion. He bowed his head in respect. "Welcome, friends of my son. You are guests in my stable. Please let me know of any-thing you need to make your stay more comfortable."

Seeing Eno open her mouth, Aeos spoke quickly, "That is very generous of you, Lord Zephyros. I am sure there are things you can acquire for us, but let us get settled in first."

Eno closed her mouth and nodded at Zephyros. Not before the older stallion saw the look she gave Aeos, however. He wondered what, exactly, he was letting into his stable. He raised his voice to be heard by all of them. "We have plenty of room for all of you to either have your own stalls or share if you wish. The soldiers built their own barracks several yards from the main compound." He looked at a black mare that was looking around with open hostility. "If any of them treats any of you with disrespect, I will deal with the offender personally."

The black mare regarded him, drawn by the steel she heard in his voice, and nodded. Zephyros turned away from them and back to Thracis.

Thracis listened to the exchange behind him with a cocked ear. He was scanning the crowd for his dam. When Zephyros joined him, he asked, "Where is my dam? Shouldn't she be here to welcome me home?"

Zephyros laughed. "She wanted to, but she and your sister had a difference of opinion this morning and now Aquina is confined to her stall. You dam is lying in wait in the stable in the event your sister tries to escape."

"Is she beautiful?" Thracis could hardly wait to glimpse his new sibling.

"She is all your dam and I hoped for." Zephyros looked over his back at the others. "Come, let's get in out of the cold."

Inside the stable, the newcomers were surrounded by servants, both Equine and Felisian, who helped remove and store the harnesses. As he was shrugging out of his armor harness, Thracis heard a familiar beat of hooves. He swung around and whinnied.

"Mother, I missed you so much in the past year." He ran to her, nuzzling her neck and shoulder.

Calypsa swung her head around to hug her youngest son. "I have missed you as well, my son."

"Mother, come here, I want you to meet someone."

Tossing her head in amusement, Calypsa followed her son.

"Mother, this is Lady Psyche."

"Thracis," the black and white mare ducked her head in embarrassment, "you could have given me a chance to clean up a little first."

Calypsa stepped forward before the younger mare could shrink away. "Forgive my son, dear, he's only a stallion." She tossed her head. "Come and let me look at you."

Psyche glared at Thracis and walked forward into an open area of the floor. She stood quietly as Calypsa circled her. "You're very pretty, Lady Psyche. My son has very good taste."

Psyche blushed with pleasure and Calypsa went on. "I think you, as well as your friends, deserve some pampering."

"My Lady, that really isn't necessary." Psyche meant to say more but Calypsa cut her off.

"It is necessary. Contrary to what all you youngsters may believe, my mate and I did our fair share of exploring and went on many adventures."

"Many of which they are too young to know about," Zephyros muttered.

Calypsa ignored him. "And I remember how much I valued a warm bath and a clean bedding box."

The new horses nodded reluctantly. Calypsa bobbed her head. "So, I propose that you all be taken to your stalls and given a chance to relax and freshen yourselves. By then it will be time for the evening meal and we can all learn about each other in comfort."

"And when will I be able to meet the newest herd member?" Thracis asked meekly.

His dam's ears lowered. "I think by then she will have calmed down enough for civil conversation."

Knowing better than to tease his dam when she used that tone, Thracis backed away. He did wonder how the sleeping arrangements would work. His stall, while spacious, was not equipped for two horses. And he was not going to point that out to his dam in a hall full of horses, both familiar and strange.

A Felisian hopped up on a pedestal and meowed to get everyone's attention. "If you will all follow me, I'll take you to your assigned wing."

The others followed the Felisian until only Thracis was left.

"What are you still doing here?" Zephyros asked.

"I thought I would have to go to my own stall."

"Why would you want to go there? It's not big enough for two."

Seeing the understanding in his sire's eyes, Thracis said, "Then I better hurry to catch up with my lady."

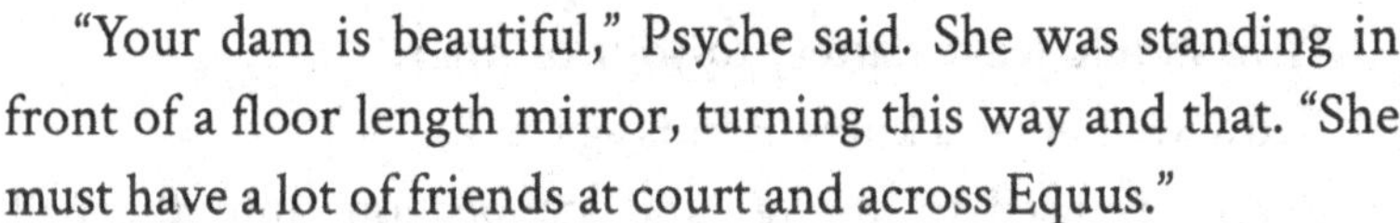

"Your dam is beautiful," Psyche said. She was standing in front of a floor length mirror, turning this way and that. "She must have a lot of friends at court and across Equus."

Thracis twitched a shoulder. "I guess she does." He was walking around the stall his parents had chosen for him and Psyche. It was a large stall reserved for high society guests. Thracis never imagined he would ever be staying here with a mare. It was exciting to him to be considered an adult but it was still embarrassing to realize that his parents would know the reason he wanted to share a stall with Psyche.

"And her friends would have daughters."

A danger here. Thracis focused his mind on the conversation. "I've met several of them."

"And?"

He walked over and nuzzled her withers. "And I have found them all lacking. You are who I want, Psyche. Nothing is going to change that."

"I am not like the mares you've known."

He nipped her gently. "My lady, that is why I'm with you and no one else. I need someone who can hold my heart and watch my back."

She turned and nuzzled his shoulder. "I can do that on the ground and in the air."

"Good to know."

"Are you two coming? I'm starving." A voice called from outside.

"Aeos seems happy to be close to home soil." Psyche walked to the door. "How do I look?"

Thracis tossed his head at her. "Better than any mare I've ever seen."

"You should leave flattery to your brother."

"How well do you know Pyrios again?"

Psyche refused to answer and stepped out into the hall where the others were waiting. All the mares had taken the time to wash and groom themselves until their coats were as presentable as possible. Aeos, in typical stallion fashion, washed himself until he was clean, ran a comb through his mane and tail and called it good. For the first time since Thracis had met them, Alcina and Titania actually looked nervous. Funny. They would charge into battle at the first war cry, but were fretting over one meal with a ruling stallion. Mares were strange, Thracis decided.

Of all of them, Alcander was the most put together. The gelding had cleaned his long coat until it gleamed and combed his mane and tail until they were free of all snarls. He had asked one of the Felisians to braid his mane along his neck and the top six inches of his tail. Thracis wondered what Alcander had been before he was captured by Zeva. Some sort of court appointed representative perhaps. So far, he hadn't seemed the least bit nervous.

Checking to make sure they were all ready, Thracis led the way to the dining hall. His parents were waiting for them at the entrance. He looked around but saw no young filly present.

Catching his look, his dam said, "Aquina is still sulking. Eventually she will get hungry enough to come down and join us. You and your brother always did."

Zephyros gave Thracis a knowing look but had enough sense not to laugh while his mate was present. "Please come and eat something. We've spent all day preparing for your arrival."

Thracis took his place next to his sire. It would have been Pyrios' spot if Pyrios had been there, but Zephyros had no objection to his younger son occupying the vacancy. Psyche stayed close to Thracis and the others fanned out from there. Every possible Calabrian delicacy was laid out on the table. Coupled with the Acarnian wine his sire had no doubt acquired from Aeos' sire, the meal would be unrivaled in all of Calabria tonight. The thought of Acarnian wine made Thracis wonder why Aeos' sire wasn't present. If Aeos thought it odd he would have mentioned it. Maybe Lord Quintus was planning on visiting Thetis Stable at a later time or maybe Aeos wanted to take Eno to his home stable of Acadia alone. Either way Thracis wasn't concerned unless Aeos brought up the topic.

"So, Lady Psyche, are you the youngest of Queen Hippolyta's daughters?" Calypsa's tone was mild enough, but Psyche had warned Thracis that this conversation was coming.

"I am, my lady. I have three older sisters. Two are in good standing. The other..." she trailed off.

"The other is involved with my older son's abduction," Zephyros finished for her.

Psyche tried to fold into herself. "Yes, my lord."

Calypsa reached across the table to nuzzle Psyche's ears. "Don't fret, little one. You cannot be held responsible for the actions of others. We realize that no matter what we think, eventually our children will make their own decisions. That is the way it must be."

"I only wish it had been someone else."

"As do we all," Zephyros said. "Tell me, what does your dam think of my son?"

Psyche shifted next to Thracis. "She has not met him yet."

Zephyros and Calypsa exchanged a look. Then Calypsa said, "Oh dear. I think I should learn as much as I can about you since my daughter will likely follow the path you have cut."

Thracis didn't know whether to rise to Psyche's defense or laugh. He hadn't met his sister yet and was already realizing that she was more of a hoofful than either he or Pyrios. Deciding anything he said would be wrong, Thracis concentrated on his meal.

"You think your dam will not approve?" Calypsa's voice held the edge it got whenever she felt one of her foals was being threatened.

"I think my dam wishes to choose any stallion I spend time with." The bitterness was clear in Psyche's voice and loud enough to draw attention from Eno and Aeos who were deep in a conversation about Acarnian wines.

"I see." Calypsa took a sip of wine before continuing. "Let me give you some advice, little filly. Introduce Thracis to your dam at the first opportunity. I cannot promise she will approve of my son but that doesn't matter. What matters is that you approve of him." She looked at Zephyros who was nodding.

"My mate speaks true. Until your dam and her court meet Thracis, they will speculate from dawn until dusk and all those speculations will be negative. Once they meet him, they will have a face instead of a name and they will know that he will stand by you no matter what they think." He looked at Thracis. "This tack will go a long way to making Queen Hippolyta amiable to your union."

"I don't think anything will make her amiable to a formal union. Diomedeans do not believe in such unions." The bitterness was gone from Psyche's voice, but Thracis knew the conversation was opening old wounds that would leak for the remainder of the evening.

"That will be something you will have to decide." Calypsa was watching the other mares from Diomedea. "I know quite a bit of Diomedean history and I will tell all of you ladies this, many of the doctrines and traditions of Diomedea came about as a way to protect the mares who lived there. From that time to this, much has changed. Including the way the younger generations think. Break with tradition if you must but always remember that those traditions served an important purpose that made you the horses you are today."

The mares all nodded at Lady Calypsa. Thracis only stared at his dam in wonder. He had never known she was so learned. He did know she had spent many years studying at the Piber University, but he never knew the subjects. He was also in shock over her earlier comment about adventuring with his sire. He never knew about that either. He doubted if Pyrios knew any of this.

"Now on to other business." Zephyros drew everyone's attention. "I have noticed that a gelding has come into my stable. While I do not doubt his integrity given his traveling companions, I would like to know how he knows all the court protocols while most of you do not."

All heads swung to face Alcander, quietly eating and listening to the conversations going on around him. The miniature finished his mouthful of grain before replying. "I attended the Levadian court before being captured. I was the personal assistant to a minor lord and was given all the privileges accorded my position. After my captivity, I was no longer welcome."

The speech must have hurt the miniature, but he gave no sign to his inner feelings. Instead he turned to face Zephyros. "If you wish for me to depart, I will leave as soon as the meal is over."

"I wish no such thing. In fact, I might have a job for you while you are here if you are agreeable. I'm in need of someone who knows the intricacies of court life to help me get some of these Felisian kittens out of my stable."

Alcander raised his ears. "I would be interested in helping you, my lord. I will have to have leave from Eno first."

"Ah yes, that brings us to you, Lady Eno."

Eno shifted under Zephyros' gaze. "Yes, my lord?"

"What are your intentions, now that you are here?"

"I was planning on continuing my fabrication of the winged harnesses. I was hoping you would allow me use of your achillium as it is durable yet light. We were eager to obtain limited mining rights and sending large amounts of achillium back to Boudica for the metalworkers."

The ruling stallion sat back on his heels. "Let me first say I have met Commander Dias and there is no doubt that you are his daughter. "

Eno lowered her head in embarrassment.

Zephyros continued, "That being said, I think I may be able to help you. Tomorrow you and I can go over mining rights with my business manager. They will be limited, I grant you, but I'm sure we can come to an agreement."

Eno nodded. "I thank you in advance, my lord."

Thracis noticed that Psyche had eaten most of what was on her plate and thought she must have settled some. That was good. He hadn't been looking forward to her tossing and turning the whole night through.

"So how long does it take to master the air?" Zephyros was asking when a clatter of hooves sounded down the hall. Calypsa immediately left the table and went to intercept whatever was causing the racket.

"Who is that?" Thracis asked. He knew if it was some emergency, his sire would have been contacted before a messenger interrupted the meal.

"That, my son, is your darling sister."

Thracis looked at the entrance to the dining hall with new interest. Calypsa entered first, making sure to block the doorway so that the filly behind her couldn't charge into the chamber. Thracis stared at the young mare who walked in behind his dam.

Tall and lanky, it would be years before she filled out, Aquina was the most perfect blue roan Thracis had ever seen. Her coat was long, but the color was unmistakable. Her ears, nose, lower legs, and mane and tail were all flawless black. She was a striking creature and he did not envy his parents at all for the suitors they would have to put up with once Aquina came of age.

Calypsa led her daughter to the table. The setting next to her had remained empty in the event Aquina joined them. Now the filly walked up proudly, with head held high and eyes challenging every mare in the room, to her place. Calypsa pinned her ears at her youngest foal. "Behave yourself or you will go right back to that stall and stay there until next week."

Aquina, smart enough not to pin her ears at her dam, bobbed her head. "I will behave, Momma."

Calypsa nodded at Thracis. "This is Thracis. He's been waiting a long time to meet you."

Aquina looked at Thracis with curiosity. "You're the one in the middle, aren't you?"

"Yes."

"I thought you would be taller for some reason." She was craning her head this way and that to get a good look at him.

"I'm taller than Pyrios," Thracis snapped.

"How am I supposed to know that?" she shot right back.

"I would think you have seen the paintings in the stable." Thracis tossed his head.

She twitched a shoulder. "I haven't really paid much attention."

Annoyed at her indifference, Thracis said, "Doesn't seem like you pay attention to much given that you were stalled when we arrived."

Aquina tossed her head at him. "You don't know anything about me."

"I know more than you think."

"How?" She looked at Calypsa. "Have you been talking about me?"

"He is your brother. He deserves to be warned about what he's in for." Calypsa turned to say something to Zephyros, effectively ending the argument before it could start.

Aquina turned her flashing eyes on Thracis. "Well, just because she told you some things don't think you know everything."

This wasn't going the way Thracis had imagined. He had thought his sister would be delighted to meet one of her brothers, ready to be regaled by stories of adventure. Her aggressive nature was a surprise. "I'm sure I will in time."

Psyche cleared her throat. "Are you at all interested in flying, Aquina?"

At that, the blue roan pricked her ears and her eyes lost some of their fire. "Most definitely. Mother says I'm too young to learn to fly. She thinks I'm going to run away to Diomedea and join the cavalry."

"I wouldn't put it passed you," Thracis mumbled.

Psyche stepped on his foot. "Well, as long as you promise to listen to Eno and I and you promise not to fly away, I think your parents might let you try."

Calypsa tossed her head. "I don't know if you are aware of what you're taking on, but if you think you can teach my filly to soar, you are more than welcome."

Aquina was dancing in place. "When can we start?"

"Not until tomorrow." Psyche and Alcina looked across the table at each other. "We don't fly in the dark unless we have to."

"And it will take you some time to get used to lift off and landing." Alcina nodded at Titania. "Titania is the best at landing. You should spend some time speaking with her tomorrow while we get you fitted for a harness."

"You realize she won't sleep a wink tonight," Zephyros said.

"Good, that means she'll be quiet in the morning." Neema was sitting on a pedestal between Titania and Eno. Until she spoke Aquina hadn't noticed her.

"Do you have wings too?" The filly's eyes were huge.

"I fly with Titania. I do not have my own harness."

"Aren't you afraid of falling?"

The calico shrugged. "I have a chute that will open and slow my downward descent."

"What if you are attacked while you are falling?"

"I am not without my defenses, little filly."

Aquina was silent as she examined that statement. Aeos took the opportunity to speak. "My lord, once you and Eno work out the trade agreements, will you give us leave to visit my home stable?"

Zephyros seemed surprised by the question. As guests, none of Thracis' new herd was required to ask for leave. They were not under Zephyros' rule and so could come and go as they wished while visiting Thetis Stable. Aeos was asking the question out of politeness as opposed to protocol.

"I don't see where that would be a problem. I spoke with your sire this morning and he indicated that you and your lady would be visiting him."

Thracis and Psyche's heads whipped around at the title Zephyros gave Eno. They had both thought Eno and Aeos were little more than nightly companions. Eno shifted her feet and wouldn't look Psyche or Alcina in the eye. Titania and Alcander looked amused and Neema was smart enough to keep her opinions to herself, for the moment anyway.

Picking up on the emotions at the table, Calypsa said, "It seems Aquina won't be the only one having difficulty sleeping tonight."

Aquina gave her dam a quizzical look before barraging Psyche with questions about flying. Alcina and Titania joined the conversation. Neema said something to Alcander. Aeos settled back and sipped his wine.

Thracis contacted the dun stallion. *Did I miss something on this journey?*

You miss a great many things all the time, Thracis. Why does this bother you?

Because I won't hear the end of it from Psyche tonight.

Maybe we should ask the mares if they want to exchange stallmates for the night.

Thracis snorted laughter which got him a scalding look from Psyche. "Something funny?"

"Nothing you want to know about."

She shook her mane. "You're probably right."

They talked late into the night. Exchanging stories, giving Zephyros and Calypsa firsthoof accounts of the Diomedean battle, telling them about learning to fly and the prototypes Eno made Thracis and Aeos try first. Aquina listened to it all with fascination and by the time Calypsa pushed her filly off to bed, Thracis had reached some level of godhood in his sister's eyes.

"You will be there tomorrow when these mares teach your sister to fly?" Calypsa kept her voice neutral but all the horses gathered with the exception of Aquina knew when a dam was fretting.

"Of course," Thracis assured her. "And don't worry. None of these ladies will let anything happen to a filly. Now a colt would be left to his own devices."

The mares laughed at the small joke. Titania yawned and looked at Neema, curled and fast asleep on her rump. "I think I am going to follow Neema's example and take myself off to bed."

Alcina, who was sharing a stall with Titania, nodded in agreement. "I have a feeling we'll have an early morning tomorrow."

Alcander was the only one who had his own stall and he shook himself from ears to hooves as he stepped back from the table. "When will you be needing me in the morning, my lord?"

"Not until after I have finished speaking with Eno. Have a leisurely breakfast, if you can with these youngsters around. I'll send for you before the midday meal."

Alcander nodded and bowed to Calypsa. "Good night, Lady Calypsa."

"And to you. All of you. I will sleep better knowing you are all sleeping under our roof tonight."

Calypsa and Zephyros walked down the hall that would lead to their private stalls. The others went back to the guest wing. They said their goodnights and entered their respective stalls.

Psyche wasn't in the stall ten seconds before whirling on Thracis. "What is your sire talking about Aeos' lady?"

Thracis twitched a shoulder. "I know as much as you do. Has Eno said anything to you about her feelings toward Aeos?"

"Eno hasn't said much to me about anything lately, but I thought she was just working out more harness designs."

Walking over to rub his head against her neck, Thracis said, "Maybe we aren't the only ones who didn't notice something going on, but Titania and Alcander didn't look very surprised."

She laid her cheek on his back. "Noticed that too, did you?"

"Aeos has always been closed mouthed about his personal feelings. I don't expect that he would bring attention to his relationship with Eno."

"He didn't seem bothered when your sire brought attention to the subject."

"I'll talk with him later when we're not surrounded by mares and parents."

She nipped his withers. "Too many ears?"

He nuzzled her neck. "Too many opinions."

"Fair enough. Let's go to bed. Your sister is going to run us all ragged tomorrow if given half a chance."

Thracis paused before joining her in the bedding box. "Do you think Alcina will be okay with all these soldiers?"

Psyche thought about it before replying. "I think she will be fine as long as they keep their distance."

"And if they don't?"

"Then they will learn quickly why the Diomedean *ammoni* are so feared."

CHAPTER 34

Psyche watched Aquina fly through a series of complicated maneuvers. The filly was doing excellently. She had taken to flying the way ducks took to water. Eno had modified one of the other harnesses to fit the yearling and Aquina was rapidly learning to read the winds and use the air currents. If she weren't so young, Eno would have recruited her into the herd. As it was Aquina would spend many years at home before Calypsa let her out of sight.

"She flies well for someone who only took off five days ago." Alcander was taking a break from the lessons he had designed for the Felisian kittens currently residing in Thetis Stable. He would never admit it, but the miniature was thoroughly enjoying his teaching position. So far he had spent four days instructing the kittens and their manners were already much improved.

"A natural talent for the winds. Thracis had little trouble when he first began." Psyche cocked an ear toward the practice arenas. Thracis had been sparring with the soldiers posted at the stable. He relished any and all practice in advanced combat. He usually sparred with Aeos, but the dun stallion and Eno had left yesterday to spend a few days with Aeos' sire at Acadia Stable.

"A lot of talent in this herd." Alcander nodded at Titania and Alcina, both airborne and explaining the proper technique for getting out of a downward spiral. "Those two are treating that filly like a little sister of their own."

Psyche bobbed her head. "Aquina is a welcome distraction for Alcina. She's been anxious ever since we landed here."

"It's so many stallions being so close."

"She could fight them off, she's strong enough in the psychic arts."

Alcander spoke quietly. "She couldn't before."

Not hearing a reply from Psyche, the gelding went on, "Old wounds heal slowly and sometimes, not ever. She is dealing as well as she can but the sooner we leave the happier she'll be."

"She and Eno both. Eno is getting antsy. She wants to start on her harnesses in Boudica and begin training her own fighting force."

The miniature tossed his head and laughed. "She is her sire's daughter."

Psyche flicked her ears. "She is."

"You seem distracted yourself today, lady, if you don't mind me noticing."

She pawed the ground and tossed her head. "The winds feel strange to me today."

He looked around, alarmed. "Like they did in the mountains?"

"No, but similar. I think we should have a short lesson today and send out scouts to be sure. It's probably nothing, but my sister is clever."

"Spoken like a queen," Alcander said. He walked away before she could reply.

Psyche watched him go, then turned her attention back to the three mares flying above her. Aquina was having a good time and Psyche felt a pang that she would end that joy without sufficient proof that there was any threat. She tossed her head. That was no way to think. After what happened to Dysis, Psyche had to listen to her gut. If something was trying to warn her, it would be in her best interest to listen.

"That's enough for today," Psyche called.

"But we've only just started."

Psyche ignored the whine in Aquina's voice and addressed Alcina and Titania. "I think we should stay inside for the rest of the day. The winds are off."

At the sound of that both older mares dropped to the ground. A sharp whinny from Titania had Aquina winging her way to land next to Alcina. Once Aquina's wings were folded and it was obvious the filly wouldn't take off without permission, Alcina turned to Psyche. "Are they the same as in the mountains?"

"No, but I would still feel better if we and the filly were safely indoors until we can equip our weapons."

Alcina and Titania nodded. Aquina looked from one mare to the other. "Is something wrong?"

Psyche nudged the filly forward toward the stable. "Nothing for you to worry about, but it would be good if you stayed inside today. If something happens we will have enough to worry about without you running around underhoof or winging through projectiles."

Aquina rolled her eyes but started walking. "I can stay out of the way."

"Would you have your brother get wounded because he's too worried about his ladies and not taking care of himself?" Alcina asked.

"I guess that wouldn't be the best way to get on his good side."

Titania chuckled, but Psyche noticed that the Clydesdale's eye was searching the sky for particularly large birds. Alcina was also searching but in a more subtle way; Psyche had felt the probing hooves of the other *ammoni* mare as she searched for occult threats. Psyche had sensed nothing, but Alcina had more experience than she and would pick up on something Psyche may have missed.

Thracis, something is wrong. Psyche felt him dividing his attention. He must be sparring.

What is it?

I'm not sure. Until we find something, I and the other mares will be staying in the stable.

She felt his relief. *I will keep an ear to the wind. If a fight breaks out bring your most damaging weapons.*

You don't have to worry about that.

I have to go. Alcander needs my attention.

Knowing Thracis and Alcander could handle the outside defenses, Psyche looked around the inside of Thetis Stable.

Built for defense, Thetis Stable was designed to be used as a stronghold in the event of any attack. The windows were large, but each had an inner covering of solid achillium that could be dropped in seconds. The doors could also be sealed with achillium plates. Nothing was getting in or out. Enemies would have to level the stable before gaining entrance. The stable was stocked with tons of hay and grain and gallons of water, as well as stockpiles of advanced weaponry. Thetis Stable would make any Diomedean mare proud.

Feeling secure in the fortress of her mate's parents, Psyche searched for Calypsa. Only the lady of the stable could tell the servants to lockdown everything. She found the dappled mare in her private inner garden, an open courtyard in the center of the stable.

"The lesson ended early this morning," Calypsa commented.

"We might have a problem." Psyche waited for Calypsa to turn from her roses before continuing. "The winds feel strange to me. I think we should lockdown the stable until scouts are deployed and return with news."

Calypsa turned from doting dam to ruling mare in an instant. "Then that is what we will do." She pushed passed Psyche and into the main hallway. As she walked, her eyes took on a slight glaze implicating that she was communicating with others in the stable. Psyche began to hear the slam of window and door protectors. Felisians sprang from one side of the hallway to the other as Calypsa called orders to everyone. Equine servants trotted back and forth, gathering supplies and closing off areas that would be off-limits until the threat had passed.

Second guessing her intuition, Psyche said, "Do you really think all this is necessary? It's only a feeling, not concrete."

Calypsa stopped and whirled. Psyche swallowed as she saw the mare Thracis would have run from whenever he did something requiring punishment. "My life has been saved by intuition many times, little filly. If you feel there is a dangerous presence in the area, that is all I need to hear. I would rather have this protection and not need it than need the protection and not have it."

"You and my dam have more in common than I originally thought."

"When you have foals of your own, you will learn that all dams have several things in common." She spun back and continued getting her stable ready for an attack.

Psyche stood where she was, watching Calypsa and flicking her ears back and forth. She wanted to contact Thracis and ask what was going on outside, but knew if something had happened, he would have contacted her. Alcina and Titania walked out of a nearby hall with Aquina trailing along behind them. The filly's eyes were white-rimmed and she was trying to look everywhere at once.

"Where is Neema?" It struck Psyche as odd that Titania's constant companion wasn't in attendance.

Titania swung her head to point down another hall. "She's helping get the kittens settled. They have a great respect for her and keeping them out from under hooves is a top priority right now. Everyone is anxious enough without the young ones panicking."

"This is all my fault. I should have waited--"

"Until we were caught unaware and under attack?" Alcina hissed. "For the sake of Lady Selene, Psyche, get yourself together and act like a Diomedean already. Stop questioning your ability." The black mare stomped off toward the main doors.

"She is still raw from Dysis' passing," Titania said, "but she is right. We all have faith in you. You need to have faith in yourself." She looked at Aquina. "Come on, little filly, let's go find your dam before she decides to find us."

"I'll come with you." Psyche waited for Aquina to fall into step behind Titania before following the roan. She wanted Aquina where she could keep an eye on her until they found Calypsa. Psyche wouldn't forgive herself if something happened to Thracis' sister while she was supposed to be watching her.

They found Calypsa standing by a large window covered with slatted achillium. The slats were wide enough for them to see out, but it would be difficult for an archer to fire into the window and hit anyone. Alcina was standing to Calypsa's left. She raised her head and whickered in greeting when the others lined up on the dappled mare's right side.

"The stallions are patrolling," Calypsa explained, "Zephyros contacted me and said he has sent out several scouts and ordered the others to take up defensive formations around the stable. So far nothing seems out of place here, but he said he has been trying to contact the horses at one of the bigger achillium mines and hasn't heard back yet."

"Is that normal?" Titania was scanning the sky she could see from the window.

"It can be. If they hit a large vein they may be too excited to contact Zephyros. But they wouldn't ignore him if he were trying to reach them."

Psyche felt the ominous feeling in her stomach grow. She knew something was wrong. Some of her guilt at warning the others faded. It was replaced by the usual nerves that reared their heads whenever she felt a confrontation was inevitable.

"I am going to prepare in the event the stallions need added support from the air." Psyche turned and bowed to Calypsa.

"We will go as well." Alcina nodded to Titania.

"Don't the three of you be thinking you're going anywhere without me." Neema's voice sounded from the hallway.

All together preparing for battle, Psyche thought, *that is how it should be.*

CHAPTER 35

Thracis shook himself, settling his armor and flying harnesses against each other. He had been on edge all morning and was relieved that Psyche had also felt something. Alcander had suggested sending scouts and Thracis had been more than happy to oblige him. Zephyros had watched as his son took charge with silent acknowledgement and Thracis felt a mixture of pride and anxiety ripple through himself. That his sire would allow him to order soldiers and make crucial decisions was something Thracis wouldn't have believed a year ago.

While they waited for the scouts to report, Thracis asked Zephyros, "Have you heard from the miners yet?"

Zephyros shook his head. He had been trying to contact the miners every fifteen minutes for the last hour and no one was replying to him. "It feels like the link is blocked by something. I can still feel their minds, but it's as if there is a wall of glass between us."

"Psyche should be here any minute. Tell her. She might be able to dissolve the block."

"Your lady is very talented in the psychic arts, isn't she?"

Thracis bobbed his head. "More than she will admit."

"She is worried someone from her herd is trying to attack us?" Zephyros tossed his head. "I find that hard to believe. The Diomedean queen may have issues with the rest of Equus but I and my horses have given her no reason to attack us."

Thracis sighed. "The mare Psyche is concerned with is an exile. Psyche's older sister. She tried to kill Psyche when my lady was hardly a yearling. For punishment, Queen Hippolyta banished Zeva from Diomedea."

"She is with the Baroquians?"

Thracis looked at his sire. "She is second-in-command to the Baroquian commander."

"Lord Pegasus grant mercy. No wonder Psyche is tied in knots." Zephyros looked toward the stable.

"She has also developed her own type of flying harness, not as efficient as Eno's, but we have already lost a companion to her flyers."

"You think she is trying to control the achillium mines by force."

"Exactly."

Alcander trotted up. "My lord, the scouts sent to the northern mine have reported a significant lack of activity. They are unable to make contact with anyone."

Zephyros nodded as if the news didn't surprise him. "Split the fighting forces in half. One to go with us to the mines and one to stay here and protect my stable."

Psyche and the others trotted up. Thracis saw they were all armed and ready for a fight. "Where do you want us, my lord?"

Thracis heard the unhappy mutterings of the other stallions. They didn't think a mare should be anywhere near the battle. The mares' presence would make them nervous, but Thracis and Alcander would be no match if Zeva sent several flyers to attack. *They would have to be flying*, Thracis thought, *there isn't any other way for an enemy to get this close to the mines.*

"Silence," Zephyros called. "For today, at least, we will all put aside our prejudices and accept aid wherever we can get it. You are a small force and we have no idea what we are up against."

The soldiers quieted, but they still glared openly at the mares. For their part, the mares didn't antagonize the stallions. They would let the males lead in this fight and act as a back-up if things got bad. That was to be their ultimate goal anyway, according to Eno, for her flyers, her Pegasi. They would help ground troops but not attack directly. In this way the males could still feel they were the stronger force.

"Some of you will have to stay at the stable," Zephyros explained. "Some of you should come with us."

"Titania, Neema, and I will stay here," Alcina said, "In this way, each group with have an *ammoni* with them. Something I fear we will need."

At the mention of a psychic threat, the stallions shifted. They had accepted Thracis readily enough and extended a grudging acceptance of Alcander. So far none of them had approached any of the mares. They had asked Thracis on several occasions if he thought the mares would object to some male company. Thracis had responded that the mare's objection would vary depending on the type of company the stallion was offering. Since then, the mares kept to themselves and the stallions stayed away.

Thracis regretted that Alcina would not be joining them at the mine. She was a formidable opponent and a priceless ally. Having her here to protect his dam and sister was something of a comfort, however, and if given the choice between her or Psyche, Thracis would pick his mate every time.

Psyche and Alcander were spreading their wings in preparation for takeoff. "We will follow you, Thracis." Psyche tossed her head to the north. "You will know if something is amiss long before we reach the mine."

Thracis bobbed his head and turned to his sire. "How many will remain and how many will go?"

"The Imperial Cavalry saw fit to send us a full platoon counting the scouts. That said eighteen will stay here. Six scouts will be returning making it twenty-four. Eighteen will come with us. The two scouts at the northern mine will hold their positions until we arrive."

"We will shadow you." Thracis looked skyward and launched himself up. The wind caught him immediately, pulling him in two directions. He righted himself and pumped his wings to join Psyche and Alcander.

"Have you contacted Eno?"

Psyche nodded. "She and Aeos are on their way. Aeos says he knows where the northern mine is and they will meet us there."

"Lord Pegasus grant they arrive," Alcander muttered.

Below them, Zephyros began moving the soldiers into a fighting formation. Sun glinted off armor as the soldiers prepared for battle. Three cavalry commanders trotted among the straight lines, calling orders and encouragement. Thracis and his companions soared lazily above, saving their strength for the fight ahead.

Thracis knew the three of them could reach the mines much faster than the horses on foot, but that seemed like a bad idea. It felt prudent to him to stay close to the main force. Despite the fact that the scouts had not reported any enemy sightings, he knew in his gut that the mine in was trouble. He only hoped they would be able to draw the enemy out into the open. The mines were narrow and low-ceilinged. A bad place for a fight, no matter how skilled the opponents. Not to mention, no matter how much technology they used, the miners still feared occasional cave-ins. Getting locked in the dark with a host of hostile Equines made Thracis' skin twitch.

The snow was unbroken beneath them, another clue that the adversaries had come by air. It was a seamless blanket as far as the eye could see. Unless the intruders came down from the north. If that were true, Eno or Aeos would have contacted Thracis or Psyche and told them. How many flyers did Zeva have? Thracis wondered. Ten? Twenty? Forty? A significant amount or she would never try to take a Calabrian mine. From what Psyche had told him, Zeva liked to stack the odds in her favor.

Banking sideways, Thracis tossed his head at Psyche. "The mine is just a mile or so ahead."

"Shouldn't we be hearing the sound of machinery then?" Psyche was slowing her forward momentum to stay over the soldiers below.

"Yes, we should." Thracis wanted to dive forward, make a large sweep over the mine and report back. What stopped him was the knowledge that any archers hidden on the ground would drop him like a pheasant.

He looked from Alcander to Psyche. "We'd best put on our own armor."

His companions nodded. Seconds later, all three of them were encased in silver achillium. Up ahead, Thracis heard the first challenging shriek fill the air.

CHAPTER 36

Zeva hovered behind a rise in the snowy landscape. She was downwind of the approaching soldiers and was aware of them when they were still a mile from the mine. Her Harpies, thirty in all, had taken the mine with little trouble. The miners were common horses, not soldiers, and were easily dispatched. Zeva hadn't bothered with prisoners. They took up too much time and effort.

Her mares had dragged the miners' corpses into one of the vacant mineshafts and covered the spilled blood and scuffed ground. They had taken the mine before dawn, killing the workers before they knew what hit them. Zeva knew exactly what time the miners would arrive and how they would go about their daily routines, thanks to that Zephyros colt.

Pyrios, while not the coveted Thracis, had given Zeva ample amounts of useful information. He had put up quite a fight, admirable almost, but in the end his mind had crumpled under her psychic attacks. Not sure if he would still be useful,

Zeva had stored him in a hideaway in the Kigerian countryside. Somehow his mind had become cut off from her and she was having trouble finding any more pertinent information. Where Thracis had holed up, for instance. Zeva had an idea that her troublesome brat of a sister had something to do with Pyrios' impromptu sanctuary, but little Psyche would have to wait. Today Zeva was in the market for materialistic gain rather than revenge. This mine was the most easily defensible and closest to Thetis Stable. She had already arranged for a mover to bring a platoon of Baroquian soldiers to this location once the mine was secure.

Zeva had been about to tell the Baroquian captain that the mine was theirs when she felt a familiar mind searching the area. So, little Psyche was much closer than Zeva thought. Well, perhaps this day would have more than one reason for celebration. Unable to contain her excitement for the coming battle, the black mare raised her head and shrieked a challenge.

Her Harpies screamed in response. They engaged their thrusters and lifted themselves higher into the air. After the attack on Eno's mares in the mountains, Zeva had altered her design somewhat, allowing armor to be added, but the harnesses still relied on the thrusters and air currents. Unlike Eno, Zeva didn't have the talented weavers to make magic wings; she had to rely on good, solid achillium. The weight was cumbersome, but these mares were the best of Zeva's troops. If any would be able to eliminate Eno and her following, Zeva's Harpies would do the job.

Ignoring the burning heat of the thrusters along her flanks, Zeva tossed her head at half her force. "Go, now, to Thetis Stable. I want the whole structure reduced to rubble. Destroy anyone or anything that gets in your way."

Her second nodded and whinnied to her mares. They banked away and formed an arrow as they cut across the sky. They would ignore the stallions on route to the mine. They had been trained to obey orders. Zeva's mares never questioned her authority.

Zeva tossed her head to the right and left, dividing her mares into two parallel lines. They would fly over the ground soldiers and release a volley of projectiles. The stallions would be wearing achillium armor, but that didn't matter. For this assault, Zeva had made sure all the weapons were crafted out of achillium.

She led her mares forward. Movement below her. Scouts. Screaming, Zeva dove down, long sharpened blades opening out of her armor. One pass and two heads. The scouts would not be a problem. Her blood singing with a fresh kill, Zeva turned her attention to finding her younger sister.

Thracis saw the two lines flying toward them. He called down to his sire. "Down, get everyone down. They're attacking from the air."

He saw his sire yelling orders, but the wind tore the words away from Thracis' ears. He looked at Psyche and Alcander. "Up."

They opened their wings and let the drafts drive them up into the clouds. Zeva would know they were at Thetis Stable, but Thracis was hoping she wouldn't be able to pinpoint their location. He felt hooves in his mind and shied away.

It is only me. Psyche sounded irritated, but amused. *Let me shroud your mind as mine and Alcander's are shrouded. It will be harder for my sister to locate you.*

Thracis opened his mind and felt as if Psyche were wrapping him in a blanket. He could still sense her, but the sense of her was muffled. He reached for Alcander and felt that same soft covering. They wouldn't rely on mind contact anyway. At Eno's insistence, they had trained in body language.

Hearing the clash of battle, Thracis glided lower. The battle had been met. Flyers dove and darted at the stallions on the ground. Both sides were using achillium projectiles and Thracis dodged away as a raptor spun past his face. He could see that at least three flyers had been brought down with retiarii, nets used to immobilize opponents. A rough count gave him fourteen flyers, including those on the ground.

Checking his weapons, Thracis folded his wings and dropped on a horse flying beneath him. The horse started to buck, throwing its head and trying to impale Thracis with spikes that ridged its neck. Thracis pulled back, opening his wings to pull up before he could become entangled with his opponent. The other horse moved up with him, intent on stabbing him. Jerking up and diving sideways, Thracis used his armor horn to impale his opponent in the belly. The other horse shrieked and fell, forgetting that it was hundreds of feet in the air.

Thracis didn't waste time watching the horse fall, he turned his attention to the next enemy. He saw Alcander, the little body easy to pick out among the larger horses. The miniature was weaving around opponents. Thracis saw a shimmering silver line attached to the back of Alcander's armor harness like spider silk. Suddenly, the miniature shot straight up and the silver line pulled taunt. Three enemy flyers faltered, then panicked when they realized the silver line had cut through their harness tracings. They fell, but not far enough. Thracis saw them scrambling to their feet to meet the stallions in battle on the ground.

Some of the flyers were landing on their own he saw, the better to get into the blood and gore. Thracis flew low and fired three raptors, striking an enemy creeping up on Zephyros' blind side. He spun away and caught another flyer in a tangle of wings and legs. He quickly got the upper hoof, his opponent already damaged from the heat of her thrusters. They grappled as they flew, tearing at each other. She was wearing some kind of cutting armor, but Thracis was in a perfect position to slice through the mare's wings with his horn. She fought to hold on to him, knowing a fall would break her back or neck. Thracis shook, intent on dislodging her. Then he saw Psyche. And the black mare pursuing her.

CHAPTER 37

Psyche folded her wings and dove between two opponents, letting fly with several raptors. The raptor's talons spun and slashed across the leather straps of the enemies' harnesses, the only point of weakness. The girths of the harnesses snapped, the wings still gliding on drafts of air as the horses fell, shrieking.

Not waiting to see where they landed, Psyche swooped low over the heads of the stallions below. They recognized her armor and halted their firing until she slammed into another flyer, hovering over two fallen soldiers. The other mare was caught by complete surprise and rolled over in midair, becoming totally confused. Before she could right herself, one of the ground soldiers threw his retiarii, effectively snaring her. Psyche darted up, her wings flapping strongly, focused on another mare and not noticing the black shape that fell from the clouds behind her.

She was almost close enough to engage her quarry, when hot fire burned along her flank. Remembering she was in the air before she ended up in a spin, Psyche opened her wings wide and shot upward on a draft of warm air. She banked around, craning her neck to see the enemy pursuing her.

"Stop running and face me, little sister."

Psyche's heart stuttered in her chest at the sound of Zeva's voice. Years had passed since her sister had spoken to her, but Psyche would never forget that voice.

Zeva hovered a few yards away and Psyche was stunned to see her sister wasn't wearing any armor. Psyche could make out the armor box on Zeva's harness, but for some reason the black mare chose not to engage it.

"Do think yourself invincible? We are taught from foalhood to never engage an enemy without proper protection." Psyche had pulled up and was hovering. Zeva was using her thrusters to keep from falling as her wings were not designed to be used as a bird's wings.

"We are high enough that those geldings down there can't hit me and your mate will do well to stay out of this fight."

"You stay away from him."

"I have no intention of chasing him when you are available," Zeva laughed. "Come, little sister, drop your armor and face me the way the Diomedeans of old fought each other."

Knowing better than to fight Zeva with no armor, Psyche tossed her head. "The Diomedeans of old would have fought on the ground." She could feel Zeva digging at her mind, trying to get through her first barriers.

"True enough." Zeva tossed her head and her own armor engaged, wrapping her in achillium. As it formed around Zeva, Psyche saw the wings shift a little, the thrusters working harder. That made no sense to Psyche; whether worn or simply carried, all armor weighed the same. Eno could have explained it, but Eno wasn't here. Psyche simply filed the information to the back of her mind for later examination.

Zeva came at her fast, her horn pointed at Psyche's chest. Psyche didn't doubt the horn was made of achillium and would pierce her armor with little trouble. She darted away, thankful Eno had insisted on constant training in the air. Zeva glanced past her, but Psyche felt something sharp and thin wrap around one of her front legs. A wire. It was starting to cut through the armor plates around Psyche's leg. The wire pulled tight, flipping Psyche forward, her wings fouling with each other.

Fighting panic, Psyche swung her head around and down, using her horn to cut through the wire. She let herself roll as she carefully untangled her wings and pulled up. She came up only twenty feet from the hard ground, the stallions below her had scrambled into a tight group, ready to break her fall. They watched in surprise as she flapped back up into the sky. Psyche knew she would have no chance against Zeva on the ground.

Zeva was waiting for her when Psyche reached the clouds again. She was laughing. "Good job, little sister. You've learned since I last saw you."

"I've learned more than you know."

Zeva cocked her head. "Have you now? Let's see." She came again.

Psyche braced herself, ready for Zeva to ram into her. At the last second, Zeva darted up. Too late Psyche saw the deathshroud falling toward her. She dodged to the side, but the shroud wrapped itself around her right wing. Instantly, the wing began to disintegrate as the acids in the shroud touched the metal fillings in the weaving. Refusing to give up, Psyche threw out the lasso Eno had built into her armor. It looped around Zeva's back foot, jerking the black mare down before she could get out of range.

Zeva shrieked in pain and outrage as she was pulled down with Psyche. Baring her teeth at Psyche, Zeva fueled more power to her thrusters, the flames burning into her even through her armor as she tried to keep herself from falling to her death. Not close enough to reach Zeva with her horn, Psyche threw out her last raptor. It flew true, cutting through the armor, and burying itself in Zeva's belly a foot behind her harness girth. Zeva shrieked again and kicked in response. The kick jerked the metal lasso and Psyche was sent into another whirl. Zeva was pulled with her and the two of them tangled together as they fell. In sheer desperation, Zeva swung her head around and impaled Pysche's shoulder where the lasso originated.

Psyche screamed as white fire shot up her neck and down her leg. She wiggled, trying to get away from that wicked horn. She slammed her head against Zeva again and again, cutting the other mare's neck and face. In the scramble, the lasso was cut. Feeling her foot freed, Zeva yanked her horn free and pushed against Psyche with her front feet, using the black and white mare as a kind of springboard to launch herself skyward. At the last instant, Psyche released a dart. It sank through Zeva's armor and pierced her left flank. Zeva bucked in reaction, but didn't stop fleeing to pull out the dart. Psyche laughed as she fell; Zeva wasn't the only one who knew about poisons.

She hit the ground with a bone jarring crunch. Desperate to get away from the shroud before it could get tangled around her body, Psyche rolled away a little, her wings trailing out behind her back. The right one was a blackened ruin, but as the shroud sank into the snow, she heard the hiss as the acids began to evaporate. It was the snow that saved her life. Had she fallen on bare earth, her back would have broken in a dozen places. Her legs too. She lay quietly, pain wracking her body as she waited for someone to find her. She had no idea where she had fallen, but she could hear the battle clearly so she couldn't be far.

Alcander had witnessed the fight between Hippolyta's daughters. And had held back. It wasn't that he was afraid of fighting Zeva. If any horse had reason to make that witch suffer it was him. He would have taken her on all on his own if he had seen her. It was that he knew Psyche and Zeva would have to face each other. Their fight had begun years before and would last until one of them was dead. It was the only way Psyche would have peace. If he had helped, the *ammoni* mare would forever doubt her ability.

Watching as Zeva retreated, wanting to finish the job now that she was wounded, but needing to see to Psyche first, Alcander tamped down his own ambitions and went to the fallen mare. He had noticed Thracis flying toward the two mares when they first engaged each other, but another flyer had detained the young stallion and he had lost sight of them once their battle had moved farther south. Alcander flew low toward the area where Psyche had crashed, his heart already mourning her as lost.

He landed a few feet from the still smoking wing and whickered softly. She shifted, trying to lift her head and he rushed forward. "No, Lady, no. Don't move. You're safe. Alcander is with you."

She shuddered as his nose touched her white cheek. He couldn't inspect her while her armor was engaged. "Lady, can you remove your armor or do you need help?" Unlike Thracis, Alcander did not feel comfortable touching Psyche in any way that wasn't strictly necessary.

"Help." Her voice was barely a whisper.

Alcander moved carefully, aware that snow could shift and he didn't want to cause her any more pain. He found the button on the armor box and held his breath as the achillium glided back, showing him the damage.

On this side, all he could see was the jagged hole in the front of her shoulder. Thank Lord Pegasus it had been the front and not the side. From the side, Zeva would almost surely have pierced Psyche's heart. Blood pumped from the wound, pooling under her chest. More blood was staining the snow under her haunches and Alcander hoped the wounds he couldn't see weren't as bad as the shoulder. He could see a shallow cut encircling her left foreleg. It was oozing blood but that was okay, it would clot on its own.

Alcander retracted his armor and folded his wings. He pulled wads of cloth from one of the bags he always carried and stuffed the cloths into the hole in Psyche's shoulder. She made a strange whining sound and tried to pull away.

"Don't, Lady Psyche. These cloths were treated with Kamuzu's special poultice mix. They will clean the wound and stop the bleeding."

"I, side hurts."

"Which side?"

She took a rasping breath. "The one under me."

Of course, Alcander thought. Using his mind, he lifted her gently, setting her up on her belly. She screamed as her shoulder shifted position. Alcander used mental stilts to keep her propped in that position, despite her begging to be laid back down.

"Can't do that. I have to see to your other wounds first."

She moaned in response.

Unlike Kamuzu and Aeos, Alcander had no formal training in healing. He knew how to splint broken legs and stitch and stop a gushing wound, but internal damage was beyond him. He didn't even know how to check a horse for internal bleeding. No point in worrying about that right now. He would do what he could.

The cut along her flank was deep, but the blood was stopping, probably because it had been pressed against the cold snow. Alcander pulled out the rest of his supplies and cleaned the wound as best he could. He didn't stitch it shut because it would need a proper cleansing with antiseptic and a healer would have to check for poison. Psyche was in pain but not showing any of the telling signs of poisoning such as bleeding nostrils, gurgling, or overheating. That made Alcander sigh in relief. She was banged up and would be recuperating for several weeks, but he felt sure she would live to fight her sister another day. He bandaged her flank with sticky adhesives and then laid her back down on her side.

"Thank you," she breathed.

"Don't get too comfortable. You know you can't stay like this. You'll have to be shifted up again soon."

"Don't fret so much, Alcander. I want to rest before all those studs come running and tell me what a fool I was for fighting my sister."

Alcander pinned his ears. "If any of them say anything like that, your mate will skin them alive."

Her brown eyes were drifting shut. "Give me warning before they arrive."

"I will." He looked along her body and began unfastening her flying harness. He would leave her armor harness on in case of attack, but he saw no reason for her to wear more than she had too.

To the north, he could hear fighting, but he thought it was coming to an end. Alcander had been to many battles and the sounds of ending were always the same. The shrieks of the dying and wounded. The final screams of challenge. The last shots fired. Then the yelling of the asklepiades and the healers as they searched for the wounded. He couldn't contact Thracis because the other stallion's mind was still shrouded in Psyche's protective wraps. Thracis would find them eventually, Alcander just had to be patient.

He looked up in fear as two shadows flowed over the snow. From his vantage he couldn't tell if the horses overhead were friendly or not. They had come from the south, but that didn't mean they weren't enemies, victorious in their destruction of Thetis Stable. The one in back whinnied loudly, getting the attention of its companion and the two swung around and back towards Alcander and Psyche.

Alcander braced himself, readying his projectile weapons. He didn't have many left but the ones he had were poison-tipped. All he had to do was puncture the armor of the attackers.

Before they could come close enough for him to hit them, one of them called his name. "Alcander. Alcander, it's Eno and Aeos. We've come from Thetis Stable to help."

Locking down his weapons, Alcander called back, "How fairs the stable?"

"Several direct hits, but all the mares inside are safe. Some casualties on the field and many wounded, but it could have been much worse." Aeos spoke as he landed next to Psyche. He immediately began assessing her condition. Eno landed and came to Alcander. "Are you alright, little friend?"

"A few bumps and bruises, but nothing I can't handle."

"You hunted well?" Her eyes held the dying fire of battle.

"As well as you, I would imagine."

She turned away before he could read her face, but her predatory stalk as she went to help Aeos told Alcander that Eno was proving herself a warrior with every confrontation.

Aeos looked up at Alcander. "Why can't we contact Thracis?"

The miniature nodded at Psyche. "She put a shroud around his mind to protect him from Zeva."

"Zeva?" Aeos and Eno said together.

Alcander nodded. "She was the one who did this."

"I hope Psyche gave as good as she got," Eno snapped.

"I'm not so sure Zeva will come back from the last dart Psyche threw."

Nodding in understanding, Eno turned her attention to Psyche's destroyed wing. "We'll have to have the weavers fix this."

"Psyche!"

They all turned to the panicked scream above them. Thracis didn't so much land as fall on the trampled snow. He failed to fold up his wings and tripped over them several times in his scramble to reach his mate.

"Calm down," Eno snarled with pinned ears. "We've already lost one harness. Don't rip your own wings."

Ignoring her, Thracis fell to his knees by Psyche's head. "Psyche? Psyche are you poisoned?" Having undergone his own poisoning when he was ambushed, Thracis was too familiar with the damage a poison could do. Alcander sympathized with the young stallion.

Psyche's eyes fluttered open. "Thracis?" She stretched her neck to reach him.

Thracis hurriedly touched noses with her, effectively stopping her movement. "Lay still, sweetheart. I'm with you. Just lay still and let the others take care of you."

Alcander thought she would argue, but Psyche only sighed and closed her eyes again. Thracis nuzzled her nose and then stood. His hooves were next to her forehead and he looked around possessively. Alcander knew no one was getting near that mare unless Thracis approved of them.

Aeos finished his inspection and looked at the rest of them. "She has several broken ribs and the front of her shoulder has received significant damage. Her leg and flank aren't too bad but given her other injuries they could become a problem if they get infected. We have to get her back to the stable as soon as possible. And we have to keep her warm."

Warm. That was something Alcander hadn't thought of. Thracis moved around Psyche and laid down so that his back was against hers. Alcander laid on her other side and placed his head on her side. It was as much as they could do but her body heat would be leaking out through the cold ground.

"I'll fly back to the stable and get blankets and tell the stallions to send movers for the wounded." Eno launched skyward and darted south.

Aeos looked at Thracis and Alcander and twitched a shoulder. "I'll go up to the main company and offer my skills. I can't do any more for her right now."

Alcander nodded. Thracis didn't move. The miniature watched Aeos push through the snow toward the soldiers, his achillium armor winking in the sunlight. Alcander looked after Aeos until the dun disappeared behind a snow drift. Then he put his head back on the mare's heaving side and waited for Eno to return.

CHAPTER 38

Thracis shifted his weight and continued to stare out the small window of the infirmary. Behind him, he could hear the whines and moans of pain, the raspy breathing, the shift of shavings as horses tried to find a more comfortable position in which to lay. The smells of blood and antiseptics and ointment and poultices assaulted his nose and made his stomach queasy.

Aeos came up behind him and cleared his throat. "Thracis? Are you ready? I'm done here for a little while."

Thracis nodded and turned from the window. The infirmary had been converted from a long hall his parents usually used for winter gatherings. The tables had been set up in one corner as an impromptu operating area. The rest of the hall was scattered with hastily constructed beds of thick shavings. The soldiers had fought off Zeva's flyers, but it had come at a heavy price. Better than twenty horses lay in the chamber, several were damaged so badly they would never fight again. But morale was high. Aeos thought most of the stallions would recover completely.

He and Thracis walked down a short hall and into another chamber, this one similar to the infirmary but much smaller. After a long debate with his mate, Zephyros had decided it would be better to keep the stallions in one area and the mares in another. The soldiers were bothered enough by the fact that Titania, Alcina, and Psyche had been wounded. They didn't need a constant reminder.

Psyche was hung in sling in the farthest corner of the stall. Thracis and Aeos went to her first. She was dozing, held in a soothing trance by the brews Aeos insisted she drink four times a day. She couldn't be allowed to lay down, no matter how much she begged. The internal damage she had sustained when she fell had been too severe. The weight of her own body lying on already damaged organs would send her system into complete shutdown. A long incision, stitched closed by Alcander's meticulous mind, ran along her left side.

Eno had come back as soon as she could with blankets and a mover. Thracis and Eno had been careful when they placed Psyche on the mover, but she was so broken inside that she had begun to bleed. Aeos had been forced to cut her open and stop the bleeding from half a dozen ruptured vessels. He and the stable asklepiade had given Psyche bags of prepared blood to replace the quarts she had lost. They couldn't give her as much as they would have liked as their supply was limited and they had several other horses with significant blood loss. Aeos had taped her ribs as best he could and seen to her other wounds. He packed her shoulder with ointments and wrapped it tight.

He wouldn't let Alcander stitch it closed as the hole needed to drain. Her leg and flank were easier to deal with and Aeos left those hurts to Alcander.

The miniature was surprising everyone. He may not have had the same training as the healers, but he knew how to care for the wounded. He split his time between both chambers, carrying water, changing bandages, and offering support. The stallions had accepted Alcander as part of their herd and once they learned Zeva was responsible for his gelding, the little horse's station in the herd was solidified. This respect gave the gelding a new confidence and he made sure everyone had whatever they needed, taking pride in his ability to help the group.

Aeos walked around Psyche, checking her vitals, her wrappings, her stitches. He spent several minutes checking the fluid draining from her shoulder before stepping back in satisfaction. He tossed his head at the other mares and spoke quietly, "I have to see to them. She is healing well. Try to keep her calm if she wakes while you're here. We have to speak with your sire once I am finished."

Thracis nodded. He waited for Aeos to leave before walking up to Psyche and gently nuzzling her from flank to ears. This nuzzling was more forceful than how he usually touched her, turning the motion into a massage. It was important to massage the lactic acid out of her muscles and keep her circulation moving well. These massages could be done with his mind, but Thracis needed the physical contact. As he touched her, he refrained from contacting her mind. If she felt him trying to reach her, she might think that he needed her and would come out of her doze no matter how many drugs Aeos gave her.

Alcina's voice came to him from the other side of the stall, telling Aeos how she was doing today. The attack had happened two days ago and Alcina was chafing under Aeos' orders that she was to stay in this chamber for a week. She could walk around the stall, but was not allowed to do more. She had nearly broken both her front legs in an attempt to bring down three enemies at once. Thracis was thankful Aeos was the focus of Alcina's anger as he was in no mood to listen to a mare's squabbling about unfair treatment. Aeos told her that no matter how good she felt, she still had five days of recovery before she could go out and start ordering the stallions around.

His examination of Titania sounded more amiable. The Clydesdale's responses were too low for Thracis to hear, but he gathered Titania was happy with the reprieve her wounds would grant her. She and Neema had fought in the air and on the ground, coming to the aid of several soldiers during the battle. Thracis had spoken to two of them, both of which were worried beyond reason that Titania would not recover from her wounds. Thracis assured them it would take a lot more than a couple of gashes to keep the Clydesdale down for long. Neema had received a couple of burns but her paws were wrapped and she stayed curled next to Titania most of the day.

Psyche whickered softly, drawing Thracis' attention away from Aeos and his other patients. He nuzzled her nose. "It's only me, sweetheart. Making sure your muscles don't seize up."

She blew a soft breath into his nostrils. Her eyes flickered open and closed. She was fighting for consciousness. Thracis pushed his nose against hers. "Don't, sweetheart, don't fight. I'll come to you."

She settled again. Her head was hanging in its own sling so she wouldn't be forced to hold it up on her own. Thracis took a deep breath and opened his mind, reaching for the other half of his soul. He saw her standing in the swirling mist of his mind. Even her projected image looked worn and beaten. It made his heart ache, but he knew she wouldn't rest until they spoke.

Thracis walked up to stand next to her. *Lean on me. I don't want to see you fall even here where I know it's an illusion.*

She pushed against him gratefully. *I only wanted to talk for a second.*

Take your time. I won't leave until you're ready. He rubbed his cheek along her back.

Psyche seemed to gather herself before speaking. *The dart I threw at Zeva was poisoned.*

We all thought as much. Will it kill her?

She shook her head feebly, staggering against him. *Anyone else, yes. But my sister won't be so easily destroyed. It will take her many weeks to recover, but she will heal.*

You fought well. Thracis wanted her to remember the good things she had done and not dwell on the negative. *I would not have had such luck against Zeva.* He felt her relax against him.

That is something I want to fall asleep on. She pulled back and looked at him. *Can I lay down here?*

I don't see why not. It's not your physical body.

Sighing in relief, Psyche folded her legs and lay down at Thracis' feet. He reached down and sniffed her ears and mane, reassuring her and himself. *Sleep well, sweetheart. I'll stay until you're deep in dreams.*

Thracis stayed in Psyche's mind until the mare was fast asleep. It killed him to leave, but he had other horses to worry about. He nuzzled her forehead and walked away, coming back to his body. Aeos was waiting for him.

"How is she?"

Thracis tossed his head. "She is healing. Her image is haggard, so I think her mind is as weary as her body."

Aeos nodded and turned to leave. "Weary and muddled by the healing brews. She will be better in a couple of days."

They went into the formal meeting chamber where Zephyros, Calypsa, and Eno waited. Aquina was off somewhere, treating wounded soldiers most likely. Not that this was anything a yearling would find interesting.

Calypsa met Thracis and nuzzled his mane. "How is she?"

"Stable. She is healing." Thracis didn't want to show how worried he was, but he could tell by his dam's sympathetic eyes that she understood.

"She is a strong mare, Thracis. She will survive."

He nodded and turned his attention to his sire. Zephyros pawed the ground. "This attack has shown us that these flyers are more dangerous than we originally thought. Far from a bit of fancy, those Harpies did more damage to my stable than a platoon of trained soldiers."

Thracis thought it better not to point out that Zeva's Harpies were trained as if they were soldiers.

Zephyros went on. "After careful discussion with Eno I have decided to send most of our stockpiled achillium with you back to Diomedea. Eno must have more Pegasi. We were nearly helpless on the ground. If not for you and your wings, Thetis Stable would have fallen." He nodded at Eno, Aeos and Thracis. "I do not doubt that what we fought was merely a glimpse at what the Baroquians are creating."

Eno spoke, "My, lord, I have already contacted Arachnae Stable. They are sending their best weavers to Boudica. The Morgans have already arrived and Master Phrenicos has begun construction on an adequate building center."

"That is heartening news." Zephyros looked at Calypsa. "We have contacted the Hippikon and told them all that has happened. The Asapatish has agreed that your Pegasi will be welcomed by the Imperial Cavalry. He will see to it personally."

Eno puffed up visibly at the mention of her sire and his pride in her ability.

Calypsa tossed her head. "Commander Dias has also requested that you contact him and 'stop dancing around the truth' as he put it."

Eno flushed and pawed the ground in embarrassment. "I will contact him this afternoon."

"See that you do," Zephyros said. "Your sire needs to know who he can count on once the Baroquians launch a full-scale attack."

Aeos cleared his throat. "We will have to stay here at least a month. I won't move Psyche, even on a mover, any sooner than that."

"We will welcome your company," Calypsa said.

"Psyche has told me that the poison she inflicted Zeva with will not kill the black mare, but it will be weeks before she heals fully. We can use that time to our advantage." Thracis was thinking that while Zeva was recovering Eno could be training dozens more mares.

"Don't worry, Thracis, we will." Eno was getting that far off look in her eyes that told Thracis she was already forming a plan.

"Aeos, your sire will be arriving this afternoon. He plans on staying a week. While he is here, he and I will formulate a proposal for King Pedasos. The king must be informed of the danger posed by the Baroquians." Zephyros was looking out a window that faced the sea. "We won't tolerate those horses coming here and killing off innocent bystanders. There was no need to destroy all those miners and by consequence, their family herds."

A look from Calypsa had the younger horses leaving the chamber; she knew her mate needed time alone to grieve for his horses. The others left the stable in silence and stood outside in the knee-deep snow. No one seemed eager to break the quiet of the winter day. They looked out over the fields at the few soldiers patrolling the area.

"I hadn't thought about the miners' herds. It must have been a heavy burden for Zephyros to inform their mates and off-spring." Eno's voice fell like rain on Thracis' ears.

"It is the weight of being the ruling stallion." Aeos spoke with conviction but he looked sick.

"Will you contact your sire and ask if he will send aid from Lipizza?" Thracis asked Eno.

The bay mare shook her head. "I will contact him, but I don't want him to send a bunch of stallions that will do nothing but grate on the nerves of the mares I am training." She looked from Thracis to Aeos. "My sire told me if I could give mares wings then we could have the sky. I will not tolerate my wings being used by contingents of stallions. We mares want to protect our own as much as you do."

"Does that mean you will take our wings?" Aeos voice was amused.

Eno softened. "Of course not. You know as well as I do, Aeos, that there are exceptions to every rule."

"No matter who you teach to fly, we have a hard road to go yet and we still have not met the Baroquian main force." Thracis' comment sobered all of them.

Finally, Eno said, "We do have a hard road, but the first steps will be easy."

Aeos and Thracis looked at her. She tossed her head. "With Zeva out of commission for a little while, at least we can prepare. And after this attack, all of Equus will know that the Baroquians will stop at nothing to get what they want."

"If we are to win the war, we will have to come together," Aeos said. "Such was the will of Lord Bucephalus."

"Do you think a leader such as he will rise again?" Thracis was watching the wind blow puffs of snow across the fields.

"Oh, I don't know. Who can tell what we might become?"

He and Eno shared a laugh before returning to the stable. Thracis stood outside for several more minutes before deciding to go down and walk along the coast. He stayed far enough back to avoid the icy waves. Other hoof prints showed that the beach had been frequented in days passed. It was the beach of his youth but not the one that called to him. It was the beach in Boudica that beckoned. The beach near Phrenicos' stable that whispered Thracis' name. This was his home but that was where he belonged. In the schooling ring with Psyche watching, honing his skills until he was ready to stand before the Baroquian cavalry once and for all.

Whinnying loudly, Thracis bolted down the beach. Seagulls took wing as he galloped into their midst, wheeling in the sky and screaming their anger. Thracis ran until he thought his lungs would burst and his legs would break. He spun and reared, voicing a challenge to the sea. The sea answered with crashing waves. Dancing on his toes, alive with the prospect of new adventure, Thracis returned to Thetis Stable.

CHAPTER 39

Before he could enter the warm confines of the stable and see to his lady, a strange mind contacted his.

On guard, Thracis cautiously let the other mind into his first barrier. *Who is contacting me?*

I am Lady Dendera. As Psyche is indisposed, I have decided you are the most logical second choice.

Thracis felt his heart speed up. *What news?*

The link filled with iron satisfaction. *We have found your brother, Lord Thracis.*

Is he well?

He is alive and we are moving him to Diomedea. He is need of the cats in Sanctuary.

Relief flooded through Thracis, making his legs turned to rubber. *Thank you, Lady Dendera. From the bottom of my soul, I thank you.*

Amusement in the link. *It was a favor asked by Lady Psyche. We were more than happy to oblige her.*

The link broke. Thracis stood for a minute, shaking. Pyrios found, in need of help, but alive. His parents needed to know. He had to tell Aeos. He had to do something else first. Making sure he hadn't drawn any attention, Thracis left the front of the stable and walked out into the open field. He fell to his knees and spoke to the snow.

"Lord Pegasus, I know a life such as mine is below your awareness. But I wish to thank you for protecting me and mine. For saving my love and returning my brother." He rose to his feet, intent on returning to the stable.

A horse stood in front of him, rainbow shimmering wings spread out over its back. Thracis had never seen such kindness and compassion in a pair of eyes.

"Young Thracis." The voice sounded like wind in mountain meadows, cool streams tumbling over colorful rocks. "I am often occupied with matters far beyond your understanding, but never think that I do not know of all my children. I have watched over you for many years and will continue to do so as I do others."

"Thank you, my Lord."

Lord Pegasus laughed. His coat had been gleaming white when Thracis first saw him. Now it was deepening to burnished bronze. "Thanks is always appreciated. Keep heart, stallion of Thetis Stable. I have given you all you need in this life. It is for you to decide what you will do with my gifts."

Lord Pegasus bunched his muscles and sprang into the air. Thracis watched as the god didn't so much disappear as dissipate, as if he had been nothing more than sculpted mists. Thracis turned back to Thetis Stable. Yes, he did have all that he needed. He squared his shoulders. The road would be hard, but with his friends beside him, Thracis knew he would reach its end.

Rebecca McCullough has lived with horses, primarily Lipizzans, and cats her whole life. Their intelligence and interactions, not to mention the author's own love for the interweaving of history and legend, were the foundations that created the realms and civilizations contained in these pages.

She lives on her family farm in Florida where she and her daughter continue to promote the Lipizzan breed through public performances.

Visit her website at www.herrmannsroyallipizzans.com for more information.